Dying Moon

Also by W. Michael Gear and Kathleen O'Neal Gear

Praise

"...richly imagined..." The Gears "succeed in blending a great deal of information about how these hunter-gatherers lived (food, lodging, weapons, etc.) together with the universal search for love, power and wisdom. It's a combination that will surely satisfy readers addicted to the series."

— *Publishers Weekly*

"One of the best novels in the whole series. The Gears have consistently captured early Native American life with precision, detail, and narrative excitement, but in *People of the Moon* they reveal their skills to an even sharper effect."

— *Booklist*

"A lively tale of warring clans...should leave readers hungry for more entries in the series."

— *Kirkus*

Dying Moon

The Earliest Americans
Book 7

W. Michael Gear

Kathleen O'Neal Gear

WOLFPACK
PUBLISHING
— EST 2013 —

Dying Moon
Paperback Edition
Copyright © 2025 (As Revised) by W. Michael Gear and
Kathleen O'Neal Gear

Wolfpack Publishing
1707 E. Diana Street
Tampa, FL 33610

www.wolfpackpublishing.com

Illustrations by Ellisa Mitchel.

Paperback ISBN 978-1-63977-579-8
Ebook ISBN 978-1-63977-681-8

| 13,000 B.C. | 10,000 B.C. | 6000 B.C. | 5000 B.C. |

Paleo Indian

Early Archaic

People of the Wolf
Alaska & Canadian
Northwest

People of the Fire
Central Rockies &
Great Plains

People of the Sea
Pacific Coast &
Great Basin

People of the Lightning
Florida

Paleo Indian

Archaic

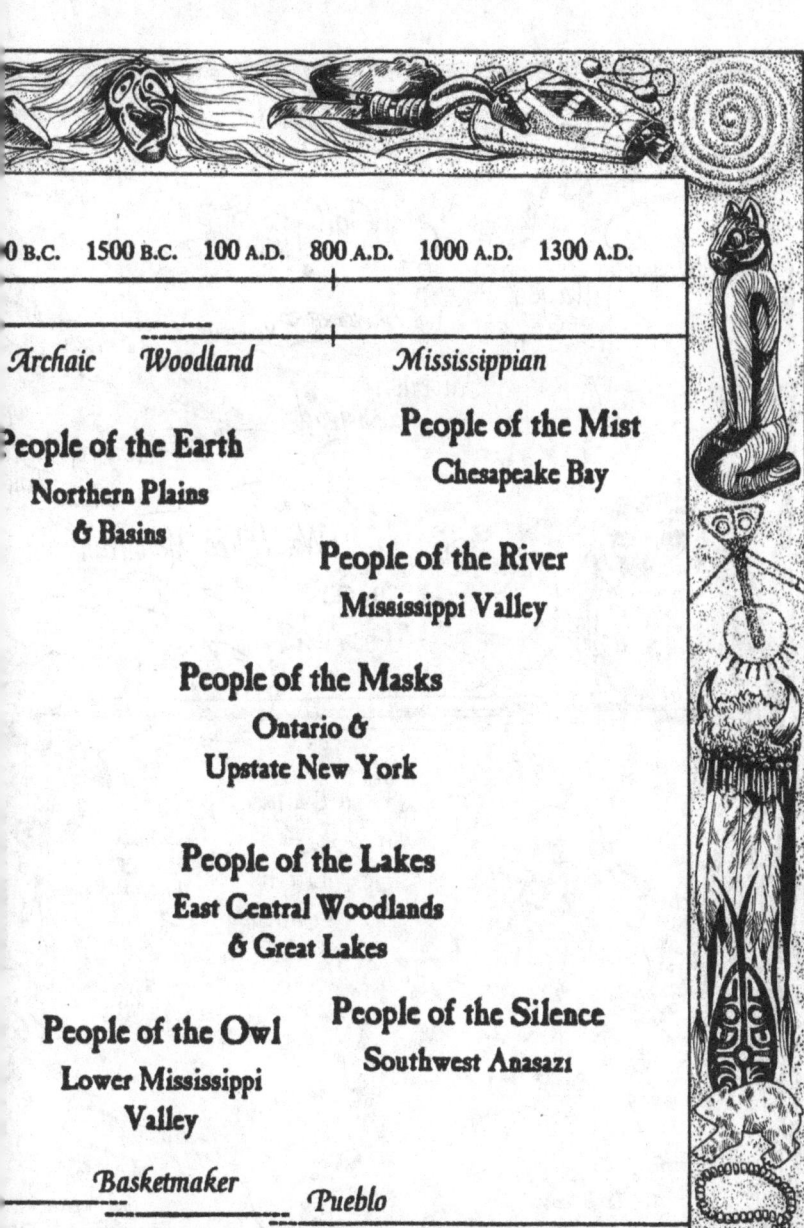

B.C.	1500 B.C.	100 A.D.	800 A.D.	1000 A.D.	1300 A.D.

Archaic   *Woodland*   *Mississippian*

People of the Mist
Chesapeake Bay

People of the Earth
Northern Plains
& Basins

People of the River
Mississippi Valley

People of the Masks
Ontario &
Upstate New York

People of the Lakes
East Central Woodlands
& Great Lakes

People of the Owl
Lower Mississippi
Valley

People of the Silence
Southwest Anasazi

Basketmaker   *Pueblo*

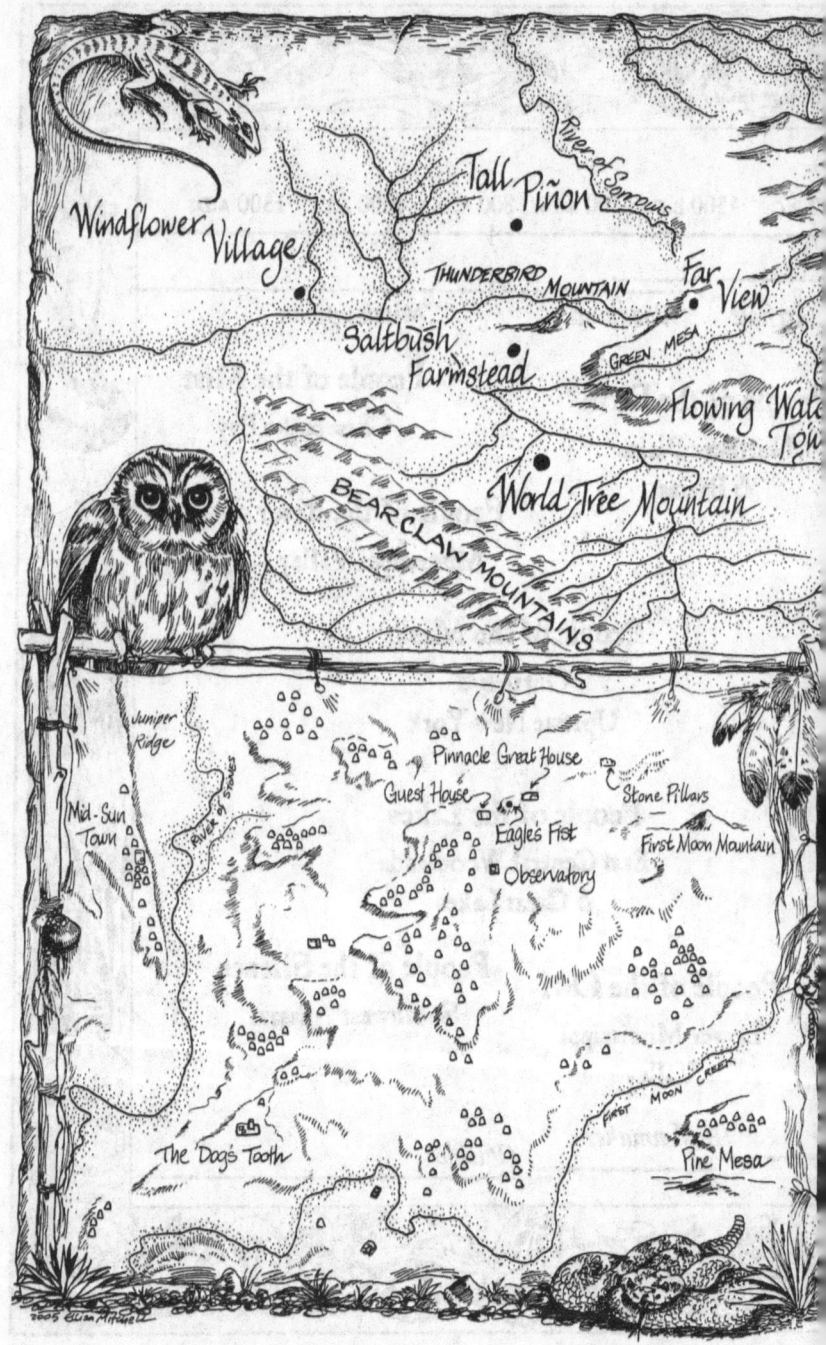

SPIRIT MOUNTAINS

River of Stones

First Moon Mountain

Ironwood's Camp

Hot Springs

of Souls

aight
ath
Canyon

GREAT RIVER VALLEY

NORTH

Dying Moon

Chapter One

The feeling of warmth grew as Ripple was pulled through a fog of gray. He could feel himself traveling, almost flying through the nothingness. The force of it was inexorable, like being at the end of a long cord that was relentlessly wound in by a strong man.

Moment by moment, the warmth grew. He could feel the cold-numbing ache melt in his bones, and sighed with relief as his flesh turned rosy, his blood spurting in every artery and vein. Yes! He lived!

The heat increased until he shifted uncomfortably. Something seemed to bind him, restricting his ability to move. Panting, cool air rushed into his lungs. Trickles of sweat began to bead on his skin; thirst pulled at his tongue.

"He's coming," a voice whispered.

Ripple moaned, then felt a cup placed to his parched lips. The delight of cool water slipped around his dry mouth. Greedily he drank, sucking great gulps of water down.

"Easy," a voice cautioned. "You don't want to choke."

Ripple laid his head back as the cup was withdrawn. Swallowing, his tongue prodded the wreckage in his mouth, explored the missing teeth on the left side of his jaw. The dull ache of pain shot up from his mangled hand as he tried to flex his fingers.

"You are safe," the calm voice told him. "You are among friends, Ripple."

He couldn't place the accent, but knew it wasn't any he'd heard before. Blinking, he realized a whitish film covered his eyes.

"Your souls have been traveling," the voice told him. "It will take a moment for them to remember your body. It is an old friend, a very comfortable and familiar home. Trust me, your souls will settle in very soon."

A damp cloth was placed on his eyes, rubbed gently, and lifted. He squeezed them shut, blinked, and was able to finally make out the fuzzy image of the woman who bent over him. Above her head, he could barely discern shredded juniper bark roofing behind the parallel poles.

"Where am I?"

"Safe. This place is Ironwood's camp." The woman wrung out the wet cloth and sponged his forehead.

"Hot," he said as he panted for air.

"Let's remove the stones." The woman bent over him, and as she did a thin, narrow-faced man leaned into Ripple's blurred vision. Together they unwound a thick buffalo robe, and from it, took what appeared to be hot stones wrapped in coarse cloth.

"We were worried that you wouldn't return," the man said with a smile. When he leaned close he had large, gentle eyes. "We think you were with Cold Bringing Woman."

"Yes." A sense of desolation grew under his heart. "She told me things."

The woman studied him thoughtfully. "Not everyone has such a close relationship with the gods."

He pressed his good hand to his eyes, rubbed them, and blinked, his vision clearing. Thank the gods, he wasn't blind, just...he gaped, seeing her: the wife from his Dream visions. He took a breath, ready to call out to her. But no recognition lay behind her eyes.

"No," Ripple answered, remembering the choice he'd made. Seeing that other future unfold in his head. "No one would want to."

The young man nodded, understanding in his thoughtful eyes. "I am called Poor Singer. This woman is known as Orenda. You are among friends, here, Ripple. Is there anything you need?"

Orenda. Her name is Orenda.

"More water." As they helped him to sit up, his stomach gurgled. "And food?"

"Of course." Orenda turned. "And while I'm at it, I'll inform your friend Bad Cast that your souls have returned. He's been worried about you."

"Bad Cast? He's here?" He tried to organize his jumbled thoughts.

"He has come by every hand of time to check on you." Orenda smiled and ducked out a flap-covered doorway.

"Bad Cast is a good friend," Poor Singer added. "He helped us know which way to go in the Spirit World to search for you."

"I'm not sure I should have come back."

3

"I know."

Ripple frowned. "You do?"

Poor Singer studied his thin hands as he flexed his fingers. The way the tendons moved behind the smooth skin seemed to fascinate him. "The ways of Power are not for the timid of heart or soul. It's nothing like the Priests say it is, is it? That's one of the more amusing ironies."

Her name is Orenda. She could have been my wife. Mother of my children.

Ripple nodded weakly. He was just beginning to understand the import and ramifications of what Cold Bringing Woman had whispered to him. Fire and ice. A lonely sense of desolation hollowed his heart.

Orenda. Children. Grandchildren. All that could be.

"They have no idea of the price."

"No," Poor Singer said wistfully.

"Neither the price, nor the pain." Ripple swallowed hard, closing his eyes. "You don't understand what this will cost."

In a hollow voice, Poor Singer answered, "Unfortunately...I do."

"Then I have a message for you. And...and then I must see the war chief."

Wrapped Wrist winced as he climbed the last steep slope onto the mesa top. The way wound around ponderosa, juniper, and piñon pine. Loose yellow-white soil slipped under his yucca trail sandals, dust rising to coat his legs. The air was redolent with pine and the scent of dry earth. Grasshoppers clicked as they rose and fell on sun-shining wings. A stellar jay rasped in annoyance, and a tuft-eared squirrel seemed to flow along an overhead branch like an undulating wave.

Crow Woman was gasping as she climbed around a tumbled square of sandstone that had cracked off the rim. The stone was taller than she was. Lichens decorated it in patterns of orange, blue, and black.

"Who comes?" a voice asked from above.

"Crow Woman, you blind wretch," she called up the slope. "And with me is Wrapped Wrist."

"Welcome home."

Wrapped Wrist paused to stare up the slope, seeing the man where he poked his head out past the high rimrock. He held a bow in one hand, several arrows in the other. From that vantage he could have skewered as many enemies as he had arrows before they could climb the narrow trail to the rim.

Crow Woman wasted no more attention on the guard as they continued the climb. Here footholds had been pecked into the exposed sandstone. One by one, Wrapped Wrist made his way up. Despite his fatigue, it was well worth it to watch Crow Woman's fine legs, muscles sliding under smooth, if dusty, skin. Her hips swayed with each step she made, swishing the war shirt in a most enticing way. That her waist was so narrow only added to the effect.

For the moment, Wrapped Wrist could almost forget his fatigue. He was grinning as he followed her through a gap in the rock and onto the mesa top.

She was panting, her breasts rising and falling as she took a moment to look around. The guard had reseated himself under a small shelter of pine boughs. "See anything out there?"

"No. Only the tracks of some hunters from down south," she told him before turning to follow a faint trail in the pine duff.

Wrapped Wrist walked by her side, the way winding among the ponderosas. "How far?"

"Not more than a finger's time now." She gave him a measuring sidelong glance. "You did all right."

She couldn't feel the exhaustion in his legs, feet, and back. "So did you."

She only grunted in response.

"Is it just me, or do you hate all men?" he asked.

For a long time she was silent, then asked, "Tell me, do men think of nothing but coupling with a woman? Is that the only notion wedged down between your souls?"

He kicked a pine cone, watching it bounce and curve off across the gray-brown mat of needles. "Actually, there's lots more stuff 'wedged in there,' as you would say. There's vanity, status, prestige, envy, fear, and uncertainty."

"That's unusual honesty to hear from a man."

"I'm an unusual man." He paused. "I noticed how you looked at Whistle that night. Did he try to lay with you?"

"Once." After a moment she looked at him curiously. "So, why haven't you tried?"

"Because you scare me half to death."

"Good."

"A man did something pretty terrible to you. What was it?"

Her only response was a glare.

As they traveled in silence, Wrapped Wrist began noticing scars where people had broken dead branches off the bottoms of the pines. Sticks and twigs had vanished from the forest floor, and the trail was more distinct.

"We're getting close," he guessed.

"In answer to your question, it wasn't a man," she said shortly. "It was men."

"Surely you've known a couple of good men thrown in with all of us bad ones."

She jerked a nod. "There's the war chief."

"And who else?"

"I said: There's the war chief."

"Just one? Out of all the men you've met?"

"Tells you something about men, doesn't it?"

At that moment a youth peered out from behind a tree trunk. He turned, running like a rabbit, weaving in and out of the ponderosa as he zipped away.

Within moments Wrapped Wrist made out the first of the structures. Two women stood, baskets in hand, looking their direction.

"We've made it," Crow Woman told him. "Go find your friends. I must see the war chief."

Wrapped Wrist made his way through the camp, nodding to women and children who nodded back. Most of the men he remembered from the camp at the hot springs. They waved, questions in their hooded gazes as they glanced first at Crow Woman where she stood talking to Ironwood and then back at Wrapped Wrist.

Probably wondering how I managed to keep my balls intact.

"Wrapped Wrist!"

He turned, seeing Bad Cast, a smile on his face as he hurried across the camp.

Bad Cast called, "Your timing is perfect. Ripple's awake." He gestured toward Crow Woman. "And I see that you've come back with the most beautiful woman in camp. I supposed you lingered in the robes like usual."

"Not with that one, old friend. Something's bent in her souls. If she offered herself, it would scare the wood right out of my shaft. You've heard the story told about the Stone Desert People?"

"The one about their women having teeth in their sheaths?"

Wrapped Wrist pointed at Crow Woman. "If ever a sheath had teeth, it would be hers."

"Sounds nasty."

"What's the news?" Wrapped Wrist embraced his kinsman.

Bad Cast's smile dropped the slightest bit. "Scary times. The Mountain Witch took Spots."

"She what?"

"Took him. Told him to carry her things and started off for Flowing Waters Town."

"To do what?"

"How should I know? Witches don't usually tell me things. But from what I can gather talking to people here, she didn't tell them, either. I get the impression that she pretty much does as she wants." He arched his eyebrow. "Would you want to question her?"

"I've never even seen her."

"Trust me, you don't want to. Spots said she was the scariest woman he's ever known."

Wrapped Wrist pointed at Crow Woman. "He's never met *that* one."

Bad Cast grasped his elbow. "Did you see Soft Cloth? What's the news from home?"

"I saw no one but White Eye." He lowered his voice. "Ironwood is brokering an alliance with White Eye to attack the First People during the Moon Ceremony."

"I know." Bad Cast led him to one of the stone-and-wattle buildings back in the trees. A dark-eyed woman with gleaming black hair sat outside the door, her long fingers weaving a basket from sumac and yucca. In the bottom was a pattern the likes of which Wrapped Wrist had never seen.

When the woman looked up at him, it was as if her eyes could see straight through him. But for those haunted eyes, he would have thought her charming.

"Be there for her," the woman said in an accented tongue. "She will need you."

"What?" Wrapped Wrist asked. "Who?"

The woman had returned her attention to the basket as if he'd never existed. As she turned the basket, he could see the design in the bottom: some sort of combination of man, snake, and bird. The very sight of it brought a shiver to his spine.

He ducked in behind Bad Cast, blinking in the dim light. It took a moment for his eyes to adjust. He squatted next to a pallet where Ripple lay.

His friend looked pale, the left side of his jaw still swollen, his hand bound in splints. Ripple's eyes, however, were clear, deep and wide, as if having seen the other side of the world's souls.

"How are you?" Bad Cast asked.

"Sore," Ripple said with a slur. "My body hurts, but nothing like my souls do."

"Why is that?" Wrapped Wrist asked.

Ripple whispered, "I've seen things. Been told things. Where is the war chief? I must see him. I have a message..."

"They've sent for him," Bad Cast said gently. "He's on the way."

"Seen what?" Wrapped Wrist asked.

"I didn't know who she was at first."

"Cold Bringing Woman?" Wrapped Wrist asked. "You mean your vision on the mountain wasn't...?"

Ripple reached up with his right hand, gripping Wrapped Wrist's arm. "Soyok! She was carrying me away when Cold Bringing Woman came and took me back."

"Who? Who's Soyok?" Bad Cast looked confused.

"That's her Spirit name," Ripple whispered, looking away. "We know her as the Blue God." He shook his head. "Odd that I didn't recognize her."

Bad Cast cried, "You *saw* the Blue God?"

Ripple nodded. "If Cold Bringing Woman hadn't found me... Gods, I hate to think about it. As it is, I've changed things. My fault. A new bargain has been struck. I have to see the war chief. Where is he?"

"He's talking to Crow Woman about attacking Pinnacle Great House," Wrapped Wrist told him.

"I *must* see him. A weasel creeps in our midst. I have to make sure he doesn't waver. He has to believe... it's just my word."

Wrapped Wrist asked, "What are you talking about?"

"Fire and ice," Ripple said numbly. "Opposites crossed. Black flakes of snow...falling from a gray sky."

"Black flakes of snow?" Wrapped Wrist glanced uneasily at Bad Cast.

Bad Cast muttered, "He's still delirious."

"He's speaking plainly," the woman at the door called, her basket still in hand. "It is your hearing that is confused. The gods have chosen you. It is through your eyes that the story shall be told."

"Does that mean we're somehow special?" Bad Cast asked skeptically.

"No," Ripple rasped. "We are cursed."

The scream sounded so close, as if someone in abject terror were just above Spots' head.

He bolted upright in the night, a cry stifled in his panicked throat.

The thin blanket fell away to leave him gaping in the darkness. He blinked, staring up at the sky. Spider Woman's constellation was just rising, telling him that it was still several hands of time before dawn. In the stillness of the night, crickets chirped, a distant owl hooted, and a slight breeze stirred.

He rubbed a callused hand over his face and stared around. Their camp sat atop a low saddle ridge that separated the River of Souls from Spirit River. The pale loamy soil was dotted by inky blotches of juniper. Even in the faint light, he could see well enough to determine that no one was close. So where had the scream...

He squinted at the Spirit bag Nightshade had given him to carry. It lay just an arm's length beyond his head.

Far enough away to dim the whispers and mute the wailings.

"Gods, what's in there?"

"Things you don't want to know." Nightshade's voice was little more than a sibilant whisper. "Heard that, did you?"

"The scream?" He looked this way and that, finally seeing her, her form hidden in the shadow of a sandstone boulder. She was sitting with her back straight, legs crossed; her hands lay on her knees, palms up. Even in the night, he could see her wide-open eyes, feel her presence rasping against his souls.

"Soyok prowls the night."

"Who?"

"You know her as the Blue God. She has run amok through the thlatsinas, sending them scampering among the clouds. They have taken refuge on their mountain."

"The one that used to be called the Rain Spinner?"

"Sternlight renamed it for the thlatsinas," she said softly. "Names, like all things, have their times. Rain Spinner is gone."

"But the mountain remains."

"Did you think it odd that the Rainbow Serpent rose at the foot of the Thlatsina Mountains?"

"I, uh..."

"The Spirits of the sky are joining with those of the ground." A pause. "Your friend, Ripple, has returned."

"Returned? From where?" Gods, what was she talking about? The subject of conversation seemed to dart around like a water skipper on a still pond.

"Soyok almost had him. Horo Mana saved him."

"The Blue God almost caught Ripple?" Who in the name of the sage was Horo Mana?

Nightshade whispered, "Opposites crossed. We shall see them Dance together across the sky."

"You talk in riddles! Where did that scream come from? I'd swear it was from the bag." He pointed at the dim shape.

"It came from a place you don't wish to travel to."

He stared first at her and then at the worrisome bag where it lay on the pale soil. She was right: He didn't want anything more to do with the thing. But for his intense fear of her, he might have just sneaked away in the night to be rid of both of them.

"You'd not get far," she told him. "They have latched their claws into the margins of your souls. The Dreams would pull you back."

"Get out of my head!" He placed his hands against his ears, flopping down in the bedding and pulling his blanket over his head. There he lay panting, smelling the warm mustiness of his blanket, eyes pressed closed.

The hunter is cowering, trying to close his souls to the calls and questions of the Spirits. I suppose I could speak to him as a mother does to her child, tell him of the things I have seen while in the arms of Sister Datura. I could tell him of the new bargain sealed by Soyok and Horo Mana. Could he withstand the knowledge, or would it send him shrieking away in the night to escape the future that continues to wrap around us?

Do I do him any favors?

I sense Brother Mud Head as he Dances around our small camp. I can feel his heavy tread, a weightless tremor that puffs dust around his bare feet. The time is coming near. He revels in the knowledge that soon we shall both be free.

It is only a matter of time until all the players are in their proper position. When the last of them is in place, the end will be irrevocable.

How do I tell Spots that the scream he heard was mine?

Chapter Two

"Let me see." Webworm leaned forward to stare at the cloth bundle Leather Hand laid upon the great kiva floor. The room was cool, dimly lit by the shaft of sunlight that streamed through the smoke hole. It shone in a square centered on the sipapu. The symbolic entrance to the Underworlds was dug into the floor in front of the decorated screens that masked the northern entrance.

On this day Webworm wore the most extraordinary bright blue shirt dyed from a thousand larkspur petals. He had used mourning dove grease in his hair and pulled the shining warrior's bun tight at the back of his head, sticking three eagle feathers into it.

Leather Hand crouched, untying a yucca cord that bound the cloth and unfolding the layers. The innermost were caked and blackened with old blood. With a hard tug he freed the last wrapping from the shrunken flesh.

Webworm bent, unconcerned with the ripe odor

rising from the old woman's head. Her features had been mashed by the cloth, the nose bent, lips twisted and pushed out of shape. The eyes had sunk deep into the skull, and streaks of gray could be seen in her matted hair.

"Greetings, Matron," Webworm said. "Far View is in turmoil wondering where your head has gotten off to. They're running around like turkeys in a cougar's shadow, not knowing which way to turn, let alone what happened."

Leather Hand stepped back, crossing his arms. "It wasn't any trouble, Blessed Sun. The few guards she had on duty were expecting nothing. Slipping past them was child's play."

Webworm reached out, shoving White Cloud Woman's head with his toe. The gruesome orb rocked back and forth like a macabre child's toy. "What of her daughter, Three Corn?"

"I whispered at her doorway that it might be better for her health if she were to leave Far View and never come back."

"Do you think she will?"

Leather Hand shrugged. "The people there, of course, will beg for her to take her mother's place as Matron."

"If they do, and if she becomes, shall we say, recalcitrant, can you repeat this triumph?" Webworm indicated the pathetic head.

"I have my ways of getting around Far View."

"You're sure that no one saw you?"

"Only one person, Blessed Sun. And I trust him implicitly."

"Implicitly?"

"Should I discover that he has betrayed me in any way, I'll have his head for my own."

Webworm stared at the grisly trophy, lost in thought. "Take it away. Bury it where no one will ever find it. Oh, and be sure that you smash it first. Preferably with a very large and heavy rock."

"Yes, Blessed Sun."

"Then I want you back here. Blue Racer arrives later tonight. I will meet with him here. Tomorrow morning. I would have you present."

"Yes, Blessed Sun."

Webworm turned, then looked back, admiring the pristine white moccasins on Leather Hand's feet. "Those are very nice."

"A gift from the late Matron." Leather Hand bent down and began replacing the cloth around the head. "Something to remember her by."

Webworm smiled as he turned away. "Memories are such sweet treats, aren't they?"

At that moment Ravengrass descended partway down the steps. "Blessed Sun? A runner has arrived from Matron Larkspur. He has urgent news for you."

Webworm nodded. "Deputy, depending on what this is, I may want your input."

A long moment passed after Webworm and Leather Hand's steps faded. Finally, the silence was broken when a sigh was uttered from behind the decorated screen. The Buffalo Clan elder Creeper stepped out from where he'd been hidden; a Dance mask he'd been repairing was still clutched in his pudgy hands.

He stared at the few dark spots of blood that had leaked onto the floor.

"Blessed Featherstone," he whispered, "what has become of the man we used to love?"

Chapter Three

louds had rolled in from the southwest. In silence Bad Cast and Wrapped Wrist watched them from the high mesa promontory. In contrast to the First People's belief that Flute Player brought the rains, Sternlight had preached that the thlatsinas Danced them from the Cloud People.

Bad Cast rubbed his chin. He wished for rain, a gentle shower that would wash the premonition of disaster from their world. Rain, however, never came.

Could it be that the Cloud People were so disgusted by the strife between Flute Player and the katsinas that they brought rain for neither?

Or was it something else? Was it that neither the Flute Player nor the katsinas called out to the Cloud People for fear that the rival would be given credit for any beneficent rainfall? Either way, most of the crops were gone in the dryland farms. The question was, could the irrigated valleys produce enough to feed the hungering masses?

Bad Cast and Wrapped Wrist walked to the open

space that served as a plaza for the little settlement. People kept looking up at the gray skies, turning their cheeks to the hot dry wind and wondering if rain would follow.

Gods, how they all missed it. Around him, the forest was dry, the duff crackling underfoot. When he plucked living ponderosa needles and bent them between his fingers, they barely bruised, so dry were they.

Overhead, the dark clouds seemed to brood, and distant thunder carried on the pregnant air.

"What do you think?" Wrapped Wrist asked as he matched step.

"I don't know. It should rain. It's the season for it."

"It's been the season for it for the last two moons!" Wrapped Wrist gestured futilely. "And what have we gotten? Blue skies."

"Drought skies," Bad Cast corrected. "Pale and white around the horizons. I heard a joke today. Poor Singer said he appreciated the drought."

"How's that?"

"He said that with all the grass gone, he could see the rattlesnakes coming."

"He worries about rattlesnakes?"

"Not anymore. He says he can see their canteens sticking through the dust before they crawl close enough to bite him."

Wrapped Wrist frowned. "A holy man should know that rattlesnakes don't have shoulders."

"What do shoulders have to do with it?"

"Without shoulders what keeps the canteen from sliding off the snake?"

They had reached the outskirts of the fire. People

sat in a ring around the blaze, turning their eyes to the trees where Ironwood, Night Sun, Poor Singer, and Cornsilk were talking. The war chief had called this meeting no more than a finger's time after he'd left Ripple's bedside.

As the gloom deepened, Bad Cast could see lightning flickering among the high peaks to the north. The wind teased them as it alternately puffed and died, as if trying to make up its mind whether or not to blow.

Most of Ironwood's warriors were present: Yucca Sock, Crow Woman, Firehorn, Right Hand, and Whistle among others.

Bad Cast noticed that Wrapped Wrist had fixed his gaze on Crow Woman. Seated, she had laced her arms around her slim legs and was talking to Yucca Sock. A glittering hardness lay behind her eyes, something sharp and cutting. From the pinching of Wrapped Wrist's mouth, the faint lines on his brow, Bad Cast knew his friend was puzzled.

"I thought you didn't like her."

"I don't. Pus and blood. What a waste. Two bent and wounded souls, captive inside that entrancing body."

Bad Cast noticed that Whistle, too, was watching her from his place across the circle. His intent stare indicated a shared an obsession with the woman.

At that moment Ironwood turned, leading his small party to the open circle. He and Night Sun remained standing while Poor Singer and Cornsilk seated themselves.

Ironwood looked around the ring of faces, nodding to some, smiling at others. Bad Cast could see the strain behind his expression, knew that the man's souls were screaming at him, tearing with fear and uncertainty. The war chief might have been stone for all he betrayed of the turmoil within.

Ironwood cleared his throat and began, "Many of you know that something is happening. We have initiated contact with the Moon People. Soon the Sunwatcher, Blue Racer, will be journeying to First Moon Mountain to welcome Sister Moon home from her passage across the sky. Webworm and Desert Willow may even accompany him for the opening ceremony. We will never have another opportunity like this to strike at the very heart of the First People."

Night Sun stepped forward. Firelight was shining in her silvered hair. She wore a black dress decorated with four-pointed white stars. "For the first couple of days after the First People reach Pinnacle House they will be wary, alert for any sign of trouble. We will wait until they grow careless. As soon as their guard drops, we will be in position to strike."

Ironwood continued, "A great many pilgrims have already begun leaving their homes, journeying northward. These people—many of them desperate because of the drought—hope to see the miracle of Sister Moon returning home after her eighteen-and-a-half-summer journey. They want to see her when she rises...right between the pillars of First Moon Mountain."

Night Sun raised her hands in supplication. "The pilgrims serve us well. With so many people flooding into First Moon Valley, we can move with ease, hide among them."

Ironwood thrust his thumbs into his belt. "The trouble, of course, is that many of us once served the Blessed Sun. Our faces are known. Beyond that, the approaches to First Moon Mountain will be well guarded." A pause. "But there are other ways. Back ways. Trails that only the First Moon People know."

Night Sun continued. "If we are to take Pinnacle Great House from the First People, it will be through stealth and audacity."

As if in emphasis, distant thunder rolled across the mesa tops.

"I suppose that's where we come in," Wrapped Wrist muttered.

Night Sun raised her hands even higher. "You should know this, too. We have recently received word that Matron White Cloud Woman was murdered in her bed. The assassin cut her throat, removed her head, and left her corpse lying in its blood. Although guards were posted, no one knew anything was amiss until late the next morning."

"Tower Builders?" Crow Woman asked.

"They would have been spotted," Whistle interjected. "Someone would have seen the strangers. An alarm would have been raised. Her guards—who were loyal kinsmen—heard nothing."

"Clan feud?" Yucca Sock speculated.

Ironwood shook his head. "Unlikely. None of White Cloud Woman's rivals claim credit—even those happy to have her gone. Word is that in Far View it's a great mystery, and there is considerable unease at the manner of it."

Night Sun had been watching the fire with pensive eyes. "We must accept that this might be an extremely adept move by one of her enemies. White Cloud Woman was a forceful critic of Webworm's policies. As long as confusion reigns in

Far View Town, Blue Dragonfly Clan stands to gain."

"Was anything taken?" Whistle asked.

"From what we hear," Ironwood replied, "only a pair of white moccasins that she was working on. The assassin left nothing of his own behind. The stories circulating around Far View claim that a witch flew in on a rawhide shield, cut off the Matron's head, and flew back out again."

"So we're to be on the lookout for a witch wearing white moccasins?" Crow Woman asked. "We do see a lot them flying around here."

A chorus of chuckles rose from the circle.

Ironwood grinned. "If any witch wearing white moccasins flies close, you're welcome to shoot him down. Just be sure he's within bow range."

Crow Woman extended her left arm, drawing back her right, and mimicked loosing an arrow at the cloud-black sky.

It was at that point that Ironwood looked straight at Bad Cast and asked, "Hunter, what are the chances that White Eye can build an alliance among your clans to attack the First People?"

Bad Cast shot a worried glance at Wrapped Wrist as all eyes turned upon him. "I—I don't know." He swallowed hard, suddenly flustered. "We're mostly farmers, not warriors. I mean some of the elders, Green Claw and Black Sage, won't want to. They would much rather pacify the First People. Others, like Hoarse Caller, will probably vote for it. It's hard to say, War Chief. My people have never been asked this before."

Night Sun was giving him a thorough appraisal. "Let me ask you this: If the clans do vote to attack the

First People, what are the chances that someone will betray us to Matron Larkspur?"

"If you wish to defeat the First People on First Moon Mountain, you will do as I say," Ripple interrupted as he walked unsteadily out of the night and entered the firelight. He looked around, eyes like crystals. "Cold Bringing Woman has told me how this can be done, War Chief. You must place your trust in me, and in your warriors here. Can you do that?"

Night Sun's quick eyes took in Ripple's worn hunting shirt, the garment apparently donated by someone. Her gaze lingered on his maimed hand in its splints and his swollen jaw. "What do you have to tell us, Dreamer?"

Dreamer? The words caught Bad Cast by surprise.

Ripple turned to Ironwood. "What is coming will demand a terrible price. We stand on the threshold. I have seen." He walked up to the war chief, firelight casting his body in bronze. His crushed hand was held before his chest. "I have looked into the face of the Blue God. She taught me terror and revulsion. Now, she is loose on the land."

"What would you have me do?" Ironwood asked.

"Are you willing to take one extraordinary chance to save your world?"

Ironwood narrowed his eye, glanced uneasily at Night Sun, and said, "I am, Dreamer."

Ripple's lips twitched as if the words elicited some painful memory. "Are you willing to pay what the gods demand?"

Ironwood's expression lined, pulling the patch taut over his missing eye. "I cannot give you an answer until I know more about what you've seen, Dreamer."

In a hollow voice, Ripple said, "I have seen you standing atop Pinnacle Great House, War Chief. Your body is bowed, the shape of it illuminated as the morning light shines through the great stone pillars. In that vision, you are victorious. But it comes at a terrible cost to you."

Ironwood stiffened. "If you have seen this, and know the way of it, I will pay that cost."

For a long moment Ripple watched Ironwood, and sadly shook his head. Then he said, "Your allies are fire and ice. Send word now. Tell White Eye that only the strongest threads of silk tether the web. If he would see the First People fall, he must call the elders to council. Spider Woman wants all of the flies in the web before we strike."

"Fire and ice?" Whistle asked. "Webs, silk, flies? What is this?"

Ripple looked to the heavens; flashes of heat lightning silently lanced the clouds. "The fire is loosened; flames rise high. The Dance is begun. In days drawing nigh, a web is spun. Sister Moon is caped, veiled, and hidden beneath a midnight cloak. Strike, great War Chief. And furl the frozen smoke."

Then he turned his gaze on Night Sun. She gasped at something deep in his expression and placed a hand to her chest.

Ripple gave her a respectful nod, turned, and walked back into the darkness.

Ironwood looked pensive as he fingered his chin. "What do you think, wife?"

Night Sun's eyes were like hollows in her face. "Is he another Sternlight? Perhaps a Dune? I don't know what to think or whom to trust."

"I do." It was Poor Singer who stood. "A messenger must be sent to White Eye. If this web is to be spun, it must be done as Ripple says." He studied Ironwood with sober eyes. "War Chief? Are you ready to pay the price?"

Ironwood's cheek muscles bunched. In a soft voice he said, "Yes. Of course."

Poor Singer glanced meaningfully at Cornsilk. "If that is your decision, Cornsilk and I must pack. Our destiny lies in the south among my mother's people."

"Are they involved?" Night Sun asked, placing a thin hand on his shoulder.

Poor Singer took her hand from his shoulder, raised it to his lips, and looked into her eyes as he kissed it. "Only in the future, my Matron."

Bad Cast felt it, a bristling in the air, as if something of great import were happening. He could see the reverence, almost worship, in Poor Singer's eyes as he held the older woman's hand.

Night Sun smiled bravely. "Take good care of my daughter, Dreamer. We shall do what we must for our people."

With that Poor Singer nodded, released her hand, and touched Ironwood on the shoulder as if in reassurance. Then he reached down to pull Cornsilk to her feet. Together they walked off toward their lodge, heads close as they whispered.

Ironwood was watching Night Sun, a frown lining his forehead. His single eye desperately sought an explanation. She shrugged but moved to stand beside him as he faced the circle of witnesses. He pointed to Crow Woman. "Can you and Wrapped Wrist make the trip back to White Eye and relate these things?"

"Yes, War Chief." Crow Woman stood, searched the circle until she spotted Wrapped Wrist, and jerked her head before starting off.

"Here we go again," Wrapped Wrist muttered.

"I might as well go with you. There's nothing more I—"

"Bad Cast?" Ironwood called. "If you would meet with Whistle and me, we have things to discuss."

"You were saying?" Wrapped Wrist asked.

"I was saying, tell Soft Cloth that I'm well—that I love her and miss her and our daughter. Tell my family I'll be home as soon as I can." Bad Cast pointed to where Crow Woman had disappeared. "I wouldn't make her wait. She doesn't strike me as the forgiving kind."

"You take care."

He slapped Wrapped Wrist on the shoulder. "I'm not the one traveling off this mountain in the middle of the night."

"We'll have light." He indicated the flashes of distant lightning that strobed the sky.

They shared a smile, and then he was gone.

Bad Cast walked through the standing people, hearing caution in their voices, feeling the growing tension. He placed himself at the edge of the circle that had gathered around Ironwood in time to hear Night Sun say, "From this moment on our fate rests with the gods." Then the Matron walked off in the direction of her lodge.

Ironwood turned, expression serious. "It appears that we have an attack to plan."

"War Chief?" Whistle asked. "If what Ripple said is true, we will be attacking in conjunction with the combined clans. How do we coordinate so many forces?"

Ironwood's smile turned wary. "Did anything the Dreamer said make sense to you?"

"No."

"Then, Whistle, as the Matron said, we must trust ourselves to the gods."

Thunder rolled, banging and crashing across the land.

Wrapped Wrist was bent on one knee, tying his pack together. He lifted his ceramic canteen, sloshing it to judge the contents: at least half full.

"Wrapped Wrist?"

He looked up to see Ripple's dark silhouette against the lightning-white clouds. The form vanished as the heavens went black.

"Ripple? What was that? What were you trying to say back there at the fire?"

"The pieces are being moved into place, old friend. I won't be seeing you again. Not like this. Not just the two of us."

"What are you talking about?"

"I've come to say goodbye, and to thank you for being my friend."

"I'll always be your friend. Don't be silly. When this is all over and—"

"I never thanked you for not telling old Half Eye that I was the one who stole her pot."

"I didn't know you knew I knew."

"I shouldn't have taken it in the first place. It was the only thing she had left of her mother's."

"She shouldn't have called you a shiftless thief. That was uncalled for. You weren't. Because you were on your own, everyone who ended up missing something thought you'd taken it."

Ripple chuckled. "We weren't very good farmers. Fir Brush got better as the years passed."

"You made up for it with meat. No one hunts better than you do."

"I did steal, sometimes, when no one was around... well, it was that or starve."

"People understood, Ripple. No one really cared because you always did something to make up for what you took. You'd bring a ground squirrel or rabbit, or even just a shiny stone if you thought it would please someone."

"I just thought you should know that I'm sorry I took that pot. Then Half Eye died, and I never had a chance to make it up to her."

Wrapped Wrist grunted. "She was a bitter old woman. No one liked her."

"You always took my side. For that, I thank you."

Wrapped Wrist stared up in the darkness. A distant flash haloed Ripple's form, betraying the worried hunch to his posture. "You sound like this is goodbye forever. Ripple, we'll make it through this. You'll see. A couple of cycles from now—"

"When your trial comes, remember this: Swallow your fear. It is meaningless. Illusion meant to keep you from what needs to be done. You have never understood that your souls are even stronger than your body.

Without death, there is no life, no future. You know that, don't you?"

"Sure, what hunter—?"

"You know that, deep down between your souls. Tell me you understand."

What was this passion in his voice? "Of course I understand."

Ripple reached down in the darkness. The instant he touched his finger to Wrapped Wrist's forehead, lightning arced in jagged patterns across the sky. From Wrapped Wrist's perspective it might have leaped from his friend's silhouetted head like a tracery to burn through the heavens.

"If you would be happy, you must save her."

"Save who?"

"Farewell, my friend."

"Don't say—"

When lightning flashed again, Ripple was gone.

Chapter Four

Morning cast a blue light through the low-hanging smoke. It rose from the breakfast cook fires to hang lazily in the trees. For as wild as the night had been, the morning air barely stirred. Voices carried as mothers talked to children. The deeper murmurs of warriors leavened the clatter of wooden dishes and ceramic spoons.

Whistle, Yucca Sock, and Firehorn knelt to either side of Bad Cast and stared thoughtfully at a drawing he had scratched into the dark earth with a sharpened stick. Bad Cast rubbed his face. Was that good enough? Had he managed to get all the details right? He wasn't sure but that the final rendition didn't look more like a too-many-legged spider than First Moon Mountain with its twin spires and sheer cliffs.

Ironwood was chewing absently at his lower lip as he studied the image. "Can they see down the slopes on every side?"

"They can." Bad Cast used his finger to point out the slopes. "These cliffs can be climbed in many places. Any young man who has spent time in rough country has the skills to scale them. The guards will be fewer, but the chances for discovery higher. A climber will be vulnerable to something as simple as a dropped stone."

He indicated the north slope. "This route is the best. The approaches to the mountain are timbered with spruce, fir, and ponderosa. The slope is steep, the footing treacherous. They won't know you are close until you are clambering up the rimrock."

"Just as we won't know where the lookouts are until we appear at their feet," Whistle noted. "What conceals us, also hides them."

"We'll be moving in force; their sentries will be standing quietly," Yucca Sock added. "It's like building a disaster block by block."

Ironwood raised an eyebrow. "Only if a guard is still there when we come. Whistle? What is your opinion? Would Matron Larkspur allow you within the walls again?"

Whistle's expression was pensive. "I think that might be arranged."

Bad Cast remembered the man's words concerning his night with the Matron. Blood of the gods, if Whistle was that bent on suicide he could just throw himself headlong off a cliff.

"If you could silence the guards along that northern slope, it might make all the difference." Ironwood took a deep breath, as if his lungs were starved. His fingers were fidgeting with the fur patch that covered his missing eye.

Bad Cast indicated the northwest slope. "Climbing here puts you behind the farthest pillar. The slope is loose, difficult, but screened by the bulk of the mountain and both pillars."

"And it's a lot tougher to traverse the slope under the pillars," Whistle pointed out. "Any body of warriors crossing there is going to make noise as their feet knock the rocks and scree loose."

Firehorn asked, "War Chief, suppose we take Pinnacle Great House? What then? How do we hold it?"

"We don't. We take our captives, set fire to the great house, and retreat back down the mountain."

Bad Cast was as surprised as the others when Night Sun calmly said from behind them, "Taking captives is not a good idea."

Bad Cast turned on his heels, staring up at the Matron.

"No captives, my wife?" Ironwood asked.

She took a breath. "Husband, am I to assume that you will take the chance of Larkspur, Desert Willow, or Webworm escaping to hide out in the mountains and foment their poison? Have you forgotten that the Blessed Sun's warriors are eating their enemies, or that White Cloud Woman's head was cut off her body inside her own quarters?"

Ironwood looked at her with an intensity that Bad Cast could almost reach out and feel. "Killing them will set a terrible precedent. In the past we have always let the Council decide the fate of prisoners."

"The Council consisted of the First People," she said reasonably. "We're hoping to build a new Council, one composed of the Made People clans as well as the last of the First People's clans. The room must be swept clean, husband. Webworm is already ahead of you on that account."

"You are assuming that he ordered White Cloud Woman's death."

She gave him a kind smile. "You still see him as he was. In your memory you are sharing campfires, remembering raids when you laughed together and enjoyed a bond of camaraderie that only a beloved war chief can share with his trusted deputy. In the years since he became the Blessed Sun, he's changed."

Ironwood stared wistfully at the drawing. "He wasn't the right man for leadership."

Night Sun continued without relent. "He is desperate. Disaster is looming before him. If we can remove Webworm, Desert Willow, Larkspur, and—gods grant us—Leather Hand all at once, the serpent will writhe without a head. We can call an assembly of the Made People clans, the last of Red Lacewing Clan, and those of the Blue Dragonfly Clan that might be called upon to effect reason over revenge. With luck we can still mend our world."

Ironwood sat paralyzed, his single eye fixed on some point beyond their seeing. His hard face revealed nothing—not a twitch of the lips, not the least tightening around his single eye. In a listless voice he finally said, "You're right."

Bad Cast watched the warriors around him shift nervously.

"When do we go?" Whistle asked.

"When we hear that Blue Racer's party is close." Ironwood's single eye locked with Night Sun's.

She said, "Discovering if Webworm is coming will be more difficult."

Ironwood considered. "Nothing would have stopped him from taking his mother's body south in the funeral procession. But Jay Bird's attack still burns in his memory. Before the Dust People stole from his larder, he might have been lured away from Flowing Waters Town, stripping the place of warriors. What if in his absence, one of the Made People clan elders—knowing his relatives are starving down south—slips a couple of basket loads of corn out of Dusk House?"

"Others might be tempted to try," Whistle added.

Night Sun settled beside them. "Quite a problem for him, isn't it? He's squatting on a wealth of food that he dare not leave. Yet he needs to have the prestige of being seen at the lunar maximum."

Bad Cast asked, "What about Leather Hand? Anyone who got caught stealing might be smacked in the head and eaten. Wouldn't that be a deterrent?"

Night Sun shrugged. "Not for someone like Creeper. Creeper has a soft heart, and Webworm knows it. In Webworm's absence, Creeper might give in to a desperate plea by one of his kinsmen. In Creeper's mind, no minor infraction like the theft of food would justify more than a severe reprimand from Webworm."

"Creeper never has been a deep thinker," Ironwood agreed. "For that reason alone, Webworm might be enticed into staying within the safe walls of Dusk House."

"If he does," Whistle noted, "that will create a complication for us. He will be at the center of his strength, and quick to dispense it against us."

"Or will he?" Yucca Sock was stroking his chin. "When he hears news of the attack on Pinnacle Great House, will the Webworm you've been describing launch an attack against us? Won't he want to solidify his power?"

Firehorn scoffed. "If he does send warriors against us, we'll run them ragged in the forests just like before. They can chase our ghosts among the trees while we pick them off one by one. Eventually they will tuck their tails and scamper back to the walls of Dusk House."

"He can't send many warriors after us." Whistle glanced from face to face. "His warriors are already too thinly spread. Why do you think Leather Hand ate those Dust People? He's doing with terror what he can't by force of arms."

Night Sun patted Ironwood on the shoulder. "This is warrior's talk. I'll go and tell the others that they should begin to get their things together. We'll be ready to leave when—"

"No," Ironwood said firmly. "I'm only taking warriors."

Night Sun stopped short, a frown lining her forehead. "We will appear more like pilgrims if women and children accompany the men. Somehow I don't believe you're going to blend in bristling with bows, arrows, and war clubs."

Ironwood's smile was warm. "No, I suppose not, but I want you to stay, wife. You and the rest. Something about the way Poor Singer said goodbye to you last night worried me."

"And?" she asked softly, love in her eyes.

"He wouldn't tell me when I searched him out later. He just gave me that irritating smile and told me what a Blessing I had been to his life. What was that supposed to mean? Me? A Blessing?"

Night Sun relented. "Oh, very well. If you would feel better, the women and children will stay."

"They'll never find you here. Among the Moon People villages, someone might recognize you. You know what a triumph Webworm would have, parading you down the Great North Road bound and disgraced."

"Plan this raid." She ran her fingers through his hair. "I'll be waiting when you finish."

Bad Cast watched her leave, wondering at the love that had shone from her eyes.

Ironwood sighed. "Now, Bad Cast, once we have filtered into First Moon Valley, I'm assuming you have houses where we can stay? Kinsmen who would keep us out of sight until the night of the attack?"

"Of course."

Yucca Sock stood up, stretching. As he looked off to the north, he said, "Did any of you notice? There's a smoke plume up in the Spirit Mountains."

"Compliments of the lightning last night," Ironwood muttered as he studied the drawing. "And that's another thing. As dry as it is, we don't want to let a fire get away from us. When we camp, cookfires are to be treated very carefully. If we set the forest on fire, everyone will be looking our direction. We want to arrive at Moon Valley in secret."

Webworm wore a resplendent yellow war shirt that hung to just above his knees. Black four-pointed stars had been painted onto the cloth, and a startling purple sash was belted at his waist. For the occasion he had chosen a wooden headpiece that mimicked sticky geranium flower petals. The effect was as if his head were the center of the flower. In his right hand he carried a solid stone war club Traded up from the south.

Matron Desert Willow was waiting when he walked through the opening created by the painted walls that masked the northern curve of the kiva. He smiled as he met her dark eyes.

She had actually tried to respond to his caresses the night before. That she had done so was a mark in her favor. When he had slid into her warm sheath and let his weight settle onto her slender body, he had found himself oddly excited. War Chief Wind Leaf had lain thus just days before him. Where his hard rod now rested, so had Wind Leaf's. Did her sheath know the difference? Did it care? Was one man's stiff shaft as good as another's?

He glanced next at Wind Leaf, seeing his war chief's reserved expression. The man wore a bright red shirt, his feet shod in intricately knotted yucca sandals, his use-worn war club hanging from the belt at his narrow waist. Behind him, Leather Hand was dressed in a dark scarlet war shirt, his feet in the resplendent white moccasins. He had a flintlike quality that Wind Leaf lacked these days. But then, Leather Hand and his companions had set themselves apart.

He cast a smile at Creeper, wondering. From his old companion's expression, one might have thought that his best friend were mortally ill. When the time and circumstances were right, he'd ask.

Sunwatcher Blue Racer was an ascetic-looking man in a spotless white breechcloth. He had a thin white cotton shawl over his narrow shoulders. The color accented his dark tan. He bowed his head and touched fingers to his forehead, calling, "Greetings, Blessed Sun."

"Greetings, Sunwatcher. You had a pleasant journey here?"

"Yes, Blessed Sun. The porters were both stout of heart and strong of limb. They bore me here in record time, and without so much as a single misstep."

"I shall reward them well. War Chief?"

"Yes, Blessed Sun?"

"See to it when we are finished here."

"Yes, Blessed Sun."

Webworm walked up to Blue Racer and stared into his dark eyes. A question lay there, as if the man were wondering something. "Yes, Sunwatcher?"

Blue Racer asked, "You will be coming to the Moon Ceremony?"

Webworm glanced sidelong at Desert Willow and then Wind Leaf. "I am not sure. I have a question of my own. You are the greatest of the Priests. Alone among them you have been charting the path of Father Sun across the sky, following the trail of Sister Moon as she inches her way toward her northern home."

"Yes, Blessed Sun."

"You have been marking the paths of the stars, following the constellations through the night sky."

"That is correct, Blessed Sun."

"Good. Then my question for you is a very simple one. It should have a simple answer."

"I would suppose so, Blessed Sun."

Webworm smiled as he leaned forward, his voice sibilant with threat. "Where is the rain?"

Blue Racer swallowed hard. "I cannot answer that, Blessed Sun. None of the signs have changed. No comets have appeared to distract the Cloud People. They still—"

"But they do not bring rain!" He narrowed his eyes. "Are you aware that most of the crops in the dryland farms are brown and dead? Are you aware that many of my people have eaten their seed corn?"

"Blessed Sun, I assure you, we have done all that we can."

Webworm glared at him, a thick black anger rising around his heart. "Sunwatcher, have you heard of the kings down south?"

"Kings, Blessed Sun? I do not know the term."

"Kings. Call them chiefs of chiefs, the Blessed of the Blessed, or so they style themselves."

"Ah, yes." Comprehension filled Blue Racer's eyes. "Far to the south, where a few of the bravest Traders venture. The stone pyramid builders. Yes, I have indeed heard of them, and the wonders of their great calendars that chart the—"

"Then you know how they feed their god. I believe they call him Chak or some such thing."

"Feed him?" Blue Racer looked confused.

Webworm smiled in a disarming fashion. "Those tall stone temples they build?"

"Oh, yes." Blue Racer nodded. "I've heard that they take captives atop them, cut their very hearts from their bodies, and tumble them down the...oh, my. Yes, I see. Feed the gods."

Webworm shot a quick glance at Leather Hand to read his face. "I am wondering, Sunwatcher, what would happen if we fed the gods here."

"Fed the Flute Player?"

"He calls the rain, doesn't he?"

Blue Racer considered that. "I'm not sure what the Flute Player would make of a man's heart, Blessed Sun. The Blue God, on the other hand—"

"Yes, yes, but the Blue God has never been one to involve herself in the conjuring of rain." Webworm waved a hand. "My problem, Sunwatcher, is drought. Without rain, there will be famine in the villages. Do you understand?" He gestured at Wind Leaf. "My warriors are barely keeping the pot from boiling over as it is. Do you have any conception how precarious our situation is?"

Blue Racer was reading the rage stewing behind Webworm's eyes. "Yes, Blessed Sun."

"Good." Webworm clapped his hand on the man's back, feeling his bones through his skinny shoulders. "Because if anyone can call the rain, it's you, correct? You're the one responsible for the rituals. You oversee the prayers and chants. You know, better than anyone else, how the thlatsina heresy of your predecessor has hurt us."

"Yes, Blessed Sun."

"Good!" He gave the man a rictus of a smile. "Since you know it all so well, you'll be perfect."

"Perfect, Blessed Sun?"

"If we don't have rain by the end of the Moon Ceremony, I shall feed you to the gods. Give your heart to the Flute Player, to be more precise. We don't have one of those tall white stone pyramids like they have down south, but I hear that they do have rain."

Blue Racer's dark eyes began to look moist and soft. His jaw worked as he tried three times to swallow. "Yes, Blessed Sun." It came out a whisper. Behind him,

Creeper's eyes had gone wide, disbelief in the set of his old round face.

"That will be all." Webworm turned, heading for the northern stairs. "Deputy Leather Hand, I have been giving a great deal of thought to Matron Larkspur's report. If you would accompany me, I have something for you and your special warriors to attend to."

"Yes, Blessed Sun," Leather Hand called as he fell in behind Webworm, followed him past the dividers and up the steps to the Priests' chamber.

"What do you think? Did I make an impression on the Sunwatcher?"

"You did."

"And?"

"Will you go through with it?"

"Feeding his heart to the Flute Player?" Webworm shrugged. "The people have to know we're trying, Deputy. Which brings me to my next problem: If I have to feed my Sunwatcher's heart to the Flute Player, I may need other hearts should his fail. There is one in particular that I would love to cut out." He glanced at Leather Hand. "I think you would like to have a crack at him, too."

"Ironwood's?"

"You seem to have a way of getting things done, Deputy War Chief. I have a plan. If it works, we will down two birds with one cast of the stone. Make this happen and you shall be amply rewarded."

Leather Hand nodded agreement. Then said, "Just one thing, Blessed Sun."

"And that is?"

"Don't ask me to make it rain."

Chapter Five

Ripple lay with his belly on a cool stone and watched the water boatmen as they stroked up to the water's surface, caught a breath, and dove, their two frondlike legs driving them down into the depths.

In the ponderosa pine that overhung the spring, cedar waxwings tittered as they searched the spreading branches for bugs. A nuthatch scampered up and down the scaly brown bark. The gray-and-white bird cocked its head, hunting for a stray grub with its keen eyes.

I have this one moment of peace.

Ripple took a deep breath and tried to carve it into his souls, hoping to savor it in the coming days. Turning his eyes back to the clear depths of the pool, he looked down into that small world and wished he could be part of it. Some other insect skittered between the pebbles in the bottom. Bees came one by one to drink at the pool's edge; and flies, moths, and butterflies lit, dipped their proboscises, and lifted into the hot dry day. Water dripped musically from wet stones where the seep trickled out of the moss-covered rock.

"Are you feeling well?" Orenda's harshly accented voice intruded on his thoughts.

"Did you know that water boatmen can fly?"

"They can?" He heard her as she came to sit on the stones above him.

He rolled onto his side and looked up at her. "I never knew that. I just watched one swim to the surface and fly away. I had always thought they were born of water."

"Born-of-Water?" She smiled. "Do you know him?"

"I don't understand."

"Nightshade and I brought him here with his brother Home-Going Boy. Born-of-Water is a white-hair. He has no color to his skin; his eyes are pink. He can't see very well, and Father Sun's light does terrible things to him. He sees the future and currently lives on the Green Mesa with his wife."

"And the other one?"

"Home-Going Boy was eaten by Grandfather Grizzly. He was born without arms." She shrugged. "A person without arms can't run very fast. Trees were close, but he couldn't climb them. Badgertail killed the bear. He was buried in the hide."

"Did Home-Going Boy have Power, too?"

Orenda nodded. "He saw the past. They were quite the pair. Forever a handful. When they learned to speak, Born-of-Water would tell of burning towns, masked Dancers, bearded white-skinned men, and silver birds trailing smoke across the sky. At the same time, Home-Going Boy would tell of Raven Hunter and Runs in Light, of Bad Belly and White Ash, and great animals with noses like elongated hands, and others with long white teeth. He'd draw them with his stubby little fingers: beasts like you've never seen. He liked one little boy in particular. He said his name would translate into our language as Tusk Boy."

"I've never heard of these things."

"Me either, but they must have existed."

"Or did he make them up?"

She studied him thoughtfully. "Did you make up your vision of Cold Bringing Woman?"

He slowly shook his head, seeing the god's white face in his souls' eye. "I wish I had."

She looked north as if to see through the trees. "Have you seen the smoke plume?"

"Lightning started it last night." He pulled himself into a sitting position. "Once again I would like to thank you for Healing me." He searched her eyes, seeing her reserve, her desperation to reach out to him.

"Healing." She smiled. "It's what I do best."

He studied her profile, aware once again what a haunting woman she was. "Why haven't you married?"

"There are reasons." She stared up at the branches where the nuthatch leaped magically up the rough bark. "For one thing, most men fear me. They think that, like Nightshade, I'm a witch."

"Are you?"

"I can't make a piece of rawhide fly, and believe me, I've tried. The mere thought of eating a dead baby's flesh makes me sick. I'd die of starvation before I'd touch it. I've tried cursing some of Ironwood and Night Sun's enemies, but none of them ever seem to keel over dead from hideous weeping wounds or fevers." She smiled at that. "What I do know are the herbs. With the right Spirit Plants, I can cure or kill."

"And the other reason?"

For a long time she sat in silence. "Something happened when I was child, Ripple. Men see it in my eyes."

She was watching him, waiting for revulsion to mar his expression.

"Then you were meant to live," he said simply. "Power had other things in store for you."

Her laughter was laced with irony. "Power never chooses a person for anything easy."

"No, it doesn't."

"I should be going. I'm sorry to have bothered you."

"You need not leave."

She gave him a skeptical look, the sort she would if his fever had broken out again.

"I just..." He shrugged it off. "I just want you to know that I don't fear you."

"Perhaps I only scare myself." She smiled wistfully. "Nightmares keep rising out of my past. I can't ever seem to outrun them."

He turned his head, as if to see through the screen of trees to the plume of fire burning high in the Spirit Mountains.

What I would give if all of my nightmares were behind me!

"Why do you keep staring at me that way?" Crow Woman gave Wrapped Wrist a sidelong glance as they wound down out of a patch of lodgepole pine and approached a small stream. "Is something bothering you?"

"Nothing." Wrapped Wrist tried to wave it off. He dropped to his hands and knees, touched his lips to the cool water, and drank. Wiping his lips, he stood and stepped across the creek.

Even from this low spot he could still see the blue-brown plume of smoke that rose above the northern peaks. As they had traveled that morning they had caught periodic glances of the fire through the trees. It had grown, the plume widening and blowing off to the east.

Crow Woman knelt on the stones of the crossing and placed her lips to the water.

He admired the sleek lines of her, wondering how such a magnificent woman could be such a bitter thorn.

She stood, water dripping from her firm chin. She wiped it away on the shoulder of her war shirt, her flinty eyes boring into him the entire time. "The look in your eyes has changed."

"Changed?" he asked. "My eyes are the same."

"It used to be you only looked at me with lust."

"I don't lust after you."

"You do...or I should say you do when you don't fear me."

"I don't fear you."

"Apparently you just lie a lot."

"I don't think you want to hear honesty."

She considered him, as if seeing him anew. "I'm not used to honesty from a man's lips."

"What about the war chief's? There must be some reason that you ran off to join his warriors."

"You need not concern yourself about that."

"But you think he's honest, don't you?"

She started up the trail, her eyes casting about the grassy valley bottom as if in search of any dangers. "He is the only honest man I know."

Wrapped Wrist chuckled. "Now you know two."

She resettled the pack on her shoulder, leaving him to watch her slim brown calves as she strode up the trail. He liked the way her hips moved.

"You're not honest." She said it so simply.

"I'm not?"

"If you were, you would tell me why your eyes have changed."

"Back to that again? All right, you said I look at you with lust or fear. What's changed?"

"Now you watch me with worry. Not for yourself, but for me. Why?"

He considered his reply as he forced himself to match her long-legged pace. She did it so easily; he was always at a half jog to keep up. Did he dare tell her what Ripple had said?

As if she heard his thoughts, she chided, "Honest?"

Throwing caution away, he said, "Ripple told me something."

"And that was?"

"He wanted me to save you."

Her laughter was melodious. "I saved myself long ago. I did it when I ran away and learned to fight. Know this, hunter: You can only save yourself. No one else can do it for you."

"I wasn't looking for a lecture. You asked for honesty. I gave it to you."

They walked along in silence; Wrapped Wrist studied the surrounding valley, seeing how the grass up the slopes had already gone tawny. The leaves on the trees had a wilted look about them. The sky above was brassy, as if filled with fine dust. Blood and bones, the world was dry.

"Do you trust this Ripple?" she asked suddenly.

"He is an old friend."

"He has always been a Dreamer?"

"He used to be just a hunter."

"But now people call him a Dreamer. I would understand what happened to him. Did he just become a Dreamer with the snap of the fingers?"

"He had a vision, one frightening enough that the First People tortured him for it."

"The Mountain Witch believes in him," she added. "You, who have known him, what do you think?"

Wrapped Wrist considered that as he watched dust puff around his sandaled feet. "He changed that night on the mountain. Something happened to him. Why would Power choose Ripple? He was never like most holy people. He was happier stalking the black timber for elk rather than seeking Power like a holy man. He never had that empty look in his eyes like a Seeker has."

"What did you see in his eyes last night?"

"Fear." Gods, yes, that's what it had been.

"For me?"

"For himself, I guess. For all of us."

"Why do you fear me? That is, when you're not lusting after me."

She wanted honesty? "I don't trust your anger. Maybe it's because I don't know where it comes from. I understand that some man hurt you, but that hard edge in your eyes can cut like obsidian."

"Good."

"The thing about obsidian," he continued as if he hadn't heard, "is that it'll slice magically through a man's flesh. Nothing is as sharp; but bend it the slightest bit and it snaps and shatters." He lowered his voice. "As I am afraid you will at the wrong moment."

She whirled, her hand going to the war club at her belt. Fire burned in her dark eyes as she whipped the weapon up to strike. "I am not that kind of woman. I refuse to be a victim. Not for them. Not for any man... let alone you!"

Wrapped Wrist backpedaled to escape her wrath. Raising both of his hands, he cried, "Easy! Pus and maggots! No wonder you don't think men are honest. If a man is, you want to break his head!"

For a long couple of heartbeats she stood there, mouth working, eyes narrowed. She finally sighed, lowered the club, and started back up the trail. He could tell from her stilted posture that she was as tense as a deadfall trap.

For the rest of the day he trotted along behind her, forcing his stubby legs to keep up.

What did I do? Which of the gods did I offend? How is it that I—who draw willing women with just a look—get stuck with this foaming she-weasel?

Chapter Six

The dusty trail led down from the gray hills, winding through desperate-looking juniper trees. Here and there along the way small shrines had been built, many with little painted wooden flowers and prayer sticks laid at their sides. Through the day they had passed farmers, Made People mostly, who trudged with packs on their backs, or pots riding in net bags across their shoulders. Round ceramic canteens had swung at their hips. All looked dusty, bestowing smiles as they nodded greetings to Nightshade and Spots.

"They seem like friendly folk," Spots ventured. The sack over his shoulder had been ominously silent, as if smoldering with some terrible presentiment.

"For the moment they hide their worry," Nightshade said as they rounded a bend that looked out over the Spirit River Valley. She stopped short, her attention fixed on the far floodplain across the river. "There it is: Webworm's rebirth of the Straight Path Nation."

Spots followed her gaze and saw the buff four-story

building. Even from this distance, it was huge: an imposing square surrounding a plaza dominated by a great kiva and its smaller clan sibling. To the east, another, more irregular structure was rising. The construction swarmed with tiny brown bodies that labored on the walls. The buildings dominated the terrace behind the shallow Spirit River floodplain.

Like so much of the valley topography they had traveled, the Spirit River bottom was verdant and green. In this continuing year of drought, ditches meant life for the corn, beans, and squash.

Spots couldn't take his eyes off the grand structures. "They make our largest buildings seem like huts."

She said, "This isn't a pimple on Straight Path Canyon. Talon Town, Kettle Town, Streamside, Center Place, and High Sun Town dwarf this place. There the paths of Father Sun and Sister Moon are written in the stone. The canyon inhales with the breath of the gods. This place is like a rain-filled playa, appearing to be an oasis. One day, not so many sun cycles from now, you will see it differently."

"How is that, Elder?"

"Learn this: All things have their time. The wisest of men, my young hunter, are those who reach out to grasp each moment of happiness to their breasts. The richest among us are those who can taste the present. Such events are rare in life. When they come to you, sink your teeth into them, savor them to their entirety. When some young woman folds you into her arms, be there with your entire body and souls. Drown in the instant and surrender yourself to it."

"Because it will not last." An empty sensation sucked at the bottom of his heart.

"Learn that at your age," she called over her shoulder, "and you shall be among the wisest of men who have ever lived."

"No young woman has ever folded me into her arms."

"Have you never seen a sunset that shot gold, orange, and purple through the clouds? Have you never savored an exceptionally cooked meal on a cold and hungry night? Gods, hunter, have you never just sat on a spring morning, listened to the birds, and felt yourself breathe?"

He frowned. "Yes, I have."

"But you cluttered it up with thousands of worries, didn't you? You fretted about what your friends said, why your elders were upset with you, perhaps you even spent that moment brooding about your scars and how they made some pretty young woman's eyes slide past you."

The emptiness in her voice sobered him.

"Ecstasy and terror await us, hunter. Let's not keep them waiting."

If that is the least of her knowledge, what is the worst of it?

As they walked ever closer to Flowing Waters Town, he could feel the Spirits in her bag: They shifted uneasily, whispering among themselves.

The way Matron Desert Willow had been acting made no sense to War Chief Wind Leaf. He squinted under the hot slant of the afternoon sun and took stock of the activity in the plaza. There, between the great kiva and the west room block, bundles, packs, and burden baskets had been laid out. Some contained corn flour, others dried root breads. Ritual clothing could be seen protruding from other packs. This was only part of the heavy load Blue Racer was accumulating for his journey northward to Pinnacle Great House. He might have been outfitting a party of warriors for a raid on the distant Stone Temple Builders that Webworm had suddenly become so infatuated with. As if people who believed in jungle gods had any merit for the Straight Path Nation. Which brought him back to Desert Willow.

She stood on the edge of the second-story roof, her arms crossed below her breasts. A frown lined her perfect forehead as she watched the slaves and Made People milling among the packs and baskets. A babble of voices rose as questions were called and commands given.

Wind Leaf stepped over beside her, saying, "Do you think they can make order out of it?"

"Probably not. I suspect the Sunwatcher will demand it all be loaded onto as many backs as he needs and carted off to the north. Blue Racer seems particularly anxious to start. He spends a great deal of time rubbing his breastbone."

Wind Leaf casually glanced around, taking note that no one seemed particularly close. "What has happened?"

"Webworm threatened the Sunwatcher's life. You were there, if you'll recall."

Wind Leaf lowered his voice further. "What happened between us? Have I offended you?"

"He knows."

"About us?"

She asked, "What happened to White Cloud Woman? I mean, how was she really killed? Who did it? One of yours?"

"I don't know. My scouts report that it remains a mystery. I have asked Leather Hand. He just shrugged."

"Webworm ordered it."

Wind Leaf tensed. "You're sure?"

"Very. He let me know in no uncertain terms that if I continued to bed you, it would go hard on me."

"You are the Matron. You could remove him."

"And put you in his place?" She glanced sidelong at him, a slim eyebrow arched inquisitively.

"No, not me. Some other more compliant—"

"I don't think I would live long after that."

"How could he get to you? With a simple command you could surround yourself with guards."

"Matron White Cloud Woman was well guarded." Desert Willow shook her head. "No, I enjoyed you, Wind Leaf. I shall cherish those memories. For now, I shall wait, and act as a Matron should. Webworm will grow tired of me again. In the meantime, I intend to learn his secret."

"He has changed since he became the Blessed Sun." Wind Leaf frowned down at the chaos in the plaza below. "Much of his old insecurity has been replaced with arrogance."

She looked up at the sky, yellowed with the haze of dust. Then she looked off to the distant north, where a flat plume of smoke vanished into the northeast. "If Blue Racer can't convince the Flute Player to call the rains, we are going to see a much more insecure Blessed Sun."

"My men have been checking the harvest, Matron. Most of the irrigated fields are doing better than expected. The corn is eared out; we should have an above-normal harvest."

She sighed. "Bless the Flute Player. Your warriors will have to be particularly vigilant during the harvest. We want as much packed into the great houses along the rivers as we can. People are going to want to hoard, but as refugees trickle in from the dryland farms, we're going to have to give them something."

"It won't be enough to feed them all."

"It won't have to be. The critical thing is that we must give them a portion large enough to carry. Enough to send them home with. It won't be our fault that they can't pack enough for several days' journey back to their starving villages."

"Many of the outlying great houses have already emptied their storerooms. There will be no harvest to refill them."

"I know, War Chief." She gave him a hard appraisal. "If there is insurrection, your warriors must be fierce, brutal, and immediate in their retaliation. I will not tolerate any abuse of our Priests or our Matrons and their families."

"Yes, Matron." He wondered at the hard set of her jaw. Didn't she understand that his warriors were going to be just as hungry trying to hold isolated great houses? Or did she think she could have runners bear packs full of corn to those distant warriors? How did she think those packs bulging with corn would ever make it through a land gone thin with famine?

She was giving him a hard look, trying to pierce his stoic expression. "You seem unconvinced of my will."

"Not of your will, Matron. I was just wondering..." The old woman caught his eye. She was walking through the opening below the east room block. Tall and thin, silver hair gleaming, she wore an oddly fashioned faded red dress. Behind her, a young man in a barbarian's hunting shirt was bearing several packs, his wide eyes almost disbelieving as he stared around at the bustling plaza.

It was the woman, though, that drew his eye. Something about her—crone that she might be—hinted of a ruler's poise. She carried herself as if she might own this place rather than just having entered it for the first time.

"Wondering what?" Desert Willow asked, then followed his gaze. "Who is that?"

"I have no idea, Matron. I don't think I've ever seen her before."

"Some Matron from a distant great house? She carries herself like one."

The old woman's gaze lifted and fixed. Wind Leaf had seen such an expression when a falcon spied a cottontail. He followed her gaze, seeing Webworm as he stepped out of his fourth-floor rooms. The Blessed Sun appeared nervous, as if something had upset his stomach. He glanced around this way and that, and finally saw the old woman. Across the distance, Wind Leaf would have sworn he felt the very air crackle.

"I think I'll go down and see just who..."

Shouts broke out below him, and he stepped forward. Two slaves were beating each other about the head and shoulders with digging sticks, yelling, "You took it!" "You're a liar!" "Give it back, dog!" "I'll kill you!"

"You!" Wind Leaf boomed, pointing at the miscreants. "I'll have your livers roasted and thrown to the dogs! Stop that at once."

The slaves desisted, stared up, went pale, and immediately scurried away.

"Vermin," Wind Leaf muttered. He glanced back at Webworm, seeing the Blessed Sun, looking shaken, his eyes blinking. When Wind Leaf turned back to where the old woman had been, the plaza was empty. He craned his neck, looking this way and that, but nowhere did he see her tall form. She might just as well have been a ghost.

Wrapped Wrist had never understood the simple pleasures of anonymity. Fearing he might be recognized, he and Crow Woman had waited until dark in a copse of piñon pine before crossing the fields in the First Moon Valley and climbing the Dog's Tooth. During the day, she had said nothing more than was absolutely necessary. So be it. Once he'd delivered her to Old White Eye, she full well knew the route back to Ironwood's.

The walled enclosure atop the Dog's Tooth reassured Wrapped Wrist when he led Crow Woman through the gap in its walls. As he'd climbed, he'd looked out across the valley. The familiar sights, sounds, faces, and places all served to comfort his anxious souls. Never would he have been so happy to simply retire to his uncle's house, to watch the fire as he shared a meal and enjoyed the company of his cousin's children as they romped on the floor, playing with corn-shuck dolls, rolling little carved wooden animals across the packed dirt, and guessing which hand held the carved ball Uncle had made for them.

"It is Wrapped Wrist," he called outside White Eye's pit house.

"Enter," the old man rasped.

Wrapped Wrist led the way up, glanced inside at the old man, and found him seated on his mat below the northern bench. His fingers cupped a small figurine. Behind his head a stone feather holder bristled with the feathers of eagle, buzzard, red-tailed hawk, and kestrel.

Wrapped Wrist climbed down the ladder, thankful to squat off to one side as Crow Woman scuttled down behind him. She seated herself, hard eyes on the old man.

His odd white eye seemed to gleam in the firelight. "What is the word from the war chief?"

"He sends his greetings, Elder," Crow Woman said. "Along with a warning from young Ripple."

White Eye heard something in her voice. "But you do not believe?"

Crow Woman shrugged ineffectively, though perhaps the keen-eared old man heard her clothing shift. "My beliefs have no importance. Ripple interrupted a council to speak with Matron Night Sun and Ironwood."

"And what did Ripple say?" White Eye turned the little stone figurine. Wrapped Wrist finally identified it as a crudely formed eagle with its wings spread.

"He said that if the First People were to be defeated, it had to be done according to what Cold Bringing Woman told him." Crow Woman appeared to fidget under that blind eye.

"How many warriors can he bring?"

"Perhaps thirty, Elder."

"Thirty." White Eye sat quietly for several heartbeats.

"We are trained, Elder. Not like the anxious young men you can recruit locally."

"The young men I will pick shall have hearts strong enough for our purposes."

"I didn't mean to imply they weren't courageous, Elder, just that the Blessed Sun will send many of his best warriors to hold Pinnacle Great House. The movement of large numbers of warriors will alert them to an attack. Knowing the war chief as I do, I can imagine that he will seek to avoid—"

"What were Ripple's precise words?"

A pause.

Crow Woman closed her eyes, speaking precisely, as if she were pulling the words straight out of her memory. "I have seen fire Dancing with ice. Send word now. Tell White Eye that only the strongest threads of silk tether the web. If he would see the First People fall, he must call the elders to council. Spider Woman wants all of the flies in the web before we strike." She took a breath. "The fire is loosened; flames rise high. The Dance is begun. In the coming days, Sister Moon's veil will be spun. When she is finally draped in a smoke-black cloak it will be time for us to strike."

"And after that?" White Eye asked.

"Nothing. He walked away."

"And Poor Singer? Did he hear these words?"

"He did."

"What was his reaction?"

"Poor Singer began to pack his family's belongings in preparation of leaving. I did hear Poor Singer say that

61

we needed to trust the gods. That wasn't encouraging to those of us who have little use for gods."

"Sister Moon's veil will be spun," White Eye mused. "Fire and ice." He nodded. "At last the pieces begin to fit."

"Fit how?" Wrapped Wrist asked.

The old man ignored him. "How does Ironwood plan on coming here? Surely he isn't going to try and sneak in among the pilgrims. The Red Shirts will be watching for him and his people."

"That I do not know, Elder."

White Eye rolled the stone eagle between his fingers. "Like you, perhaps he should arrive in the night. Bring me word, and I shall have places to secret his warriors. First Moon Valley is big, with a great many towns, villages, and houses. We can find places where the Blessed Sun's warriors cannot weasel you out."

Wrapped Wrist asked, "Do you believe we can do this, Elder? I mean, can we take Pinnacle Great House while the Blessed Sun holds it with his best warriors?"

The old man smiled wistfully. "What did Ripple say? Fire and ice? The key lies there."

"But what does it mean?" Crow Woman asked, and glanced at Wrapped Wrist with a camaraderie that surprised him.

"We shall just have to wait to find out." White Eye smiled. "And trust to these gods you seem hesitant to accept, Crow Woman. They have their own needs here."

"So do our clans." Wrapped Wrist stared thoughtfully at the fire. "I was there that night of the meeting when you decided to rescue Ripple. Some of our clan elders won't want to participate."

"No, I suppose not." White Eye tilted his head back. "We will have to be very discreet."

Crow Woman yawned, the warmth of the fire obviously playing upon her fatigue. She shook it off, adding, "What message do you wish me to take back to the war chief?"

White Eye said, "I will have an answer for you in the morning. Meanwhile, I must think."

"I need to take a message to Soft Cloth." Wrapped Wrist rose to his tired feet.

"Take Crow Woman with you," White Eye ordered. "See if you can find her another dress to wear while she's in the valley. That war shirt stands out like a burning brand in the dusk. Rest at Soft Cloth's. I will send Fir Brush and Yellow Petal to see you. They have been wondering about their kin. Then return to me tomorrow night. Should anyone show interest in you, you are a husband and wife visiting from down valley."

Wrapped Wrist knew he looked just as horrified as Crow Woman.

"Your lives may depend on it." The old man's voice snapped like a whip. "Act like it!"

It was only after they had climbed back out into the cool night that Crow Woman asked, "How could he know I wore a war shirt?"

Wrapped Wrist shivered, dreading her presence. "Oh, you wouldn't believe the things he knows."

"Act married? To you?"

"I think he's still punishing me for leaving my buffalo hide at his doorstep."

She pointed her finger. "If you so much as touch me..."

"Go ahead and kill me. It'll be a Blessing."

Chapter Seven

Monsters

The stories about giant horned rattlesnakes, Underwater Panther, flying spiders, deer-antlered men, and all the other creatures of evil and darkness have filled my imagination from the beginning. I know them all: blood-sucking, meat-eating creatures that lurk in darkness, prowl the Underworlds, and the tie snakes that hide in springs. They are tied to rivers, deep forests, and hidden places below the earth.

In Dreams I have battled them. While soul-flying, I have escaped their clutches or outwitted them while in search of the dead. I have enchanted some, lured and baited others, and even brought a few into my embrace.

I have little fear of monsters, demons, or evil Spirits. For the most part, they seek only to tear the heart from a person's breast, or perhaps devour his soul. In any event, their strike is quick—usually without warning. An instant of excruciating pain, a heartbeat of terror, and then...nothing. Blackness. Void.

While Dancing in Sister Datura's arms I have looked into the darkness and seen the monsters staring back. The first time, so long ago, an abject fear almost paralyzed me. I survived by the barest chance of fate.

Knowledge is Power. As I came to understand the monsters, my fear ebbed and evaporated away like a muddy pond in a drought. Familiarity with their ways taught me to respect and understand them as a hunter knows and avoids the great bears, cougars, and poisonous reptiles.

I have watched the unease grow in people's eyes when I describe the monster beasts that inhabit the Spirit Worlds. I've seen them shiver in mindless terror at mention of a cannibal owl. For days after, they cannot sleep, their Dreams filled with images of huge monsters.

How can they be such fools? Those selfsame individuals who toss and turn in terror of a Spirit Beast will fawn over some soul-twisted priest who just pulled the intestines out of an infant in a futile attempt to scry the future. Tell people that a certain spring is inhabited by underwater witches, and they will flee in screaming panic. Mention a giant winged scorpion, and they will cower in their houses until they starve. But show them a great chief infected with evil and watch them flock to his side. They will compete to curry his favor, mindless of the demented gleam in his eyes as he turns his smiles upon them.

Do I fear monsters? Oh, yes.

Spots glanced nervously at Nightshade as he busied himself about their small camp. Nightshade had picked this place in the thickets beside the river after she had slipped away from Dusk House that afternoon. She had said she needed time to think. He had cooked their supper of steamed cornmeal and lily root over a handful of fire. Fuel had consisted of sticks, rabbitbrush, and bits of driftwood he'd found lodged in the riverbank willows.

Nightshade seemed oblivious to the water lapping just beyond the yellow-brown stems, or the star-speckled night sky above. The whining mosquitoes that plagued Spots seemed to ignore her as she sat, back straight, hands neatly folded in her lap. Her wide eyes stared, unblinking, at something beyond this world. Periodically her lips moved, as if speaking. Her black cloak with white stars gave her the appearance of a night creature.

Spots used river water to wash out their little round brownware pot and replaced it in his pack. Then he squatted, limp hands dangling from his knees. He snorted at a mosquito that had flown up in his nose, and shook his head to keep them from whining in his ears.

"Elder?" he whispered. She might have been dead but for the occasional twitch of her lips. Watching closely, he couldn't even see her breathe.

Grunting to himself, he shot a nervous glance at her pack. The faint whisperings carried to his souls with greater clarity. He'd sensed their disturbance growing from the moment they'd crossed the Spirit River and walked across the cornfields to Dusk Town. They'd positively shrieked when he'd borne them into the plaza that afternoon, only sighing with relief after Nightshade had suddenly turned and led them away.

He was sure he didn't hear them with his ears—not that such sibilance would penetrate the incessant whining of mosquito wings. No, these were voices who spoke to the souls. The whispering was interrupted by a new nervous chattering—the sort that might have been made by tortured bats.

How could this happen to me? I never wanted anything to do with Power; now it falls around me like ash from a forest fire.

Something inky and unseen flapped through the night over his head. He caught just the faintest shadow passing across the stars. A shiver ran down his spine. He could feel things shifting and watching from the surrounding willows.

He tossed the last of their scanty firewood onto the dying flames. In the renewed light he unrolled his blanket and pulled the coarse weave through his fingers, wondering what protection it would give from the wavering cloud of mosquitoes, let alone the occasional soul-craving Spirit that might reach out of the darkness.

"Tomorrow," Nightshade said suddenly, "you need to be very careful. No matter what you see or hear, do not interfere. Do you understand, Spots?"

"Do not interfere with what, Elder?"

"In the morning, when I enter Dusk House, you are free to go. I thank you for your help on this journey. You have been a brave and worthy companion."

He frowned. "Elder? Aren't you going back to Ironwood's? Won't you need me to carry your pack? Cook for you on the return journey?"

"I am not going back."

His anxiety grew as his souls heard the Spirits in her pack crying out.

"No!" he cried, unsure about what.

She cocked her head. "You have responsibilities to your family and clan. In appreciation for your help and company, I will tell you this: Take your relatives—all that you can convince to accompany you. Go from this land. Save those you can...and run."

"Elder?"

"This is your chance to break free. You have very little time. Just enough to run back to your home and try to persuade your closest kin to leave."

Spots frowned. "That man you looked at in the plaza today. I saw your eyes meet, felt the change in the air. I heard the voices of the Spirits I carry cry out. Who was he? You wouldn't say. You just came straight here."

She almost smiled as she said, "Webworm."

"That was the Blessed Sun?" The notion stunned him. He had actually seen the Blessed Sun? The man hadn't looked like a magical figure; his body hadn't glowed in golden rays of light. He'd been average, overweight, and somehow soft. When his attention had turned to the fighting slaves, Nightshade had stalked away—walking with vigor he hadn't suspected the old woman capable of.

"I have come for him," Nightshade said simply. "It is between him and me."

"What is?"

"The future. The past. What might have been. And what might not."

"I don't understand."

"But for a choice made by a far-off Dreamer many sun cycles ago, I would have become Matron of the Straight Path Nation, the last of my clan, and the most Powerful. Would it have been better or worse for our peoples, I cannot say."

"It must be a terrible thing to have such responsibility placed on your shoulders."

"My shoulders?" She laughed. "That morning you decided to climb the mountain to help Ripple with his elk, did you think about it first?"

"Well...no."

"Choices. Who knows how decisions you make here will change your life and the lives of thousands of others?"

"Elder? I can't leave you alone."

"Go with the sunrise, young friend. Save yourself and your family."

Spots stared at her, trying to fathom what she was up to, how she would defeat Webworm in the safety of his lair.

The voices in her pack whimpered in fear.

At the sound of people talking, Crow Woman blinked awake, startled to find herself in a pit house. Morning light slanted through the smoke hole to illuminate the inside of a mud-daubed wall. Several white-slipped pots, corrugated-ware cooking vessels, and plain brown seed jars occupied the bench beneath the rectangle of light. Folded clothing rested on a willow mat next to them. The four roof supports had a honeyed look in the morning. Beside her, Wrapped Wrist still slept. With dismay she realized that his chest was pressed against her back, her buttocks neatly formed into the angle of his crotch.

Panic clutched at her heart, a fist squeezing her lungs. She willed herself to take a breath.

It's all right. This is Wrapped Wrist. He's safe... inconsequential.

Her heartbeat slowed as cool air entered her lungs. It was just an accident of the way they were sleeping that they'd ended up this way. It had been cold in the night. That's all.

How long had it been since she'd felt comfortable near a man? She swallowed nervously at the memory of his soft voice, cooing as he climbed on top of her and looked down into her eyes.

Snake Head. A witch.

He'd eaten whole pieces out of her souls—left them a patchwork that she'd sewn back together with the greatest difficulty.

"He's here," a woman's voice said from outside. "He arrived last night."

A pause. "With a woman." Another pause as Crow Woman tried to make out the second voice.

"I don't know. She's some woman. She was wearing a war shirt, carries a war club, bow and arrows. And she's tall!" Laughter. "You should see her. She towers over him like a ponderosa!"

Crow Woman rolled her eyes.

"When I left they were moccasined."

Moccasined? What did that mean?

Crow Woman eased away from Wrapped Wrist's warm body and sat up. Loose strands of hair fell about her face and shoulders where it had come loose from her bun. She reached back, pulling the deer-bone stiletto and spilling the whole mass of it down her back.

"I'll see if he's awake," the voice called. "Or if you're interrupting anything."

The tone in the woman's voice left no doubt what she might be interrupting. Crow Woman balled a fist and thumped Wrapped Wrist's thick muscles with a hard punch. Gods, the man was solid steak. He slitted an eye, mumbling, "I never touched you."

"Someone's coming. I think it's a woman."

Wrapped Wrist sat up, rubbed at his eyes, and stared at her as if he'd never seen her before. "Gods, you're absolutely..."

"Yes? What?"

The walls were trembling as someone climbed up and stared down the smoke hole.

"Absolutely—"

"Wrapped Wrist?"

Crow Woman looked up as a young woman clambered down the ladder. She wore a brown skirt woven from some fiber or other, her bare breasts small, the nipples smoothed by the indirect light. She stopped short to give Crow Woman a hard measuring assessment.

"Fir Brush?" Wrapped Wrist asked as he smiled. "Blood and dung, it's good to see you! I see you've kept out of the First People's grasp."

She gave Crow Woman a meaningful jerk of the head. "It looks like you haven't. Who's she? Another one of your conquests?"

"Uh, my wife," Wrapped Wrist muttered.

Crow Woman slitted her eyes just long enough to

promise retribution, then cleared her expression in time to say, "I hope worms infest your hair, little forest imp," in First People's tongue.

"She doesn't speak like a human," Fir Brush said in amazement. Then her brow furrowed. "Are you sure you're married? I mean, without approval from the clan? No one even knows! And if you've married in opposition to the clan, you'd better hope the Blue God has mercy on you. Old Rattler sure won't."

Wrapped Wrist grinned sheepishly. "I'll tell you... but only because you're being hunted by the First People, too. We're only supposed to act married in case the Red Shirts come by. No one is supposed to know she's here."

Fir Brush nodded, then smiled at Crow Woman, saying, "Welcome to First Moon Valley."

In First People tongue, Crow Woman replied, "I hope locusts eat your crops down to stems." Then she smiled politely.

At that, Wrapped Wrist leaned forward, hugging Fir Brush to his breast, eyes closed, a smile on his face. She returned his ardor, clasping him awkwardly as she tried to encompass those broad shoulders.

"I'm glad you're safe," Fir Brush whispered. "I've been sick with worry." She backed away, staring into Wrapped Wrist's eyes. "How's Ripple? I've heard... well, terrible things. He's alive, isn't he? Does he need me? I can have Slipped Bark packed, ready to go. We could meet you along the trail."

"He's fine. Fine." Wrapped Wrist made a face. "Gods, how do I explain? He's not Ripple anymore."

Fir Brush tensed, expression hardening. "Because

of what they did to him? His hand, his mouth?" She winced. "I heard they cut him. Took his…"

"He's healing. As to whether it will ever work, who's to say?"

"Who cares for him? The Mountain Witch?"

"She's with Spots."

"Is he injured, too?"

"No, she's traveling with him."

Fir Brush's eyes widened. "Why?"

"How should I know? I was running messages when she took him. Bad Cast says that he Dreamed her, or she Dreamed him, or some such thing."

Crow Woman arched an eyebrow. How long had it been since she'd seen people act so normally? The scene touched something she'd thought long dead inside her.

Fir Branch shook her head. "This Dream thing will pass. When's he coming home?"

"I don't know." The mood faded, turning serious again. "He may be in Ironwood's camp for a time."

"The war chief?" Fir Brush's eyes widened again. "You've seen him?"

Crow Woman couldn't help but smile at the young woman's awe.

"He's…well, impressive," Wrapped Wrist said. "Scary when you first see him, scarred, and his one remaining eye cuts through you like a knife. Then you watch him with his wife, or children, and he's just like anyone else. But sad. Maybe the saddest man I've ever known."

"And Night Sun, you've seen her?"

"Yes."

"What's she like?"

"A stunning woman," Wrapped Wrist answered. "I think she's the greatest lady I have ever seen. She walks with perfect grace, and when she looks at you, a deep serenity lies behind her eyes."

Fir Brush sat back, an expression of amazement on her face. "And Ripple's in the middle of this? Our Ripple? I just can't believe it!"

The walls vibrated again, another face poking into the smoke hole. "Wrapped Wrist? Is that you?"

He looked up. "Yellow Petal?"

Another young woman, this one scarred, thickset, but self-possessed, came climbing down the ladder, followed in turn by Soft Cloth with baby at breast. They both beamed, smiles as if for Wrapped Wrist alone.

Gods, what did he do? Collect young women like a flower drew butterflies?

She sighed; her stomach was empty and her bladder full. She had never had the chance to share a normal woman's society. Had never had female friends like these. Watching them was like observing some strange and distant people. The inside of the pit house looked like a potter's circle.

It was going to be a long day.

From where he lay in the willows, Spots watched the long procession wind out of Dusk House. Like a huge multicolor millipede, it marched down from the first terrace onto the floodplain. At the front strode a thin figure in bright blue robes. He bore a tall walking stick, his eyes thoughtfully on the ground. Behind him came a double line of Priests; dressed in white, their long hair hung down past the middle of their backs. Then came the warriors, ranks of them wearing red war shirts, their weapons packed in bundles on their backs, most bearing round wicker shields that made them look like bulbous figurines. Four parallel ranks of Made People marched in turn, and finally, at the end, came the slaves with their backs bent under full burden baskets. Warriors trotted along their flanks, calling orders, raising yucca-leaf scourges to swat at any who would tarry.

At the ford, the party waded across and took the eastern trail Spots and Nightshade had come down. East? And he knew: It had to be Blue Racer and his party. They were on their way to First Moon Valley to prepare for the Moon Ceremony.

Spots propped his chin on his right fist and scratched a mosquito bite with his left.

Travel in safety. The words echoed between his souls. Nightshade had wished him well as he stuffed his blanket into his pack that morning. She had given him the little round brown pot to cook his meals and had ordered him to take the last of their food.

He had touched his forehead in respect, then wound through the willow trails to this last stand of leaf-green stems. Here, he had stopped, suddenly unsure.

Rot it all, he could still hear the plaintive voices calling from her Spirit pack.

Just go!

He knew what few others did: Their world was about to shatter into mayhem and conflict. Nightshade had given him leave to save himself.

Not just myself. Yellow Petal and her baby. Perhaps as many as I can talk into it.

He grimaced as he imagined Yellow Petal's response: "What? You want to leave? Spots, the corn is a moon from being ready to harvest! Do you really think we'd be stupid enough to walk away from our fields? Just leave an entire winter's supply of food? To do what? Go starve in the mountains? All on the word of a witch?"

He chewed his lip, stomach churning in a battle of indecision. The voices in Nightshade's pack were calling.

"We all have choices," he whispered to himself. "Choices on one hand, and the cages that bind us on the other." Yellow Petal was so completely ensnared in the cage of her responsibility that he would have to bind her, gag her, and carry her away from First Moon Valley.

"I should go and try to warn them." He could feel the warp and weft of his own responsibility to his people closing around him.

Of course they would listen to him. Just as they had listened to Ripple? Old White Eye had been the only one who understood, the only one to act.

Yellow Petal's voice chided, "Don't be a fool, Spots! This is our home. Nothing's going to happen to us."

To her, to the majority of his people, it was inconceivable. Generations of the First Moon People had lived there. How could they comprehend that their world was coming to an end?

Gods, but for having lived what I have in the last half moon, how could I?

He still wasn't sure he believed it.

As he watched the last of the procession splash across the river and begin the winding climb up the silty gray trail, he listened to the grinding of his teeth.

Nightshade's expression that morning haunted his memory.

She knows she might not win, the unified voices whispered to his soul.

Spots frowned as he clawed at another of the mosquito bites. It was sobering to think of what it would take to frighten Nightshade.

Choices.

He groaned, climbed to his feet, and slipped back through the willows. Twice he had to stop, crouching, as women from Flowing Waters Town followed trails through the brush to fill water jars. Only after they had balanced the heavy jugs on their heads and turned back did he proceed.

He approached the little camp he'd shared with Nightshade, using all of his hunter's skills to sneak up on the place.

Nightshade sat there, back straight by the dead fire. He could see a thin gray paste drying on her temples, her eyes glazed and black in her slack face.

She made no move, then smiled slightly, blinked, and reached for her pack.

Spots heard the voices sigh as she shouldered the pack. He almost nodded with the sense of inevitability.

Like a fox he crept along behind her.

Once in the open, she took the shortest trail through the cornfield.

Spots hesitated. Then, throwing caution to the wind, he ran, taking one of the paths through the willows until he crossed the major trail the women followed to get water. Turning, he trotted out into the open, approaching Dusk House from an angle to Night-shade's path. Through occasional openings in the corn he could see her, walking ever so stately in her red dress and black cloak.

Gods, I must be mad.

Chapter Eight

To avoid the hot morning sun, the Blessed Sun had seated himself in the shady angle created by Dusk House's eastern and northern walls. Back braced in the corner, Webworm's butt rested on a comfortable triple fold of split turkey-feather blanket. A tall mug of berry juice stood by his side; he whistled and scraped at the little stone carving he was making.

War Chief Wind Leaf had the sudden thought that Webworm reminded him of a fat toad. Banishing the thought, he glanced up at the morning; despite the early sun, the sky was already pale, the air hot. A single buzzard could be seen—a portent of the bounty drought could provide. When Wind Leaf looked south, beyond the green band of the river fields, the hills were scorched. The grasses had gone dormant before spring ever began. Even the stones looked thirsty. Slowly dissipating dust marked Blue Racer's path to the east.

Wind Leaf considered the contrast between the spare world around him and the Blessed Sun. The man's round belly was beginning to bulge out over his hips. The toad image was right. Webworm's light summer shirt had been spun of fine white cotton; it stretched around him like a toad's sides.

The Blessed Sun was whistling softly to himself as he proceeded with his carving. Having seen Blue Racer's procession off, he might not have had a care in the world.

"The last of them have vanished into the hills, Blessed Sun." Wind Leaf shuffled as he waited for some response.

"Good." Webworm finally looked up from his carving. Wind Leaf could see that it was some sort of snake curled inside an egg-shaped jet pebble.

"I've detailed runners to keep us informed of the Sunwatcher's progress, especially once they have reached First Moon Valley." He cleared his throat. "One of my deputies, Leather Hand, hasn't reported to me."

"I'd be surprised if he had. What? Did I forget to tell you?" Webworm cocked his head. "I've given him and his men a special project."

Wind Leaf's stomach tightened. "Did you send him off with a packet of seasonings? I hear that chilies and squash blossoms add a delightful sweet tang to boiling meat."

At that, Webworm threw his head back, laughter bubbling from his belly. "Quite so, War Chief. I should have thought of that on my own."

Gods, the man hadn't even caught the irony? "I've begun the process of collecting supplies for your journey, Blessed Sun. I wish, however, that you would tell me why you countermanded my order for another twenty warriors to accompany us to First Moon Valley."

"I am planning on going in secret," he replied. "A large party, as I'm sure you could see with Blue Racer's passage, raises too much dust." He glanced up, smiling. "When we go, it will be quickly, with no warning."

Wind Leaf took a deep breath. "You expect trouble, yet will not allow me to prepare to meet and destroy it?"

"There are too many places along the trail where a party can be ambushed. Were we to follow the river bottoms, a smaller force could inflict terrible damage in the canyon narrows. If we were to take the ridges, we would be vulnerable again, either when we climbed up onto the caprock, or when the mesa tops narrowed." He gestured with the stone graver he held. "I learned my lesson well, War Chief."

Wind Leaf exhaled his frustration. After Jay Bird's raid, Webworm had been in charge during the pursuit. His war party had climbed through a treacherous canyon, then out onto an easily defended rim. As they passed into the open—and what should have been relative safety—they'd found a dead captive left behind by Jay Bird. It had been a cunningly devised ambush that had sent Webworm reeling back to Straight Path Canyon in staggering defeat.

"So you will go with a small party? If Ironwood should hear—"

"He won't. That's why I will decide on my own exactly when to leave and which route to take."

"But the additional warriors—"

"I want them here," he declared emphatically. "They must protect the corn!"

"The corn? I'd rather that you not go than waste warriors protecting corn."

"War Chief, a little more than eighteen sun cycles

pass between Sister Moon's homecomings. I didn't see it last time, and at my age, it's a sure thing that I won't be here to see it next time. This is my opportunity."

"But the extra warriors, Blessed Sun!"

Webworm looked up expectantly. "They must patrol the river fields. The farmers already have their hands full just battling the raccoons, worms, crows, and other vermin."

Wind Leaf scuffed the packed clay under his feet. Webworm could read displeasure in his expression.

"People are hungry out there." Webworm gestured randomly toward the south. "What good does it do me to travel to Pinnacle Great House to watch Sister Moon come home if the country is starved into revolt over the coming winter?"

Wind Leaf nodded, thinking, I'd rather fight a disorganized hunger-weakened rabble than one better fed, led by a resurrected Ironwood, and emboldened on by the murder of a Blessed Sun.

Webworm gestured with his chert graver again. "I've had some of the Priests out counting."

"Counting?" The change of subject surprised him.

"Yes, counting the number of fields, looking at the corn, beans, and squash plants. We have a chance to avoid calamity. To do so we must confiscate as much corn as we can, carry it here under guard, and parcel it out throughout the winter. I'll pack every room in Flowing Waters Town, Northern Town, and the rest of the great houses. People may starve this winter—some obviously will—but the First People must be seen to help. Everyone must know that their Blessed Sun is working for their good."

"What you are hoping is that something will be

better than nothing? That you can buy the goodwill of the people?"

Webworm went back to his carving. "The Priests think that the harvest from the irrigated river fields will be substantial. At least enough to feed people within a seven-days walk of the valley great houses. Meanwhile, we have another problem."

"And that is?"

"Protecting the harvest. Most of the storerooms in the great houses are depleted. Some, in the dryland areas, have already been stripped bare. By harvest, the Matrons will have no more corn left to distribute. All those hungry people will be looking our direction. If they should descend on these northern river valleys during harvest, it will be like a swarm of locusts."

"Then, what is the choice?"

"I will need patrols of warriors to guard the roads, War Chief. The choice is: Do we pull the warriors away from the Moon Ceremony to guard the harvest?"

Wind Leaf cocked his head. "Absolutely not!"

"You need not worry about the harvest," a soft voice said.

Wind Leaf turned. The old woman wore a black cloak decorated with white stars over a faded red dress. Then he saw her eyes: large and glassy, as though seeing things beyond this world. They dominated her once-beautiful face. Long gray strands of hair fell over her shoulders. She was slim, nearly as tall as he; a worn pack hung over one shoulder.

Something about her sent a shiver down Wind Leaf's spine, as if he could feel prickly insect feet slipping about his skin. Of the verge of dismissing her, he remembered having seen her the day before.

"Who are you?" he asked.

Evidently the Blessed Sun felt the same stirring unease.

"The Witness."

"Witness? What witness? To see what?" Webworm glared at her. Even Wind Leaf noticed that he was suddenly rolling the little carving around in his hand.

The woman's eyes had fixed on it. "Curious, isn't it? Only now can you feel its Power."

Webworm looked down at the carving. "This? It's nothing. Something I saw once. I think the design came from the Hohokam."

"It's called a basilisk: a snake born of a cock's egg. A perversion of Power. You are getting ready to inlet a red coral eye into the serpent's head," she told him. "Do you remember the first time you looked into the snake's loathsome eye?"

"It was years ago, just after I became Blessed Sun."

"That was the moment the slithering evil entered your souls."

"You will address me as Blessed Sun, old woman. And unless you tell me your name and your clan, I shall have your tongue pulled out by its roots."

Delicate mocking laughter rolled out of her. "A few sun cycles in charge and already you are hardened by selfish authority. You really don't know me, do you? Your souls have grown so full of you that they cannot see past themselves."

"Drag her away from here," Webworm muttered, returning to his carving.

Wind Leaf took two steps toward the woman before she fixed her dark eyes on his like a slap. In that instant, his thoughts swayed, and a weakness ran through his blood. He stopped short, shaking his head to clear it. He blinked, confused.

Webworm gave Wind Leaf a glare. "I thought I told you—"

The old woman spoke slowly, each syllable perfectly enunciated in the formal address of the First People. "I am Nightshade, Matron of the Hollow Hoof Clan, Keeper of the Tortoise Bundle, daughter of Matron Yarrow. My father was Red Crane, Sunwatcher of the Red Lacewing Clan. In fulfillment of a long-ago promise, I have returned to the Straight Path Nation."

"What promise?" Webworm asked.

"One given my mother...long ago." Her odd eyes enlarged. "Brother Mud Head has seen to the dead. My concern is with you, Webworm."

"Nightshade?" Webworm asked, thinking. "I'm supposed to believe you are the Mountain Witch?"

Wind Leaf swallowed hard. Gods, what was she doing here? He reached down, his fingers caressing the handle of his war club.

"The stories they tell about you"—Webworm sounded bored—"you just wouldn't believe them. Did you really get carried off to the land of the distant Temple Builders?"

"I was called to be a witness there, too."

He studied her from under heavy lids. "Are the towns of the forest kings as great as ours?"

She never even hesitated as she said, "The entirety of the Straight Path Nation could fit into the province of one lesser chief. Some of their cities are surrounded by walls forty hands high. Their rulers derive from bloodlines that go back to the beginning of the world."

"What about their warriors? Could they be a threat?"

"You can muster a large war party. The Great Sun can dispatch armies. In battle they are invincible."

"Then why don't they ever come here?" Webworm had begun to smile, as if he'd caught her in a lie. "They took you—never to return."

"Why should they?" Nightshade tilted her head back, staring down her fine nose in disgust. "We have nothing the lords of Cahokia want or need. Don't you understand? They are old. Their traditions go back to the beginning of the world. While our ancestors were moving from camp to camp, theirs were already building temples to the sun. It was their Trade that awakened the Stone Temple Builders in the south hundreds of sun cycles ago. To the forest kings we are nothing more than curious barbarians living somewhere out in the dimly perceived desert wastes."

"Barbarians?" Wind Leaf snorted.

She spared him a quick glance. "The sort—barely above animals—that eat other human beings."

Webworm made an irritated sound and continued scraping on his little snake effigy. "Go on back to Ironwood and Night Sun. Tell them their days are numbered."

"The patterns are cast, Webworm. I've come to Dance with you."

"What? Dance with me?" He looked up, taking in her age and smiling at the insanity of it. "It might strain you too much."

Her voice dropped to a conspiratorial whisper. "I can send you to them."

"Them? Who?" Webworm demanded.

"Cloud Playing and Matron Featherstone. I can free you."

His face had gone white. He looked at Wind Leaf. "You know the bear cage? The one we kept the young grizzly in? I want it placed in the plaza. Put her there, stripped naked, where everyone can see her. It's time the myth of the Mountain Witch is finally put to rest."

Nightshade laughed, turning, and as Wind Leaf reached for her, she called over her shoulder, "I can free you, Webworm."

"That's quite a family you've got," Crow Woman said as they followed the path that led across the valley bottom.

Wrapped Wrist glanced over his shoulder at the sunset. The sky was glowing red and orange over the ridges. To the north, the smoke plume was cast in evening bronze by the slanting light. Compared with that morning, the plume was larger, puffing like a giant mushroom over the high peaks and trailing off into the east in a dirty smear.

"They're clan kin. Surely you grew up with the same."

"No, Wrapped Wrist, I didn't."

Gods, did everything he said have to set her off?

Then she seemed to relent, saying in a softer voice, "I had no relatives."

"Everybody grows up with family, cousins, lineages, and clans, although I hear some of the Tower Builders up north don't have moieties."

"No," she replied shortly, "not everybody does."

Cautiously he asked, "What about your mother?"

"Why do you want to know?"

"We travel together. I'd like to know something about who I'm traveling with."

"She died when I was little more than five."

"And your aunts and uncles?"

"I never knew them."

"How could you never know them?"

"Do you have granite for brains?"

Giving her a sidelong glance, he could see her pinched expression. "Well, you surely weren't a slave. You'd have..." The bitterness in her face was all the answer he needed.

As the light fled, he tossed the revelation back and forth between his souls. What must her childhood have been like? How on earth had she ever escaped to become one of Ironwood's most trusted warriors?

"What incredible courage," he whispered.

"Courage?" she whispered softly. "I've been scared all of my life." As if she realized what she'd said, she hissed angrily at herself.

After a time he asked, "Where did you grow up?"

"I don't want to talk about it."

The red ember of sunset faded in the west; gloom settled around them as they entered the trees. A party of hunters, packing deer, turkeys, rabbits, and several porcupines, passed, calling greetings.

"Someone's going to be happy," Wrapped Wrist noted. "The dryer it gets, the harder the hunting is."

She said nothing.

"It'll be a long dark walk to our divide camp. There's a little meadow ahead that would make a good camp."

Silence.

"Are you always infuriated?"

"Don't worry about me, stumpy."

Stumpy? He hadn't deserved that ember being stuck between his blankets.

"You must be the most unhappy person alive."

A hand of time later, Crow Woman agreed to make camp. In silence they ate the corn cakes that White Eye had provided for their return trip.

Wrapped Wrist rolled into his blanket, listening to the crickets and hearing the occasional cry of the nightjar. The night lay heavily on the land.

She surprised him, saying, "I grew up in Fourth Night House—a town on the Turquoise Trail east of Straight Path Canyon. It's a dismal place, dry and dusty, constantly windblown. The land is dull yellow— the soil, the rocks—even the sky takes on that color.

"As a girl I carried water, removed ash from the heating bowls, emptied waste pots, and trapped rodents. I helped prepare and cook food, mixed plaster, carried stone and timbers, and sweated in their miserable excuse of a cornfield."

She paused for a while.

"The thing was, the other slaves treated me differently. So did my Made People masters, and even the First People who lived there. I got more to eat than the others. I even was allowed to sleep in the Matron's storeroom." She hesitated. "The rumor was that I was Crow Beard's daughter. That he'd taken a liking to my mother on his trips through." She shrugged. "I never allowed myself to believe it."

Wrapped Wrist kept his peace.

"I only had one friend. The girl who taught me your tongue. She was sleeping with the Matron's oldest son at the time. On occasion he would sneak into our room after dark and lay with her."

Wrapped Wrist wondered if he should say anything.

"I was in love with him, too. I used to listen to them, hear the kindness in his voice as he whispered into her ear, and muffled cries of delight from their fierce coupling." She sighed. "Then his younger brother came to my bed just after my first moon as a woman. Everything his brother was, he was not. I bled for days after he jammed himself into me."

An owl hooted in the trees.

"My friend and her lover left for Straight Path Canyon. The younger brother had always been considered something of a nuisance, never having his brother's courage or talent at doing things. He took out his parents' displeasure on me."

In the long silence that followed, Wrapped Wrist could well imagine the ways a spoiled young man could abuse a woman under his command.

"I ran off," Crow Woman continued. "It was a spring storm. Wind Baby had blackened the sky with blowing dust. In desperation I charged off into the middle of that. Gods, the sand felt like it would scour the skin right off my face. It plugged my nose, ground in my teeth, and burned in my eyes, but I continued, walking into the wind, following the road to Straight Path Canyon. It was the only place I could think of to go, since my friend and her young lover had gone there."

"Did you find them?" he asked softly.

"Oh, yes. She was glad to see me, and while he understood my reasons for running away, he was a new warrior in the Blessed Sun's guard. It was his 'duty,' he said. He took me to Talon Town to ensure that I was taken back to Fourth Night House when..."

She tossed in her blankets, unable to finish.

Wrapped Wrist waited for a moment before asking, "Did they ever take you back to Fourth Night House?"

In the dim darkness, he thought he saw her shake her head.

"Snake Head," she whispered, "wouldn't let them."

"The one they said was a..." He wouldn't utter the word "witch," afraid of what if might do to her.

"By the gods," she almost whimpered, "he was a monster. The things he..." Her dry swallow was audible.

In a reasonable voice, Wrapped Wrist said, "He is dead, his souls howling forever. You are alive."

In a half-frantic voice she said, "Why am I telling you this?"

"Have you ever told anyone else?"

"No."

"Then maybe you needed to tell someone. I've heard from the Healers that sometimes just speaking the words can start the souls on the way to Healing."

"If you ever speak of this to anyone, I swear..."

He chuckled at the fury behind her words. "Yes, yes, I know. My death will be painful and long."

She sat up in her blankets. "Do you mock me?"

"Quite the contrary, I honor you."

For long moments she hovered in indecision before lying back in her blankets. "Good night, Wrapped Wrist. In the morning I don't want to be reminded that I said any of this."

He rolled over onto his side. No, of course not.

Still, sleep wouldn't come. His fertile mind kept conjuring the images of things that she might have endured at the hands of various evil and violent men.

When Wrapped Wrist finally awoke, morning was breaking; dawn looked bloody and dull as sunlight fingered the smoke-blackened eastern horizon. He glanced over, only flattened grass marked the place where she'd laid her bed the night before.

Chapter Nine

S pots made a face. To think about walking unafraid into the middle of the First People's world by himself was one thing; to actually set foot inside Dusk House without Nightshade's protection was something else.

Terrible stories were told of the First People late at night by crackling pit house fires. Tales of their evil deeds, of the hideous rites they practiced, and of how their heartless cruelty knew no bounds. Of course, they had enslaved many of Spots' people over the years, and those few whom fate had spared often broke into tears as they related their experiences in the quarries, or of building the great roads, ramps, and stairways that tied the Straight Path Nation together.

"I should be on my way home," Spots mumbled as he stared at the massive buildings. The symmetrical perfection of Dusk House contrasted to the thriving activity as tens of tens labored to raise Sunrise House. He could hear the distant clattering as the masons used stone hammers to true sandstone slabs for the walls.

His attention kept going back to that immense construction. One wrong move and that's where they would put him: just another slave to build their great house. Assuming, that is, that they didn't just crack his skull and toss his body out to rot in the cornfields.

We all have choices to make. Nightshade's words echoed hollowly within him.

Gods, did a choice have to include the runny feeling of fear that coursed through his guts?

Did Nightshade really need him? Surely, if she had, she would have kept him at her side. On the other hand, he remembered that clear look of fear and resignation behind her eyes as she'd dismissed him.

Something terrible is going to happen to her.

"Then don't let it happen to you," he growled to himself as he watched the dawn light grow brighter.

He stood, throwing his pack over his shoulder. That's it: Be gone. Back to First Moon Valley. He had obligations to his kin. Yellow Petal had to be warned— for what little good that would do. He made a face as he imagined her mocking eyebrow as he told her to pack her things and leave. And what about his kiva? He owed it to his brothers to warn them. And then there was his clan. His duty was to take Nightshade's warning straight to Elder Rattler. Tell her to prepare for disaster.

He nodded, his mind made up. He made no more than four steps toward the ford on the Spirit River and stopped.

Who did he think he was? Worse, who would his people think he was? A young hunter? Bearing warnings from the Mountain Witch?

They would brand him a fool.

He groaned aloud as he fingered the rough fabric of his sack. Placing himself back in time, to the person he had been before Ripple's vision, he knew how he would have reacted to hearing another young hunter give such a warning of disaster: He'd have dragged him kicking and screaming to have a Healer return his lost Dream soul to his body, for this was obviously the ranting of a sick man.

Choices.

He looked back over his shoulder, turned, and started forward. As he broke the cover of the willows and set foot down the path toward Dusk House, he glanced at the corn. The immature ears were thickening, the kernels green within them. It would be a good crop.

Enough to keep them from stripping First Moon Valley bare? he wondered. As he walked, the smoke plume in the north could be seen. The entirety of the northeastern horizon had turned murky. It matched the Rainbow Serpent's smudge to the southwest.

Fire on two corners of our world.

That notion kept repeating itself as he tried to figure out what he'd say if one of the guards stopped him.

"I'm a Trader."

"Oh, and what did you bring to Trade?"

"Well, nothing. I thought I'd see what they needed here."

He wrinkled his nose. This was Flowing Waters Town. They needed nothing. They took everything.

"I'm here looking for my brother."

"What might your brother's business be here?"

"He's a stonemason."

"Then you'd better go down, put on a slave's work shirt, and join him."

Spots didn't like that one, either.

"I'm here with a message for the Mountain Witch."

This time, the guard didn't respond; instead his wrist flicked and a war club caved in the side of Spots' head.

"Gods," he muttered as he left the cover of the cornfields and stepped out onto the Great North Road. He stopped for a moment, looking at the wide thoroughfare.

He imagined it, running straight as a stretched cord southward, across high desert to Straight Path Canyon, and from there on down in the distance. How far south? To the end of the world? It was said that the souls of the dead were released at Center Place to travel this road northward to the sipapu that allowed them to descend into the Underworlds. There they would find the Land of the Dead and their ancestors. Did Spirits walk this way even as he stood here? Did they pass him, wondering at the poorly clad barbarian hunter with his pack?

"Are you planning to be a tree?" a voice asked in Made People tongue.

Spots jumped, heart racing as he turned. The darkhaired Trader had a medium build, three pack dogs at his heel. The man was looking him up and down. "Sorry, didn't mean to scare you."

"I—I was thinking about the Great North Road."

"Glad to see you speak a little of my tongue." The Trader cocked his head. "You look like you're straight out of the hills. Come down to see how real people live?"

Spots swallowed hard and nodded. "I can't believe it. I'm actually standing on the Great North Road?"

"Of course you are. The gods know I've trod it long enough," the Trader added wearily. "What people are you from?"

"First Moon."

"They about ready for the ceremony up there? The Sunwatcher left yesterday." A question lay behind the man's eyes.

What do I say? "Among my people, a great many stories are told about this place. I just thought...oh, it's probably silly."

At that the Trader smiled. "No, not silly. Me, I left the Green Mesas so fast the pollen from my kiva initiation was still sifting out of my hair. Sometimes the people at home don't understand those of us who have to see the rest of the world."

Spots gestured at Dusk House. "Can I go in there, or will they take me prisoner, or something? I can't just walk up and say, 'I want to see inside,' can I?"

The Trader chuckled. "Sure. No one will care unless you climb up the ladders onto the second floor. That's only for the First People and those others who have reason to be there. If you stay in the plaza, no one's going to say a thing. You can poke your head inside the south entrance to the great kiva, but stay off the First People's kiva. Last, don't touch anything that's not yours."

Spots nodded. "Thank you. I won't."

The Trader narrowed his eyes as he took in the scars, along with the smooth muscle in Spots' body. "I'd say you had a close call with that fire."

"It changed my life. When you come that close to your end, you see the world differently."

"Interested in traveling down to the Mogollon country?" He pointed at the pack on his back. "I've got some fine First People pottery here. The Fire Dogs will Trade their redware, two for one. I could use the company on the way south. Introduce you around, teach you some of the tricks of the Trade."

Spots grinned, genuinely liking the man. "I thank you from both of my souls, but no. After I see this place, I must get back."

"Ah, yes, Moon Ceremony and all." The Trader puckered his lips, brow lined in thought. "You know, I've never seen...no, no. That doesn't make sense. As much as I'd like to see Sister Moon come home, I don't think I can Trade my pots to the First Moon People for anything anyone else would want." He reached around to pat his pack. "Me, I specialize in luxury goods, not that bulk stuff."

"May your travels be safe."

"Yours, too." The Trader passed him, calling, "See you on the trail someday."

Spots turned, taking a deep breath, and headed straight toward Dusk House.

Stay in the plaza. Don't touch anything that's not yours. Stay off the First People's kiva.

That wasn't so hard, and the last thing he was going to do was linger there any longer than it took to have a good look around and see if Nightshade's situation could be discerned.

Still, his heart refused to obey his head's instructions as he approached the huge building. It was a wonder how much courage Nightshade's mere presence had given him the last time he'd strode up to the tall walls.

Like last time, people were squatting outside the walls, many sitting on blankets. Some wove baskets in the morning sun; others knapped stone tools from blanks. Two old women were hawking Spirit Plants, bundles of herbs laid out on white cloths.

Another old man saw him coming and cried, "Charms! I have charms! Young man, for a pittance you can free your souls from fear! Ward off the evil eye!" He waved something that looked like a dried raccoon's foot on a thong.

A little girl ran up to him, asking, "Do you have corn? Please? I haven't eaten in a week! Mother is dying."

He smiled uncertainly at the little waif, avoiding her grasping hands as she pulled at the bottom of his pack.

"Didn't expect this," he told himself. No one had bothered Nightshade that first time she'd approached.

A young man in a white tunic spread a black blanket on the ground and laid out lines of turquoise, jet, coral, and polished shell jewelry. The pieces literally shone in the sunlight. It was more wealth than Spots had ever seen in one place.

He thanked the gods he was smart enough not to meet their eyes, hoping desperately that they wouldn't take him for the naive barbarian he was.

The tall wall before him curved ever so slightly. To his unease, a red-shirted warrior stood on the southeastern corner. Spots battled with the urge to turn tail and run. He wasn't sure his legs weren't shaking as he passed around the end of the wall past a young woman offering corn cakes for Trade and looked up at the high east room block of Dusk House. Yet another guard stood there, his bored eyes noting Spots, lingering for a moment on his scars, and passing on to the slave who walked past with a stinking pot of night earth in his hands.

Spots swallowed hard and hurried past. The plaza opened before him, and he stopped. To his right, the First People's kiva rose waist high above the ground. To its left the huge cylinder of the great kiva gleamed in the morning light. But it was the splendor of Dusk House—rising four stories high and cupping the plaza like a mother's arms—that took his breath away. For long moments he just stared, trying to comprehend what he was seeing. Last time the size of the place hadn't sunk in. Nightshade had been in a hurry—coming and going.

"Surprised?" asked a young woman who appeared at his elbow.

"I never suspected."

"You have a strange accent."

He spared her a glance. She was a little shorter than he, an odd weariness in her eyes. Her breasts stretched her too-tight dress, and her hips seemed to struggle for liberation against the restricting cloth.

"Tall Piñon," he lied. "I'm of the Deep Canyon folk."

Her knowing eyes fixed on his. "No, you're not. First Moon, or somewhere up there in the north, if I don't miss my guess."

"Does it make a difference?"

"No. You just here for the day?"

"I don't know. I just came to see."

"I'm called Cactus Flower." She smiled. "I could guide you."

"You could?"

She indicated his pack. "Depends on what you've got in there. I Trade for services. Let's say for a jar of corn, I can take you around the plaza, show you the great kiva, point out the Blessed Sun's quarters—"

"Up there." He pointed to where he'd seen Webworm while in Nightshade's company.

"You've been here before."

"Once."

Cactus Flower added, "For a shell comb, I could put you up for the night. I have a farmstead up on the terrace. The bed is nice, no fleas or lice. An abalone pendant? Well, I could make your stay most memorable." She swished her hips in a suggestive way.

He tried not to gape. "Thanks, but I don't have any of those things."

"I'm always around." Cactus Flower shrugged, took two steps, and matched stride with a Trader who entered between the walls. He laughed and shook his head, waving her off. She gave a saucy flip of her long black hair and retired to the shade of the wall to await new prey.

Spots felt his heart begin to settle into its normal rhythm. He'd just take a turn about the plaza, maybe look inside the great kiva, and slip out, assured that wherever Nightshade was, he didn't need to...

He stopped short, seeing the stout wooden cage. The thing was as tall as a man. Lengths of wrist-thick lodgepole pine had been used for bars. These had been fitted into holes bored into larger ponderosa logs. Thick willow stems had been woven between them for strength. Through the bars, Spots could see something crouched inside. A group of small children were staring in, one little boy whacking at the bars with a stick. Others were making faces.

Spots followed the walls around, glancing up at the upper floors. Nowhere did he see Nightshade among the visible people. While some comfort came from the fact that no one gave him a second look, he could feel the faintest sense of something.

"Must be the Spirits of this place," he muttered as he walked along under the west room block. A most notable man dressed in a bright red war shirt stopped to give instructions to a warrior who stood with a shield over his back. Then the fellow proceeded at a fast clip for the ladders leading to the upper stories.

"War Chief?" Spots wondered. What was his name? Wind Leaf? Or might that have been the dreaded Leather Hand?

At the thought, he whispered, "Check the kiva, and get your skinny self out of here."

He turned, approaching the great kiva. The big cage squatted no more than fifteen hands before the kiva entrance. Spots took long enough to lean his head in, marveling at the huge timbers that made up the roof. The painted images between the illuminated vaults dazzled him. A smoldering fire sent fingers of smoke toward the massive ceiling.

"Witch!" a child spat in Made People's tongue. The stick clattered on the wood again.

Spots turned, shaking his head at the magnificence of the great kiva. Just imagine the spectacle of the gods as they came Dancing into ...

He frowned, watching as a young man, a short slave

limping on a bad ankle, hesitated long enough to dash the contents of a night pot onto the bars of the cage. He smiled crookedly as the children scampered away, holding their noses.

Spots frowned, giving the cage a wide berth. Nightshade was nowhere to be seen. It was time for him to start home.

The voices! He cocked his head, hearing them. Instinctively, he wanted to shift the pack on his back, only to remember that Nightshade had taken it with her.

He stopped short, listening.

Yes, a desperation lay behind their urgent plea.

"Gods," he whispered. Something made him look closer at the cage. His very body willed itself to walk up to the bars.

"Elder?" he muttered, seeing her in the shadowed interior. Her long silvering hair draped her shoulders, apparently her only protection outside of the bars. She sat naked, legs crossed, her hands palm up on her knees.

He stepped around, calling louder, "Elder?"

"All things in their time, hunter." Her voice was emotionless. "Mine has not yet come. No matter what choice you have made, do not tarry here."

He glanced back and forth between the bars. "Do you have food or water?"

"For the moment, I am still a novelty. They are watching. Do not let them see you. Go now. If you would help me, it must be through stealth and cunning."

"Where is your pack?"

"The Blessed Sun kept it." She looked up, her eyes

boring into his. "If you do not go now, all will be undone. I am just where I need to be. Go!"

He backed up, and must have had a funny look on his face as he started for the gate.

"See!" the urchin with the stick cried. "She's just an old woman. She's no witch."

Spots surprised himself when he pointed at the little boy's chest. "If you torment her again, your stomach is going to hurt. In four days, your bowels will be passing bloody stools. Unless you seek her forgiveness, you will die screaming."

The urchin's eyes widened, and in an instant, he was gone, little feet pounding.

Gods, why did I do that?

Or had it been the Spirit voices speaking through him?

"Oh, Spots, what are you going to do now?"

Chapter Ten

Where he lay on Orenda's bed, Ripple jerked awake, sweat trickling down his sides. He gasped and ran his hand across his face. To his relief it was late morning, a muted light angling through the door. Gods, had he slept half the morning away? Or had the Dream—so very Power-filled and haunting—refused to free him from its grip?

Images were still wheeling around his souls, so clear, the colors so bright: High atop First Moon Mountain, Cold Bringing Woman was Dancing in the darkness. As she wheeled, her cloak sailed through the night sky. She would lean close, eyes glowing red. Her cold breath blew a numbing frost over the burning building. Ripple had looked up through the flames leaping yellow around him. He could still hear the screams and piteous wailing. An odd tingle remained in his legs where the Dream fire had burned them.

It was with amazement that he looked at the clear morning air inside Orenda's small room, surprised not to see sooty flakes falling around him.

Beside him, Orenda sat up on the narrow bed, the blanket slipping from around her shoulders. "Are you all right?"

He nodded, running his tongue over the ruination of his teeth. Several of the jagged roots had loosened and come free the day before. He'd spit them and the bloody pus they'd produced onto the hard ground.

"Dream?" she asked, eyes widening.

"Yes. I was atop Pinnacle Great House. Standing in the middle of a raging fire. People were screaming. Terrified women clawed at my legs, trying to climb them to safety." He closed his eyes, reliving the details. "Blood was running down my legs, trickling out in pools that fed the fires. As smoke rose from the burning blood, it turned black, falling as flakes."

Orenda laid a hand on his shoulder. "Are you all right?"

"I have to be there."

She narrowed her eyes. "Ripple, you don't need to go back. Your message has been delivered. We know Cold Bringing Woman's vision. Ironwood is already plotting how he will take Pinnacle Great House. Leave it to the warriors."

He reached up, placing his palm against her cheek. Her skin was soft and warm. "I must be there. It's my blood, you see."

She stared into his eyes, trying to read his souls. "Your blood is better off in your body. If Pinnacle Great House must burn, let the fire feed from its wood and matting. You're not even fully Healed yet. You need to stay here where I can tend you."

Trying to find the right words, he said, "I am part of this. A circle. A beginning that must become the end.

Without me, I can sense that there will be a wrongness. Some part of this will be incomplete. I am part of the pattern drawn by Power. I must weave myself into the final fabric." He paused. "Does that make sense?"

She nodded, a weary acceptance in her eyes. "Yes, yes. I know the ways of Power. Oh, do I ever. And I'm tired of it, Ripple. Tired of being at the center of great events. By Birdman's sacred mace, I'd break free if I could. I want to go away somewhere, build a house by a stream and grow corn and squash. I want to lie with a man who won't hurt me, and learn what love is. Can't I be left alone, have the chance to conceive and have children? I want to watch them grow, and play, and smile at them as they sit by the fire. Why is it impossible for me?"

He stared down at his left hand where it rested in a mass of splints. The bones were itching, most of the swelling gone. Through gaps he could see scabs crusted and loose atop pink skin on what had once been knuckles.

"Answers are always hard to find," he said mildly. "From the day I watched my mother and father die I have wanted nothing but the First People's destruction. I had not thought to find anything I would want as much." He smiled sadly. "I haven't told you before, but Raven Hunter gave me a vision. In it, I saw your face."

"Then don't go."

"I made a promise to Cold Bringing Woman."

She said nothing. Perhaps Orenda of all people knew what came of breaking promises to the gods.

Oh, the gods, what capricious beings they are. As woven into the ways of Power as humans, but with the ability to use it for their own purposes. Once I feared the gods. That was such a long time ago, before I realized that they, too, were as mortal as I. True, the lives of gods are longer, and the Spirit World in which they live has more twists and turns than the earth that people walk; but in the end, they, too, shall die.

I have yet to truly understand how gods harness the Power they use. I think it resembles the whirlpools and eddies along one of the great eastern rivers. Power is the current, constantly flowing through time. Somehow the gods concentrate that current for their own, holding it for a time, using it for their petty aims. But in the end, they can no more hoard Power than any of us can hoard life. As a god's Power drains away, he wilts, fades, and finally whimpers into a memory. Memory as we all know is ephemeral as a summer rain.

As I sit in my cage, I ponder the irony: In the beginning, people depend on gods for their survival; and in the end, it is the gods who desperately depend on people for theirs. Time will defeat them both.

I cock my head, listening. The faint whisper of the Spirits in my pack carries from Webworm's room. By now they are sending their tendrils down into his souls. What a fool he is, inviting Power into his Dreams.

All the while he carves another basilisk.

Meanwhile, I sit in my cage. I have heard them say I'm harmless.

Let them believe.

"Fool! Fool! You stupid fool!" Crow Woman cried. What on earth had gotten into her? She'd told him things she'd never said to anyone. What was it about him that had conjured such idiocy?

Crow Woman trotted down the sinuous trail, winding her way between patches of pine and lodgepole. She had crossed the divide into the River of Souls Valley. The ford that would take her to Ironwood's camp lay no more than three hands' journey ahead. As she hurried along, her shield, bow, and arrows clattered on her back; with a willow switch she slashed angrily at the brown grass.

She had awakened in the night, morning still hands of time away. Shivering from the nightmares that had haunted her, she'd stared over to where he slept so peacefully. Regret, like a thing alive, had been twisting in her breast.

How would she dare face him in the morning? She'd never be able to look him in the eyes again, knowing that he knew. By letting her words run like a brook, she'd given him bits of her souls, pieces he could use against her.

And he would.

He was a man.

Maybe he wouldn't.

She viciously squashed the voice that tried to wedge its way into her thoughts. Of course he would. What man hadn't tried to harm her, humiliate her, bend her to his purpose?

The war chief.

Very well, there had been one. But his respect for her hadn't been shared by his warriors. Her lip lifted in disgust as she remembered the night Whistle had caught her in the willows. How his hands had groped her breasts, how his hot breath had purled across her neck. Or the look of surprise on his face when she'd dimpled his throat with a deer-bone stiletto she used to pin her hair.

Yes! By the gods, that's how you deal with them!

Through a patch in the trees she glared up at the brown pall that cloaked the east. Stellar jays screeched in the trees. The morning smelled of dry grass and dust.

On top of everything else she was an escaped slave with Dreams of something better. She could make no claim on family, kin, clan, or tribe. Her only defense lay in her ability with weapons and in the cold aloofness she maintained with her comrades.

So why had she confessed so much to Wrapped Wrist?

She shook her head, deluged with self-disgust as she stormed down the trail. Around her, muted light gave the ponderosa and lodgepole pine a ruddy tone as it filtered through the smoke-hazy eastern sky. Through patches in the trees she could see the distant plume. With each passing day the pall grew larger as it was carried off to the east.

If the sky was a bowl—as some people maintained— eventually it should fill up. But for days now, the smoke had just vanished over the eastern horizon. That being the case, just how big was the world? Not even Night-shade had seen the eastern edge of it, and she had lived out there for years.

A memory of Wrapped Wrist smiling, eyes sparkling as he talked to his kinswomen, lingered down in her souls. Was that it? She'd seen him so at ease, watched the warmth as he talked to Yellow Petal, Soft

Cloth, and Fir Brush. They had genuinely enjoyed each other's company. It had touched some part of her souls she had long thought cold and dead. The very notion of a man at ease with women had confused her.

Enjoyed? In her experience, no woman had ever enjoyed a man's company. If he wasn't ordering her around, working her until her fingers bled, or trying to ram his rod into her, he was asleep.

Wrapped Wrist had thought his relationship so normal; that had confused her even more.

"They're clan kin. Surely you grew up with the same."

He might have been saying, "The sky is blue."

It's not blue, you fool.

If only it had been. She thought back, way back. She'd accepted the beatings and humiliation that came with being a slave. She'd never known any different. As a girl she had come to admire Wraps His Tail, the Matron's son. For a brief instant when a hard warm body slid into her bed that first night, she'd thought it was he. Only to discover it was his brother who clamped a hand over her mouth, groped her breasts, and jacked her legs apart with his knee.

She'd started to cry out when his hard shaft began prodding at her, but a hand had closed like a rawhide clamp over her throat. He hadn't even forced himself inside when he stiffed and groaned, his seed trickling hot across her skin.

Cursing under his breath, he'd slumped. For long moments she'd lain in fear, taking shallow breaths, feeling his semen soak into the blanket beneath her buttocks.

"Put your hands on me," he'd finally growled into

her ear. "If you don't, by the Blue God, come morning, they'll never find your body."

Somehow she'd managed to overcome his ineptitude, contributing to her own rape that night.

So she'd run away—right into worse trouble.

Leather Hand had been nothing compared to Snake Head. She remembered his face, triangular to the point that his cheekbones seemed to stick out of the side of his head. That first night the firelight had glowed red on one side of his face; he was grinning down at her as he twirled a greased stick painfully inside her. The worthless weasel had been absolutely gleeful as she chewed on her wrist to keep from screaming. And all the while, his guards had remained oblivious just beyond his door.

She looked down in the morning light and could still see the faint scars marring her skin. Generate enough pain, burn with a hot-enough anger, and she could endure anything—even Snake Head. Even the memories, and the bits of her souls he had ripped out of her.

"I saved myself!" She knotted a fist, feeling familiar anger come bubbling up from inside. Anger had been her ally. It had nerved her when Whistle grabbed her in the willows. He'd seen it burning behind her eyes, felt it in the stiletto tip she'd pressed into his throat. The knowledge was in his eyes every time he looked at her: I made him fear!

So why should she think Wrapped Wrist was any different? Perhaps he did treat his kin well, but they were off-limits, family, and thus safe. But let him have a vulnerable woman in his control, and yes, the beast would come out.

She was thinking of Wrapped Wrist, her souls seeing that sparkle of good humor in his eyes, when the trail entered a thick patch of serviceberry. Her thoughts were on his smile, on his unassuming manner, so different from the men she had known.

Gods, yes, he watched her body with the same desire other men did, but not with that covetous need to possess. No, he watched her with something akin to worship. When had a man ever looked at her that way?

She couldn't help but smile as she remembered the first day when he'd tried to run her into the dirt. A stubby sawed-off chunk like him shouldn't be trying games with a long-legged distance runner like her.

Still, he'd given it a—

Two hard hands clasped her from behind.

She'd just raised her hands to claw free when another body exploded out of the brush. Then another, and another, until she was driven down into the dusty trail, pinned by the weight of hard bodies.

"A woman, by the gods," a man cried. "Look what a prize we have here."

She tried to struggle as they stripped off her shield, her bow and arrows, her war club. A pinning knee jammed painfully in the small of her back. Hard hands groped her, ripped the stiletto out of her hair bun, and invaded her clothing. They found her obsidian blade and tossed it away.

She fought as they bound her hands behind her and tied a short length of braided leather between her ankles.

As they stood, she rolled onto her back, ready to kick out, and looked up at the four hard-eyed men. They were muscular, fit-looking, their bright red shirts and weapons proclaiming them to be the Blessed Sun's.

"Now," one said, "before we take you to the deputy, where might you have been headed?"

"Eat pus, maggot!"

Funny how I'm always carrying firewood these days. The notion amused Spots as he picked his way down the dusty trail out onto the high terrace. Evening was darkening the east, sunset having turned the smoke plume up north to deep lavender mixed with splashes of ruddy orange. Meanwhile in the southwest, the Rainbow Serpent had risen in a high column of blue-black backlit by the sinking sun.

Smoke. The skies were full of it. To the chance eye, it brought a quickening of the heart, only to crumble with the realization that it wasn't cloud, that it bore no promise of rain.

Spots trudged down the trail from the uplands and onto the flat terrace. Straggly rabbitbrush speckled the flat. Here and there the powdery soil had been blown away to expose old river cobbles.

Farmsteads dotted the land as if cast out from an irregular hand. The fields around them were barren, nothing more than plots of disturbed soil. As he passed the households, he could see a faint glow in fire pits as the occupants attended their evening meals.

Thank the gods for the fire. People always needed wood, and Spots was prepared to serve that need. The closest source was a hard day's run to the northwest. Wood for Flowing Waters Town was at a premium;

with each load he could not only Trade for food, but it gave him a reason to linger around Dusk House that the guards could understand.

He was approaching a low mounded pit house that stood just off the trail. The thing looked like an oversized swallow's nest, more mud than anything else. The style was different than he was used to, the doorway being a covered arch in the side instead of in the roof. Someone had built a ratty ramada to one side, and a couple of brownware water jars were propped near the wall.

Spots was passing when a woman called, "Hey! You!"

He turned, staring out from under his load of wood. A woman ducked out of the doorway. She wore a white skirt belted at her hips, her top bare. Her long black hair was pulled up into maiden's buns on either side of her head.

"Yes?"

"I need some wood."

She stepped forward, and in the half-light he said, "Cactus Flower?"

She squinted at him as he swung his heavy load down. The blanket he'd used to pad his shoulders fluttered away, and he straightened, gasping with relief.

"Do I know you?"

"We met at Dusk House. You wanted to Trade for favors."

She shrugged. "I meet a lot of people I want to Trade with for favors. Right now I want to Trade for firewood."

"My name is Spots. I'm from the First Moon villages."

"With all the scars. I remember." She cocked her head. "What are you doing with the firewood? Going to try and burn the place down?"

"I intend on Trading it. You know, for food. And maybe some kind of special thing to take back home. A copper bell, perhaps. Or one of those Hohokam pots. Something to remember the place by."

She nodded, eyeing the firewood. "Do you have any food?"

"A little." He indicated the pack Ironwood had given him.

He could see her sucking on her lips. "I'll cook it for half of your load. You can stay the night for all of it."

"Thanks, but I'll go on and camp by the river. Tomorrow I should be able—"

"I'll cook and you can stay for half of your load."

Spots shook his head, looking down the trail. "Thank you, but I think I'll—"

"A quarter?"

"A quarter? You wanted an abalone pendant the other day."

She shrugged. "Trade hasn't been so good recently. Not with this drought. Things have tightened up. Who'd have ever thought a Trader with a painted seed jar would rather Trade for a sack of corn than a night with me?"

He shrugged. "I've never given it much thought."

"Come on, a quarter's not much. Not for a bed and a hot meal. And you can drink all the water you want. I just packed it up from the river."

Spots chuckled to himself. Besides, he wasn't going to get in and see Nightshade at this time of night. "All right. A quarter."

"Good!" She stepped forward, grabbing the length of rope he'd used to tie the bundle together and dragging it possessively toward her house.

Spots followed her to the ramada, where she bade him sit.

"Want a drink?"

"Yes. It's a long day's journey. I was looking forward to making the river." He produced his cup, and she filled it from the brownware jar.

As she busied herself with a fire bow and kindling, he sat and sipped. The water was cool, kept that way by evaporation as it permeated the clay sides of the water jar. The evening was quiet, only broken by a dog barking in the distance. Every muscle in his body felt tired.

She rose from the fire pit in front of the ramada as flames crackled up. "There. Now, what did you have in that pack to eat?"

"Rabbit and corn cakes. The rabbit I stunned with a throwing stick today while I collected wood."

She was in his pack in an instant, pulling out the stiff rabbit.

"So, how did you get those scars all over your body?" She glanced up at him as she placed her foot on the rabbit's head, grasped it by the back feet, and jerked the head off. The latter she tossed into the flames.

"House fire." Spots watched her peel the rabbit out of its hide. "Only my sister and I escaped."

"Must have hurt." She hesitated only to use a sharp obsidian flake to cut the feet free as she turned the rabbit inside out.

"More than I could ever tell you."

She sliced the gut cavity open, slinging the

intestines, stomach, and lungs into the fire. The rest she dropped into a corrugated cooking pot she produced from just inside the door. Adding water, she placed it in the fire, wiped her hands on her skirt, and dropped all of his corn cakes into the pot.

"Hey! That's all of my corn cakes!"

She stared at him, irritation on her face. "Well, what do you expect? You don't think I'm just doing this for you, do you? Not for just a quarter load! I'm hungry, too!"

Spots opened his mouth, then shook his head as she refilled his cup with more water. Instead of complaining, he asked, "What happened at Dusk House today?"

"Nothing much." She settled herself cross-legged on the ramada matting and added another stick to the fire. "With most of the warriors headed to First Moon Mountain, the place is dead. Matron Desert Willow cut War Chief Wind Leaf off. He's fuming."

"What do you mean, cut him off?"

She gave him the same look she'd give an idiot. "They were lovers. Every other night he was slipping himself into her sheath. Well, just before and after her moon."

"Why only then?"

The "you're an idiot" look returned. "She didn't want his child growing in her belly. Remember what happened to Night Sun?"

"Oh."

She was squinting at him in the firelight. "You don't know much, do you forest boy?"

He shrugged, embarrassed.

"Do you have a wife back up in the hills?"

He shook his head. "Uh, I'm not very attractive to

women. I've never pushed my clan to find a wife. At least, not yet."

She was sucking on her lips again. He was starting to think it was something she did when she was thinking. "But you've been with a woman?"

"Of course."

"Bleeding gods, you're lying!" She laughed at the horrified expression on his face.

"I am not!"

Her laughter increased. "Oh, don't worry." Then she seemed to consider. "Of course, for the rest of your firewood, I could change that."

"No." He raised his hands. "No, thank you. I'm fine. In fact, after dinner, I'll just take the rest of my wood and make my way—"

"I see," she said with a smirk. "Afraid, huh?"

"Well, I wouldn't be any good."

"You're sure? For the rest of your wood I'd—"

"No!"

She stared at the fire, sucked at her lips, and sniffed as the first tendrils of steam rose from the pot.

"Desert Willow and Wind Leaf," Spots said to change the subject. "Who would have ever thought?"

"Anyone with eyes in their heads." Cactus Flower used a stick to stir the stew. "But then, the First People are as blind as moles."

"How's that?"

"Their world is about to catch fire, and they remain oblivious."

"Catch fire how?"

She gave him that "look" again. Curiosity overcame his irritation. "Listen, I'm not from here, all right? Tell me about this fire. Does the Mountain Witch have anything to do with it?"

"Gods, no. She's just an old woman in the wrong place at the wrong time." Cactus Flower shifted, laying her hand on his thigh. She didn't seem aware of the scar tissue. Her touch felt cool on his skin. "You have to understand, the First People have dominated the Made People for years, just like they've controlled everyone else in the world. The Made People clans have built their buildings, farmed their fields, fought their wars, and done their errands. Then Night Sun and Ironwood have a child?" Her eyes glowed. "Think about it! If they can have a child, the First People aren't any better. They aren't any different from the Made People. It's all been a sleight."

"A what?"

"A sham, a trick. A way the First People have kept themselves above everyone else. When Cornsilk was born it was proof that she had souls."

"I don't get it."

"Cornsilk is Red Lacewing Clan. She's alive. A person can't live without a soul. The First People have always said the rest of us have animal souls. Cornsilk is half Bear Clan from Ironwood. A First Person's soul can't live in a Made Person; a Made Person's soul can't live in a First Person. Put it together."

He nodded, seeing the dilemma. "You say the Made People are full of resentment?"

"The clan leaders are having secret meetings." Cactus Flower rose and checked the stew. "They're planning what to do if the harvest fails. So far, only Creeper is keeping them in check."

"Who's he?"

"The Buffalo Clan elder. He practically raised Webworm. It's a measure of how worried he is that he hasn't said anything to the Blessed Sun."

"Why doesn't Webworm do something to appease the Made People?"

She shrugged as she walked to the doorway and returned with two bowls. "I really don't think he has the slightest idea that anything's wrong. None of them do. They're so involved with themselves, they consider no one else important."

Did Nightshade know this? He pondered the notion as he ate the hot stew. If she had truly gone to Flowing Waters Town to destroy Webworm, she must know the ramifications.

"You seem to know a great deal about the Blessed Sun."

Cactus Flower grinned. "All it takes is eyes and ears. Most of us know these things. The First People don't even see us anymore. To them, we don't exist."

Later, after they had eaten, she set fire to a pine cone on a stick and led him inside her house. Four posts supported the roof, while two concentric benches were crammed with different Trade items. A fire pit had been dug into the floor behind the reflector—the night much too warm to merit its use. To either side were rush-mat pallets covered with soft deer hides.

"That's mine." She pointed in the flickering light. "Yours is there." She glanced at him. "Assuming you insist on keeping that last quarter of firewood."

"I said you'd get a quarter for cooking and a bed."

She grinned. "You've got a good memory."

"And don't forget it."

He had no more than lain down, sighing at the feel

of the soft hides cushioning his body, when the little cone torch burned out. In the darkness, he could look up at the small smoke hole and see stars.

"You've really never had a woman?" she asked.

"I agreed to a quarter of my wood for dinner and a bed."

Silence.

He closed his eyes, thoughts on what she'd told him about the Made People. Could he really believe they were plotting against Webworm and Desert Willow? If that were the case, then what did—

Fingers picking at his hunting shirt brought him bolt upright.

"What are you doing?"

"Trying to get you to sit up and take this shirt off."

"What?"

"I've never been anyone's first before. That's a pretty good Trade, if you ask me."

Chapter Eleven

Making a miniature was a stroke of sheer genius. The notion of building a small copy of First Moon Mountain would never have occurred to Bad Cast, but Ironwood had said, "Can you make it for me?"

"What? The mountain?"

"And the valleys as well."

"I don't understand. Make it?"

"Re-create it. Here, in the plaza, with stones, dirt, and grass stems for trees. The way a potter makes a representation of the world when she forms a clay bowl. Pile up the rocks in as close a representation of the mountain as you can. Draw in the streams in the valleys. Make it so that my warriors can study it, know it, as if they were giants looking from above at the actual mountain."

Bad Cast, with Whistle's help, had gone to work, stacking rocks, laying a sandstone slab at a cant, and dumping soil over it along the slopes. Two round stones replicated the pillars. He used broken potsherds to indicate the villages, scratched lines marking the major trails, and stuck pine needles into the dirt to indicate trees. Making the model took him most of a day, for he had to portray Juniper Ridge, the mountains to the north and south, as well as their major villages.

When it was finished, Whistle fingered his chin, standing back. Afternoon sunlight cast shadows from the waist-high peak, and the lower rendition of Juniper Ridge.

The warrior said, "I think that's it. Even the orientation is correct."

Bad Cast nodded, arching his back and wincing at the pain from being bent over most of the day. "I think we should stick more pine needles into the slopes."

"It doesn't have to be perfect," Whistle reminded. "Just good enough."

"And you think that's good enough?"

Whistle chuckled. "It's a war map, not a sacred offering."

Ripple's voice surprised them from behind. "Sometimes they are one and the same."

Bad Cast turned. Ripple stood silhouetted by the reddish light that filtered through the smoke-hazy sky. His skin might have been copper burnished with blood. Gods, how he had changed: Something about his eyes—they seemed larger, darkened by sadness. A pinching around his once-youthful face expressed an incalculable sense of loss. Before his vision, his frame had been bulky, flesh smooth; now it was composed of bone and fibrous muscle that slid under too-tight skin.

"What is this?" Whistle asked. "One or both?"

Ripple's lips quivered. "That is for you to decide,

warrior. Will you give up First Moon Mountain? Or your souls?"

"I don't understand." Whistle looked suddenly nervous.

"You will. Soon you must choose between your life and your souls. The only thing left to be discovered is how you will justify it."

Whistle's frown darkened, and then he waved it away. "I serve the war chief. If doing so costs me my life, so be it."

Ripple nodded with the sagacity of one who knew more than he let on.

Whistle seemed to shiver, saying, "If you will excuse me, I must see to some things."

Bad Cast watched him walk away, steps hurried and jerky. "What did you say that to him for?"

"So that he may prepare himself."

Bad Cast stared at his friend. "Ripple, come on. If you know something, tell him. He's Ironwood's deputy. The war chief is sending him to meet with White Eye as soon as Wrapped Wrist and Crow Woman return with their report."

"Events are moving faster than you would think." Ripple inclined his head toward the room block back under the dull green ponderosas. The mud-splashed line of stone dwellings had taken on the reddish hue of the sky. Protruding roof poles were hung with net bags full of dried corn, chilies, and squash.

Ironwood and Night Sun had emerged from one of the rooms and were talking to Whistle and a dust-covered runner who had appeared out of the trees. The latter was a skinny youth in a brown pullover shirt. He talked hurriedly, arms waving in excitement. He carried a bow and a quiver of arrows.

Ironwood listened to the runner, expression growing stern. He turned and said something to Whistle. The Bee Flower Clan warrior jerked a grim nod, pivoted on his heel, and, with the runner, trotted off toward his shelter back in the trees.

Ironwood spoke tersely to Night Sun, then started across the beaten plaza. Night Sun followed at his heels, a determined look on her face. The tall war chief and formidable woman made for a provoking image: he resplendent in a red shirt and feathered kilt, she in a black dress, strings of gleaming beads at her throat. Her gray hair was twisted and pinned atop her head.

"Bad Cast?" he called as he approached. "Is it ready?"

"Yes, War Chief."

Ironwood shot Ripple a wary glance. "Good evening, Dreamer. We have just received word: Sunwatcher Blue Racer is on his way to First Moon Mountain. He is traveling slowly because of the size of his party, but should be there in another four days."

Night Sun added, "We have just ordered Whistle to travel to the First Moon villages. Perhaps he will intercept Crow Woman on the way; if not, he will give White Eye our proposed plan of attack."

Bad Cast frowned. "We have a plan of attack?" He indicated his piles of stone and dirt, so laboriously crafted. "I thought you'd make that based on my re-creation of First Moon Mountain."

Ironwood gave him a cunning smile. "Actually, I've had the plan in my head for some time. That's why I wanted you to build this copy of your mountain as faithfully as possible. I want my warriors to study it intimately. We will begin as soon as I can have them assembled. We are going to learn your mountain front and back, every drainage and crack, every village, forest, and cliff."

"But what about Whistle?" Bad Cast said in confusion.

"Whistle knows."

"But he didn't say anything about it while I was working on this. Only that it had to show all the mountain's features."

"I'm sure he didn't." Ironwood was inspecting the panorama, squinting as he walked around. "He will tell White Eye what I need from his First Moon clans. With their help, I can crack Pinnacle House like a pinion nut in a mortar."

Ripple's face blanched. "Then it's begun."

Night Sun had a flinty look in her eyes. "It has Dreamer." She stepped over to the miniature and pointed to the steep northern slope of First Moon Mountain. The loose dirt bristled with needles that Bad Cast had carefully planted to indicate forest. "Our warriors will scale this side in the darkness of the second night after Sister Moon comes full." She bent, pointing to the flat incline of the southwestern slope. "The First Moon clans will assemble their warriors here. Whistle will tell White Eye to make an attack toward Guest House at first light. They need only draw the attention of Webworm's warriors to the slope."

Ripple's voice had a singsong lilt. "No matter what plans are made, success eludes us until blood is paid."

"What does that mean, Dreamer?" Night Sun demanded.

"We shall succeed, but we will each, in our own way, pay a terrible cost."

Ironwood stepped forward, demanding, "What cost? I must know."

Ripple raised his hand. "Ask yourself, War Chief, do you really want to add my burden to your own? Are your shoulders that wide and strong? No, I thought not. I can see it in your eyes. You have accepted your destiny; now allow me to accept mine." With that, he turned, walking slowly, head down, toward the forest.

"Ripple?" Bad Cast called, starting in pursuit. "Is there anything I can do?"

"No, old friend. But soon. Very soon."

Bad Cast slowed to a stop and would have sworn Ripple's shoulders were heaving with sobs, but it might have been caused by his friend's stumbling pace.

Wrapped Wrist puzzled over what to do next. He hurried from tree to tree in the darkening forest. Dry needles crackled under his feet. The ponderosa had turned gloomy and dark; their thick boles barely hid his wide frame. The pungent odor of smoke from the distant forest fire carried on the wind.

A chickadee chattered. Some of the evening birds warbled in lonesome melody. The first of the night creatures were stirring.

He had always liked this time of day—the quick transition into night—because of the stillness that leached from the trees, rocks, and soil. Even the air seemed to grow heavy, lethargic. In silence, the shadows swelled, encompassing the world. He'd always felt at peace.

This time as darkness settled around him, he dared not. His heart hammered, skin hot and sweaty. Nerves made his guts squirm. Fear was proving an uncomfortable and unwelcome companion. He wondered how the heroes in the stories dealt with this sense of incipient panic. All he wanted to do was run away.

Instead he continued creeping from tree trunk to tree trunk, each time hoping that none of the warriors would look back in his direction.

In the gloom they had become slinking shadows, and worse, the forest floor here was littered with old cones, crackly duff, and fallen branches that could snap underfoot and give his presence away.

Four of them! The notion rolled around in Wrapped Wrist's head. Four dreaded Red Shirts, trained warriors! What in the name of the gods was he going to do?

Since he'd been a babe on a teat, it had been beaten into him that Red Shirts fought like Spirit Demons unleashed. They trained for war, perfecting their arts the way hunters perfected the stalk, or potters their vessels.

I'm just a hunter. How can I hope to prevail?

They were armed with bows, each carrying a full quiver of arrows. He had only his atlatl and three darts. A good bowman could have six arrows in the air before the first landed. The atlatl allowed Wrapped Wrist but three casts, each demanding that he stand, step, and release. Atlatls were weapons suited to hunting, not war. If they discovered him, he'd have no better chance than a rabbit caught on sandstone slickrock.

"Maggot!" Crow Woman's voice was filled with loathing.

One of the Red Shirts laughed.

Wrapped Wrist ground his teeth. Whatever they were going to do with Crow Woman, it wouldn't be nice. He knew what Red Shirts did with captive women, had seen the aftereffects among his own people when a Red Shirt fixed his attention on a young woman. Her clan might protest to Matron Larkspur. Sometimes some small offering might even be made in restitution depending on how egregious the warrior had been; but in cases of simple rape, without a beating or disfigurement, rarely was a word of consolation even granted.

Not so long ago a young woman's brother had taken matters into his own hands, attacking the warrior who had raped his sister. The retaliation of the Red Shirts was rapid and remorseless: they burned the young man alive, killed his closest clan kin, and gutted the young woman who had had the temerity to complain.

What can I do? Wrapped Wrist wondered as he sneaked quietly after the warriors. How can I hope to set her free?

Frightened, but unwilling to give up, he continued creeping through the deepening gloom. Step by careful step, he followed, hope draining away with the last of the light. What if he lost them in the darkness? Worse, what if he blundered on top of them? They'd kill him without a second thought. The image of whistling war clubs sent a quiver through his guts.

Why am I doing this?

He wasn't even sure he liked her. Just thinking back to her caustic comments was enough to give him pause.

Stumpy? That had hurt! Maybe this was the gods paying her back for her arrogant attitude?

Then her confession in the night returned to haunt him. She probably didn't even know that hidden in the tones of her voice had been a desperate longing for simple friendship.

Why does it have to be me? If she hasn't been able to trust another human being up to now, I'm not going to be the one.

Nope. Fact was, her souls had been wounded and scarred long ago. Far be it from his responsibility to try and fix them. The mere notion of damaged souls scared him half to death. She'd made her way this far, she could see to herself. This was lunacy! A smart man would veer off from the trail and vanish into the night.

Wrapped Wrist hunched and hurried forward, his darts grasped between his fingers so the wood wouldn't rattle. He could barely make out the shadows of the warriors ahead.

Don't be a fool! Leave!

Down between his souls, Ripple's last words burned like cactus under the skin: "You must save her."

Hummingbird

The Fire Dogs who live in the south have a wonderful story about Hummingbird. It is said that one hot summer day lightning struck the mountaintop where Hummingbird had her nest, and a great fire roared to life and began devouring the forest. All of the other birds flew away. The animals raced down the slopes, and the lizards and snakes crawled into holes trying to find cover.

But Hummingbird refused to leave her eggs. Day and night, she soared to and from a high mountain lake, carrying water in her tiny beak to drop on the enormous flames sweeping toward her nest.

Her courage so touched the hovering Cloud People, their tears poured down in a great flood and drowned the fire.

The Fire Dogs say Hummingbird proves that even the smallest efforts of a selfless heart can bring about salvation.

I see another teaching in the story.

Hummingbird teaches me that the tiniest act of courage can draw the most powerful allies.

Firewood was a lucrative business. The environs around Flowing Waters Town had been stripped of fuel. Spots was on his second load. He'd laid it out on his blanket just before dawn, and now watched the sunrise over the eastern horizon. Its light cast long shadows from the rising walls of Sunrise House.

The hucksters were still arriving, claiming the best places along the eastern wall for their blankets of Trade. Cactus Flower and Spots had arrived in the half-light, getting a position close to the southeastern gap in the Dusk House wall.

The world was just beginning to stir. The guard above them on the first-floor roof called lazily to a farmer leaving for her day in the fields. Spots grinned.

He liked this place and the odd people who made their living bartering with travelers.

Squinting into the sun, he could see someone emerging from a newly completed room in Sunrise House a dart's cast away. He recognized the form. Though just first light, the Ant Clan elder, Yellowgirl, was already on site, planning her day's work.

"She has no other life," Cactus Flower said from where she'd laid out her own Trade. Her trinkets consisted of several pieces of raw clamshell, a couple of Green Mesa pots, four ears of blue corn, and three rabbits. "She just lives for her building."

"Oh, I think not." Spots pointed as a rotund figure stepped out of the room Yellowgirl had just left. The man glanced this way and that, hurrying past Yellowgirl. He said something as he passed, and Yellowgirl gave a curt nod.

"That's interesting," Cactus Flower agreed. "I'd know that shape anywhere. It's old Creeper. Normally you can't get him out of bed until midmorning."

"Maybe Yellowgirl gave him a warm bed last night?" Spots raised an eyebrow. He'd stayed at Cactus Flower's for a second time last night. She'd been alone when he arrived with his load of wood, and happy to Trade a night for a quarter of his load.

As he watched Creeper approach, he wondered yet again about his relationship with Cactus Flower. He liked her. Apparently clanless, kinless, and irreverent, she made him laugh. Her wry sense of humor, cynical disbelief in anything sacred, and earthy appetite left him completely charmed. Or was he just ensorcelled by her enthusiasm when she tightened her sheath around his shaft? The memory of her face in the fire's glow,

133

gone slack, mouth open as she gasped and stiffened, would be with him forever. Nor had he anticipated that coupling could go on all night. His penis stiffened just at the memory.

Creeper came plodding past, head down, expression dark and brooding. He never even glanced Spots' way as he pounded by in a stiff walk.

"Good Morning, Elder," the guard called from above.

"Yes, yes," Creeper called back absently. "Clan business. It's never done." Then he was inside the walls.

Cactus Flower lowered her voice. "Something's happening."

"Oh?"

She pointed. "That's not how Yellowgirl usually acts."

The Ant Clan Matron had been standing, head bowed as she kicked at the dirt with a sandaled foot. Now she shook her head, as if at something distasteful, and seated herself on a pile of stacked stone, her head in her hands.

"She looks worried."

"All the Made People are. You can feel it." Cactus Flower pursed her full lips, the sunlight casting her smooth face in bronze. "It started three moons ago, clan elders sneaking around in the night, attending meetings in other clan kivas. Not only that, they leave watchers, sentries, to see that they're undisturbed. Once, when the Blessed Sun walked out from his rooms to look up at the stars, one of the sentries pitched a stone into the kiva where they were meeting. It went silent as a log. Just like that."

"I thought you stayed at your farmstead."

She shrugged. "Sometimes a Trader asks me to stay here with him."

Which left him wondering. How was he going to feel the first time he came in with a load of firewood and found her occupied by another man?

"Do you ever think you'll want to stay with just one man?"

She gave him a hard look. "Don't start."

"Start what?"

"Do you know how many times I've heard that?"

"I was just asking. It wasn't—"

"No! And it isn't going to be, either." She chewed her lip, glaring at him. "I like you, Spots. Just don't get any ideas about becoming the one man in my life."

"Sorry. Don't yell at me. I was just curious about—"

"Gods." She sighed. "It's all right. You're young."

"No younger than you."

"I wasn't talking summers. I meant in living. It's different. Time means different things to different people." She shrugged. "Besides, I'd never get attached to you anyway."

"Why not?" He winced. "Because of the scars?"

"No, fool." She jerked her head toward Dusk House. "Because of her. You keep sneaking her food and water, and they're going to catch you. Any man who's best friends with a witch isn't headed for a long and happy life. You're just lucky I'm brave enough to lay my blanket next to yours."

He thought about that. "She's my friend."

"Make friends with something safe next time, like a rattlesnake or scorpion."

Spots ground his teeth, frowning at the distant figure of Yellowgirl. She looked as miserable as he felt.

135

Cactus Flower relented. "Sorry. It's just that they put her in that cage for a reason. When the Blessed Sun gets tired of her, he'll haul her out, have her whacked in the head, and buried under a big rock. That's all."

Spots shook his head in disbelief, voice lowering. "It won't happen that way. Trust me."

She gave him a sidelong appraisal. "Is there more to her than I know?" He gave a brief nod of the head. "What?"

He bit his lip, refusing to answer. "Oh, come on, give it up, Spots. What?"

He kept his gaze locked on Yellowgirl. Was it the distance? Or was she crying?

Chapter Twelve

A fire crackled. Yellow light illuminated the camp the warriors had chosen. Thick scrub oak, sumac, and wild rose was interlaced with nightshade vines, the latter rich in black berries. Overhead, smoke from the distant fire damped most of the stars. From this ridge, distant flames could be seen as they sparkled on the high-country slopes.

Crow Woman swallowed hard and fought the urge to tremble. They had tied her feet, waist, hands, and neck to a slim pine pole. She couldn't bend without tightening the thong at her neck. She could barely shift her feet and wiggle her arms. Trussed like a hunter's carcass she could only stand, her back to a sandstone boulder, and hope she didn't fall over.

The four warriors watched her from the fire, eyes like ferrets' in the hot yellow light. They were muscular men, wearing new war shirts. One, a narrow-framed man, kept giving her an oily smile. After they had stopped for the night, he had donned a pair of spotless white moccasins. Something about him, the way he looked at her, scared the breath right out of her.

She had watched as they fixed a stew of corn, yampa root, chokecherries, and goosefoot seeds. Two had emptied their canteens into a small corrugated pot after the ingredients had been added. They had watched her in silence while it boiled. One by one they dipped from the steaming pot using spoons crafted from mountain sheep bones.

Silence. They just ate, savoring each bite, their eyes fixed on her. She wanted to squirm, to hiss and spit, to curse their mothers as camp bitches, but fear had a stranglehold on her voice. It would have been so much better if they'd cursed, leered, tormented, and threatened. They just watched, jaws chewing, eyes eating into her courage.

Silence. It left her trembling. She couldn't stop the sudden shiver that racked her. It was as if they weren't men, but some kind of feral predators. Wolves gone into men's bodies. Or worse, mute evil that watched from those gleaming eyes.

The narrow-framed man scraped the bottom of the jar, tilted it, and scooped the last of the stew. He lifted the polished bone spoon, letting it slip past his lips as he sucked the last of the liquid from the hollow.

In silence they replaced their spoons in their packs, retied their canteens, and wiped out the stew bowl with grass before packing it away.

Why don't they speak?

She swallowed hard to keep her breath from catching in her throat. Her mouth had gone dry, her knees weak.

They stood, stepping around the fire, each

inspecting her with eager stares. The narrow-framed man was smiling. Not a leer, just a lilt to the lips. A hint of expectation in his expression. He knew how terrified she was.

"What do you want from me?" Her voice came out as a croak.

They might not have heard.

The narrow-framed man raised his hand, and she was surprised to see a long, hafted obsidian blade. She winced, almost toppled, and caught herself as he slipped the sharp blade across the skin of her cheek. He didn't press hard enough to cut, just to tickle.

"Get it over with, maggot!" she cried. "Kill me, and have done with it!"

Silence, but the men smiled, two showing missing teeth. Another laughed with silent mirth.

The only sound was the crackling of the fire.

"If you want me, take me," she said between pants of fear.

The narrow-framed man leaned close. She could smell his sweat, the smoky tinge to his hair. His breath carried the faint scent of stew. Lips to her ear, he whispered, "Where's Ironwood?"

She jerked back, teetering, falling. But one of the men caught her, holding the pole she was bound to upright.

"I—I don't know." Her voice was catching. They could see her shivering now. Blood and spit, if they'd only beat her, give her the pain to cling to! Anything but this slow silent promise. She leaned her head back, throat straining at the thong, and screamed her terror into the smoky night.

It echoed in the quiet air.

With slow deliberation, the narrow-framed man inserted his obsidian blade beneath the neck of her war shirt and carefully severed the fabric. He worked his way out, over her shoulder, and down her arm until the cloth fell away, exposing her arm and right breast.

"What are you going to do?"

"Shhh!" He placed a finger to his lips, leaning forward to add in a whisper, "We follow Leather Hand. He has sent us to find Ironwood."

"I don't know where he is!" she insisted doggedly.

"Oh, yes," he whispered. "You do. But we have time."

She had trouble taking a full breath. "I said, if you are going to take me, get it over with. Come on. Untie me. You're men, aren't you? Your staffs aren't made of wet clay, are they?"

He nodded, and the rest followed as if at some unseen signal. "Time." He mouthed the word. Inserting his knife on the other side, he began the process of slitting the fabric over her left shoulder.

Crow Woman watched in fascination as the faded red fabric parted and fell away to expose her smooth brown skin.

They're peeling it away.

And when they had removed her clothing, what then?

I will no longer be a warrior.

She clamped her eyes closed, insisting, Yes, yes I will!

That was when the blow caught her. A smacking impact that blasted her kneecap sideways. She would have fallen but for strong hands fixing her pole. The thong cut into her neck, causing her to stiffen, gasping for breath.

She blinked. Each male face leaned close, peering, as if to see her fear from a hand's breadth away.

"Where is Ironwood's camp?" Narrow-frame whispered.

"I don't know," she insisted. "In these mountains somewhere."

"Good," came the whispered reply.

For a moment they watched; then Narrow-frame reached out and cupped her breast. His touch was light, little more than a caress of her nipple. Nevertheless the hard callus on his hand made her stiffen.

He lifted the knife. "You heard about the Dust People?"

She jerked a nod.

He ran the keen blade in a circle around the swell of her breast; the sharp edge left a white scratch on her dark skin. "If I cut this off, we will eat it. And you will watch us." His hand went to her other breast. "Then we will eat this one."

She tried to speak, to deny it, but a croaking came from her throat.

He was playing the obsidian blade up and down her stomach, following the line from her sternum down to the navel. The rope at her waist parted, and the remains of her dress fluttered down to wad around her ankles. She stared down in horror as the obsidian blade traced around her abdomen, then patterned a spiral above the black thatch of her pubic hair.

"I will eat your womb when I cut it out," another of the warriors whispered. This was a thickset man who was missing two of his incisors.

She tried to shrink away from the gliding blade. Faint white scratches on her smooth skin marked its course.

"Tell," Narrow-frame whispered, his voice barely audible above the wind in the distant pines.

She leaned her head back, screaming, "By the gods, just kill me!"

"Oh," the sibilant whisper assured, "it won't be that easy." A pause. "Unless you tell us where Ironwood—"

"If...if I do...you'll just kill me?"

Narrow-frame nodded, voice rising. "After we enjoy you, yes. You will make it good for us? You won't just lie on your back like a sack of corn?"

"No." She tried to nod through the shivers. "I'll make it good."

He smiled, eyes glittering. "And you won't lie about Ironwood? If you did, well, we can eat you slowly. A piece at a time until you die."

Gods, kill me now! "I...won't lie."

"Good." He reached up with the knife, slicing a line across her chest just above the swell of her breasts. Then he severed the thong at her neck. Two of the warriors stepped back, pulling their war shirts over their heads, grinning. One already had an erection that bobbed as he tossed his shirt to one side.

The hiss might have been the exhalation of the gods —the meaty slap, a clap of thunder.

Crow Woman tried to make sense of the image. The two naked warriors jerked up and down like Dancers, their muscular bodies writhing back and forth, out of step. When one moved, the other twisted. She could see the point protruding from the thickset man's side like a misplaced second erection.

"What in...?" The narrow-framed man stepped back, his knife in hand, ready to attack. His darting gaze took in the brush, and he blinked, night-blinded by the fire.

The last man leaped for his weapons as the first two warriors staggered and stumbled, then fell to the ground. The thickset man had lost his erection, his hands clutching the spearhead that stuck out of his side. A wild scream broke from his mouth, only to be cut off by a bubbling froth of blood.

Another hiss ended with a thud as the third warrior stood, his war club in his hands. He stared down stupidly at the dart point that extended half a body length from his chest. He grabbed it with his left hand, sagged to his knees, and gasped out a hoarse rattling cry.

"Show yourself," Narrow-frame cried. "Come fight like a man!"

Something warned him. He threw himself sideways, a long dart cutting the air where he'd been standing but a heartbeat before.

Narrow-frame lunged for his dying companion, plucked the war club from his hand, and backed quickly to where Crow Woman balanced precariously, her pole held only by her hands and the rope at her ankles. Her knee was an agony of pain.

"Show yourself!" he cried. "Or I kill her!" He jabbed the knife at Crow Woman.

She tried to squirm away; the pole slipped sideways, toppling her onto the grass. Her knee wrenched, but she bit off the shriek.

Narrow-frame grinned as he placed his foot on her neck and pressed down. She could see him lift the war club, knew how warriors practiced this stroke: the death blow for executions.

"I am a White Moccasin! Come and get me, you cowardly filth! This woman is dead! I will eat her flesh!"

From the corner of her eye, Crow Woman watched the stone-headed club rise in the firelight.

A sense of peace filled her. It would be over now. A sharp pain, and then her souls would be free. Free. It wasn't so bad.

The blur came from the sandstone boulder. She felt the impact, heard her neck crack, and then the white moccasins flashed before her eyes. The warrior was driven into the grass before her, his breath making a whuff as he hit. It might have been wild animals given the howls and screams that tore from the men's throats as they rolled and kicked.

Crow Woman gasped for breath, watching as a bulky form emerged from behind the warrior. She caught the firelight on a litter-matted hunting shirt as thick hands grasped the warrior's throat.

"You are no stronger!" the apparition bellowed. "Without death, there is no life! No future!"

Narrow-frame made a gagging sound as Wrapped Wrist's hands tightened on his throat. The warrior was flailing his arms, the obsidian knife flashing this way and that, whipping backward in an attempt to find Wrapped Wrist's body.

Wrapped Wrist threw his head back, away from the blade, and a wild "Aaaragh!" broke from his lips.

Crow Woman watched as Wrapped Wrist's legs tightened about the warrior's waist. She saw the muscles swell, knot, and strain. The crackling sounded like breaking pottery. Wrapped Wrist heaved again, and a final pop carried on the still night.

Wrapped Wrist tossed the twitching body away. For a moment he stared at his hands, perhaps seeing them for the first time. A shudder racked his body; then he turned, seeing her where she lay trussed. Blood streaked his right cheek.

He asked, "Gods, why am I so scared?"

Bad Cast watched with a curious reluctance as Ironwood held Night Sun in his arms. The war chief cradled her to him like a precious and delicate bird; his face was a reflection of pained love.

Bad Cast would have walked away, but he had to wait his turn by the cleft in the rimrock where the trail led down the slope. Faint morning light filtered pink through the pall of smoke that masked the north and east.

Most of the warriors had already started down the narrow defile. Bad Cast shifted from foot to foot beside Ripple. Oddly, his friend had a sad look on his face as he turned to Orenda and said, "I need you to do something for me."

She gazed thoughtfully at him. "Yes?"

"In three days, I need you to pick mint from the river just below the hot springs where the Mountain Witch tended my body."

Bad Cast expected her to say something like "What? That's silly," but she didn't. She just nodded as if this was the most ordinary of requests despite the fact it meant a half-day's journey for her.

Bad Cast glanced back to where Ironwood's powerful arms were wrapped around Night Sun.

"I'll see you soon," the war chief promised. "Remember, each breath I take is for you."

"You stay safe for me, my love." Night Sun's smile carried the warmth of the sun as she reached up and stroked the side of his scarred face.

Bad Cast swallowed hard and looked away. Were the roles reversed, would he and Soft Cloth have had that same Power of affection between them? Or was this something born of a different trial? The worship reflected in Ironwood's and Night Sun's eyes would cling to his memory for a lifetime.

Ripple had turned away from Orenda, noticed Bad Cast's attention, and pushed him toward the trailhead, whispering, "He knows. Just not the way of it."

"The way of what?" Bad Cast took his turn, easing himself down through the cleft, oddly reassured by the rock closing around him.

"The sacrifice he has to make for the world," Ripple added. "I wish I had her courage."

"Whose? Night Sun's?"

"Her love is greater than mine."

Whatever Ripple might be talking about, Bad Cast could agree. When had he ever seen devotion like that reflected in lovers' eyes?

Love? Just what was it? Oh, granted, he missed Soft Cloth something terrible, and he had always thought he loved her. But did what he felt in his heart mirror what he'd just seen shared by Ironwood and Night Sun?

"Gods," Ripple whispered behind him. "It hurts."

Bad Cast glanced over his shoulder, seeing the hollow expression of loss on his friend's face.

"I'd think it was you leaving something behind, rather than the war chief."

"I am." Ripple smiled sadly. "I wish I'd never gone up after that elk. If I could, I'd go back, change it."

"Does that mean you'd deny Cold Bringing Woman's vision?"

"No, not at all." Ripple placed a reassuring hand on Bad Cast's shoulder. "Don't mind me. I'm just complaining. Cold Bringing Woman came to me, and I made my choice. What's different now is that I know what the alternatives would have been. Had she not come, I wouldn't have known. So most likely in that other life I would never have met Orenda. Might never have shared what little time we've had. So I live with my decision."

"You and Orenda?" Bad Cast asked. "You still don't know that in the end, after this is all over—"

"Yes, I do. From this moment forward, lips will never smile, children will never laugh, and hearts will remain empty. Promise dies today. The future won't even mourn over its corpse."

"Ripple, don't be so sure. Anything can happen." In that moment, missing Soft Cloth became an even greater need.

"Will you promise me something?"

"Of course. Anything."

"When you've finished your duty with the war chief, find Soft Cloth and your daughter and go as far away as you can."

"What about you? Can't you come with us?"

The smile Ripple gave him was bittersweet with longing. "I've made my bargain with fate."

"What kind of talk is that?"

147

"The kind that speaks of the death of Dreams."

"You're going to have a wonderful scar," Crow Woman said gently.

Wrapped Wrist flinched and hissed as she slipped another cactus thorn through the cut on his right cheek. Narrow-frame's blade had made a neat but deep slice. To bind it, Crow Woman squeezed the flesh together and pierced the skin through both lips of the incision with a long cactus spine. Next she looped thread from her war shirt around the thorn ends so that it pulled the skin together. The process was incredibly painful.

Wrapped Wrist shot an uneasy look at the scrub oak; broken branches could be seen where he'd dragged the bodies out of the little clearing. He could imagine them there, sprawled among the stems and leaves, limbs akimbo, expressions slack as flies crawled over their eyes and into their open mouths.

He gasped again as Crow Woman's steady fingers lanced his cheek with another of the long thorns. The sting was terrible, burning as cactus always did.

A stew was simmering on the fire, the last of the warrior's goosefoot, corn, and water. Knowing that they were Leather Hand's men, Crow Woman had opted to burn the dried meat she found in one of the packs rather than take a chance it might be human.

"Are you feeling better?" she asked, concern in her voice.

"I still feel shaky." He took a breath as she pulled her make-do suture together. "I guess a real warrior wouldn't have thrown up afterward."

She laughed, the sound of it nervous. "A real warrior?"

"Someone like you," he added. "You wouldn't have been a trembling mess. Pus and blood, you should have seen me. I was shaking so bad. That first cast had to be perfect. I had three darts, so I had to wait until I could get two with the first throw. They were close. I was scared. I had to wait." He tried to glance away. "I'm sorry it took so long."

She grabbed his chin, turning his head to see his eyes. "A warrior is smart first, Wrapped Wrist." Then it was she who looked away. "I was shaking pretty badly myself. If you hadn't come..."

"You'd have escaped, killed every last one of them," he told her positively.

"Shut up."

He clamped his jaws as she finished pinning and binding his cheek. Her capable fingers tied the knot off, and she sat back, legs crossed.

He dabbed at the binding with his fingertips. His chin and neck were stiff with blood. It had soaked into his hunting shirt. "Where did you learn this?"

"It's an old warrior's trick. Be careful and don't snag it on anything, or you'll break the cactus spines. They're going to soften anyway. It's going to make pus, so I might have to redo it tomorrow."

"Thank you." He could see the places on her ankles and wrists where the binding had chafed her skin. Her knee was swollen, and she held it out stiff before her. She wore a blanket over her shoulders, the ruins of her war shirt tied about her waist like a double-flapped skirt.

"Why don't you let me sew your war shirt back

together?" He indicated the folds of red cloth hanging at her waist.

"I'm no warrior," she replied dully. "I am unworthy of this shirt. When they cut it off me, it was as if I lost myself." She leaned her head back, her hair spilling loose from the bun at the back of her head. "Nightshade was right. There was nothing but anger inside me. I became the shirt. When I lost it, I didn't know who I was. I never knew I was such a coward."

From his memory the words came: "Swallow your fear. It is meaningless—illusion meant to keep you from what needs to be done. You have never understood that your souls are even stronger than your body. Without death, there is no life, no future."

She gave him a disbelieving smirk. "Words, Wrapped Wrist."

He frowned, wincing at the pain in his cheek. "Ripple...the Dreamer told me that last time I saw him. He said I had to know it down between my souls. That I had to understand."

"What else did he tell you?"

"That you would need me." He made a gesture. "Who'd have thought? Ripple. My old friend." He glanced up skeptically. "Did he really see the future?"

She stared vacantly at the fire where the stew boiled. "Maybe, like Nightshade, he knew I was hollow."

"You're not hollow." Wrapped Wrist reached for his pack, recovered his little clay cup, and dipped up the hot liquid. "You going to eat?"

"Not hungry."

"Well, you'd better eat. We lost a half day when they started back toward First Moon Mountain."

She shook her head. "I'm not going."

Wrapped Wrist made a face. "Ironwood is depending on us."

Crow Woman said wearily, "I would have betrayed him. Wrapped Wrist, I've got to think about this." At that she got awkwardly to her feet and limped away.

Wrapped Wrist watched her go, the ruined war shirt swaying around her long legs. Sighing, he turned his attention back to the fire and sipped the hot stew. If only he could get the memory to go away, but all night long he'd relived the fight. He could still feel the warrior's neck as the bones popped. Could feel how the man had twitched, how the head had flopped, a dead weight in his hands.

The queasy sick feeling tickled his stomach again.

Chapter Thirteen

Soft white light shone through the small window in the north wall; Leather Hand knew that morning had come. He looked down into her dark eyes, seeing them widen as he slid into her warm sheath. She locked her legs around his hips, pulling the blanket lower on his back. The morning chill prickled his skin.

A satisfied purr came from deep in Larkspur's throat as she tightened and arched her hips against his.

This was a delightful way to awaken. He'd been lost in Dreams when her fingers had found him under the blanket. Only after she'd awakened his manhood had she pulled him onto her warm body and opened herself to him.

He surrendered himself to the moment, tried to concentrate on the sensations. Unlike the slave girls he emptied himself into, she moved with him, grinding her hips against his. The stifled gasps in her throat were refreshment for his soul.

His loins exploded with an intensity that left him

breathless. The muscles in his legs and buttocks cramped and locked as he rammed himself into her and stiffened. Her body thrashed under his as she dug her fingers into his back, a scream locked behind clenched teeth. She ended, arched against him, panting, her eyes blazing as she tightened her grip on his shoulders.

"You have to learn to be quiet," she whispered. "Only the slaves would have heard, but at the wrong time…"

"I made no sound."

She laughed, digging her nails painfully into his back again. "Really? A rutting bull elk doesn't bray with that much passion."

He rolled off of her, aware that his sweat was drying in the cool air. She stood, the pale light lovely on her smooth skin, her nipples like hard thumbs as she stepped over and squatted above the chamber pot.

He gasped and threw his arm over his head, the nerves in his body still quivering.

"I hope your warriors are getting as much relief," she told him as she reached for a blue cloth dress that hung from a peg. She slipped it over her tawny body and belted it at her slim waist. Pulling her long hair out, she fluffed it by running her fingers through it.

"Your orders were explicit. They were to be granted every request." He grinned under the weight of his arm. "I saw the looks in the eyes of the Made People. What your authority does not dictate, the wrath of my men does."

She was watching his face closely when she said, "News arrived last night. Matron Husk Woman was found in her sweat bath. Her head was missing. Tall Piñon has been without a Matron for over a week."

Leather Hand allowed no reaction to cross his face. "Too bad. She and I might not have agreed, but she served her people fairly."

Larkspur cocked an eyebrow. "Rumors have begun to circulate. Traders carry the most outrageous stories."

"Oh?"

"They say that witches fly past the guards in the dead of night, murder the Matrons, and quietly fly away with their heads again."

"Clever witches."

"Yes," Larkspur agreed. "Odd, isn't it, that these witches are so clever they only seem drawn to the Blessed Sun's enemies?"

"Curious indeed."

Larkspur's voice dropped. "Then perhaps it's lucky that I serve the Blessed Sun as faithfully as I do."

Leather Hand looked at her from under his arm. "You need fear no witches here, Matron."

A faint smile played at the corner of her lips. She gave him a slight bow, took a feathered cloak down from the next peg, and climbed up the ladder to her top-floor room.

He drew the blanket back, used the chamber pot himself, and pulled on the coarse-woven hunting shirt he'd wadded beside the sleeping pallet the night before. His red shirt was tightly rolled inside his pack, as was his war club. He'd dressed thus, looking like just another hunter, since he and his men had filtered into the First Moon Valley by ones and twos. Like him, they, too, kept out of sight, lodged in certain Made People's pit houses where they were fed, bedded, and sheltered.

He walked around the long room, fingering her

dresses, examining her turquoise, jet, coral, and shell jewelry.

Matron Larkspur. The title intrigued him. Heiress of the Blue Dragonfly Clan. She was in line to inherit the clan Matronship should anything happen to Desert Willow. Not only that, from what he'd seen, she was smart.

He lifted one of her dresses, a beautiful black thing with white four-pointed stars, sniffing at the fabric and filling his nostrils with her scent. The future was an uncertain place. There were so few of the First People left, and he was Red Lacewing Clan. If something happened to her husband? An accident, maybe?

Voices could be heard from upstairs. He froze, aware that a man was speaking in low tones. He couldn't quite make out Larkspur's cautious reply; then he heard her say, "Stay right there."

Her body darkened the hatch as she climbed swiftly down the ladder, shot him a warning glance, and grabbed up a small turquoise brooch from a cedar box. As quickly, she was back up the ladder, saying, "Well done. This is for special service. Come back when you have more."

Leather Hand heard sandals scuffing as the man left. Moments later, Larkspur leaned into the hatch, one eyebrow lifted. "One of my little songbirds just arrived. He tells me that a messenger has arrived from Ironwood. All of the clan elders will be atop the Dog's Tooth tonight. They are going to have some sort of meeting."

Leather Hand matched her smile with his own. "Tonight. On the Dog's Tooth?"

Larkspur nodded. "That nest of vipers has been a thorn in my bed for long enough."

"What of the Moon People?"

"Do this right, Deputy, and they won't dare try anything."

War Chief Wind Leaf found the Blessed Sun absently wandering Dusk House's plaza. He had just taken Deputy Ravengrass's report and had been on his way to find Webworm.

"Good day, Blessed Sun."

"What's good about it?" Webworm wondered.

"Excuse me?"

"Oh, nothing. I didn't sleep well last night. Hideous Dreams. Smoke, fire, people screaming." Webworm gestured with the basalt graver he held. "And voices, whispering, all night long. Can you believe, War Chief, I even got up and checked the Matron's quarters on one side, and Blue Racer's on the other to see if people were hiding there?"

"What of my guards? Did they hear anyone?"

"No, nothing. I asked." Webworm waved it off. "I could see by the man's expression that he had no idea what I was talking about."

Now it's voices?

Wind Leaf squinted up at the sky. A hot sun burned down on them, baking the packed earth. As they followed the wall of the great kiva, he took note of the few hucksters who had placed their wares in the shade of the single-story rooms on the south. Others would have retreated to the greater shade of the north wall behind Dusk Town.

He grimaced as Webworm worked on his hideous little carving. Each scratching sound seemed to resonate, grating clear down to Wind Leaf's bones. The malignant thing was clearly defined now; a coiled serpent inside a broken eggshell. Webworm was using his basalt graver to detail the triangular head.

In an effort to keep from staring at the loathsome fetish, Wind Leaf looked out across what vista he could see through the gaps on either side of the southern wall. The land baked in the heat, waves of it rising off the cornfields and the distant uplands. The southwest wind seemed to suck at his very souls. It carried a cloud of ash from the Rainbow Serpent that settled atop them; at times he could catch its foul breath: sulfurous and noxious.

He said, "I have everything in readiness, Blessed Sun. Supplies are packed. I have detailed a handful of scouts to precede us along the route. Five of my best warriors will accompany us dressed as slaves. If Matron Desert Willow goes with us, I will detail another eight warriors to act as her litter bearers."

As he talked, they rounded the great kiva. Webworm seemed not to hear, carving as he walked. Nevertheless he said, "Oh she will go. She won't want to miss Sister Moon's homecoming. I don't know if she wants to attend the opening ceremonies at equinox or pick a time during the next three moons to travel up there."

"Fire and ice!" The cry came from the bear cage several paces beyond the great kiva's southern entrance.

Webworm stopped suddenly. Did his face go pale?

Then the Blessed Sun shook himself, pacing up to the wooden cage. He peered into the shadowed interior. "Are you enjoying your stay, witch?"

Wind Leaf could see the old woman. She sat cross-legged, naked, her aged skin hanging in loose wrinkles. She should have been half-delirious from thirst by now, let alone famished. Instead her eyes gleamed with an otherworldly intent as she studied Webworm.

"You don't look like you've been sleeping, Webworm." Her voice carried more conviction than a prisoner's should.

Wind Leaf frowned. No, she couldn't have heard. They'd been on the other side of the great kiva.

"My sleep isn't your concern." Webworm snorted, shook his head, and continued with his carving. "Were I you, I'd be contemplating my journey to Spider Woman's fire."

She smiled, her gray hair hanging in ratty strands. "That's a curious thing for you, of all people, to say. I'm not the one carving a serpent born from a cock's egg."

Webworm held the carving up.

As quickly, the old woman had turned her head to the side, refusing to see it. "I know it very well. Didn't you hear the voices warning you? Just having it in the same room with the Spirits sends them into a frenzy. I'd be careful, Webworm."

"You'll be dead," he growled.

"Not just yet. You and I still have business between us."

Webworm looked mystified. "What business?"

"I have come to free you of evil, Webworm. I am the Witness."

Wind Leaf thought it was all rantings, but when he

looked at Webworm's face, he could see a deeper worry. "Free?" the Blessed Sun whispered under his breath. "What good would freedom do me?"

"If I kill you without freeing you from the serpent, your soul will never find Cloud Playing. She's waiting for you."

To Wind Leaf's amazement, Webworm nodded slightly, frowning. Blood and pus, he wasn't believing this, was he? "Blessed Sun? About traveling to First Moon Mountain?"

"Hurry," the old woman added. "The sooner you get to First Moon Mountain, the sooner the people can rise against you."

"What have you heard?" Wind Leaf demanded. "Speak, or I shall have your tongue stretched and pierced with cactus thorns."

She glanced at him as if seeing him for the first time. He couldn't help but gasp as her eyes met his.

"So, you've heard the rumors? Reported it to your Blessed Sun, have you?"

Wind Leaf flinched.

"Rumors?" Webworm asked.

Wind Leaf waved it away, uneasy at the old woman's manner. "It's nothing. Talk, is all. The story is that the Made People are ready to revolt. Supposedly even the clan leadership is conspiring against you. I haven't been able to prove any of it."

Webworm chuckled at that. "Nor will you. Rest assured, Creeper would tell me at the first hint of trouble."

"You are indeed your namesake," the witch said. "A worm caught in your own web. A treat for the robins, kingbirds, spiders, and wasps. I wonder, which will get you first?"

"You could be dead at a moment's notice, witch!" Wind Leaf pointed a hard finger. "Let me kill her, Blessed Sun. We don't need to put up with her spreading her poison."

"Not yet," Webworm said, frowning.

"Hurry," the old woman whispered. "Away with you. Go, Webworm. The sooner you reach First Moon Mountain, the sooner the world will be rid of you. Go, before the Rainbow Serpent snatches you for fouling his realm with your little carvings."

Webworm stepped back. "You couldn't know..."

"It was a Powerful Dream, wasn't it?" The old woman put her head back and laughed. "You call for me when the nightmares become too real. Then, and only then, will we Dance, you and I."

At that, Webworm turned, hurrying away. He almost kicked over a pile of firewood that a young barbarian had packed in to Trade.

"Blessed Sun?" Wind Leaf called as he hurried after.

"Stupid old hag," Webworm growled under his breath. "Thinks she can scare me, does she? I'll show her." To Wind Leaf he said, "Unpack. If she thinks she can drive me out of my own great house, she's sadly mistaken."

Wind Leaf slowed to a confused halt. Behind him in the cage, he heard the witch chuckling.

A southwest night wind had blown the smoke pall away. Powerful gusts moaning through the trees had awakened Bad Cast. He blinked after rolling in his blanket and looked up at the midnight sky. The stars were haze-grayed, Sister Moon nearly full. He could see a ring around her, as if some sort of storm were coming.

Bones and stones, it was a storm indeed. He made a face, sitting upright in his blankets. If this went wrong, the Red Shirts would take it out on his family. Somehow he had to get word to Soft Cloth and his kin.

Several paces away a single fire still burned, the flames whipped this way and that by the capricious winds. Ironwood sat like a bowed god, his scar-filled face illuminated by the flickering light.

Bad Cast unwrapped from his blanket, picked his way past sleeping men, and squatted opposite the war chief.

"You should be sleeping," Ironwood said softly. The wind pulled at his hair, slapping it around in a wild display. The patch over his eye made a black streak across his deeply lined features. The shadows cast by the fire lent him a terrible expression.

"So should you."

"A great many things are on my mind."

"Mine, too."

Ironwood's single eye gleamed in the light; his scars interrupted the lines on his face. "Oh?"

"My family. If the First People discover who is leading you up the mountain, they will hunt down my brothers, sisters, mother, and uncles. They will find Soft Cloth, and my daughter, and who knows how many others."

Ironwood reached out, dropping another broken

pine branch into the deeply dug fire pit. "That is a possibility."

Bad Cast waited, watching the war chief as he stared into the flickering fire. His broad shoulders sagged.

When he finally spoke, he didn't meet Bad Cast's eyes. "I will make a bargain with you."

"A bargain, War Chief?"

"Once you lead us up the back side of First Moon Mountain, you may go. Find your people and warn them. Tell them not to take part in what's coming, but to pack and leave. Personally, I'd take them east to the Great River. There's good land there."

"But what if you need me?"

"If we do not completely surprise them, Bad Cast, my warriors and I will have no need of anything." A faint shrug of his shoulders. "Your presence will not affect the outcome."

Bad Cast frowned. "Somehow, it doesn't feel right just leaving you, Yucca Sock, Firehorn, Right Hand, and the rest. I would always wonder if my being there might have made a difference."

"Ah, so you're a man with a conscience. It's a terrible thing to have." He rubbed his face with his large bony hands. "But in your case, I am going to play on this conscience of yours and ask you if you will do something for me."

"Of course, War Chief. It will be my honor."

"When I dismiss you before the attack, go and warn your people. Then, when the fighting plays out, I want you to return to my settlement and tell Night Sun and Orenda what has occurred. I need you to make sure they are safe."

"I don't understand. Why won't you send one of your warriors for them?"

He ignored the question. "Your people know this country; you have kin that you can count on to hide them, keep them safe. If the worst happens and we are all killed, the Blessed Sun may have warriors searching under every bush. You might have to move them around, travel by night until Webworm gives up. When things finally quiet down, please promise me you will take Night Sun down to Cornsilk and Poor Singer. Chief Jay Bird will know where they are."

"You can take care of her yourself."

Ironwood turned his head, looking where Ripple had lain his bed. Bad Cast followed his glance. He would have sworn Ripple's eyes were open, that he was listening. "When you bargain with the gods, they expect you to keep your word. From the things both Nightshade and Ripple have told me, I know that I must suffer something terrible. No, don't protest, Bad Cast. I've done unspeakable things during my life. Being granted the few summers I've had with my wife and daughter are more than I deserve."

"War Chief, you can't—"

He reached out, taking Bad Cast's hands in his strong grip. "Do I have your word that you will take care of my wife?"

Bad Cast swallowed hard, and nodded. "Yes, War Chief."

From where he lay in his bedding, Ripple made a soft whimper and turned onto his side.

Chapter Fourteen

Throughout the afternoon Leather Hand's men had filtered down off the mountain. In ones and twos they had made their way, packs over their shoulders. Some had dressed in hunting shirts, others in farmer's kilts. The patches of trees that surrounded the base of the Dog's Tooth became their lair. There, they secreted themselves, burrowing into brush, hunkering under duff-covered blankets among the rocks.

In the last fingers of light, they had emerged, opened their packs, and removed their bright red shirts. They strung their bows, counted the arrows in their quivers, and practiced swinging war clubs to loosen their muscles.

Leather Hand himself had taken the scout's position, secreting himself beside the trail. Motionless as a snake, he had covered himself with a gray blanket and watched as five slow processions of the elders made their way no more than two arm lengths from his hide.

He had heard their soft barbarian speech, listened to the tension in their voices.

Matron Larkspur's informant had been right.

He waited for a half hand of time, watching the stars slowly rise on the southern horizon. Then, the moon appearing, he rose and took up his weapons. The only sound he made was a hooting, the sort one of the cliff owls would have made. Another hoot answered. And then another.

Step by careful step, he began the climb up the Dog's Tooth. The first sentry was a mere boy, the lad so stupid he asked something in his incomprehensible tongue. Leather Hand's whistling war club thudded into his neck, snapping the spine.

He could see the walled enclosure, now little more than a dark blot against the moon-bright sky. There would be other sentries, some perhaps smarter than this one had been.

Whistle, still caked with trail grime, stood tall, a war club in his hand. The central fire in the Black Shale Moiety kiva cracked and popped, sending sparks toward the wide opening in the roof. Firelight reflected amber off of the support posts as well as the ring of watching faces. The elders sat on the kiva bench as was their due; the war chiefs, such as they were among his people, sat on the floor—ten young men of dubious valor and experience.

Old White Eye sat in the preeminent center of the bench, his snowy eye cast red from the fire. "How will we know when the war chief is in position?"

Whistle said, "We will have runners, people you delegate to us. As we prepare our assault, we need you to make a demonstration lower on the mountain. If each of our clans deploys their warriors and begins to ascend toward Guest House, Burning Smoke will mass his warriors there. Given the narrow approach to Pinnacle Great House, he'll want to concentrate his forces."

"You're sure?" Hoarse Caller of the Strong Back Clan asked through her rasping voice.

Whistle gave her a nod. "Burning Smoke is no fool. The clans will outnumber him. His strategy will be to narrow our front of attack. He knows his fighters are better than ours. His warriors are trained. Ours will be made up of hunters and farmers. Most of our people still use atlatls. Knowing this, Burning Smoke's warriors will be close to cover, far enough away that they can duck and dodge. His goal will be to hold us back, or induce us to charge. If the latter, he's counting on the effectiveness of his bowmen. In the time it takes for our fighters to close, his men can send a hail of arrows down. Then, our ranks weakened, morale lowered from the casualties, his warriors attack with war clubs. They need only to break our attack and send our fighters fleeing back down the hill."

Rattler, of the Blue Stick Clan, said, "And that's the one thing we cannot allow to happen."

"Correct," Whistle replied. He looked at the uncertain war chiefs. "It is imperative that we hold back. Do you understand? This will be a game of nerves. We must keep the threat up, but never allow ourselves close enough where they can rain arrows upon us."

One young man said, "We have to tease them."

Whistle nodded. "That's right. You may allow some

of your most fleet young men to dance in and out of the danger zone. Burning Smoke's warriors will be anticipating this, so don't expect them to draw many arrows." Whistle steepled his fingers. "You see, they, too, will be playing the game. They will try to tempt your young men farther and farther into the killing area."

Wizened old Black Sage asked, "How long does the war chief expect us to keep this up?"

"As long as it takes," Whistle replied. "Now, here is the final thing: On the day before the attack, each of the clans needs to send a small party of fighters around the base of the cliffs below Pinnacle Great House."

"Why?" Red Water asked. Firelight gleamed in the white streak in her hair. "They'll be able to see us from above."

Whistle clapped his hands. "Precisely." He turned to the war chiefs. "You are to order these scouts to retire immediately after being spotted. Do you understand?"

"No," Dead Bird muttered. "That's as crazy as a stone-struck grouse. They'll know we're coming."

Whistle said, "Of course. Pay attention. We want them to know that we know the rim is guarded. We want them to think that because of those guards, we have no other option but to try and force our way past Guest House and onto the ridgetop."

White Eye asked, "Does the war chief really think this will work?"

Whistle spread his hands wide. "Elder, in war no one can know."

"Precisely!" a voice called from the kiva entrance.

Whistle turned, seeing a familiar figure enter. It took him several heartbeats to realize this man spoke in First People's tongue. And then the red shirt, dark in the firelight, sent a stab of fear into his heart. As the man approached the stunned elders, his face caught the firelight.

"Leather Hand!" Whistle's heart skipped, his gut sinking. He raised his war club, dropping into a crouch. He had a fleeting glimpse of the elders, the war chiefs, all frozen as if thunderstruck, expressions of panic on their faces.

Even more warriors were pouring into the kiva, spreading out, bows drawn, arrows nocked and held for release.

Leather Hand's white moccasins flashed in the firelight. "No one need die here," he said in Made People's tongue. One of his warriors repeated the words in First Moon language. "You may leave this place, alive, and accompany my warriors up to the great house. There you will remain for the duration of the Moon Ceremony."

"What then?" Whistle's voice cracked with sudden understanding.

"Well..." Leather Hand shrugged. "We will see. Your futures will depend upon the obedience of your people." He grinned. "If the Moon Ceremony proceeds peacefully, you may be allowed to return to your clans. If it doesn't, who knows? Perhaps my warriors and I shall toss your bones down the slope after we roast your bodies." He made a face as he inspected wizened old Black Sage. "Much too tough. We might have to seek out some of your younger kin to fill our pots."

The grim red-shirted warriors chuckled at that.

"So?" Leather Hand asked. "What will it be? Live, or have your souls devoured by my human wolves?"

Whistle leaped, bringing his war club up.

He wouldn't have believed it. Leather Hand blocked his blow, pivoted, and before he could recover, hammered a blow into Whistle's rib cage.

The pain was agonizing. A second blow smashed his hip, tumbling him to the dirt. Then Leather Hand dropped, his knee spearing the center of Whistle's broken chest.

"Now," Leather Hand said softly, "let's you and I talk about Ironwood."

He bounced his weight on Whistle's sternum. The resulting scream might have split the sky.

From the screen of the trees, Ripple stared out at First Moon Valley. The twin pillars of rock dominated the great mountain. From this angle, Pinnacle Great House remained hidden behind the mountain's shoulder. He could feel the place, like a darkness on his souls. The First People waited there—waited for him.

"Smoke," Bad Cast said as he walked out of the trees.

"What's on fire?" Ironwood asked as he led the rest of the warriors to the tree line.

"The Dog's Tooth," Ripple replied, seeing it in the Dream. "The kivas are gone; bodies lie broken and mutilated on the slope."

"What?" Bad Cast cried, stepping beside him, a hand on Ripple's arm. "You saw this?"

Ripple nodded sadly. "It is as it must be."

"Must be?" Bad Cast cried, grabbing his other arm, shaking him violently. "Why didn't you warn us?"

Ironwood's hard hand clamped on Bad Cast's

shoulder, tightening, fingers digging into the nerves. "Let him go."

Bad Cast's hands fell away, but he kept his frantic eyes on Ripple's.

"I'm sorry," Ripple whispered. "Bad Cast, do you think this is easy? It's not! It's tearing me apart, wounding my souls, but it's got to be this way!"

"In the name of the gods, why?"

Ripple took a breath, slapping his hands to his sides. "In the name of the gods. That's exactly why. It's a battle, Bad Cast. You're a hunter; you know that it's one thing to bait a trap, but the game has to be reassured before it will walk into the kill pen. There are things going on that you don't know...can't know\"

Bad Cast's expression pinched in the old familiar way. He nodded, shooting Ripple a submissive glance. "All right. I think I understand."

Ironwood glanced back and forth; the warriors were muttering among themselves.

"What's next, Dreamer?" Ironwood asked.

"Would you let the trap spring before you act?"

Ripple watched the conflict behind the man's eye, could see his souls struggling, writhing with indecision. In the end, desperation won out. "Yes, Dreamer, I would."

Ripple swallowed hard, hearing the man condemn himself to the path of the gods. "Then you must follow my orders." He paused, aware that every warrior was listening. "Will your men follow you?"

Ripple was aware of cautious nods as the war chief said, "I'm sure they will," with more authority than he felt. The old warrior's single eye was rife with indecision.

"All is not lost," Ripple said quietly. "As it was planned, you'd never have won. Now our victory is assured."

"How?" Bad Cast demanded. "If the Dog's Tooth is burning, Matron Larkspur found out about Whistle and White Eye! For all we know, they're up there waiting for us!"

Ripple nodded, seeing the confusion in his friend's eyes. "Oh, yes. The Flute Player has moved his pieces. He thinks he has won the game. Now we must wait. Be patient."

"For what?" Ironwood demanded, his resolution beginning to fray.

"For Cold Bringing Woman and the katsinas to move theirs." He stepped close to the old warrior, staring into his eye. "Will you trust me, War Chief? Trust Cold Bringing Woman's vision? I promise, allies are coming from unusual directions."

He could feel the tension, see the struggle as if it were smoke that rose from each man in the party.

"Yes," Ironwood said angrily. "Tell me what you will have of me."

"A place to wait." Ripple turned to the surrounding warriors. "And a patience worthy of your greatness."

"What are you doing?" Bad Cast demanded.

"Fulfilling a promise to a god," Ripple said hollowly.

In the evening light, Bad Cast sat with Soft Cloth. He hadn't known how precious it would be just to see her again. To hold her. They perched on the sandstone rim and looked out over the River of Stones. Juniper Ridge cast a deep blue shadow over the fertile fields in the floodplain below. Across from them, First Moon Mountain rose, the twin pillars touched with the last strokes of orange. Even as they watched, shadow slipped up the rock, as if their world were drowning in darkness.

In the north, the sky was black, yellow, and red, billows of smoke rising as the northern mountains continued to burn.

Bad Cast tightened his grip on his wife's hand. "There they go."

On the other side of the valley, in the dip below the blackened ruins of the Dog's Tooth, the first white specks of Blue Racer's Priests emerged onto the trail that would take them the rest of the way up to Pinnacle Great House. Like a slow snake, the column of men emerged, winding its way upward.

"It can't be that bad," Soft Cloth said.

"How bad can it be?" Bad Cast was past reassurances. "I'll tell you." He pointed at Pinnacle Great House where it squatted on the peak. "Leather Hand will kill and eat Elder Rattler, White Eye, and the rest of the clan leaders. The war chiefs will be gutted and tossed over the cliff. We are back where we were when the First People came here. They'll take many of the lineage elders off as slaves; the rest of us, well, we have to be punished. Expect our harvest to be confiscated. All of it. Every last kernel."

She shook her head. "They wouldn't do that. If we starve to death, who will they find to farm this land next year?"

"Dust People," he said quickly. "Yellow Soil People, people from the Green Mesas, refugees from the lowlands. The Blessed Sun can offer it to anyone he wishes."

Soft Cloth frowned, a rebuttal rising.

"No," Bad Cast said firmly. "You haven't seen the things I have. You don't understand." He tightened his grip on her hand. "Look at me, wife, and listen very carefully. I want you to think about leaving this place."

"What?"

"You, me, our baby, and any of our relatives that we can talk into it."

"That's crazy! We have property here, fields." She pointed to Mid-Sun House, the two-story building where even now Ironwood and Ripple sat with her lineage elders. "This is where my family is. Our house is right over there."

He nodded. "Soft Cloth, our world is coming to an end. Ripple and the Mountain Witch have seen it." He gestured at the winding column of worshippers climbing First Moon Mountain. "Equinox isn't that far away. A matter of days." He pointed to the distant watchtower that perched on the high rim of First Moon Mountain. "How far north is the sun?"

"Less than a finger. But that's the point. Harvest will begin soon. You don't expect me to just walk away from my responsibilities, do you?"

Bad Cast sighed. "I was afraid of this."

"Afraid of what?" She shook her head. "What's wrong with you? You're not the same man who left here."

He chuckled bitterly, looking down the slope. "Remember when you caught us gambling down there under that tree?"

She nodded.

"Gods, Soft Cloth, what I'd give to be that man again. What I'd give if only I could go back and keep Ripple from going after that elk."

"You really believe this, don't you?"

He met her eyes. "I want a chance to love you. I want to watch our children grow up and marry and have children of their own. Do you understand? I want to love you. Not just now, but forever."

"Bad Cast?"

"I have things to do, responsibilities I must see to. But if I ask you to leave with me, I need you to say yes."

He could see the deep confusion in her eyes. Perhaps it mirrored his own. Pus and blood, what was he going to do if she said no?

Spots gazed in awe at the northern sky as he walked up from the river. A deer bladder full of drinking water hung in one hand; a thin net bag from his other. Seven baked corn cakes were within.

"Some fire," Cactus Flower greeted him as he approached the southeastern gate. She stood up from her blanket and stretched.

"It is. Must be spectacular from home."

She considered him. "You miss it?"

"Well, sure. My sister must be half-crazy without me to do my chores in the fields. This is the critical time. The corn is headed out, starting to mature. This is when the raccoons, worms, deer, and human thieves get ready to raid our fields. As dry as it's been, she's been working sunup to sundown carrying water."

"But you'd rather run back and forth like a Trader,

packing firewood so you can Trade for her?" She inclined her head toward the gate.

Spots chewed his lip, aware of Cactus Flower's wary arch of brow. "It's just something I have to do."

"Oh, yes, sneak food to a condemned witch. You know, if they catch you..."

"That's why it's got to be done right at dusk."

She frowned at him. "Well, if you're convinced you need to have some warrior stand on your neck and smack your brains out, go ahead. If you escape getting caught again tonight, I don't have anyone staying over."

He cocked his head. "As you well know, I'm out of firewood."

"You've got a string of shell beads. White Lizard gave them to you."

"I'd better get this inside." He lifted the bag, glancing up at the roof where the bored guard watched the southeastern gate.

"Oh, just come by," she said huffily.

"Trade or no?"

She shrugged coyly. "Sleeping with you is fun. I'm starting to like it."

He thought about that as he walked through the gate, nodded at the guard, and called, "I'm just going back for my blanket."

He received a wave in return.

Evening light had softened the interior of Dusk House. It had masked the hard lines of the great kiva, gloom filling the doorways. Here and there people went about their evening activities. Most would be leaving soon, headed back to their farmsteads. For all of its massive size, few people actually lived here—only the

Blessed Sun, the Made People clan elders, Priests, warriors, and the slaves who served them.

He found his blanket where he'd left it, to one side of a doorway leading into one of the southern rooms. He glanced surreptitiously around as he folded his blanket. No one seemed to be watching.

He stretched, flopped his blanket over his shoulder, and walked toward the great kiva. He could hear singing from within. The entrance had a soft yellow glow, and several people crowded at the doorway, watching the events inside.

He felt his heart lurch as he angled past the bear cage. Every time he did this, it scared the liver out of him. He always expected shouts of alarm and red-shirted warriors charging to capture him. The interior was dark in shadow, Nightshade a mere representation of her name.

"Food and water," he said softly, reaching through the bars as he passed slowly by. To an onlooker, it would just seem that he'd barely brushed the cage.

Nightshade said, "Bring me a hafted chert knife the night before equinox."

"Yes, Elder." He passed on, a feeling of relief filling him. The night before equinox? Good. That would be what, four days? Maybe three?

He paused, peering over the shoulders of the onlookers. Down the long rectangular stairway he could see masked Dancers, their bodies festooned with green cornstalks. They swayed and bent to the Song, each step of the sacred Dance made to assure the fruitfulness of the coming harvest.

If the Full Corn Dance was tonight, equinox was four days away.

He turned then, waving at the guard as he passed out through the gate. From the wall shadow, Cactus Flower appeared and took his arm. She had a canteen hung over her shoulder, and it bounced on her round hips.

"So," she teased, "you live another night."

"It would seem."

"Good." She tightened her grip on his arm. "I don't know what it is about you. You're certainly not handsome with those scars all over. You're not smart, or you wouldn't be feeding the witch. You're not even a very good Trader."

"Thank you," he muttered dryly.

She shoved him playfully sideways. "Have you had your witch put some sort of spell on me?"

"No! Why are you asking all these questions?"

"Because my sheath has been itching for you all day long, and I can't figure out why."

Chapter Fifteen

Orenda bent to pick another mint plant and glanced up at the sky where the drifting haze of blue smoke spread from the north across the entire eastern horizon. Through it, Father Sun's face was a huge ruddy smear of red-brown light.

Ripple had been so intent when he'd asked her to come pick mint. Why? Had it been some curing he wanted her to do? The desperation in his eyes hadn't allowed her any response but to agree.

Ever since he'd asked, she'd been puzzling over it. His simple gaze affected her in a way that left her forever uncomfortable.

One by one she stripped leaves from the stem and dropped them into her coarsely woven collecting bag. Discarding the stem, she was about to reach for another when a flash of red caught her eye. She eased down to one knee.

They were some distance away, just emerging from the trees on the other side of the valley. Even from this distance she could see it was a party of warriors. And, no, this was not the war chief returning. These war shirts were too bright, and two of the men wore white moccasins. They came on at a trot, heading for the river just below her.

She sank slowly to her belly before she began wiggling her way like a salamander for the stand of willows that stood just below the hot springs.

Once she had slithered into the concealing stems, she waited and watched. Hopefully they wouldn't see the trail where she'd crushed the grass, mint, and daisies.

Her view was obscured as they stopped, drank, and then trotted into sight traveling in single file. She watched them work their way, panting, up and into the trees.

By the Long Nosed God, they couldn't know where the village was, could they? Fear began to pound brightly.

What could she do? They were between her and the settlement. Were she to run with all her might, she could never circle around them in time to warn Night Sun.

The tall ponderosa cast slanting shadows as Leather Hand led his warriors across the mesa top. Dry pine needles crackled under his tough yucca trail sandals. He carried his bow at the low ready, an arrow nocked in preparation to be drawn and released.

To either side he could see his White Moccasins. Like the human wolves they were, they slipped from tree to tree, only the faint crackle of the pine needles audible.

Faint trails crisscrossed the mesa top, and here, for the first time, he found a tree where someone had just recently broken the dead branches from the lower trunk. A slow smile crossed his lips.

The young man was oblivious as he came walking down the trail. In his midteens, he appeared on the verge of manhood. Smooth brown skin covered a triangular face, his large brown eyes fixed on the ground before him. A load of firewood had been slung over his shoulder, and the perplexed frown on his forehead betrayed his preoccupation.

Leather Hand raised his right hand in the "ready" signal, and his men shifted silently behind the nearest cover.

Leather Hand stepped behind the thick trunk of a ponderosa, his heart quickening with the fever of war. He could hear the youth's footsteps before he made out the muttering under the young man's breath.

"Pick up firewood. Take out the ashes. Clean up after your brother." A pause. "I hope lightning strikes them all dead."

Leather Hand kept the tree between him and the youth, then stepped out, no more than half a body length from the youth. "Stop right there! And if you scream, this arrow goes right through your heart."

The youth halted, wide-eyed, mouth dropping open. He blinked as Leather Hand's warriors surrounded him.

"Who are you?" Leather Hand demanded.

"Ra-Ravenfire," the youth sputtered, his head

turning this way and that as he took in the hard-eyed warriors around him.

"Cornsilk's get," Turquoise Fox growled from behind the lad.

"Cornsilk's get," Leather Hand repeated.

"What—What are you going to do with me?" Ravenfire's fear sent beads of nervous sweat to shimmer on his skin.

"Why, kill you," Leather Hand said easily. "Just like we did the Dust People."

"You?" Ravenfire's throat worked. "You're Leather Hand?"

"The very same. In less than a hand of time, we'll be carving those tender muscles from your bones. Then we will deliver your head to your mother."

"She's—she's not here!"

"Where is she?"

"Gone south with Poor Singer to Jay Bird's village."

"But Ironwood is here?"

Ravenfire shook his head vigorously. "Gone to First Moon Valley."

"With how many warriors?"

"I—I'm not telling."

"Hold him." Leather Hand glanced at Turquoise Fox. He laid his bow to one side as he pulled a long obsidian blade from his belt pouch. Several of his warriors had grasped the youth, holding him while he kicked, and one clapped a hard hand over his mouth to keep him from screaming.

Leather Hand stepped close, using the keen blade to sever the belt at the young man's waist. "See how easily the rope parts?" He traced the glittering blade along the base of Ravenfire's throat. "Your neck will cut just as easily. Now, how many warriors did Ironwood take to First Moon Valley?"

"Th-Thirty." It was hard to hear, mumbled against the gagging hand.

"Not enough to threaten Burning Smoke," Turquoise Fox said with relief. "When Ironwood hears that the First Moon elders have been taken, he'll retreat like a whipped puppy."

Leather Hand nodded. To Ravenfire, he said, "You would like to live, wouldn't you?"

Ravenfire swallowed hard, jerking his head in affirmation.

"Then you will tell us where Ironwood's village is?"

The terrified Ravenfire nodded again.

"You won't scream?"

He shook his head.

"Good." Leather Hand fingered his chin. "When you approached, I heard you. So you're tired of running errands and doing chores like a common slave?"

He might have been young, but Ravenfire was quick of mind. Leather Hand saw the calculating behind his eyes. Good, he could still think, even when frightened half out of his skin.

"Help us, prove your worth to us," Leather Hand encouraged, "and your rewards could be greater than anything you have ever hoped."

Ravenfire's cunning eyes narrowed. "How great?"

"I want Ironwood. I'll Trade your life for his."

Ravenfire took a deep breath. "All right. Night Sun is over behind those trees. Once you have her, you can lure Ironwood anywhere you want him to go." He glanced around. "But if I were you, I'd grab her, and run for someplace where you can control all the approaches. The longer you stay here, the more vulnerable you are."

"Is it that easy for you?"

Ravenfire actually smiled. "They've never recognized my talents. I can do a great many things for you. After all, I'm Red Lacewing Clan—and I deserve a better life than scuttling around like a wood rat in the forest."

For years Night Sun had lived the nightmare. In it, she imagined red-shirted warriors popping out of the trees, charging, their war clubs lifted. She had imagined the expressions of surprise and terror as people looked up from their chores, turned, and bolted in all directions.

That fateful moment when it finally happened, she stood, stunned, staring in disbelief as the warriors appeared out of the trees. Unlike her nightmares, however, they made no sound. The only thing she heard was the patting impact of their sandals on the hard dry ground.

It took her a moment to find her wits. In that instant, as she watched, Cedar Loom was struck down from behind. Then Night Sun turned, willing her old legs to run. She had made no more than six steps before she heard Ravenfire scream, "Grandmother! Help!"

She slid to a stop, turning, hesitating as she saw him running toward her. "Come on!" she cried. "This way!"

To her great surprise, he ran up to her, and hugged her with his strong arms.

"Let me go! We've got to run."

"Sorry," he told her with a smug smile. "But I've made a better deal."

She struggled, confused, unable to understand. She was still beating at his confining arms as he plucked her off her feet, carrying her back toward the grinning warriors.

"I wish you would just run ahead," Crow Woman complained as Wrapped Wrist led the way down the trail. "You needn't fuss over me like a hen turkey over her chicks."

Wrapped Wrist perched precariously on the slope to hold a low-hanging ponderosa branch to one side. Crow Woman hobbled past, leaning on the makeshift crutch he'd made.

"Good thing they didn't whack both knees," he said as the branch whipped back in place.

"Too bad Narrow-frame didn't cut straight down the center," she muttered. "If you had a split nose and four lips maybe you wouldn't talk so much."

Wrapped Wrist trotted around and ahead of her. They followed a game trail that wound down the side of the slope. Through gaps in the conifers, he could see the broad River of Souls Valley. It wouldn't be long now before they broke out of the timber. The footing would be better, less chance that Crow Woman would turn her swollen knee.

She cried out as she stepped over a log and jammed her leg. "Bloody pus! Why does that have to hurt so?"

"Knees are funny that way." He stepped around, taking her hand, helping her over the obstacle. Was it his imagination, or did she hold onto him for a moment longer than necessary?

He shot her a wary glance. Had to be his imagination. This was Crow Woman, after all. Even subdued by her run-in with the Red Shirts, he didn't trust her to remain that way. What would it take? A sideways glance? A wrongly inflected word? And then she'd be her old prickly self again.

"What?" She'd realized he was thinking about her.

"Nothing."

"Must be something."

He kicked the remains of a rotten log out of the way and held another branch. A red squirrel chattered above them, which set off the stellar jays. She was shooting him pensive looks. "Gods, am I really that bad?"

"Kind of like one of those macaws the Traders bring up from the distant south. Really pretty, but I like you with your claws tied and a string around your beak."

He caught the slightest bit of smile at the corner of her lips. "Good."

She continued hobbling down the trail. The slope was gentler here, and she made better time, slowing only to clamber over a deadfall.

"It's just that we've lost so much time. First they made us backtrack and took us off the main trail. Then this knee." She shook her head. "My fault. All my fault."

"Stop it." He wanted to scratch his face where the makeshift stitches itched and burned.

"If I hadn't been so bullheaded. Gods, I can be such a buffalo sometimes."

"You do all right."

She bit her lip and said nothing more.

Wrapped Wrist kicked a stone out of the trail and craned his neck. Yellow sunlight could be seen between the branches. Good, another couple of paces and they'd be out of the trees and into...

Wrapped Wrist raised his hand, stopping short. Yes, those were voices. He dropped to a crouch, trying to peer under the branches.

The timber below them gave way to scattered rabbitbrush, patches of sumac, and tall grass. In the bottom, the River of Souls coursed between willow-bounded banks. Several stands of cottonwoods clustered along the river.

He scuttled forward, taking a position behind one of the last pines. Leaning out from the trunk he could see them: red-shirted warriors. They seemed too well dressed. A line of them, perhaps thirty, were leading a small group of women and children. And there, on a pole litter, he could see a woman being borne along on six of the warriors' shoulders. Worse, they were headed right down the valley. Given their route of travel, they would pass no more than fifty paces in front of him.

Wrapped Wrist eased back up the slope, motioning Crow Woman to get down. He took position behind yet another of the trees.

"Who are they?" Crow Woman whispered.

"Warriors."

"Ours?"

"I don't think so. They've got women and children."

Crow Woman made a face as she crawled down beside him to peer through the screening branches of the pine. "I can't see much."

"Shhh! They're coming this way."

He felt his heart begin to pound and anxiously reached around for the war club he'd taken from one of the dead warriors. It had a good feel to it. He considered his options. He'd left his darts in the bodies of the dead. The one that had missed Narrow-frame had shattered on a stone. Now he cursed himself as a fool, but at the time the thought of pulling them out of human flesh had been too much for him.

If I live through this, I promise, I'll never be squeamish again.

With the appearance of the lead warrior all other thoughts were stillborn. He was a tall man resplendent in a bright red war shirt; gleaming necklaces hung at his throat. Three jaunty eagle feathers had been thrust into his hair bun, and striking white moccasins clad his feet. They rustled in the tall grass.

Crow Woman gasped before she clamped a hand to her mouth.

For a second Wrapped Wrist thought the warrior had heard, for his head snapped to the side, his fierce eyes searching the forest. But his step never faltered, and he continued on his way.

Behind him came two ranks of warriors, bows unstrung, quivers packed with perfectly fletched cane arrows. Some carried the long curved wooden war clubs the Blessed Sun's warriors favored. They talked in low voices, some laughing. The light of triumph seemed to Dance over them as they smiled and nodded amid animated talk.

The litter jounced into view, and Wrapped Wrist gaped. The expression of disgust on Matron Night

Sun's face might have been chiseled in stone. She wore a dark blue robe, strings of beads at her throat. Bejeweled and decked out, she might have been heading for some great house ceremony. She rode with her back stiff, head forward, imperious of posture; but even from this distance, Wrapped Wrist could see fear glitter in her eyes. The leather binding on her wrists betrayed her true status.

Several of the camp children followed; they were being herded by Ravenfire, Cornsilk's firstborn. He carried one of the thin wooden war clubs, and walked with a jaunty attitude. Nor were his hands bound.

"Ravenfire?" Crow Woman hissed under her breath. "Gods!"

Wrapped Wrist recognized several of Ironwood's warriors' wives. All were naked from the waist up, wrists bound, lengths of thong tied between their ankles to keep them from running. The bruises on their faces, legs, arms, and breasts had that new cherry color. Each one had a bloody pack slung over her shoulder. To Wrapped Wrist's practiced eye, it looked like they carried freshly butchered meat. One woman held her arm as if it was broken. Several were crying, while others looked tear-streaked, eyes dull.

A squad of warriors brought up the rear; mindful of their charges, they lashed out at any who tarried.

After they passed, Wrapped Wrist remained as if planted. Gods, what had happened? Who were these terrible warriors? He glanced over, seeing Crow Woman's expression. She looked on the point of tears.

"What in the name of the gods has happened?" Wrapped Wrist asked in a whisper, still unsure whether to trust his voice lest the terrible warriors hear despite the distance.

Crow Woman exhaled wearily. "How?"

Wrapped Wrist waited, his heart beating anxiously.

"That warrior in front," Crow Woman finally said. "That's Leather Hand. Somehow, some way, they've captured Night Sun."

"What about the war chief? Orenda and Ripple?"

"I don't know." She swallowed hard. "We've got to go after Night Sun and Ravenfire."

Wrapped Wrist reached out, clamping her arm as she started up. "No. Think, Crow Woman. They have thirty warriors. There's just the two of us, and you're half-crippled. Before we do anything, we have to find out what's happened. See if any of the others survived." He hesitated. "And I'm not sure, but Ravenfire looked like he was one of them."

She shot a hot glare his direction, started to struggle, and bent her leg. She bit off the groan of pain and relented. "Yes, you're right."

Leather Hand! Wrapped Wrist took a deep breath. He'd looked right into the eyes of the cannibal! "I pray that the gods guard Matron Night Sun."

The climb up the slope to Ironwood's mesa seemed interminable. Wrapped Wrist chafed, loose soil and pine duff slipping under his feet. Crow Woman, her face a mask of dismay, levered herself up, step after painful step. The way was marked by disturbed ground, churned needles, and tumbled stones.

Wrapped Wrist noted a spot of color: a little boy, his body wedged around a tree trunk. He'd been smacked in the top of the head with a war club, blood having spattered the dirt as he rolled limply down the slope.

Crow Woman shook her head, taking a moment to catch her breath as she leaned on her crutch. "People called him Kit. He wanted to be a warrior like his father, Yucca Sock. He must have angered them."

At the cleft in the caprock, Wrapped Wrist reached back and bodily lifted Crow Woman onto the top.

They found Orenda at the village. She sat in the center of the plaza, a little dead girl in her lap. Her absent gaze was fixed on the smoke plume that hung over the mountains to the north. Her hand moved like a delicate bird as she fingered the girl's limp hair. Tears streaked her dusty face, the corners of her mouth trembling.

"How did they find us?" Crow Woman demanded as she hobbled forward.

Orenda shook her head, mystified. "They came straight here, as if they knew. They didn't even search."

Crow Woman sighed and seated herself on a stump, her stiff leg out before her. "We saw Ravenfire. He was armed and seemed to be guarding the prisoners."

Orenda nodded, looking stunned. "I saw him. They were treating him like he was one of them! Clapping him on the back. Thanking him for capturing Night Sun! He was strutting and bragging. Night Sun herself spat on him."

"I always thought he was a worm," Crow Woman said in disgust.

For Wrapped Wrist, the sight in the plaza was ghastly. Several women could be seen, partially naked, limbs askew, hair loose and tangled with dirt and detritus. He stepped over, curious to see that some had long sections of leg muscle cut from the bone. One woman's entire leg was missing, neatly cut off at the hip.

Then he got a close look at the children. He'd last seen them alive— bouncing, smiling, and squabbling as children do. Could these broken bodies be those same expectant little people? Flies were already swarming to the wounds.

"Where is the war chief? Where are our warriors?" Crow Woman asked. "I see no men here."

"Gone. They left three days ago for First Moon Mountain."

"So they could have been captured, too?" Wrapped Wrist asked.

Orenda shrugged.

"We've got to find out." Crow Woman hitched herself back to her feet. "Get anything you need."

Orenda blinked. "What about...?"

"Their souls have already fled," Crow Woman said gently. "This is just flesh. When it's all over, when we know what's happened, we can come back for the bones. The living may need us more."

Just flesh. Wrapped Wrist glanced again at the stripped bones. How could such an evil have entered the world? Worse, what could they do about it?

In the sky above, the smoke plume had shifted, curling around in the sky and pointing off to the southeast.

Leather Hand pushed his warriors and captives until full darkness obscured the trail. They would camp for several hands of time, and then when Sister Moon rose in the northeastern sky, he would order them on. Or so he hoped. When he looked up at the east, smoke had blotted the stars. Would Sister Moon be able to pierce the darkness with her glow?

At his feet the River of Souls flowed, water lapping under the bank. The current was calm here, though he could hear the faint roar of rapids in the distance downstream. Overhead, cottonwood leaves rattled with the breeze blowing down the canyon.

He walked back under the trees to the place where Turquoise Fox had kindled a fire. In the leaping yellow light, he could see his captives. Night Sun sat cross-legged, her bound wrists before her. Back straight, face forward, no expression crossed her stern features.

The other captives, bound together in a line, were overseen by four of his warriors. They, in contrast, looked broken, heads down, shoulders slumped.

Turquoise Fox stepped close, voice lowered. "What do you think? Could Ironwood be close?"

Leather Hand avoided night-blinding himself on the flames as he looked out at the darkness beyond the cottonwoods. "I have no idea. If we are to believe the things Whistle told us, he's camped somewhere outside of First Moon Valley, waiting for the elders to send him word."

Turquoise Fox grinned. "Then he'll wait a long time."

"Without his allies, he won't dare to attack. What can his little band of warriors do against Pinnacle

House? No, he's nothing without the Moon People clans. Even Whistle agreed with that."

"Whistle." Turquoise Fox shook his head. "I thought he'd have been tougher than that." Turquoise Fox glanced at Night Sun, sitting like a wooden statue.

"We didn't get everyone," Leather Hand reminded. "Someone will have escaped. Perhaps a boy out hunting rabbits, some woman picking berries. Ironwood will know soon enough."

"And when he does?" Turquoise Fox asked.

"He will abandon First Moon Valley and come looking for his wife and young Ravenfire." He looked toward where the youth was talking with the warrior called Fast Fist.

"Do you trust him?" Turquoise Fox asked, lowering his voice. "He betrayed his people. What would it take for him to betray us?"

Leather Hand rubbed his fingers together, as if sampling the air. "I don't know. He did grab Night Sun for us like he said he would. And he captured her alive. He ate his share of meat tonight."

"He told Fast Fist he's never had a woman before."

Leather Hand chuckled. "Well, he'll have plenty tonight. And he says he knows how to lure Ironwood into our grasp. As long as he continues to be a benefit, he lives. The second he seems to waver, don't even think about it. Just kill him."

"And Ironwood?"

"I expect him to try and sneak into Flowing Waters Town. I'll send you with a warning for the Blessed Sun when we get closer. With any luck War Chief Wind Leaf will round him up before he has a chance to make trouble. It's not like he's hard to miss. How many towering gray-haired men are missing their left eye and covered with scars?"

"Night Sun," Turquoise Fox said softly. "By the gods, I never would have thought we'd take her alive."

Leather Hand smiled his satisfaction. They might not have, but for Ravenfire's deception of Night Sun. The raid had been perfect. In less than a finger's time, those not captive were dead. Some of the women who had fled were run down and dragged back. On his orders they were beaten and raped before they were killed. His men had cut steaks from the bodies.

When Ironwood returned, saw what Leather Hand's men had done, he would be coming. Yes, old enemy, feel your blood boil. Know that Leather Hand and his human monsters have your wife and grandson. Lose your senses to rage and desperation. I shall be waiting.

He walked over, squatting to look into Night Sun's eyes. She stared back with an unexpected serenity.

"Well, Matron, it appears that you have been brought low."

In a firm voice she replied, "This is not the first time I've been taken captive. The only difference is that last time, my captor was a great man, not a piece of walking two-legged filth."

"He's your grandson. It must run in the blood."

"I was referring to you."

With a lightning strike, he slapped her. The force of it stung his hand and nearly knocked her over.

"Do not use that tone with me, Outcast."

She righted herself, working her jaw. He could see the red rising on her cheek. Her necklaces, the ones he'd placed on her as a symbol of her rank, were askew.

"Unlike you," she said angrily, "I was declared Outcast. You have placed yourself beyond the society of honorable humans by your own outrageous actions."

"Do not mock me. I hold your life in my hands."

She snorted derision. "You hold nothing. Our world is coming to an end, and you are but a symptom of the last days. Look at you, one of the First People, a monster who chooses to eat human flesh. Leather Hand, when I see you, I see the rot that the First People have become."

Glaring into her eyes, he said, "I can make your death particularly ghastly."

"Just take me before Webworm. In the end, we shall see who makes whose end ghastly."

He could see no fear behind her hard black eyes, only revulsion to his proximity. He leaned closer, whispering, "My dear Matron, I'm not taking you to Webworm. Far from it."

"Stop playing silly games. Your Blessed Sun is far too vain to miss an opportunity to preen and brag in front of me."

Leather Hand rubbed his hard palms together. "Sorry, Matron, but you could become a symbol within the walls of Dusk House. Some of the Made People might foolishly rally to your cause. Even members of your Red Lacewing Clan might attempt something stupid. No, we have a safer place to hold you. You are going home."

At her slight confusion, he added, "I'm taking you back to Talon Town. It's deserted. A huge hulking warren of empty rooms. And when I get you there, you will scream, Matron. And then you will scream some more."

Only then did he see the quickening of her fear.

"That's right. And unlike at Flowing Waters Town, where Ironwood might find allies, I will lay my trap for him in Straight Path Canyon. In that abandoned valley, we'll have ample warning before his arrival."

Satisfied, he nodded as he straightened. She'd betrayed herself under his gaze. It was as if he'd seen into her very souls. Down deep inside, she was seeing Ironwood's death.

Chapter Sixteen

The hubbub broke midmorning. Spots was standing in the shade of the south wall. His firewood pile had been halved by the morning Trade, during which he'd obtained a sturdy gray quartzite knife hafted on a chokecherry handle. Cactus Flower's trinkets lay on the blanket next to his. He caught various glimpses of her as she led a Hohokam Trader around, pointing out various sites, taking him through the great kiva. Spots leaned back against the cool wall, shoulders and one foot braced against the plaster.

"I can't imagine what it's like down south." He was talking weather with a Trader from the Deep Canyon country. "The trails I take leading up to the forest are ankle deep in dust."

The Deep Canyon man, with a display of finely crafted black-on-white drinking mugs on a red-and-brown blanket before him, shook his head. "In all my days I've never seen a fire like that up in the Spirit

Mountains. The night sky glows orange. Thank the gods we're upwind."

Spots crossed his arms, watching a squad of red-shirted warriors pass, nodding politely to them. How funny, he'd become a fixture. They had come to consider him part of the landscape. "Smoke in the north, smoke in the south. Between the fires and the Rainbow Serpent, it's enough to make you wonder."

"I tell you, it's the Priests' doing. They've angered the katsinas to the point..." He didn't finish, staring instead to where one of the guards atop the fourth floor began shouting, pointing off to the northeast.

"I wonder what that's all about?" Spots saw Webworm, Wind Leaf, and Desert Willow emerge from their high rooms, climb the ladder, and stare off to the northeast.

"If you'll keep an eye on my Trade," the Deep Canyon man said, "I'll step out the gate and see what I can."

"Yes, go." Spots waved him away. More people were climbing out onto the roofs, staring off into the distance.

He frowned. Yesterday news had come that Blue Racer and his party had arrived safely at First Moon Mountain. So, too, had rumors circulated that all of the First Moon elders had been taken captive by Leather Hand.

Spots wasn't sure he believed it. But, if true, some Trader would no doubt arrive today with confirmation. That begged the question of how it had happened. He remembered the night he'd been escorted to the Dog's Tooth and seen the gathered elders. How, in the name of the Blue God, would Leather Hand have learned of their meeting?

Cactus Flower emerged from the great kiva, bowed to the Hohokam, and received a beautiful cotton shawl from him in payment for her tour. She almost skipped as she passed the bear cage and stepped into the noontime shadow beside him.

"Look! Isn't it magnificent?" She had the fabric laid out over her arms. It was indeed striking, the red, blue, yellow, and green colors lifelike, so good were the dyes.

"Something's happening." He pointed where Webworm had begun leaping from foot to foot on the high roof. Wind Leaf was nodding vigorously, slapping his thigh. Even Desert Willow threw her head back. The laughter carried faintly.

"In the northeast?" Cactus Flower wondered. "More news from First Moon Mountain?"

Spots shrugged. "Anything that might be good news for the First People is probably bad news for me."

The Deep Canyon man came trotting back through the gate, his expression neutral. He nodded to Cactus Flower, having already avoided losing any of his ceramic mugs to her wiles. "It's a signal fire, a black smoke. One of those warriors who passed earlier, he said it was a message. War Chief Wind Leaf called down that it was the prearranged sign for Night Sun. Evidently she's been taken prisoner."

"Night Sun?" Spots asked, stunned. "Someone captured the Matron?"

"Apparently." The Deep Canyon man returned to the shade beside his mug-covered blanket. "It has to be Leather Hand who did it. That's why no one's seen him recently. When he's around, people talk."

"You know him?"

"Seen him. That's bad enough. He spent quite a bit

of time at Tall Piñon. I'd rather stand on a high peak in the middle of a lightning storm than be close to him."

Up on the rooftop, Webworm was clapping his hands and Dancing with joy.

"Excuse me." Spots walked forward, stepping around behind the bear cage. He could see Nightshade seated inside. The old woman gave him a curious glance.

"The word is that Night Sun has been captured." Spots made sure that no one was within hearing distance as he kept his back to the cage, his attention on the roof of the great kiva.

"The Flute Player is lulled," Nightshade replied.

"Lulled?" Spots asked, trying to keep his voice low. "Gods, what if the rumors about the First Moon elders are true? My people won't risk their elders' lives by attacking Pinnacle Great House. If Night Sun's been captured, can Ironwood be close behind?"

Her laughter had a hollow echo. "Live well, Spots. These are the last days."

With unerring precision, Turquoise Fox kept them on secondary trails that followed ridgetops and avoided the more heavily traveled valleys.

Leather Hand held a hand up to block the last shafts of reddish gold as he stood on bare caprock and watched the sunset. The light set the northern horizon ablaze as it bathed the smoke-filled skies.

He cast a final look into the valley below, seeing the scattered farmsteads where isolated farmers kept their fields. Here, so close to the River of Souls, the floodplains were watered by ditches, or were so close to the river that water could be carried in jars and fed to the corn plants.

With a final glance at the distant horizon he turned and walked back along the wind-smoothed sandstone to the tree line. He could smell the juniper fires as he walked through the trees to rejoin his little band of warriors. Several of his men were already taking their pleasure of the captive women. He could see Raven-fire's bare buttocks gyrating as he took his turn. The children watched from the side, wide-eyed, disbelieving.

Turquoise Fox had been amused to discover that Ravenfire had never lain with a woman. Now the boy was making up for lost time.

"What do you think that does to a child?" Night Sun asked as he walked up to her fire and seated himself.

"Pardon?" He glanced up, pulling out a piece of fine leather he'd been working on.

"Watching their mothers being treated like receptacles," Night Sun elaborated, jerking her head toward the grunting men.

"The children do not worry me, Matron." He chuckled, using his rabbit-bone awl to poke a hole into the soft leather. He was carefully beading the strip with patterns of chevrons; Larkspur had given him a supply of the finely crafted beads. A token, she had said, of their future alliance.

"They do not worry you?" She had lifted an eyebrow.

In the beginning, it had irritated him that she looked at him as though he were some sort of loathsome parasite, perhaps similar to a tick or gray louse. He'd considered beating it out of her, but thought better of it. She'd travel better in good health.

He smiled. There was always the future. Until Ironwood showed up, he'd have all the time he needed to hear her scream.

"The children," he told her, "are temporary. They are a lure, like a stuffed rabbit placed atop an eagle trap. When we have drawn Ironwood and his warriors into the trap, they will be of no further value. He glanced at them, snot-nosed, filthy-faced, their skinny arms bound behind them."

And then there was Ravenfire. "Your grandson, however, has turned out to be an unexpected prize. While I have you, and will soon have Ironwood, I still need to deal with Cornsilk. The young man assures me that he has no problem sending the sort of frantic message that will draw her into my web."

"I'd worry more about Poor Singer than my daughter."

"What's another silly Dreamer? Jay Bird might take him seriously, but the old chief isn't long for this world. He's elderly Matron. Just like you. Somehow I can't see skinny Poor Singer rallying warriors to accompany him north in search of me."

"You have this all thought out, have you?"

He nodded at Night Sun as he strung another chevron of beads onto a flax thread and stitched them down. "Something happened to me the night that we ate the Dust People."

"Yes, you became a walking abomination."

Ignoring her, he continued. "I felt a presence in the night. I'm fairly sure it was the Blue God herself. She was watching me, but I didn't sense that she'd come to devour me."

"I'm sure she has better taste than that," Night Sun agreed. "Given a choice between you and six-day-old carrion, I'm sure she'd choose the latter."

He gestured with his awl. "I've felt her since then. The last time was atop First Moon Mountain. I'd had a most enjoyable night with Matron Larkspur. It's the oddest thing, but I just knew that my future was being decided."

"Spider Woman's fire might be closer than you think," Night Sun said coldly.

He chuckled. "Ah, you do tempt me, Matron. But I can be patient. It's a necessary virtue for a man in my position. So as much as I'd like to hurt you now, we'll consider it a future obligation. No, what I was saying is that I could feel the Blue God's presence that night. She heard Larkspur and me making plans, and I have to tell you, I'm sure she's on my side."

Night Sun's expression hardened. "Any normal human being would burn himself alive before surrendering himself to the Blue God."

"You're probably correct, but I'm nowhere near a normal human." He gestured to his men where they sat at their fires, slabs of meat from the bloody packs extended over the coals. "Nor are my men normal. You've seen the white moccasins?"

"Of course."

"To be granted a pair, the warrior in question must not only have eaten man-meat, but must have eliminated one of the Blessed Sun's enemies by stealth."

"Matron White Cloud?"

"These are her moccasins." He indicated his

footwear. "I took them as a trophy, but the Blessed Sun really made the idea stick."

"What will you do when he no longer thinks your services are necessary?" she asked.

Leather Hand met her distaste with a warm smile. "I've always liked the sound of' 'Blessed Sun,' haven't you?"

"A wise man wouldn't be telling me such things."

"Why, Matron, what on earth makes you think that you'll ever live to tell anyone?" He finished the last row of bead, and stepped around behind her. The piece was done in chevrons of alternating colors.

She went stiff at his touch, but he was very careful as he placed the beaded slave collar around her throat. "There," he said proudly, and quickly stitched the ends snug. "It's very becoming, but I wouldn't advise swallowing a large bite of food. It could end up choking you."

She was seething as he stepped away.

"Matron, I want you to remember, I made that from untanned leather. If you should anger me, or cause me to pour water on it, it will shrink as it dries. It would be a pity. As it slowly strangles you, the beadwork will be distorted. You wouldn't want that, because, well, it's absolutely magnificent just as it is."

She hawked and spat in his direction as he walked off to take his pleasure from one of the captive women.

A stillness lay in the air as Wrapped Wrist paused on the outcrop where he'd first looked out over First Moon

Valley with Crow Woman. This time, Orenda accompanied them.

The day had turned to dusk, sunlight fading into red. Muted light cast the blue-shadowed valley with a golden rime. The smoke from hundreds of fires softened the hard edges and darkened the green of junipers, pines, and agricultural fields. Overhead, in a huge curl, the smoke plume from the high-mountain fires was painted in gaudy red, orange, and black.

Looking to the north, he could see entire slopes denuded and charred, pale feathers of smoke rising into the larger mass.

"By the gods," he whispered, awed at the contrast of his peaceful valley and the distant conflagration.

"How would you ever describe that? Words don't have the ability to make it real." Crow Woman leaned on her cane. "I've never seen such a huge fire. People wouldn't believe it if they couldn't see it. The whole north is in flames."

"I've already seen too many terrible things," Wrapped Wrist said softly, images of the warriors he had killed mixing with those of brutalized and broken women and children at Ironwood's camp. "Let's just pray those flames stay north."

"I guess we're just lucky for these southwestern winds," Crow Woman agreed. "It would have gone poorly for us if they'd shifted while we were up on the divide."

Orenda was staring soberly at the fire, and then down at the valley. "Ironwood is down there? It's so huge. So many villages. How will we find him?"

Wrapped Wrist tightened his grip on the war club. The feel of the wood reassured him. "The elders will know. We'll go find White Eye. He'll tell us what to do."

Crow Woman pointed. "Look at the Dog's Tooth. Is it the shadows, or has it been burned?"

Wrapped Wrist squinted into the fading light. "Gods, I think you're right." A sinking premonition grew in his gut. "What's happened here?"

"I have the feeling this homecoming is going to be particularly painful for you," Orenda said soberly.

Ripple walked slowly through the night. He picked each step, setting down one foot and then the other. The dark climb wasn't particularly hazardous, but he feared what he would find when he reached the crest. The vision Cold Bringing Woman had given him hadn't been explicit about this part.

The trees waved around him as the breezes changed direction, teasing the piñon and juniper. The night air remained warm, carrying the fragrance of dust, pine, and cook fires. A cold breath danced across his cheek as an eddy carried cooler air, trapped from the bottomlands. As quickly, it was gone.

He could see the walls now, dark and straight where they topped the Dog's Tooth. No head broke the silhouette. He could feel Power in the air. Unseen eyes watched as he climbed the last bit and entered the unguarded gap in the wall.

The smell of charred wood still lingered here. Ripple walked past the collapsed remains of smoldering pit houses, feeling the heat that radiated from their ovenlike interiors. The two great kivas were flattened piles of rubble. In the darkness, he could see gleaming red eyes: coals that refused to die as they ate into the incompletely consumed roof supports. Inside the eastern wall, the upper story of the clan building had collapsed when the roofing burned through.

Broken pottery cracked and popped under his weight. Bits of torn matting, cloth, split baskets, drying racks, and other household debris were scattered about.

Curls of smoke rose around him, the acrid odor clogging his nose. He closed his eyes, inhaling the stench of destruction into his souls. When he opened them and looked north, he could see the distant forest fire: a thousand winking eyes that vanished and reappeared in the smoke palls.

Those were the mountains of his youth. He had traveled every trail, scaled every peak. He'd known them as intimately as this valley he called home. The clearing where Cold Bringing Woman had appeared to him was now turned to ash. Had the great bear survived? Or had that shared meal of elk been among his last?

He blinked at smoke-induced tears and remembered the cool forests where he'd hunted. The mice and voles wouldn't have escaped. Many of the deer and elk would have been trapped in the blind valleys. How many of the stately trees now existed as burned snags?

The time has come.

He threw his arms wide, aware of the heat that radiated from the burned buildings to warm his skin.

In the vision he had seen the River of Stones running black with ash; then that afternoon, it had been as he had seen. The image was burned into his memory. The farmers he had overheard were discussing how it would help finish the corn, the added nutrients sure to guarantee full kernels and large ears.

"What an empty promise the gods have made." He let the first sob rise from his chest. Hot tears trickled down his cheeks.

Cold Bringing Woman? Can I cancel my bargain? Can I just go away and save this world? Will you allow me to escape with Orenda? Can I have my children? Can I die of old age, having lived a ripe and full life?

He felt rather than saw or heard the dark rasp of wings in the smoke-laden air. Smoke and tendrils of ash whirled about him.

No, the bargain was long since struck. Only now, as the immensity of it was brought home, did he wish that he'd been left to die in his prison deep inside Pinnacle House. That end, painful as it was to his body, was preferable to what his souls were about to suffer.

He heard the crunching steps behind him. Then Ironwood said, "You asked me to meet you here."

"In the vision, Cold Bringing Woman said I would face you in the smoking ruins of my people's house. I didn't know what that meant. But here I am, and here you are."

"Face me?" Ironwood cocked his head. "Does this have anything to do with the signals we've seen flashed from Pinnacle House?"

"Cold Bringing Woman said you would have to decide if you would save one, or many. Tonight you must choose if you are a husband or a chief. Will you save your souls, or your people? Power awaits your decision."

Ironwood was silent, a towering dark form in the

night. "My souls or my people? I don't understand. I have always chosen my people."

"As you did the night you lay with Night Sun and conceived a child? As you did when you refused the temptation to kill Snake Head before he could become Blessed Sun? How many times have you ignored your responsibilities to salve your heart?"

"Many," he said reluctantly. "What are you trying to tell me?"

"That when the time comes, the choice of the heart will oppose the choice of leadership. You may choose either way, War Chief. There is no wrong answer."

"I still don't understand. What you are trying to get me to choose?"

Ripple turned, pointing up past the dark pillars of First Moon Mountain. There, behind the billowing black of the smoke-filled night, Sister Moon appeared for the briefest of seconds, her round shape but a faint reddish disc in the murky sky. She shone for less than a heartbeat before she faded into nothingness.

"Sister Moon has donned her smoke-black cape, War Chief. By this time tomorrow, we must commit ourselves to the Dance."

Chapter Seventeen

The wind brought Bad Cast awake. He lay curled against Soft Cloth, thankful for her warmth under the thin blanket. Another gust whistled through the ladder uprights where they protruded from the roof.

He sniffed, aware that the odor of smoke was stronger. Outside a basket tumbled across the plaza, pushed by the wind. He hoped nothing fragile or important had been inside. Something wooden was blown over to an accompanying clatter.

"Storm?" Soft Cloth asked.

"Sounds like."

She sniffed. "That's not our fire, is it?"

"No. Sure is strong." He glanced around, assured that no flames were licking at the inside of their pit house. House fires terrified his people, especially because escape was through the roof smoke hole. Just ask Spots; he could testify to the terror of a burning house.

Now that he'd thought about burning to death in

his sleep, any kind of meaningful repose was out of the question. If he tried, it would be to constantly crack one eye, sniff for smoke, and worry.

As he threw back the blanket, Soft Cloth asked, "What are you doing?"

"Taking a look."

"Don't wake the baby."

He climbed up the ladder and stuck his head out. The wind was from the north, the smell of smoke worse. His first glance took in the plaza they shared with Soft Cloth's two sisters. Everything was inky black. Blood and pus, it was one dark night.

Then he looked into the wind and froze. From Soft Cloth's pit house, there was no clear view of the northern horizon. The shoulder of Juniper Ridge and the tree line obscured it, but a dreadful reddish-orange glow could be seen.

"Snake's blood," he whispered.

"What?" Soft Cloth rustled the bedding below.

He climbed back down, reaching for his clothes. "The whole northern sky is glowing. It's like nothing I've ever seen."

To his surprise, she checked the baby, dressed, and followed him out into the night. Hand in hand, they felt their way along the trail that led past the Mid-Sun Village great kivas and up to the rimrock.

At the rim, Bad Cast stopped, heart leaping. Flames dotted the entire northern horizon. Yellow at the bottom, they raced upward, illuminating the smoke in orange, red, and then a dull crimson that faded to black.

Another gust of wind shook them, powerful, tearing down from the north.

"Maybe it's a rain cloud," Soft Cloth said over the gale. "You know how it can blow under a thunderhead."

Bad Cast sniffed again. All he could smell was wood smoke. "Do you smell rain?"

She sniffed. "No."

They staggered under another gust.

"If it's not rain, it's unusual for the wind to blow out of the north this time of year. You'd think it was winter solstice instead of coming up on equinox."

Bad Cast felt something pattering on his skin. Reaching up, he expected it to be rain, but it was dry to the touch, powdery.

"I hope that wind doesn't keep up. At this rate, it will push that fire right up to the edge of the valley."

"Come on, let's go back to bed. I'm scared."

Another gust pattered the invisible specks against him. When he rubbed his finger over his skin and touched it to his tongue, he tasted ash.

Wrapped Wrist led the way to Yellow Petal's house, figuring she was a kinswoman; and after all, Spots was his best friend. Yellow Petal had built a large, tight, two-room dwelling. The bigger main room contained the hearth, two stone benches, containers, and ventilator. The smaller chamber was separated by a wattle-plastered wall and accessed through a hide-covered door. It was there that Spots kept his bedding, tools, weapons, and personal possessions.

To his surprise, the place was empty. Food, however, was plentiful, and he felt no guilt as he pawed through the jars. In a wood-lidded white-slipped jar he found cornmeal. A net bag produced smoked turkey meat. He lifted the lid off of a globular brownware jar to find hulled pine nuts. Pulling the stopper from a canteen, he sipped, delighted with the taste of chokecherry juice.

"Are you sure this cousin won't mind us eating her food?" Orenda asked skeptically.

"Pretty sure. What's the point of having kin if they can't help you when you're in need?" He mixed cornmeal, pine nuts, some dried rose hips, and the turkey in a corrugated cooking pot. Then he went about stoking the coals in the fire pit to life. Yellow Petal had stacked a liberal supply of firewood along the south wall.

"What are you smiling at?" Crow Woman asked as she awkwardly lowered herself onto one of Yellow Petal's blankets. She had her leg stuck straight out in front of her. Wrapped Wrist was hard pressed to keep from jarring it as he prepared the meal.

Orenda looked worried as she removed the wrapping she'd placed on Crow Woman's knee. The bruise looked black and ugly, but the swelling had gone down.

"What's wrong?" Crow Woman asked cautiously.

Orenda prodded the knee, eliciting a gasp from Crow Woman. "Nothing. You're healing fine."

"That's a relief. From the expression on your face, I thought maybe I was crippled."

Orenda failed when she tried to produce a smile. "It's not you. First Nightshade walks away, who knows to what purpose or fate. Then this Leather Hand...well, I can't do anything about the dead, but I'm sick at the thought of what they'll do to Night Sun and the others."

Crow Woman's eye narrowed. "The war chief will see to it. But, by the Blue God's soul, Leather Hand will rue the day if he so much as yanks a hair out of that woman's head."

Wrapped Wrist kept his attention on his cooking, wondering all the while what Ironwood's handful of warriors could do against the might of Flowing Waters Town.

To change the subject, he said, "I was thinking of what a good worker Yellow Petal is. She's always after Spots to do this or do that. Fortunately for us, she's laid in a goodly supply of everything we need."

"I'd say she's going to skin a piece out of your hide if you don't replace what we use," Orenda told him. Too worried to simply sit, she pushed him out of the way, busying herself with the corrugated cooking pot on the coals.

"I wish she were here," Wrapped Wrist replied as he sat back. He was aware of Crow Woman. She'd been watching him with a peculiar intensity all day long. Whatever motivated the penetrating interest in her eyes, Wrapped Wrist was sure it boded him no good. He'd probably said something during the last day that she'd been stewing on. The thing was, she didn't look mad at him. And twice, he'd swear she'd been on the verge of smiling at him.

"Stop that!" Crow Woman snapped as he started to pick at the cactus thorns holding his cheek together. It itched like a thousand lice were under his skin.

"Sorry." He lowered his hand, unsettled by the concerned look that Crow Woman gave him. "I'd sure like to know what's happened here since we left."

"Tomorrow," Orenda said, "I can go around and ask. No one will recognize me. To them, I'll appear as another pilgrim."

They ate in silence, but Wrapped Wrist was acutely aware of Crow Woman. She was watching him, a veiled speculation in her eyes. Whatever it was, he tried to avoid her as he attended to the task of filling his belly. Odd, though, that she hadn't just lit into him with her usual vigor.

After they had cleaned the pots, Wrapped Wrist retired to Spots' room. There, to his satisfaction, a bundle of darts had been stacked. He fingered each of the long shafts and wondered where Spots was, and how he was faring. Wherever he was, Wrapped Wrist figured Spots wouldn't begrudge him this cache of desperately needed darts. Given the change in affairs, he swore he wasn't going to be unarmed again if he could help it.

He flopped out on Spots' bed, careful to lie on his back so as not to snag his stitches. What an odd sensation to be home, safe for the night in a kinswoman's house. As he thought about it, the last half moon might have been lived inside a whirlwind.

I killed four men.

And after what he'd seen at Ironwood's village, he'd have no hesitation to kill more.

Who have I become?

Until this one moment of peace, he hadn't had time to ask.

As the fire died, he watched the light fade, then heard Orenda's deep breathing. Well, at least one of them was sleeping well.

Then the wind began to blow. He heard it whistle around the ladder uprights, felt it stirring inside the house as it sucked through the ventilator shaft.

Crow Woman surprised him when she slipped

through the entry and carefully sat on the bedding beside him.

"What's wrong?" he whispered.

"Nothing." A pause. "Everything."

He waited.

"Wrapped Wrist, I have a sense...a premonition."

"Good or bad?"

"Bad. Is there any other kind these days?"

He remembered the mutilated bodies in Ironwood's camp, the look of fear in Night Sun's eyes as she was borne past their hiding place.

He started when she lay down beside him and was surprised when she placed a hand on his chest to push him back down.

"Can you hold me tonight?" she asked.

"What's wrong?"

"I think I'm going to die soon. It would be nice, just once...Rot and blood, how do I say this? I've been alone all of my life. And then, for the last quarter moon..."

"I know. Sometimes it's hard to remember what life was like before you started to make me miserable."

"I'm sorry. I'll go now."

He tightened his arm around her shoulders. "Don't. Maybe it turns out I like having you make me miserable."

"That day I was captured?"

"Yes."

"They caught me because I was thinking about you. I was imagining..."

He waited. "You seem to have trouble finishing phrases."

She sighed in frustration. "Look, I don't know if I'd be any good at this. I'd never be a normal wife. Nothing like your adored kinswoman, Yellow Petal. Snake's blood, I don't even know what you want in a woman."

He smiled, feeling the tightness in his stitched face. "How about a simple friend and companion?"

"Is it ever simple between a man and woman?"

"Absolutely positively never."

She tensed, taking a deep breath. The wind hammered at the house. "This coupling business. It's always been an unpleasant experience."

"Doesn't have to be."

She hesitated, then sat up in the dark and pulled her brown shirt over her head. "If you hurt my knee doing this, I'm going to rip those stitches right out of your face."

"Sometimes your charm leaves me dazzled."

He wriggled out of his own hunter's shirt and stretched out beside her. Every muscle was rigid, as if she were primed for combat instead of love. She spread her legs, whispering bravely, "I'm ready."

"For the moment," he said softly, "let's just hold each other. I want to feel your heart beating against mine, and your breath against my neck. Then you need to touch me, gently, as I touch you. We have plenty of time, you and me.

"Careful of your knee." He reached out, pulling her tense body onto his. Sighing, he hugged her to him, her hair falling around them like a veil.

After tonight, you'll never call me Stumpy again.

As the wind moaned past Cactus Flower's little house, Spots lay awake. She was sleeping with her head on his shoulder, her arm draped over his chest. Her firm brown thigh lay atop his groin, her right breast soft against his ribs.

Angry gusts pattered sand against the north wall of the house, and he could smell dust on the wind. Outside he could hear the matting on the ramada flapping, and something rattled as it blew away.

He breathed deeply, taking in the scent of her hair. He had watched her turn down a Trader's offer that afternoon when the man offered her an abalone pendant in exchange for a night at her place. It seemed that every time Spots was around, she was mysteriously unoccupied. Even more odd, she no longer even hinted that he Trade any of his goods in exchange for her bed.

He found a lock of her hair, running it around his finger. By the bloody gods, he'd come to enjoy this. It was more than the wondrous sensations she conjured from his shaft. He enjoyed the sparkle in her eye, the anecdotes she told about the Fire Dogs and First People, the Hohokam, and the Tower Builders. She just seemed to know so much.

From the moment they returned to her little farmstead, they talked—and talking was remarkably easy with her. He had learned that her father had been a Trader and that she'd grown up in a town down along the border with the Fire Dogs. She'd just passed her tenth summer when a mysterious coughing disease sickened most of the inhabitants. Cactus Flower's mother had asked her father to take her north, away from the miasma. When they'd returned the next spring, her entire lineage—mother, aunts, and uncles—had perished.

"So I just traveled with Father from then on."

He smiled at that, amazed at the differences between his upbringing and hers. He'd never been more than three days' travel from his mother's house. Cactus Flower had been from one end of the world to the other. Had seen the Rainbow Serpent where it belched out of the ground, had visited the Hohokam cities with their ball courts and river-wide canals. She had followed the trails north into the land of the Tower Builders and had tried her hand at their ceremonial game of divination: They rolled stone balls across their pit house floors as they Sang and prayed.

"Then Father was killed," she'd said simply. "It was a river crossing. Among the Hohokam, I learned to swim. He didn't."

As he stroked her hair, he could almost sense the presence of the sharp quartzite knife where it lay hidden in his pack beside the door.

Tomorrow would be the day. He would slip it to Nightshade when the opportunity presented itself.

And then what? He swallowed hard, hearing the patter of wind-driven gravel against the house walls. A fine filtering of dust hung in the air, muting the scent of her hair. It ground between his teeth, and he could feel it on his face.

Choices. Nightshade's benediction and curse balanced between his souls. He could slip her the knife, and then come home with Cactus Flower. Together they would kindle the dinner fire, make a meal, and then she would take her clothing off and entwine her soft brown body around him.

And Nightshade? Was she really a witch, or a madwoman?

What makes her think she can defeat Webworm?

Chapter Eighteen

A howling north wind ripped and tore its way over the weathered sandstone cliff behind Talon Town, whirled past the column of rock called Propped Pillar, and made a low moaning, as though the very stone was tortured.

Buffeted by the gusts, Leather Hand stood atop Talon Town's fifth-floor roof and stared up at the black sky. He ran his fingers over the smooth stone of the serpent-in-egg carving Webworm had given him. His souls were slithering around inside him—as if his gut were mimicking the carving. It was an eerie feeling, perhaps stimulated by the snake's head he rubbed under his thumb. Or perhaps his souls were hearing the cries of the dead. The First People had been living in this canyon for hundreds of years; their Spirits called from the stone, log, and soil that composed Straight Path Canyon.

He shifted against the wind, pierced by the lance-driven chill that seeped past his clothing. In the room below his feet, Night Sun lay securely bound. She was back in her old quarters, the ones she'd lived in before her exile. What was it like to return to that very room where she'd bedded Crow Beard, borne her son, Snake Head, and betrayed the Straight Path Nation when Ironwood crept into her blankets? Was she reliving those days, unbidden memories drifting up from her souls?

Wind Baby tugged at him, whipping his hair this way and that. The prickling in his souls continued.

"War Chief?" Turquoise Fox asked as he climbed the rickety old ladder onto the roof.

"Yes, Deputy?"

"I have seen to the warriors. They are in place just in case Ironwood is closer behind us than we think. I will rotate the men three times a day to ensure that everyone stays crisp and vigilant."

"Excellent."

"We are home," his deputy said softly. "It's almost as if we'd never left."

Leather Hand frowned, musing, "Home. The souls of the dead Dance here. It is to this place that the Dreams of our people return. From this dry canyon, the plant that would become our nation sent down its roots, sprouted, grew, and flourished." He sighed. "Deputy, I first entered this canyon in awe, my heart literally beating in my throat. I remember the sense of disbelief when Webworm and Featherstone decided to move north."

"Many of us couldn't believe it."

"By abandoning this place, we left the essence of what made us ourselves." Wind Baby pushed him again, trying to shove him backward off the roof.

"How do we find ourselves again, War Chief?"

"To whom does your first loyalty belong?"

"War Chief?"

"If you had to choose, would you serve the Blessed Sun, or your companions?"

Turquoise Fox was silent, searching for the trap, aware that the wrong answer could kill him. "I would have to say, after the most careful consideration, that I serve my companions, War Chief. It is they who serve the Blessed Sun."

He let Turquoise Fox stew in suspense. Finally he said, "I can feel the Blue God tonight. She is stirring, driving Wind Baby across the world as a warning."

"A warning of what?"

"That a mighty change is coming. There is a reason we've had no rain."

"Yes?"

"The Blue God is in ascendance, my friend. Webworm, Blue Racer, and the rest—they don't understand her cravings and appetite. I can imagine her sniffing around the Flute Player, mocking his music, fingering the pack he carries on his back. What is seed and fertility compared to blood and terror?"

"I don't know, War Chief. My concerns are not with gods and chaos, but with obedience and service."

"Did you check on the boy?"

"I did. Fast Fist tells me Ravenfire has done nothing to incite his suspicion."

"What do you think?"

"The youth wanted me to ask you something."

"And that is?"

"Is there a way to blame this on the Made People?"

"Ravenfire asked you that?"

"He did." Turquoise Fox squinted into the wind. "It

would have to be done carefully: a rumor planted here, a Trader bribed there. There are those among the Made People clans who dislike Night Sun and Ironwood even today. Those individuals would likely brag about it. Before long, people will believe that what happens here was the work of the Made People."

"I notice that you gave the youth one of your war feathers."

Turquoise Fox nodded. "I told him he's a man now. He participated in the raid, captured Night Sun, and has bedded his first woman. You should have seen his face when we first approached Talon Town. 'The home of my ancestors,' he said."

Another gust blew out of the black night. Leather Hand turned his back to it. "He's right. We stand on the same spot where the rulers of the Straight Path Nation have stood for generations. Look out there. The canyon is black, deserted. From here they would have seen thousands of lights gleaming up and down the canyon. Now only darkness remains."

"Would you bring the lights back?"

"Yes." He slapped Turquoise Fox on the back. "Come, let us sleep. Tomorrow, Night Sun is going to have a very, very long day."

In his high room in Flowing Waters Town, Webworm sat on his sleeping pallet. Wind Baby howled out of the north, whistling and moaning as it savaged Dusk House's balcony. His door hanging jumped and jerked as though alive. Embers flickered in the fire bowl he'd ordered a slave to bring him. In their blood-glow the paintings of the Flute Player, Spider Woman, the Blue God, and Father Sun seemed to pulse on the plastered walls.

He lifted a tall ceramic pitcher and sipped at the blackberry juice. Grit grated on his teeth. Dust. It was everywhere: blowing on the wind, leaving its scent in his nostrils.

A hollow moaning was spun where Wind Baby howled through doors, around corners and protruding roof poles. Spirits were out. He could feel them, hear them as they slipped about in the dark wind. Yes, a dark wind indeed.

He peeked out and found the night stygian despite the promise of a full moon. He wondered how Blue Racer was going to fare up on First Moon Mountain; thousands of people would be watching, and Sister Moon was nowhere to be seen on the equinox of her homecoming.

Something whispered behind his ear, and he turned, staring. He heard them all the time now: chittering little voices. Or he'd hear a shout; but when he turned, only the echo remained, hollow between his souls. The laughter was the worst. Just that afternoon, he'd spun around and shouted, "Stop it!" at Wind Leaf. His war chief had looked at him with shocked eyes, and quietly asked, "Stop what?"

Did no one else hear the voices?

Chortles of delight fluttered around his ears, and his eyes were drawn to the witch's pack where it hung from a peg in the corner. He'd looked through it, found a Spirit bundle, and inspected its worn leather. No telling what it's Power might have been. The beautiful black bowl was like nothing of local manufacture. He'd sniffed the gray paste it contained, and supposed it was datura. Other items had included a thin copper man-snake-bird image he'd never seen before. A huge shell gorget had been decorated with a spider effigy circled by a snake that was eating its own tail. Small sacks made of colorfully feathered bird skins held various powders and potions. Bits of bone, dried animal feet, and other amulets defied any explanation of their purpose.

Fact was: He hadn't had a good night's sleep since he'd gone through the pack. As he stared at it, he wasn't sure but that he ought to set fire to it. He'd picked it up the day before with just that intent, but at the last moment, rehung it before pacing back and forth. Then someone had called that a black signal fire burned in the north. Black, but not white. Leather Hand's signal that he'd only captured Night Sun.

Night Sun. I've got her. Where Night Sun goes, Ironwood will follow.

An image formed: Ironwood, years ago. Webworm had been his deputy back then. What fine friends they'd been. Life had been so simple. Ironwood gave the orders, and Webworm carried them out. Ironwood's youthful words clung like cobwebs in Webworm's memory: "Be strong, my friend. Never forget your warriors in arms. Your life is theirs, theirs is yours."

The corners of his lips quivered. How had they lost such a perfect friendship? He would hate to see Ironwood's body, to have to remember how it had been between them. Gods, how he missed that life. He'd been so happy back then. But for a twist of fate, he would have married Cloud Playing and been happy for the rest of his life. A man could only love like that once.

"Webworm?"

Was that his mother's voice? He cocked his head, struggling to make out the words, but they faded right out of the air.

Voices, voices. Where do they all come from? It hadn't been this bad until the Mountain Witch had walked into his room.

Yes, Nightshade.

He glanced over at the corner where Nightshade's bag hung from its peg. Even as he did, the voices grew louder. Some spoke in a tongue he'd never heard. The language of the Mound Builders, he supposed.

"I really ought to burn you," he muttered.

Whisperings and rustlings made him whirl and stare owlishly at his bedding. Something had been there, hadn't it? He'd just caught movement from the corner of his eye. Jabbing at the blankets with a nervous hand, he found only cloth atop the cushioning layers of buffalo hide.

Webworm muttered under his breath, sipped more of the berry juice, and scratched beneath his arm. Was that smoke he smelled on the wind? If only he could sleep.

No, he dared not. When he drifted off, it ended in disastrous nightmares.

He blinked, yawned. A child began to cry, sadness and grief in the driven sobs. He scrambled to the doorway and pulled the hanging back. Nothing.

"Did you hear a child?" he asked the dark shape of the guard who huddled in the windblown dark.

"No, Blessed Sun." The warrior sounded wary.

Rot it all, that was the third time he'd asked the guard if he'd heard anything. Maybe the man's ears were plugged with the thrice-accursed blowing dust.

He crawled back to his bed and slumped onto the blanket. Blinking, he forced himself to stay awake.

Gods no, you dare not Dream.

When he did, it was more than just voices.

He was just drifting off when he heard the serpent's Powerful hiss.

Jerking up, he spilled berry juice over the floor, crying, "What was that?"

From outside his door, the guard asked, "Blessed Sun? Are you well?"

Webworm winced, blinked, and stared down where his hand was planted in the berry juice. Thoughts. Scattered thoughts.

I have Matron Night Sun. With her for bait, I will have Ironwood. "And then I will have murdered the last of my friends."

In the light of the glowing coals, he could see his latest carving. The serpent lay curled within its eggshell, a black hole where the eye should be. Tomorrow he would set that eye. Perhaps he would make a little gift of the carving to Desert Willow.

He lifted his hand and began licking the sweet juice from his palm.

Chapter Nineteen

I n the course of a night, the world had changed. The knowledge lay deep down between Bad Cast's souls. When he and Soft Cloth had returned to their house after watching the fires, it had been with a sense of some great portent. After she had fed the baby, they had coupled with a tender violence that left them both limp and drained.

Still entwined in his wife's arms, he had awakened to the stench of smoke. The light through the smoke hole was a dirty gray. Outside, the wind alternately roared and eddied, and bits of ash, like flakes of snow, drifted down from the skies.

Bad Cast kissed Soft Cloth's shadowed cheek and rolled out from under the blanket. Locked in Dreams, she murmured and rolled over.

To his relief, the baby was still asleep. He pulled on his hunting shirt and climbed up the ladder and out into the day. He coughed, hawking up black phlegm. Looking to the sky, he was amazed to find the heavens blackened with smoke. He could see the stiff north wind rolling patterns of darkness across the skies.

Making his way through the gloom, he walked up the path to the rimrock and looked out over First Moon Valley. Wind gusts pushed at him, relented, and pushed again. Was it his imagination, or did the gusts have an unaccustomed bite to them? Through the haze he couldn't even make out First Moon Mountain.

Someone coughed on the trail behind him, and he turned to see Ripple as he emerged from between the juniper trees.

"What a morning." Bad Cast squinted up into the soot-filled air. "I've never seen it this bad."

"No, I suppose not."

Bad Cast waved. "Look—you can't even see across the valley. Everything's blue-brown. Even my spit's black."

"It's the Dance."

"What Dance? No one's Dancing." He looked out into the thick haze. "Equinox is coming. They should have started the first ceremonies up at Pinnacle House last night. Our elders should have been at the sipapu. With this wind, I'll bet Blue Racer couldn't even keep his costume on."

"They Danced," Ripple assured him, his thoughtful eyes on the gloomy valley. "Tonight, they shall Dance again."

Bad Cast took a breath, wanting to cough. "This is part of Cold Bringing Woman's vision, isn't it?"

Ripple nodded.

"Can you tell me about it?"

Ripple smiled softly. "Do you remember the trail

that leads up the north side of the mountain? The one that passes the old lightning-riven tree?"

"Sure. It passes through the trees on the north side. Ah, I recall. You're thinking about the time that the four of us climbed up that way to spy on the First People's solstice ceremonies."

"They never knew we were there." Ripple smiled. "Spots wouldn't let me climb onto the top. He was afraid I might go in search of my father's skull."

"We climbed up that crack in the rocks," Bad Cast remembered. "You couldn't climb over the rim because Spots was holding your ankle." He smiled at the memory. "You know, he probably saved your life."

"Could you find that trail again?"

"Sure. I just have to look for—"

"Can you find it in the dark?"

Bad Cast frowned. "I don't know." He glanced at Ripple, seeing his friend's sad expression. "Why?"

"They will be depending on you tonight."

"Ripple? What's wrong? You know something, don't you?"

He seemed not to hear, but smiled, as if seeing something in the distant past. "We had some times, didn't we? Remember when you made that willow-stick doll for Slipped Bark? And the time when Wrapped Wrist was coupling with that Strong Back Clan girl down by the river?"

"We stole their clothes." Bad Cast laughed. "They had to wait in the willows, swatting mosquitoes until midnight before they could dare to sneak home without anyone seeing them." A pause. "When I was courting Soft Cloth, we coupled in the willows once. She thought I was demented because I insisted on keeping one fist balled in our clothing the entire time."

"We have all been so jealous of you."

"What?"

"Spots and I—and even Wrapped Wrist—thought you were the luckiest man we knew when you married her."

"Why?"

"We imagined you going home to her every night. You have what we all wanted: a capable and caring wife. The two of you just fit together. That's how I want to remember you. Not pulling pranks, not sharing the hunt, but with her. I want to imagine you in the future, not the past."

"What's to imagine? You'll share our fire for years to come. Maybe you and Orenda."

His smile was wistful. "Orenda will travel over to the Green Mesa after this. There, she'll live for a while with Born-of-Water. Then she'll marry one of Cornsilk's sons."

"That's no way to—"

"I know these things, Bad Cast. And it's all right. I made my decision. I'm at ease with it. I have one last responsibility to my people; and, after that, well, the ghosts will rest easier."

"Ripple, why don't you just take Orenda and go? You've already made a difference."

"Funny, isn't it? I spent my life hating the First People. Now, with their end looming, I'm just tired." He placed his good hand on Bad Cast's shoulder. "Deeply and soul-weary tired. Do not mourn me, dear friend. As much as I hated the past, I couldn't bear the future. Take care of Wrapped Wrist and Spots. They will need your sober counsel even more in the days to come. And whatever you do, make sure Soft Cloth and the baby travel with you when you leave for the Great River Valley."

"You're talking as if you won't be there."

He shrugged. "I told you: I'm tired, Bad Cast. Our world is about to be cleansed. I would rather rest than endure the storm—but if I am to serve my purpose, I have one last duty to perform. I promise, tonight, finally, you will understand."

"You are talking nonsense." When Bad Cast stared out at the roiling smoke where his pristine valley should have been, it looked anything but cleansing.

"It only seems that way now." Ripple tightened his hand on Bad Cast's shoulder. "I just wanted a moment with you. Thank you for always being there for me. I know what risks you took on my behalf. I will be forever grateful."

"We have always been there for each other."

"Go now," Ripple added gently. "The war chief is meeting with some of the lineage leaders in the Soft Earth Moiety kiva. He's going to need you before this is all over."

Bad Cast gave Ripple a furtive inspection. His friend was staring thoughtfully into the north, eyes squinted against the thick and rolling smoke and blowing ash.

Coupling, Crow Woman decided, had definite therapeutic value. Her limp was decidedly better, the pain nowhere near as intense. She followed close on

Wrapped Wrist's heels, placing her feet in his footsteps.

In the smoke-thick morning, they climbed a well-traveled trail, each step something of a trial for her, but nothing like yesterday's trip. The smoke, however, burned the eyes, nose, and throat. She coughed periodically. Between wind gusts, bits of ash filtered out of the murky air.

Wrapped Wrist nodded to the people they encountered coming down the hill, many burdened with hoes, baskets, or water jars. Everyone looked worried and nervous, usually pausing long enough to ask if he had news on the fire.

Gusts of wind still batted at them, and the whirling flakes of gray-white ash reminded her of perverted snow. It coated everything: hair, cloak, her pack. The merest touch left gray-black streaks on her skin.

Orenda coughed as she followed them up the steep trail. The woman seemed more subdued than ever, expression pinched, worry behind her soft eyes.

"It's up to me to tell him," Orenda had said over their breakfast in Yellow Petal's house. She had been so preoccupied with what she would say to Ironwood that she hadn't noticed the secret glances and smiles Crow Woman and Wrapped Wrist had shot each other.

Flashes from Crow Woman's experiences during the night before kept popping up in her memory. The first surprise had come from his tender hands, the way he'd brushed his lips lightly across her skin. The sensation of his tongue on her nipples had charged her with excitement. His sensitive fingertips had sent pleasure through her sheath.

At his urging, she had touched him back, fascinated

by the feel of his hard shaft in her hands. By the time he had gently shifted his weight onto hers, the fear of his imposing organ had vanished. She couldn't believe that she was literally aching for him. She'd sighed with relief as he slid into her, and miracle of miracles, it hadn't hurt.

She'd moved with him, eyes closed, arms around his muscular shoulders. He'd been slow, patient and careful, his breath purling on her chest as his hips rotated against hers. If only she could have kept those honeyed sensations forever.

So this is what it's all about?

The thought had barely formed when her loins exploded. She was panting, hugging him to her, when the sensations faded.

"Shhh!" Wrapped Wrist had whispered. "Orenda is trying to sleep."

She'd swallowed hard. "I've heard women talk...it's just never happened to me before."

"Well, let's see if we can do it again."

When she'd awakened in the predawn, his muscular arms had been around her, his body sending its warmth into her night-chilled flesh. She had turned, finding herself face-to-face. He'd looked her in the eyes and given her a happy smile. After he brushed his lips across her cheek, his hands began smoothing her sides, rounding her hips, and stroking her legs.

His touch lit the fires inside her pelvis, and they were at it again. Not once, but twice before she had to dress, leave his bed, and find her way outside for the purpose of relieving herself.

Gods, what has happened to me?

She ached to be alone with him, to ask him about

what had been kindled between them. Did he share the same mad desire she felt for him? Was his memory as filled with her as hers was with him?

Snake's blood. 1 What if he's planted a child in me?

Dumbstruck, she wondered what the consequences of that would be.

They stepped out onto the crest of Juniper Ridge, and Wrapped Wrist took the moment to catch his breath. A biting chill was rising, and she shivered against it. Two pit houses stood back in the trees. First Moon Valley was masked by the thick haze.

She caught his eye. "I have to speak with you."

He nodded, a reassuring smile on his lips. To Orenda, he said, "We'll be back."

The woman nodded, granting them a wistful smile before returning to her gloomy thoughts.

Wrapped Wrist walked several steps down the ridge. "It's hard when there are three people, isn't it?"

"There are so many things," she began. "I'm confused. Delighted. I'm half-scared. What happened to me last night?"

He took her hands, grinning. "I'm hoping you fell in love."

"It's impossible!" She dropped his hands, limping off and crossing her arms as she stared out at the smoke and falling ash. The wind gusted, whipping the trees. The cold seemed to intensify. "Wrapped Wrist, you have a life here. I have duties to my war chief."

"Crow Woman, I've lain with a lot of women, but last night my souls were Singing." A conspiratorial grin crossed his lips. "And yours were, too. You're anything but quiet when your moment comes."

"I wasn't that loud."

"Orenda didn't get much sleep last night."

"She knows?"

"Well, it was pretty hard to miss."

"She didn't say anything, didn't stare at us."

Wrapped Wrist raised his hands to calm her. "Because what we did is normal for two people who really like each other."

She swallowed hard. "Do you really like me?"

He nodded.

"Most men, and nearly all women, think I'm unlikeable."

"You never let men see the souls you keep locked inside that wonderful body of yours. As to the women, you'll have to find your own answer to that." His voice dropped. "When this is over, I want to go away with you. Just you and me, where we can be alone with each other."

"Why?" she almost cried. His words kept stirring feelings she'd thought long dead. Hope, longing, and dread all mixed together. By the gods, she hated being confused—especially by herself.

His grin was contagious. "I like you. I think I love you. But I want to know that you and I can love each other forever. It will take time for both of us, but I want to try."

"What if you made me pregnant?"

"We will deal with it," he replied reasonably. "If, for some reason, you don't want me to help raise the child, that's fine. On the other hand, if your life precludes raising it, my clan will be happy to adopt. I'll raise it." He arched a teasing brow. "Who knows? Maybe we'll decide to raise it together."

She stared at him in disbelief. "It can't be that easy."

"It's not." He turned deathly serious. "There's nothing harder on earth than a relationship between a man and a woman. It'll even be harder between you and me because of what fate and other men have done to you."

She sighed. "I'd swear you put some sort of charm on my souls. For the moment all I can think about is you and what happens when we lay together."

"Good." He stepped close, pulling her head down and brushing his lips on hers. "Trust me; we'll work it out."

The problem was, they were heading into a war; and the last thing she needed was to have her thoughts constantly distracted by either his smile or his body.

A long-legged man could cross the Soft Earth Moiety kiva in Mid-Sun Town in eight paces. The roof with its large opening was rattled by the wind, and bits of ash drifted in. A fire had been lit in the central fire pit, a concession to the growing chill. Bad Cast had slipped inside after returning from his meeting with Ripple. He'd found his wife seated on the corner of the foot drum and had taken a seat beside her. Her expression was grim, her brow lined. She'd taken his hand in hers, grip tight.

Around the walls, lineage leaders sat cross-legged, eyes thoughtful. Ironwood stood in the north, a grim expression on his thin-lipped face. His single eye had fixed on the fire.

"Ironwood has asked for help in attacking Pinnacle House," Soft Cloth whispered into Bad

Cast's ear. "Without the elders, it's up to the lineage leaders."

Under normal circumstances, the kiva would have been the preserve of the Priests and Shamans who were preparing for the equinox, a most special time this year since it coincided with Sister Moon's homecoming. Now, however, with the presence of the war chief, the captivity of the elders, and Ripple's looming vision, a special meeting had been called.

A Strong Back Clan man, Black Bush, who had married Yellow Petal, held the floor, a long dart in his right hand. "I have talked with my opposites," he said forcefully. "My own inclination is to attack Pinnacle Great House according to the war chief's plans. It seems, however, that others in my clan do not share this conviction." He shot the war chief a sad smile. "It is their fear that if we help you attack, our Clan elder, Hoarse Caller, and War Chief Rose will be put to death by the First People. I must, therefore, respectfully decline your invitation, War Chief."

Ironwood nodded. He'd obviously heard enough of this already.

Black Bush relinquished the long dart, symbol of a speaker during a war council, and returned to his seat beside Yellow Petal. She nodded encouragement to her husband and took his hand as he seated himself.

Bad Cast looked around, waiting for someone else to come forward. No one did. An uneasy silence spread through the room.

Someone, do something.

Bad Cast glanced over his shoulder to where the Whisper and Muddy Water Clan leaders sat. Most of them looked down at their hands, or anywhere but toward Ironwood.

Bad Cast nerved himself. Gods, he'd never done anything like this, but he took a deep breath, winked at Soft Cloth when she gave him a questioning look, and stood. His heart was hammering as he picked his way between the seated people and walked up to Ironwood. His hand was trembling as he took the long, fletched dart and turned.

He froze as every eye fixed on him. Words stuck in his throat. The carefully rehearsed argument vanished into air. For long moments he stood petrified.

"Bad Cast?" Ironwood said gently. "It is traditional to introduce yourself."

A chuckle came from the floor, and Bad Cast grinned sheepishly. "I am Bad Cast, of the Blue Stick Clan." His mouth was dry. "I am not a lineage leader. I'm a hunter, not a leader."

He happened to glance at Soft Cloth and saw the surprise and amazement in her eyes. As their eyes met, she smiled, nodding her encouragement. He stiffened his spine, planting his feet. "What I wanted to say here is that I was one of the first to hear Ripple's vision. I was one of the men who rescued him and took him to the Mountain Witch. She believed his vision and took it as a sign. In the meantime, I have lived with Ironwood's people, and talked to the Dreamer, Poor Singer. He believes Ripple's vision."

He glanced at Ironwood and drew strength from the slight nod. The dart shaft was slick in his sweaty hands. "Cold Bringing Woman told Ripple that the First People could be broken. I know it is difficult to decide what to do when our elders' lives are at risk, but

I think in my heart that we must support the war chief and Ripple."

Was he making any impression at all?

"I cannot speak for my clan, not even for my lineage. I can't even speak as a warrior. I speak only as a man. But I want every person in this room to understand that when the war chief and his warriors move against Pinnacle Great House, I will be with him." He paused, looking out at the faces. "I do not ask you to come and fight with us, only that you be ready to do what your souls and honor ask of you. That is all."

The room was silent.

Bad Cast tightened his grip on the dart and tapped it against the kiva floor before handing it back to Ironwood. "That is all."

He knew that Ironwood's single eye followed him as he went back and seated himself beside Soft Cloth.

Ironwood pursed his lips as he stared thoughtfully at the floor. "Well, at least I have one of you with me. Thank you, Bad Cast."

A voice from the door called, "Whatever Bad Cast has gotten himself into, you can count on me, too." Wrapped Wrist ducked through the entryway, followed by Crow Woman and, most surprising of all, by a worried-looking Orenda.

Ironwood jerked a curt nod. "Thank you, Wrapped Wrist. Your support is deeply appreciated." To Crow Woman, he said, "Good to see you, warrior. We've been worried."

He stiffened when Orenda said, "War Chief? Might I have a word with you outside?"

Ironwood addressed the room. "If you would excuse me for a moment, I'll give you time to digest Bad Cast's words." Then he followed the others as they stepped out.

Bad Cast stood, retraced his way through the crowd, and ducked out into the smoky day. Behind him, voices rose in sudden bedlam, although a voice shouted, "Order! Order! One at a time!"

Bad Cast slapped Wrapped Wrist on the back. "Good to see you. Where've you been?"

Wrapped Wrist gave him a sober grin. "Having interesting times. What happened on the Dog's Tooth?"

"Leather Hand surprised the Council of Elders up there. He captured White Eye, Whistle, and the elders, and burned the place on the way out. He's taken them up to the great house. No one has seen him or them since."

Orenda had led them several paces into the center of the small plaza. She turned, looking Ironwood in the eye. "I have no way to tell you this, but the camp has been attacked. Leather Hand killed many, took others." She drew a breath. "Night Sun is his captive. He and his troops have taken her south. Perhaps to Flowing Waters Town."

Ironwood's flinty expression began to sag. "How long ago?"

"Three days now." Orenda wrung her hands. "They went straight to the camp, Ironwood. It was as if they knew exactly where we were."

Crow Woman asked, "You said they caught Whistle?" A pause. "That's how they found us."

Orenda threw her hands up. "One other thing: Ravenfire was with them. It was he who captured Night Sun. I swear it, War Chief. He gave her up to them."

Ironwood looked stunned.

"We saw her," Wrapped Wrist added. "They were carrying her on a litter. Some of the other women and children were walking. Ravenfire was with them, walking freely and carrying a weapon."

Crow Woman cocked her jaw. "You should also know they butchered some of the bodies. Took the flesh with them for meat."

Ironwood's face was as ashen as the sky. "By the gods."

Bad Cast fought the urge to reach out and steady the man.

"War Chief?" Crow Woman asked, stepping forward.

Aware of Soft Cloth as she walked up behind him, Bad Cast said, "Come. My house is but a stone's throw from here. Let us have some tea and consider what to do."

"We can save her," Crow Woman insisted. "It will have to be done quickly and carefully. They'll most likely have her in Dusk House. We can sneak most of our people inside, then, with a good diversion, break her out."

"Do that," Bad Cast said, "and we'll lose any element of surprise here."

Crow Woman shot him a withering glare. "Who are you, hunter, to advise the war chief?"

"He's my husband," Soft Cloth said, stepping forward.

"Well, woman, our Matron has been taken, and that supersedes any attack on First Moon Mountain. Besides, the situation here has changed. If the First People took Whistle, they know everything." Crow Woman turned to Ironwood. "He would have talked rather than endure Leather Hand's torture." Even as she said it, her face blanched, and she turned away.

What was that all about? Bad Cast wondered.

Soft Cloth, fuming now, started forward, lifting a finger to launch into Crow Woman. Bad Cast held his breath as he interposed a warning hand. One could never predict results when dealing with enraged women. Fortunately, Soft Cloth stopped short.

"Easy," Wrapped Wrist said in a calming voice. "We're all on the same side here. The smartest thing that's been said is that we go somewhere and think this through. Hasty action now could lead to disaster, whatever action is finally chosen."

To everyone's relief, it was Orenda who took Ironwood's arm and started him in Bad Cast's direction.

"My choice," Ironwood said woodenly, as if speaking to himself. "Oh, how bitter the gods have made this."

"What choice?" Crow Woman asked.

Ironwood said hollowly, "The Dreamer asked: Do I serve my heart, or my people?"

"Your people," Crow Woman rapped.

"Your heart," Orenda countered, concern on her face as she looked up at Ironwood.

Soft Cloth leaned close, whispering, "Whatever you must do, husband, I am behind you."

Bad Cast anxiously took Soft Cloth's hand, feeling blessed by her love and camaraderie. As much as he loved her, how much more painful was this for Ironwood?

Ironwood stopped suddenly, shaking off Orenda's arm and staring off into the smoke. There, between the trees, stood Ripple, a phantom figure in the haze.

Then, as suddenly, an eddy in the wind obscured his form.

"Yes, Dreamer," Ironwood whispered miserably. "I know. My pride and arrogance have at last come home to curse me." He looked about, face working. "I need no tea, Bad Cast. Let us go back to the council and tell them this news."

Crow Woman asked, "War Chief?"

"Sister Moon's cloak is no blacker than the one around my heart," he said, waving at the smoky heavens. "Prepare yourself, Crow Woman. Our souls and our world hang in the balance."

"You will save the Matron?" Orenda asked.

"She knows the depth and extent of my love. Perhaps someday the world will know what this decision has cost me." Ironwood straightened. "Come. We've a rescue to plan."

Ripple could sense Ironwood's decision. Once again Cold Bringing Woman had gambled well. He smiled wearily to himself as he turned and walked through the trees. They surrounded him like shadows, ghostly gray wreaths of smoke blowing past.

The temperature was dropping, and when he turned his nose to the wind, he could smell the blowing fire as it raced and raged through the thickly forested mountains to the north.

My beautiful world. He had spent most of his youth up in those densely forested slopes. The dark trails that had known his sandal-clad feet were ash now. The creaking trees but black spears that smoked and smol-dered against a flame-streaked sky.

Fire was clearing the way for Cold Bringing Woman.

He remembered cool springs, places where he had bent and touched his lips to drink. The once-crystal waters would still be flowing, choked with ash. He could imagine the streams where trout slipped over the brown mottled rock. They'd be turgid and black, much of the water boiled away. Did anything live there anymore?

My world is dying.

One thing left to endure now.

He glanced over his shoulder, seeing a dark form slipping from tree to tree.

Yes, only one thing.

Chapter Twenty

The morning had dawned gray. Spots and Cactus Flower walked down to Flowing Waters Town with the wind howling from behind. It whistled through the heavy load of firewood that bowed Spots' back and kept trying to blow Cactus Flower's pack around in front of her. Grains of sand stitched their backsides with stinging effect. The combination of wind, the smell of smoke, and the dropping temperature had combined to ensure that few Traders had displayed their wares around the Dusk House walls; and those who did had chosen the lee of the south wall, where they could huddle in the wind shadow.

Only in the far west did any blue remain, while to the southwest, the Rainbow Serpent rose into the sky, curled south, and then merged with the thinning smoke plume.

Spots just had a feeling that it boded ill to see the fires of the north and south merged into one. The eerie feeling that had ridden his Dreams and dogged his bones deepened.

"Must be a terrible fire," Spots muttered. "I hope it's not too close to home."

Cactus Flower staggered under a wind gust. She'd done her hair in twin buns on either side of her head to designate herself a maiden. A split-turkey-feather cloak slapped and floated about her shoulders. "We don't usually have this kind of wind at this time of year. You'd think it was winter."

"Tomorrow's equinox." He glanced up at the sinister heavens. "Sister Moon's coming home. Maybe it's the end of the world?"

"Maybe." She shrugged. "Spots?"

"Yes."

"Why were you so quiet this morning? Every time I tried to get you to laugh, you just stared at the fire. Did I do something?"

"No."

"You're sure?"

He nodded, dread thickening around his heart. "It's not you. Well, yes, it is."

"What did I do?"

"Nothing. Everything." He glanced her way, only to have the wind whip hair around his face. "I want you to know: I have something to do tonight. I have to do it alone, so I'd like you to go back to your house and wait for me there. I'll come if I can."

"This doesn't sound like you. What are you doing? It involves that witch, doesn't it?"

"No." He hoped she didn't hear the lie. "It's safe, I promise. And don't even ask if it's another woman. You know better than that."

She pursed her lips in that familiar way, then said, "I never did believe you were here just because. You arrived just after the witch. In fact, I'd swear I saw you walk in with her the day before. I see most everybody who comes through the gate."

"Will you promise to wait for me at your house?"

"Why should I?"

"Because I want you to." He sighed. "That's the problem. I want you to be away from this. Safe."

"Safe? You're not going to kill anyone, are you?"

"No!"

"Are you going to steal something?"

Only the Blessed Sun's souls!

He forced himself to sound reasonable. "No one's property is in danger. I just have to give something to someone and then see that she's safely out of Flowing Waters Town. That's all. After that, I'll do whatever you want me to. Perhaps go off to Trade with the Hohokam. I don't care."

"I want to help you."

"I'll Trade you. A week's worth of firewood. Whatever you want, for as long as you want it. Just promise me you'll stay home tonight."

"This thing must be very important to you."

"It is." Besides, if doing this got him killed, it wouldn't matter what he'd promised.

Choices.

She was silent until they dropped down the hill to the earthen berm behind Dusk House. He could see the high balcony that ran the length of the third floor. This day no people lounged there. The doorways were blocked off. Only a few water jars stood on the clay-packed surface.

"I'll be there for you," Cactus Flower said. "But you worry me. What if someone finds out what you're doing?"

He made a face. "I might have to leave for a while. Go home. I wouldn't want you to get blamed."

She'd pinched her lower lip, eyes wary. "You're not going to bring the Red Shirts down on top of you?"

"No, nothing like that." He hoped.

"Gods, Spots! What kind of trouble are you in?"

"Helping an old friend, nothing more. It's not like I'm declaring war on the First People." Or was it? "I just have to attend to a duty, that's all."

She gave a toss of her head that he'd come to know as irritation. "Sure. Well, pay no attention to me. It's none of my business."

"That's right," he added somewhat coldly, hoping she'd be so angered she'd ignore him for the rest of the day.

"Rat dung!" she spat. "You're as cold as this wind. You'd think it was winter instead of equinox."

He sniffed, smelling the windblown smoke that streamed down from the north. What was happening up there?

They waved to the guard as they entered the southeastern gate. On this day, Spots wouldn't have much trouble selling firewood.

Mid-Sun Town had been precisely located atop Juniper Ridge. It lay in direct line between the watchtower, the sipapu, and the spot where Father Sun rose on the equinox horizon. The town should have been a hive of ceremonial activity. On this day, with the clan elders imprisoned atop First Moon Mountain, with blowing smoke and rapidly falling temperatures, it was a gloomy and depressed place.

Normally people gathered on the rim, watching for the equinox sunrise as it gleamed over the distant watchtower and then onto Mid-Sun Town's mud-plastered buildings.

Few had ventured out into the choking smoke to leave pahos on the high rimrock.

Then the meeting with Ironwood had been called in the Soft Earth kiva. Those people who could had congregated there. From where he sat Wrapped Wrist could cock his head and hear the shouting and argument inside the kiva. He longed to be there, to hear what the clans were deciding.

Instead he stood just outside the Black Shale kiva, keeping an eye on the door as Ironwood met with Yucca Sock and Crow Woman. The big kiva had been the only place large enough for Ironwood to assemble his warriors. Now Wrapped Wrist and Bad Cast strolled casually around the perimeter, ensuring that no one intruded.

"You saw Ripple this morning?"

"I did." Bad Cast gestured off toward the rimrock. "He was out there at dawn. Wrapped Wrist, I'm worried. He wasn't himself."

Wrapped Wrist snorted irritably. "Are any of us?"

"No, perhaps not." Bad Cast shook his head. "And where has Spots disappeared to? For all we know, the Mountain Witch has stolen his souls, left his dead corpse by the side of the trail."

"Who knows?" Wrapped Wrist coughed and

sniffed in the smoke. "What was it about Ripple? I need to see him, ask him things."

"He was...I don't know, wistful and sad. Resigned to his fate. It wasn't anything he said, just a sense."

Wrapped Wrist nodded. "Whistle and the elders have been captured. The First People know our plans. Leather Hand has taken Night Sun." He glanced uneasily at the Soft Earth Moiety kiva. "The way they're arguing in there, our people are fraying about the edges. Everything that could has gone wrong. Ripple knows it. Now Ironwood's gone into council with his warriors to plan this rescue?"

Bad Cast nodded. "So, Cold Bringing Woman was wrong? What are we going to do?"

"Try to survive, just like Ripple is going to have to." He glanced at Bad Cast. "You know, don't you, that neither one of us can stay here now. After the First Moon Ceremony, the First People are going to come down off that mountain. They're going to be looking for us. All of us. Anyone that had anything to do with Ripple's vision and Ironwood."

Bad Cast missed a step, shock registering on his face. "That's what he meant. Ripple, I mean. He said I had to take Soft Cloth and leave."

Wrapped Wrist took a deep breath. "I want you to think of something else. What if Cold Bringing Woman was working with the Flute Player all along? What if her vision was meant to bring us all to disaster?"

"You mean she used Ripple to destroy us?" Bad Cast made a face. "But why?"

A scream was followed by a smacking impact in the trees just east of the plaza.

Wrapped Wrist wheeled, turning to run, his darts

gripped in his left hand. He rounded a ramada and dodged through the trees. The gloomy smoke obscured anything more than a couple of body lengths away.

Bad Cast was off to one side, keeping him in sight as they hurried in the direction of the rim. Yes, the shout had come from here, somewhere. He could hear questions being called back and forth in the plaza behind them.

Bad Cast made a questioning gesture, and Wrapped Wrist pointed. A wreath of denser smoke blew past. The effect was eerie: warm smoke mixed with cooler, clearer air. He might have been in a Dream land, the trees ghostly, somehow unreal.

He stopped just in time to hear clothing rasp on rock ahead of him. Dropping to a crouch, he started forward, nocking a dart in his atlatl.

Bad Cast had matched his pace, eyes searching the trees.

At first the shape didn't register; it looked like a hunched beast. Then the man straightened from the body he bent over.

Wrapped Wrist stepped forward, lifting his atlatl and dart. "Stop where you are," he called, closing the distance.

To his surprise, the man spun, and in that instant leaped for him.

Wrapped Wrist's release was instinctive. The hurried cast drove the dart through the assailant's shoulder, causing him to whirl. The man staggered, raised a war club, and bellowed.

Wrapped Wrist dropped his atlatl, catching the man's upraised arm. He grabbed a handful of fabric, lifting with his considerable strength, and threw the fellow over his shoulder.

The assailant arched, then slammed into the unforgiving rock with a jarring thud.

"You all right?" Bad Cast asked as he ran up.

"Fine." Wrapped Wrist realized he'd started to pant; his arms were shaking. "What is it with me and people?" He gestured to the moaning man. "Keep an eye on him."

Then he stepped over to the prone form, squinted, and bent down.

Ripple's skull leaked blood from the crown. More blood seeped from the jagged slash in his neck.

"By the gods!" Black Bush cried as he arrived, panting. "What's happened here?"

"It's the Trader," Bad Cast said, retrieving the man's war club. "The one called Takes Falls." He drove the head of the war club into the man's shoulder. "Why? Why did you do this?"

The man screamed as Bad Cast's blow landed on the broken dart shaft. He grabbed his bleeding shoulder, crying, "For turquoise, you fool! The Matron will pay anyone who can deliver his head!"

Wrapped Wrist stood, a feeling of despair rising in his souls. "Ripple's dead. The Trader was trying to cut his head off."

Word passed like from lip to lip as people hurried to the scene. "The Prophet is dead!" "They've killed the Dreamer!"

In the dim gloom of evening, Priest Water Bow stepped up onto the third-floor roof of Pinnacle Great House and squinted into the north. The Sunwatcher, Blue Racer, stood there, his long form wrapped in a blanket against the bitter chill. He, too, watched the flames. They could see spot fires burning on the other side of the valley.

Throughout the day, runners had come bearing news about the fire. At first it had blown southward, forming a long and sinuous front. Reports came in of walls of flame that literally blasted down the mountain valleys. High winds carried burning ash and glowing cinders that lit more fires in advance of the flames. By the time the wall of fire caught up, they'd been fanned into conflagrations of their own.

One runner reported the fate of a colleague. He had observed the man fleeing down a mountain trail on the next ridge. A fleet runner, the fire had proved faster, engulfing him and even a small band of panicked elk. The runner had never seen fire move so fast; he'd sprinted from the area, energized by a panic of his own.

"Will it stop?" Blue Racer asked.

"It should," Water Bow replied with a certainty he didn't feel. "This cold will help. The fire will slow, burrowing deep into dry wood. Perhaps by morning the winds will cease. If they do, the valley will protect First Moon Mountain. We have water on two sides, and exposed shale on the other."

Blue Racer puffed his irritation. "I cast the auspices four times atop Spider Woman's Butte. In none of the auguries did I see this. From the alignment of the Star People as well as the casting of the bones, Sister Moon's homecoming should have met with fair weather."

Water Bow could see his condensed breath. "This feels more like snow than anything."

"How would you tell?" Blue Racer asked. He indicated the blowing ash that slowly spiraled out of the darkening night sky. "As it is, Sister Moon will rise between the pillars this night, but no one will see her. Not with a murky black sky like this. Even sunset has been cloaked."

"Will you conduct the welcoming ceremonies?"

Blue Racer shrugged. "I haven't decided. If we can't see Sister Moon, she surely can't see us. What's the point of welcoming her if she remains ignorant of our greetings?"

Water Bow wasn't sure how to reply to that. He glanced down the slope where the Eagle's Fist was just barely visible. Beyond that, people crowded the mountain below. Most were Made People, relatives of the ridge inhabitants whom the warriors had allowed to pass Guest House. As the temperature dropped, their numbers had declined in favor of warm fires in accommodating pit houses.

"Blazes," Burning Smoke muttered as he climbed up from below. He squinted into the wind and wrapped his cloak around his body against the bitter cold. "You'd think this was winter solstice instead of equinox."

"I've been hearing that all day," Blue Racer said caustically.

"We having a ceremony?" Burning Smoke asked.

For a long moment, Blue Racer considered, then shook his head. "I'm not sure if we should or not. I hate having to wait. The Blessed Sun has expressed his strongest interest that we ensure the ceremonies are a success."

"That's assuming we're not battling fires on the slope below us tomorrow night." He looked down at the thick forest on the northern slope. Gods, if that caught, it would roast anyone on the summit like a rabbit on a stick.

Burning Smoke wiped a hand over his face, smudging the soot that had accumulated there.

Hands, faces, clothes—ash and soot coated everything. Water Bow's once snowy white robes would have to be sent down and thoroughly washed in the rivers, assuming the waters ever ran clean again. Just that afternoon Matron Larkspur had poured a cup from a freshly obtained water jar, only to find the water dark with ash. For the next while they would be drinking from the storage jars.

The war chief turned his attention to the stone pillars. In the faint light, they loomed as mere shadows in the thick haze. "As the night darkens, I'm not sure your Priests will be able to see each other. It's going to be black as pitch. And with this wind, torches will blow out. If we light bonfires, the gusts will blow the fire sideways."

Blue Racer hugged himself for warmth. "Nevertheless, we shall Dance tonight. But the last thing I want is for one of my people to be blown over the cliff, or to fall just because he couldn't see in this miserable gloom."

Burning Smoke jerked a curt nod. "Very well, I'll alert the guards." He turned, stocky frame disappearing as he descended the ladder.

"Time for a hot drink," Blue Racer said. "I'd better warm my heart as often as I can these days. If it keeps up like this, the gods alone know how soon the Blessed Sun is going to want to cut it out."

Water Bow nodded, thankful to escape the cold. How could the fire keep burning when it felt ever more like freezing? "The gods pity those poor guards on a night like this."

"They're the lucky ones," Blue Racer rejoined. "They can just cover themselves in their blankets and doze."

Gods, it was cold! In the darkness beneath the trees, Bad Cast could barely make out the seated forms of Ironwood's warriors. Everyone crouched under his blanket and wore his warmest clothes. Yucca Sock, Firehorn, Two Teeth, and Right Hand sat close to the war chief, their heads bent. Warriors were looking uneasily at Ironwood in the gloom. Conversations were whispered, everyone in a dark mood after Ripple's death.

No one was sure what to believe, or if this was just more madness driven by the end of the world.

Off to one side, Wrapped Wrist sat close beside Crow Woman. The way they huddled, it seemed to be more than just pre-raid camaraderie. Bad Cast had seen more than one speculative glance cast their way, at least until Crow Woman shot back with a hot glare.

The other warriors waited, some shivering as they fingered their bows, checked arrows, and hefted their war clubs.

What am I doing here? Bad Cast had to wonder. He carried his atlatl and an axe. He had never considered himself a warrior. Truth be told, he barely made it as a hunter. Sneaking around in silence had never seen him at his best.

"All right," Ironwood said, rising. "I need you to hear my final orders. This is a rescue first and foremost. The Moon People elders wouldn't have been taken were it not for my initiating contact. They are our responsibility."

The warriors shifted, some nodding, others watching with wooden expressions. They would follow their war chief, no matter what they thought of his motives.

Ironwood continued. "Bad Cast knows a trail that will lead us up the slope. When we reach the rimrock, we will stop. Bad Cast will climb up first, making sure of the route. Yucca Sock will follow and take care of any guard he finds up there. At his signal, we will climb one by one. The place we've chosen isn't that difficult, but taking shields will be too cumbersome. Leave them here. Those of us who live will return for them."

Ironwood reached out. "Friends, companions, we have shared so much. Now, like yours, my heart is worried sick. We don't know if your wives or children are alive or dead. Tonight, we will strike a blow in retaliation for them.

"I want you to think!" He smacked a fist into a hard palm. "Our first goal is to free the captive elders. Our second is to take First People for hostages. If you kill all of the First People, we will have nothing left to bargain with. Do you understand? We can Trade Matron Larkspur, or Blue Racer, or Water Bow for Night Sun and our women and children."

Grunts of assent were muttered around the dark circle.

"Good." Ironwood clapped his hands together. "Next thing: We have no support from the First Moon

People. I can't blame them. Their Prophet is dead. They can't take the chance of having their elders killed, or even face the Blessed Sun's retaliation." He paused. "We are on our own. We have no one but ourselves to depend on."

More grunts sounded, and Bad Cast could just make out the shadowy warriors as they touched hands and thumped each other's shoulders, a physical demonstration of their solidarity.

"This night," Ironwood's voice dropped, "is a gift from Cold Bringing Woman. I still believe in Ripple's vision. I think it is she who has blown this dark wind down from the north."

"As long as she doesn't blow the fire into this forest," Yucca Sock added warily. "We could be burned to a crisp before we reach the summit."

"On your feet," Ironwood ordered. "Keep the noise to a minimum. If they hear us, if someone has betrayed us...well, fight like the fury—but run faster."

Nervous chuckles broke out.

"Bad Cast?" Ironwood asked. "Can you lead the way?"

"Follow me." A terrible weight had settled in his chest. Step after step, he placed his feet and started up the dark slope. Behind him, Ironwood tried to place his feet in Bad Cast's tracks.

Find the trail by the lightning-riven tree!

Bad Cast hadn't expected the blowing smoke, the inky darkness of the gloom. Behind him, warriors coughed, their throats smoke-tight and lungs clogged.

Overhead, the trees waved and thrashed as the cold north wind ripped through the timber. Bad Cast muttered under his breath. Any fear of the coming fighting vanished as he waged his own battle with dark branches, slanting deadfall, and treacherous footing. Worse, what if he lost his way?

"Here," he said, indicating a handhold, or, "Watch your foot. Step inside of the log here."

It seemed an eternity later that he found himself panting, half-winded. He stared up into the black tangle of fir, pine, and spruce. How far had they gone? Where was the summit? It seemed they'd been climbing all night.

"Bad Cast?" Ironwood asked, a darker question in his voice.

"It has to be above us somewhere, War Chief." He wiped his face, feeling the dryness of soot, the grit from the forest. Then he resumed his ascent, testing his footing, pulling himself up with branches, scrambling ever upward. Behind him, the line of warriors kept climbing.

Over the wind in the trees, Bad Cast could hear them, wood knocking on wood, the rattle of arrows. Sometimes a person slipped, a curse under his breath. Sticks snapped under misplaced weight. The warriors kept coughing from the smoke.

They couldn't hear that up above, could they?

Bad Cast's dire imagination filled the heights with armed Red Shirts, each with a nocked arrow or a perched boulder, just ready to rain death down on the foolish little band that dared to scale the impregnable heights. He kept seeing Ripple's expression, one of longing, his dead eyes wide, blood dripping from his head and neck.

Did you see that coming? Was that why you looked so resigned this morning?

Bad Cast blinked away a sudden tear, wondering at the grief that threatened to flood his breast.

A stone broke loose, and someone gasped in pain before the rock crashed down into the trees.

"Who's hurt?" Ironwood hissed over his shoulder. The question was whispered down the line.

"Thorn Petal," came the whispered reply up the line. "The stone knocked him off his feet. He's fallen into a tree."

"Go." The hissed command went back down the line. "Thorn Petal will catch up if he can."

Ironwood tapped Bad Cast on the back, and the relentless climb continued. A branch slapped him in the face, and painful grit smarted behind his eyes.

If I could just see!

Instead he worked his way up, making his way by feel. When he couldn't brace his foot on a stone or fallen log, he had to dig his sandaled feet into the thick duff. Needles pricked and pierced the tender skin between his toes. Often his first foothold collapsed, and more than once Ironwood stopped him from sliding down atop the others.

More to the left.

Bad Cast hesitated. The voice had sounded like Ripple's, merged with the wind in the trees. He began edging to his left.

Onward they climbed, the slope getting even steeper, more dangerous. When his foot slipped, and he skidded down onto Ironwood, the war chief braced him. "Easy. Don't rush. If we start a landslide, they'll know we're coming."

Bad Cast filled his lungs, puffing in the cold air. His fingers were growing numb. Once again he put himself to the task. Hand, foot, hand, foot. Test the toehold, step. Feel around for sticks. Check for loose rocks that could roll underfoot. Hand, foot, hand, foot.

Something wet landed on the back of his neck. Water? Gods, it couldn't be raining, could it?

He glanced up at the blackness; the wind was still slashing through the trees. They were creaking and grinding, covering the sounds of die climbers. Well, for that, at least, he could be thankful.

She comes!

Bad Cast swore he heard Ripple's glad cry.

Something else cold and wet spattered on his shirt. He could smell it now: the damp scent of soot. Snake's blood, they had to hurry. If it rained, every piece of wood would become slick; the rocks, already treacherous, would make each handhold precarious. Fingers growing numb from cold would add to the danger.

He pulled himself past the thick trunk of a fir tree and felt the wind twirling in the night. And what was this? He tilted his cheek, aware that something light pattered down around him. He caught one on his tongue, tasting water and soot.

"Snow!" he whispered in disbelief.

"Snow?" Ironwood asked, confused.

"It's snowing," Bad Cast affirmed, and scrambled up on all fours before his fingers encountered wet sandstone. He felt his way up, could see the blacker rock against the night sky.

The rimrock!

He bent down, whispering, "Shhhh! They're right above us." But where was he? How close to one of the cracked chutes that could be scaled to the ridgetop?

"Fire and ice!" He barely heard Ripple's call over the storm. "Cold Bringing Woman has come for us."

Bad Cast started along the rim, feeling his way, hearing dirt and stones as they periodically rolled down into the trees. He could feel the snow as the wind swept it around him. The cold had increased, and he could hardly feel his wet fingers.

He stopped, exploring a crack in the rock. Yes, here he could find a foothold. "Rope?" he whispered. Moments later Ironwood passed him a coil of braided leather that he hung around his neck and shoulder. Bad Cast began to climb.

He levered himself up, searching for a handhold. His wet, numb fingers clawed at the rough stone, found purchase, and he muscled himself up another half body length.

"Well?" Ironwood whispered, his voice hidden in the wind.

"Wait." Bad Cast grimaced as his sandal slipped off the rock. In desperation, he kicked it off, using his toes, and gained another half body length. A strong gust of wind plastered his back with snow and almost tore him from his hold.

He reached up, grasped the rim, and pulled. Sandstone crumbled in his hand. At the last moment, he saved himself, but heard a soft thump, and a grunt as the rock dropped onto whomever waited below.

"Are you all right?" he called softly.

"I'll live," a hoarse growl answered. "Climb. Then toss the rope down."

He stuffed a fist into a vertical crack, lifted, and swung a bare foot onto the rim. He toppled onto his side, blinking and panting. Snowflakes pattered onto his face, melting, and trickling down his skin. To the north, half-hidden in the storm, a wicked red gleam marked the fire.

Fire and ice. He shook his head. Ripple had been shown the future. Bad Cast pulled himself upright, unslung the rope from his shoulder, and tossed one end down. He felt a hand give a tug, and braced himself.

Dearest gods, don't let my grip slip.

Everything depended on him.

Chapter Twenty-One

They had taken Night Sun to the old Red Lacewing kiva, a large cylindrical room built into the third story of Talon Town. Turquoise Fox had preceded Leather Hand, having a large bonfire kindled in the fire pit. The floor and benches had been plastered in a deep red, the upper walls in white. On the pilasters between the pole-shelved niches, images of the thlatsinas had been painted. Rendered by Sternlight's own hand, they had graced the walls since Crow Beard's day.

Leather Hand studied one—the Long Horn thlatsina—and stepped up to it. He gave Night Sun a sidelong glance, then spit on the image.

She just continued to stare at him as if he were some detestable insect.

To his men, he said, "Destroy these."

He stepped back, watching as his warriors attacked the images, raining blow after blow onto the hated thlatsinas with their war clubs and stone-headed axes. He had found a room full of snowy white capes, which, given the frigid temperatures, his man had adopted with appreciation. In the process, he had allowed them to ransack some of the storerooms, decking themselves with jewelry the likes of which they would never have been allowed otherwise. Loyalty deserved to be rewarded.

"Your gods are dying, Night Sun," he said evenly. "As they go, so, too, shall you."

She looked around. "Where is my grandson?"

"He came to me earlier today, saying that he had heard of a special room. A place here in Talon Town where the most wondrous treasure had been hidden."

"Anything in this building belongs to the Red Lacewing Clan."

"I am Red Lacewing; you are Outcast." He smiled, hearing steps on the kiva roof. He looked up as a large fabric bag came tumbling down the ladder. It clattered to a stop over the sipapu in the northern floor. Ravenfire's sandaled feet came stamping down the rungs.

"I found them!" he cried. "Just where Poor Singer said they'd be." He leaped the last three rungs to the floor, grinning maniacally.

Leather Hand watched the tightening of Night Sun's expression. He'd purposely kept the two of them separated while he and Turquoise Fox worked on Ravenfire. The young man was desperate for special recognition. When he'd asked to go in search of something he'd heard tell of in Ironwood's camp, Leather Hand had immediately dispersed Fast Fist to accompany him.

"So, you found them?" Leather Hand asked. He glanced around; his men were finishing the job of mutilating the wall paintings. The timing was perfect.

Ravenfire had a smug look on his face as he untied a cord that bound the bag and upended it. A pile of wooden masks clattered onto the hard-packed floor.

They were beautiful, painted in bright colors with striking eagle, macaw, and hawk feathers. Some had long noses, others white-rimmed eyes or gaping toothy mouths. One—covered with fitted pieces of turquoise, coral, and jet—gleamed in the light.

"Blessed gods," Turquoise Fox whispered. "Look at the wealth they represent!"

Leather Hand made a face, his gut crawling as the obscene masks stared up at him. Then he glanced at Ravenfire. How committed was the young man to his new life and friends?

"Burn them," Leather Hand ordered.

He caught the look of horror on Night Sun's face, the sudden reservation on Ravenfire's. Even Turquoise Fox hesitated, saying, "But War Chief, the turquoise alone—"

"I said, burn them."

He turned, his white cape whirling. He pointed at Night Sun. "Tonight we dedicate ourselves to the task of destroying the thlatsina heresy. You, woman, were as much responsible as anyone. And since I don't have Sternlight here to atone for this blasphemy, you will."

"I will do nothing you ask of me." Night Sun lifted her chin defiantly.

"Cut the cords that bind her," Leather Hand ordered as several of his warriors bent and began pitching the gorgeous masks into the central fire.

"She no doubt Dreams of escape, of slipping away in the night." He was watching Ravenfire's expression as he said, "Tonight, Matron Night Sun, you will Dance atop the burning thlatsinas. After this night, you will never walk again."

Ravenfire only swallowed. He looked slightly ill as two warriors prodded Night Sun forward; then one shoved her into the fire pit, her bare feet stumbling over the burning masks.

She tried to flee, but with each step she took, the ring of warriors pushed her back.

Even when the smell of her burning flesh began to fill the air, Ravenfire's expression remained strained, but not sympathetic.

Perhaps he is suited to be one of us?

Through it all, Night Sun locked eyes with his, as if her souls were untouched by the pain she had to be feeling.

Very well. He could always raise the stakes.

Dusk bore down on Flowing Waters Town, the sky black and cross. The smell of smoke had intensified while tiny black flecks of ash drifted down from the surly sky.

Spots crouched, his blanket around his shoulders, and wondered if it was the end of the world. A couple of sticks of firewood remained. His pile would have been gone by midday but for the horrendous return he asked for each piece.

People had been wary. He'd seen it in their eyes, felt that sense of foreboding as the wind sawed at Dusk House's tall bulk, prodded at the doorways, and whistled around the square-cornered rooms.

Each time he glanced over at Nightshade, her dark

eyes were fixed on his. No expression crossed her impassive face, but he could feel her anticipation. The question lay deep behind her eyes.

Yes, I'm here for you.

Spots exhaled worriedly and realized his breath was white before his mouth. Gods, how cold was it going to get? Worse, the old woman was still naked, her thin bones having no protection against the increasing chill. People were staying inside, walking quickly, with wraps around their shoulders when they had to travel outside.

The circular bulk of the great kiva resembled a big head, vaults like eyes, the entrance a square muzzle with a yawning mouth. Atop the southeast gate, the guard huddled under his blanket, looking particularly glum. His expression left no doubt about his misery. The guard on the southwestern gate looked similarly preoccupied as he shivered in his war shirt. When he'd come to take his place, he'd been poorly dressed, having given no thought to the fact the chill would intensify.

"It's almost dark," Cactus Flower said from where she huddled in the next doorway. "Let's just go home, Spots. Whatever you have to do, wait until the weather's nicer."

"I can't." He stepped out, shivered, and walked to where she'd taken shelter. Wind Baby had nipped up the corners of her blanket, mostly covering her pile of shells, jet bracelets, and locally made ceramic jars with their pretty black-on-white patterns.

She shook her head, a sober reserve in her eyes. "It smells like snow. You don't want to be out in this."

He smiled. "Would you do me the greatest of favors?"

She tilted her head. "In return for what?"

"Me."

"What do you mean, you?"

"Will you go back to your farmstead, fix a warm dinner, and eat it? Then I want you to go to bed and have the covers warm for me when I show up. I don't know how long I will be, but when I do finally get there, I will be yours for as long as you want me."

"You will be mine?"

He nodded. "To do whatever you want. To stay here and farm if you wish, or to go on the road, Trading where we will. I would be happy to continue fetching firewood for Trade here just as we've been doing. You decide, and I will agree to it."

"Assuming you live through this?"

He shrugged.

"You know," she told him, "the Blessed Matron suspected a young man and his dog of aiding a witch who was cursing people by using bits of buffalo fur soaked in menstrual blood. She had that young man walled up in one of the interior rooms. People said they could hear the little dog scratching at the walls for days."

"I'm not cursing anyone."

"Can you imagine what that must have been like?" Cactus Flower asked, looking past him to Nightshade's cage. "Slowly dying of thirst in the dark, all the sound deadened by the thick floors and walls." She paused. "Do you think in the last days he clawed at the walls? It's been said that people will rake their fingernails off in desperation."

"Go home, Cactus Flower." Spots smiled gently. "I will be there as soon as I can. Then, well, you decide.

You may even grow tired of me and decide to go back to your old life."

She gave an irritated shake of the head. "You're not going to be talked out of this, are you?"

"What good would my word to you be if it weren't good to anyone else? Oh, and take my Trade. I got a nice piece of turquoise today."

He helped her pick up her things and fill her pack. When she was ready, he gave her a final hug, relishing the feel of her cold body against his. In a last act, he brushed his lips across her forehead.

"Take care, Spots," she said with resignation, and he watched her walk through the southeast gate. The guard didn't react to her wave.

Spots took a deep breath, picked up his blanket, and folded it into a square. Taking the knife from his belt pouch, he slipped it between the folds of the blanket and had a final look around. Both guards seemed completely oblivious to anything but shivering.

Spots walked forward, passing by the side of the cage as if on his way to the kiva entrance. He hesitated beside the thick poles only long enough to slip the blanket inside.

"Cold Bringing Woman comes," Nightshade said from within. "It's our night, Spots. Wait for me in the kiva entrance."

He continued on his way, the gloom of evening darkening around him. Several of the remaining Traders had packed their goods and were walking out of the plaza, tossing waves to the guards.

Did they keep track? Were they aware that Spots had remained? He'd never seen them keep a count of who went in and out, and besides, the numbers of people passing was large. Who was to say if someone came in one way, and left through the other gate?

He could see Nightshade's dark figure as she sawed at the ropes that secured the door to her cage. Moments later the old woman stepped out, the blanket over her head. She hobbled toward him, ducking into the shelter of the kiva entrance.

"I swear, my joints have stiffened during my days in there."

He sniffed, wincing at her odor.

"Come," she said evenly. "There will be water in the Priests' room behind the altar."

"We can't go there! It's forbidden!"

She snorted derisively. "Who's going to notice? It's equinox. All the Priests are out Blessing the fields in preparation for the final moon before harvest. None will be back within the walls for another hand of time."

Heart in his throat, Spots followed Nightshade down the stairs, across the great kiva floor, past the altar, and behind the screens. She made her way slowly up the northern stairs into the Priests' room.

Spots peered around in the gloom. Large cedar boxes held different costumes. Masks hung from pegs on the wall. It seemed to Spots that the black eye holes were watching his every move with displeasure.

"Here." Nightshade removed a wooden lid from a large water jar. She used a piece of cloth taken from one of the boxes and began sponging herself. The air picked up the odor of damp excrement.

"I'm sorry, Elder," Spots whispered. "There was nothing I could do. It was hard enough to sneak you food and water."

"You did just fine, young hunter. More than I

would have hoped for. The filth is only on the outside, and the body but a husk." He could see her smile. "What counts is in the souls. Look at yourself. That pretty young woman has seen past your scars. Your courage, humility, and kindness spoke to the longing and loneliness in her life. In you she found a part of herself that was missing. You made her whole, as she made you."

"She wasn't lonely," he pointed out. "She had men there all the time."

"Is that what you think? That a warm body beneath the blankets is company? For her it was only illusion, the image of what life should be. Then you came along with the real thing and she'll never be happy until she finds it again."

He wasn't sure he believed that.

Nightshade continued sponging herself and asked, "Could you pick that jar up? I want you to pour it slowly over my head so I can rinse all of me clean."

He picked up the heavy jug and hesitated. "It will splash all over!"

"After this night, that will be the least of the Priests' worries."

He did as directed, feeling the water splattering against his legs and feet as she washed her hair and wrung out the last of the water. A long white robe served her for a towel before she dropped it to the floor to dry her feet. Then one by one she picked through the robes, finding a short white tunic. In a box she discovered buffalo socks and yucca sandals that fit her feet. Fingering through the garments she took down a beautiful macaw-feather cloak that hung down almost to her knees. Finally she picked a particularly gruesome mask from the wall. She held the piece at arm's length, staring at the white-rimmed eye holes, at the long muzzle and wicked-looking teeth. Stringy gray hair had been pasted to the domed skull.

"That's hideous," Spots said, backing away.

"Soyok is meant to be hideous."

"Soyok?"

"You call her the Blue God."

"You'd better put that back."

"Oh, no," she whispered. "The gods of terror and I go way back. For tonight's purposes, the Blue God is just right." Then she bent, rummaging through several more boxes for items Spots could barely make out in the gloom.

She straightened, head back, eyes closed, and took a deep breath. Was it his imagination, or did she swell, expand, a renewed vitality radiating from her?

He could imagine her as she once had been: a raven-haired beauty, eyes flashing, Power like lightning crackling from her fingertips. No wonder the Mound Builders had stolen her away. And who knew how the world would have been changed had she stayed to rule the Straight Path Nation?

"Come, Spots. The time has come to begin the Dance." She didn't look back as she walked regally toward the doorway that led out onto the plaza. "Let us unleash the Power of the Blue God!"

Deputy Sunwatcher Water Bow sat on his most beautiful rug: a piece woven with yellow, black, red, brown, and white interlocking diamonds. The thick wool cushioned his old bones from the hard floor of the First People's kiva. Fortunately for him, he'd managed to stay warm for the most part. It had been Blue Racer and his Priests who'd born the brunt of the storm as they'd called the Blessing to Sister Moon. Most of it had been torn away as Wind Baby howled over First Moon Mountain, pelting the procession first with ash and cinders, then with brutal cold that numbed the bones, and finally finished the ceremony off with driving flakes of soot-encrusted snow.

Even as he stared around the brightly lit kiva, the effects of the weather were obvious. Everyone's clothing was blackened; some, who'd been afforded less protection by their robes, had black-streaked faces where they'd rubbed at the wet soot sticking to their skin.

No one had been happier to beat a retreat to the warm kiva than Blue Racer. The Blessed Sunwatcher sat before the crackling fire, his hands out, long face pensive and worried. And well he ought to worry. Who had ever heard of such a terrible storm so early? The Sunwatcher had chanted less than half of the Blessing before people broke and ran for shelter. The four lines of Priests behind him didn't look any too happy either.

Matron Larkspur was sitting to the side, War Chief Burning Smoke just behind her shoulder. She was one of the ones who'd smeared soot when she wiped away the melting snow. To her right, Deputy Ravengrass had a dower look. He was responsible for the security of the First People's party while at First Moon Mountain.

"The storm worries me." Blue Racer placed another piece of firewood into the blaze. "I cast the auguries four times. The weather was supposed to hold. I can't believe that the Flute Player would allow this to happen to us."

"The gods have their own ways," Water Bow reminded. "And do not fear for the weather. At this time of year it is not uncommon for a storm to blow through. Tomorrow it will be warm, sunny, and all shall go well. You will see. And do not chide the Flute Player. But for this storm, the fire might have jumped the valley, and had it done so, we would now be fleeing the fire's wrath, not just enduring a little snow."

"The flakes are black," Ravengrass said in amazement. "In all of my life, I have never seen black snow."

"And with luck," Larkspur added, "you never will again. My concern is the harvest. The valley is literally bursting with corn."

"It will not last," Water Bow predicted. "And what we feel here, atop the mountain, is much colder than the valley bottom. When snow blows here, it falls as rain below."

"You don't seem concerned," Blue Racer said warily.

Water Bow kept his mocking smile in check. After all, it behooved Blue Racer to worry. His heart was on the line if the weather didn't break. "Blessed Sunwatcher, you bear too many responsibilities on your weary shoulders. We have asked for rain, and this storm is a good one. You forget you are atop a tall mountain. Were I you, I would send the Blessed Sun a message telling him the Flute Player has brought moisture. If anything this is a further affirmation that the Flute Player has forgiven his people."

"We have neutralized any threat," Larkspur added. "Even as we speak, Leather Hand should be leading

Matron Night Sun into the safety of Straight Path Canyon. He will be laying his trap there, awaiting the arrival of Ironwood. The Outcast war chief's warren of vermin has been cleaned out. Neither can we forget the other service that Leather Hand has done us: We have the First Moon elders locked away under our guard. The local population dares try nothing against us. Everything is happening in our favor."

Water Bow couldn't stop his dry smile. Fortunately, no one interpreted its true nature. He'd been out at midnight the night before Leather Hand left to hunt down Ironwood. Unable to sleep after hearing Whistle's screams, he'd gone to check the moonrise. He'd walked in the shadow cast by one of the stone pillars and had approached the signal fire when he heard a woman's panting.

On the verge of calling out, he'd heard a man grunt and the rustle of cloth on stone.

Water Bow had stopped, unwilling to intrude on what was a private moment.

"Gods." Larkspur's throaty whisper had barely carried to Water Bow's straining ears. "I miss a man's hard staff."

"There is always opportunity in the wind."

"How is that?"

"You and I work very well together, Matron."

"Is that ambition, Deputy?"

"You have Desert Willow's confidence, and you are in line to be Matron of the First People should anything happen to her."

"She's young."

"So are you."

"I'm married."

A pause.

"Do you love him?"

"How could I? I haven't seen him for seasons on end. He's not an imaginative man. There's a reason Webworm sent him south. He follows orders, but thinking is too trying for him."

"I see."

"And?"

"You think a great deal, and you long for more."

Larkspur had shifted. Peering around the tall pile of wood, Water Bow could see her arms where she tightened them around Leather Hand's back. She said, "Tell me, Deputy, if we were to work together, do you think we could achieve more?"

"If our bodies are this good together, think of what the mating of our souls could bring."

"I would like to explore that," she'd whispered, "assuming I was to find myself suddenly without a husband."

Water Bow had eased himself away before Sister Moon could rise high enough to reveal his presence. The next morning he'd seen one of Leather Hand's warriors sneaking out of Pinnacle Great House, a large travel pack on the man's shoulders. To Water Bow's surprise, the man hadn't been wearing his red war shirt, preferring to travel unrecognized.

I wonder how long it will be before Larkspur's husband is found lying in his blankets, his head mysteriously missing?

Now, as he sat in the kiva, he knew Matron Larkspur's cunning smile was based on more than just the weather. For her, things were looking very good indeed.

"We are more secure than we have been in quite

some time," Burning Smoke agreed. "With the elders in captivity, any threat from wild prophecies and possible attacks by Ironwood are nullified. With this moisture, the crops should be abundant. First Moon Valley can contribute even more to the famine relief in the south."

Water Bow watched Larkspur's growing smile. Apparently she was already imagining pack after pack of corn as it was borne out of the valley, headed for Flowing Waters Town. She was seeing another feather for her hair, and an even higher status in Desert Willow's eyes.

Beware Matron Desert Willow. Let us hope that the serpent you have created in Leather Hand does not strike you sometime in the night.

It would, of course. Leather Hand's ambition would only be rivaled by Larkspur's.

"We still have no idea where Ironwood is," Ravengrass said as he looked from face to face. "I first served under him. It doesn't pay to underestimate the man."

"I think we can be assured that he'll be headed south as soon as he hears of Night Sun's capture." Larkspur's eyes had narrowed. "He has surrendered his ambitions for Night Sun before; there is no reason to think he is a different man today than he has always been."

"You must admire him," Water Bow said, curious to elicit her reaction. "It's hard to condemn a man who would sacrifice so much for the woman he loves. Such an undying love is hard to find and should be appreciated."

Her smile was wooden. The kind she'd give a doddering old fool.

"I've half a mind to call the guards in," Burning

Smoke said. "In this weather, they're not going to be able to see an arm's length in any direction. And the Matron's right: With the First People elders in our hands, no one will try anything."

"Do not delude yourself," Ravengrass said. "Until we hear that Ironwood is spotted in the south, we must remain vigilant."

"I have twice the number of men on the ridge below us." Burning Wood insisted. "In this weather, no one could find their way up the slopes. Not even Ironwood is that crazy. Besides, he'd lose half his command to treacherous footing. Those who didn't slip and break bones would be lost within moments of entering that thick timber."

"You're probably right." Ravengrass steepled his fingers, eyes on the leaping fire. "But I'll take a chance on the sentries just in case."

Burning Smoke had a big smile on his face, and said, "Oh, you won't have any worry. Matron Larkspur's right. The Flute Player is on our side. Nothing could go wrong now."

Larkspur had drawn a breath to say something else when a voice outside cried, "Alarm!"

Chapter Twenty-Two

Wrapped Wrist waited his turn in the dark and leaned close to Crow Woman. "How's your knee?" Around them, the trees swayed and thrashed as the storm intensified under the First Moon Mountain rim.

"Stiff and sore," she growled back. "But I'm not missing this."

"Can you climb?"

He heard her swallow hard before she admitted, "I'm not sure. Whatever happens, I've got to get up there. I won't let the others down."

"Wait. When I go up, I'll pull you. All you have to do is keep your grip on the rope and keep from banging your knee on the rocks. No one will know."

He got a quick squeeze from her hand before he turned to the rock face and scrambled up. Like Bad Cast, he'd been climbing since he was a boy. It was just part of growing up in the First Moon Valley. Ready hands pulled him onto the caprock.

"Here," Wrapped Wrist told Yucca Sock. "Let me

do this." He handed the man his atlatl darts, took the braided leather rope, and shook it. He felt Crow Woman take her grip and give him a ready tug.

He stood, bracing himself against the wind, which blew snow and acrid smoke. Gods, the stench of it: wet ash and slush. He knotted his grip and flexed his muscles. Crow Woman wasn't light by any means, but he pulled her up with ease. She caught herself as he lifted her past the rimrock. She swung to the side, getting her feet under her. For a brief instant, she put her arms around him, hugged him, and then vanished into the dark.

"Which way?" Ironwood asked.

Wrapped Wrist squinted in the blackness. Trickles of water from snowflakes stung his eyes. When it ran into his mouth, he could taste soot. Gods, it was cold up here, the wind blowing a blizzard.

"We're but a stone's throw," he said. "Pinnacle Great House is just above us, the Eagle's Fist below."

"I will attend to the Eagle's Fist," Yucca Sock said. "I have business with the First People." He turned, vanishing into the blowing snow.

Wrapped Wrist had bowed his head, letting his shoulder take the brunt of the blizzard. Snow was packing on his side. Amazed, he realized he could see faint images.

"Sister Moon has risen by now," Crow Woman said, voice hollow. "She stares down at the cloud and smoke. She is come home to watch the destruction of our world."

"Let's go," Ironwood ordered. "Pairs of two. First group take the building's west wing; second group with me attacks the east. Remember, we want as many of the

First People taken alive as possible, but your first concern is the rescue and safety of the elders."

Wrapped Wrist stayed close to Crow Woman, trudging against the wind. The big flakes of snow pattered against the side of his face. Any trace of heat had vanished from his claylike flesh. Gods, how could the warriors manage to wield a bow in weather like this? Their fingers had to feel as wooden as his own.

He tapped the atlatl darts he had taken from beside Spots' bed. Thank the Spirits his people remained some of the last holdouts for the atlatl. He could nock and cast no matter how numb his fingers became.

The wall loomed out of the night, dark and foreboding. In the faint storm glow, Wrapped Wrist could see snow beginning to crust on the rocks. A shivering fit left him shaken and miserable.

Then, from the night, a sudden cry: "Alarm!"

Crow Woman hissed. "Hurry up! We're spotted."

Wrapped Wrist pounded his way forward and followed Two Teeth up the stairs onto the first-floor roof. Dark figures were spilling out of the kiva as well as from the lower-floor rooms.

He charged forward, nocking a dart. Before he could use it, a man seemed to rise from the very roof. He heard the whistle of the war club, turned, and took the blow meant for his ribs on the shoulder. At the impact, his entire left arm went numb.

Wrapped Wrist staggered, gasping with pain. He heard the warrior laugh as he stepped in, bringing the war club high. In that instant, a dark shape twisted out of the night; a smacking slap came as Crow Woman drove her war club down on the warrior's suddenly lifted arm. In lightning movements, she literally danced around him, slashing, chopping, and finally crushing the enemy's skull with a snapping blow.

"Thanks," Wrapped Wrist said through gritted teeth.

"Broken?" she asked, crouching beside him, eyes on the wavering figures who fought around them. Was it just Wrapped Wrist's inexperience, or were there a lot of warriors emerging from the rooms?

Wrapped Wrist flexed his elbow and raised his arm. "I don't think it's broken."

"Stay behind me. Watch my back."

"Glad to." It was sobering to think how close he'd just come to death. The fight became a melee of whirling figures, screaming men, and hissing arrows.

Spots could have turned and run—should have bolted like a panicked jackrabbit—but something had kept him walking obediently at Nightshade's heel as she climbed up the tiered levels of Dusk House, into the forbidden territory of the First People.

No one seemed to give her a second glance as she walked regally in the macaw-feather cloak, the hideous mask tucked beneath one arm. She crossed the second-floor roof and climbed to the third. She never hesitated as she turned and walked straight past a guard, the poor fellow huddled under a deer hide cape. He stared out from under his blanket. "Elder? Excuse me. That's the Blessed Sun's room. Do I know you?"

Unconcerned, Nightshade ducked into Webworm's personal quarters.

The guard muttered, stared uncertainly at Spots, and stood while he fumbled for his war club.

The action was instinctive. Spots stepped close, ripped the man's stiletto from his belt, and drove it straight into the warrior's breast. At the same time, he clamped his left hand over the man's throat, squeezing his cry short in his windpipe.

Hot blood spilled over his hand. Within moments the guard's flailing ceased, his body limp in Spots' arms. The man sank, tremors running down his legs and arms.

Spots' own breath came in fast gulps. He shivered and stumbled toward the doorway.

What did I just do? What came over me?

In the Blessed Sun's ornate room, coals glowed in the fire bowl. Spots stared in amazement at his blood-slick hand.

"Come sit," Night Sun whispered.

Spots staggered forward, still in shock. Looking around, he recognized several of the pieces of wood he'd Traded that day in the Blessed Sun's woodpile. Who would have thought? Then, to his amazement, he realized that the form under the blankets was none other than Webworm himself.

He must have looked like a gaping idiot when Nightshade motioned him to be seated atop a pile of buffalo hides that had been stacked against one wall.

I've got to run! I just killed a Red Shirt!

But his muscles had frozen.

Moving quietly, Nightshade retrieved her familiar pack from where it hung on a corner peg. She reached inside and withdrew several pouches. Her long fingers took a pinch of something from one. This she sprinkled atop the glowing coals. A faint but pungent smoke rose from the hearth.

Nightshade lifted a narrow pitcher from beside the bed and poured water into a striking white cup decorated with thin black lines and patterns of dots. Into this she poured yet another potion from one of her little bags. After she removed her shining black bowl, she dipped a thick dab of paste onto her fingertip. This she touched ever so lightly to Webworm's temples. She made a faint grunt of satisfaction.

Spots just stared, wondering what had possessed him to follow her here. Nightshade was inspecting the line of pots and jars. She picked one—a wide-necked black-and-white Green Mesa design with a wooden lid. Raising the lid, she dumped the red cornmeal it contained onto the floor and set the open jar by her side.

Finally, she gave Spots a warning look. "No matter what, say nothing. Do nothing." Then she sat back, donned the hideous mask, and began to chant.

How long they sat there, Spots couldn't say, but periodically Nightshade would reach out to dab more of the datura-laced paste and rub it with ever more vigor onto Webworm's temples. Meanwhile, the wind howled outside, and Spots grew ever more frightened.

Someone will come and find me here. When they do, I am going to die.

In all of his wild nightmares he would never have believed that he would be seated like an idol, terrified to the point of jumping out of his skin, across from the Blessed Sun's bed.

Webworm tossed and turned, mutters and moans coming from deep in his throat.

"That is Sister Datura wrapping her souls around you, Webworm." Nightshade spoke gently. "Let yourself go. Rise and twirl in her arms. Surrender yourself, Webworm." She paused while Webworm mumbled, swallowed hard, and groaned. "Yes, tell Sister Datura what you desire more than anything."

"Cloud...Playing..." Webworm whispered.

Spots made a face. Power was loose in the room. He could hear the subtle whispers and hisses as the voices from the sack began to tease the deep recesses of his souls. It seemed that each time the voices grew louder, Webworm's mutterings increased.

"Free yourself," Nightshade repeated as she reached forward and rubbed the datura over Webworm's lips.

"Elder?" Spots barely mouthed the words. "Are you trying to kill him?"

Spots jumped when Webworm screamed, "Gods, no!" The man sat bolt upright. "Night Sun! Don't burn! Stop the fire!"

Webworm blinked, eyes fixed on the distance. He rubbed his face, smearing the gray paste over his skin. With fumbling fingers, he reached for the white cup Nightshade had filled and sucked down large swallows. As he finished the drink, he froze, eyes sliding sideways to take in Nightshade's masked form. The now-empty cup sagged in his nerveless fingers.

"Who—who are you?" The words came with difficulty. His glazed eyes were wide with fear.

"I have come for your heart," Nightshade said in the formal tongue of the First People.

"My heart?" Webworm blinked, his eyes glassy

from the drug. Sweat was beading on his skin, trickling down around his loose gray-streaked hair.

"You are no longer using it. Only the serpent lives there now. It is black, polluted by your actions. Your orders are reaping the storm, Blessed Sun. Your world is dying. If you doubt, go out and look to the north. See the wrath of Cold Bringing Woman. Feel the bitter flakes of snow that she blows out of the north."

"Snow?" he asked stupidly.

"Your harvest is freezing, Webworm. The Flute Player has been caught by surprise. The thlatsinas are Dancing even now. With each beat of their feet, they drive snow from Cold Bringing Woman's storm. The old gods never saw them as they left Cloud Maker Mountain, climbed the Rainbow Serpent, and crossed the smoke pall to help Cold Bringing Woman Dance the storm out of the north. By this time tomorrow, the ripening corn will be frozen solid on its cob. The beans will blacken in their pods, and the sunflowers will turn dark and wither. Some of the squash may be saved, but the immature gourds are lost."

"What snow?" he repeated, then crawled on wobbly hands and knees to the rear of the room. There he fumbled for the handles and pulled down a wooden door that had been carefully fitted into the north wall.

A gust of wind immediately blew through the room, and with it came a chilling brace of winter air. Spots could see snowflakes as they blew in, landed on the floor, and melted into damp spots. Webworm stared out into the stygian night, sniffing at the damp smells of smoke and snow.

"Fire and ice," Nightshade said with an empty

voice. "Opposites crossed. You sit at the crossroads of the old world and the new."

It took Webworm three tries to fit the doorway back in place. As suddenly the fire died down to a gleam. Nightshade added another piece of wood.

Webworm collapsed onto his butt, one leg crossed, an anxious look on his drug-slack face. "I can't lose the harvest. Thousands will revolt. They will blame me."

"You are too late." Nightshade's voice echoed from inside the mask. "The cock-hatched serpent cares only for itself. The only way to save yourself is to surrender your heart."

"Who are you?" He shot her a glassy glance. His voice began to slur. "Is that you, Seven Stars? Wait, you must be Blue Racer. But no. You're supposed to be atop First Moon Mountain. Yes, that's right, and if you don't bring the rain, I'm taking...taking your...heart." Even as he said them, the words choked in his throat. He shot a fearful glance at Nightshade's mask, eyes bulging, sweat popping out on his face.

"The time has come, Webworm. Your tortured Dreams must end. I've heard you crying and moaning in the night. You want to be free of that, don't you?"

"Yes." His head wobbled as he stared at her mask.

"I can save you from the serpent in the egg. He possesses your souls, and as long as he has them, your breath-heart soul will never escape to travel to the Sky Worlds. You will never see your beloved Cloud Playing, never hold her in your arms. You will never fly up toward Father Sun in the company of your mother, Featherstone. She has so many things to tell you now that her wits have returned."

"I can't give you my heart!" Webworm cried.

"You looked into the serpent's eye," she told him. "That was the moment it entered your body and wound its way into your heart."

His eyes had lost their focus, and he blinked in confusion. "I don't understand."

"Tell me," Nightshade asked. "Are you happy?"

"Happy?"

"Are you? Do you ever awaken, glad to be alive? Do you ever finish the day, thinking, 'I have a good life'?"

Webworm's face went from slack, to squinting, to slack. "My life stopped when Cloud Playing...my precious Cloud Playing...was...was murdered by Swallowtail. He took my Dreams away..."

"And you took his evil fetish," she hissed. "You looked into its eye, and your souls, like his, were swallowed by the serpent. It coils inside you, Webworm. Only I can take it out, relieve the pain."

He nodded slowly, crawling back to his bed. "You swear? If you do this thing, I can go to Cloud Playing?"

"You can."

To Spots' amazement, Webworm began tugging at his shirt. The effort to pull it over his head was tremendous and came perilously close to defeating him. The fabric fell from his senseless fingers, and he sank back naked on his bed.

"It won't hurt?" Webworm slurred.

"Do you feel yourself flying?" Nightshade asked as she leaned forward.

"I'm floating. Lighter...lighter."

"That's Sister Datura, bearing you aloft. She can't take you all the way to the Cloud People until I remove your heart."

"... The Serpent...stays with ...?"

"It will."

"I will...be free?"

"You will be free."

He yawned. "...Sleepy...now..."

"That's the morning glory powder you drank filling your veins. Let go, Webworm."

Spots gaped as the Blessed Sun closed his eyes, breathing deeply. His left arm skipped off his belly, landing on the bedding like dead meat.

"Elder?" Spots whispered his horror.

"Shhh!" Her masked head swiveled, and he found himself staring into the Blue God's hard eyes.

His breath locked in his throat.

The terrible face swung back to Webworm. The man's breathing had slowed, his head lolled to the side. Spots could see his eyes rolled back in his head. His tongue lay in the side of his gaping mouth.

The curious chant rose on the air again as Nightshade reached into her pack and carefully laid out a spindle whorl, a length of thread, and a long obsidian blade.

"Elder, you can't—"

"Do not meddle, boy!"

He started, as if slapped. The voice issuing from behind the mask hadn't been Nightshade's.

The Blue God extended her bony hand, and the glassy blade glittered in the red light. With one swift motion, she cut a long slice that followed the V of Webworm's ribs.

The man jerked, air hissing as the blade sliced the diaphragm. Without effort, Nightshade batted his flailing arms aside, leaning over him as her hand disappeared under his breastbone.

Spots watched in disbelief as the old woman worked the blade this way and that. When she withdrew her blood-slick hands they gripped the quivering heart. Webworm's mouth worked like a fish's in air. Bug-eyed, he stared into eternity.

"Yes," the old woman said solicitously. "I hear you in there." Turning, she laid the heart inside the wide-necked jar, slapped the lid down, and sat back, sighing wearily. "Go, Webworm. You're free now. The serpent is safely removed."

Spots rose off his seat to stare into the slit in Webworm's chest. He could see pooled blood in the cavity where the man's heart had been. The Blessed Sun's feet were kicking weakly, his hands grasping at air. A gurgle sounded from his throat.

Nightshade was stringing thread around the spindle whorl. "Go now, Spots. Take the heart with you. No matter what, do not remove the lid until you are in the great kiva. The Priests will have returned from the fields and kindled a bonfire. Tell them you come with the offering of an elk heart. Cast it into the flames yourself. Stay only long enough to see that it is indeed burning, and then leave. Once outside the walls, smash the pot." She glared at him, and once again he was staring into the Blue God's eyes.

"I...understand." His voice sounded weak.

He took the vessel, a beautiful thing, white-slipped and painted in the striking Green Mesa mountain-and-cloud designs.

He wasn't prepared for the weight. Gods, a man's heart couldn't be that heavy, could it?

"It's the evil inside," Nightshade told him. "Now, go. Your duty to me is finished, Spots. When you have smashed the pot, find your woman, but speak nothing of what you've seen here."

He almost stumbled, legs gone curiously awkward and stiff; he stepped out into the cold night. Snow twirled down to melt on the roof. The guard lay sprawled, a darker stain of blood on the wet roof.

The gods help me! Gods, please help me!

In the silent night, Spots made his way down the combination of ladders and stairways to the plaza level. With each step, the pot seemed to grow heavier. He skipped sideways as a serpent hissed from the night.

"Silly, in this temperature, a snake would be as slow as a stick." But he kept a hand atop the lid, clamping it in place as he rounded the great kiva. At the southern entrance several people waited, taking their turns one by one. Each carried a package, jar, or bundle of cloth: all equinox offerings tied to some sort of prayer for the coming season.

When his turn came, Spots carefully entered, bearing the beautiful pot. He made his way down the stone-and-pole steps and crossed the floor to the great crackling bonfire.

"You come to do honor to the season?" a white-robed Priest asked.

"I—I have an elk heart."

"We receive your offering," the Priest intoned. "Place it in the fire. Let the smoke rise and bear it to the Star People."

A swallow stuck in his throat as Spots grasped the bowl, tossing the lid and bloody heart into the center of the flame.

Even the Priest stepped back as the heart exploded in a loud hiss.

"You'd think it was a snake." The Priest laughed.

"Yes," Spots agreed absently. "You would."

He was turning to go when, to his amazement, he swore he saw a bloodred serpent come slithering out of the big severed artery. It whipped and twisted in the flames, growing smaller until it was but a flicker of red leaping this way and that over the coals.

"Gods," Spots breathed.

"Tell the next to enter," the oblivious Priest told him.

Once outside the Dusk House walls, Spots lifted the beautiful vessel high. As he smashed it on the hard-wet ground, he heard a faint cry in the snow-thick night.

Blessed Gods, what did I witness this night?

Then, in panic, he ran as he'd never run before.

Chapter Twenty-Three

As wind-whipped snow whirled out of the night, Bad Cast kept to the shadows below the Pinnacle Great House wall. The sound of fighting rose above the moaning of the storm: wood clattering on wood; screams that tore from wounded throats; shouts of anger and insult; the meat-smacking sounds of war clubs hammering home.

The war chief had given him permission to leave after he'd guided the warriors to the mountaintop, but Bad Cast lingered. His heart pounded in his chest. His mouth was fear-dry, and his breathing came in gasps. Every muscle was charged to the trembling point.

A body sailed off the roof, thumping loudly as it landed in the snow a hand's length from Bad Cast's foot. The dying man issued a rasping gasp, twitched, and went still.

Peering, Bad Cast was able to determine that the face belonged to a stranger. A well-crafted war club lay beside the man's limp hand.

Bad Cast grabbed it up, surprised and awed that the

handle was so warm. He hurried to the stairway that led up to the first floor. As his head cleared the wall he could see knots of warriors surging back and forth. They twisted, leaped, dodged, and slashed at each other, mere shapes in the falling snow.

A sprawled figure was alternately screaming and weeping as it kicked and bucked on the packed clay. Bad Cast stepped onto the roof, bending to see one of Ironwood's warriors. Was it Thorn Petal? The man had two feathered arrow shafts protruding from his chest. Even as Bad Cast extended a hand, the man uttered a croaking rasp and went still, his eyes staring into the falling snow.

Something hissed through the air beside Bad Cast's ear, and he leaped for the shadow of the dividing wall.

I'm not a warrior!

That fact repeated down in his souls as he crept along the wall.

One of the white-robed Priests emerged from the Blue Dragonfly Clan kiva in the plaza floor. The man carried a pine-pitch torch in his hand as he emerged like some bizarre worm from the smoke hole. He stood on the ladder, torso protruding, waving the torch as he peered at the melee.

Bad Cast saw Crow Woman turn and hammer the man in the crown of the head; she skipped away. Wrapped Wrist trotted behind her, jabbing this way and that with a handful of hunting darts.

The Priest toppled, his robe snagging on one of the ladder uprights, and there he hung. The torch, pinned by his robe, set the cloth on fire. Yellow light leaped, illuminating the tumbling patterns of snowflakes where the wind whipped them in and out of the fighting.

Bad Cast suffered a sudden shiver. Ironwood's warriors were most definitely outnumbered. Six of them had been crowded back toward the western room block.

Where are the elders?

Bad Cast forced a swallow down his tight throat and ran for the ladder leading up to the third-story roof.

Yes, that's where they'd be.

Outside of Wrapped Wrist, he was the only one who knew the way. Assuming, that is, that the elders were being held in the same northern room where they'd kept Ripple.

On the third floor, he ran to Burning Smoke's room, hesitated at the doorway, and glanced back at the kiva. The dead Priest's robes flared as the man's hair caught fire. The corpse had a gruesomely black char to the skin. Then, the cloth burning through, it fell, one leg across a ladder rung, the body half in and out of the smoke hole. Smaller flames were licking on the dry wood of the entry.

Bad Cast ducked inside, ran to the shield, and tossed it aside. He clambered down the ladder into the darkness, felt for the second cover, and tossed it aside. Leaning his head over the dark hole in the floor, he called, "Anyone here?"

"Who comes?" a voice answered in his First Moon tongue.

"Bad Cast, of the Blue Stick Clan. Stand back. I'm lowering a ladder."

He felt around, located the ladder close to where they'd found it before, and lowered it into the depths. No sooner had the rungs thumped onto the floor than someone began climbing.

"What's happening?" the first young man asked as he emerged.

"Ironwood's warriors are fighting the First People," Bad Cast said. "It doesn't look good. There are weapons in the room above. Hurry."

Bad Cast assumed the young men who climbed out were the clan war chiefs. In the darkness he couldn't really tell. Then, bracing the ladder, he helped the elders as they climbed one by one from the lower level. They were old and frail, and he wasn't sure how they'd make it past the fighting, across the perilous ridge crest, and through the storm to safety.

"Bad Cast?" a raspy voice asked.

He helped an old white-haired man off the ladder. "Elder White Eye?"

"Has Cold Bringing Woman come?"

"Yes, Elder."

"And the fighting?"

"Not good. We are outnumbered."

"Then let us not waste time. Lead me to the way out."

In the confusion of the dark room, he wasn't sure, but he thought Elder Rattler, Green Claw, and Red Water climbed out before he led White Eye to the ladder. He followed the elder up into Burning Smoke's room. A wavering shaft of yellow light illuminated the doorway.

One hand on White Eye's arm, Bad Cast led the old man to the doorway and looked out. Fire still licked around the dead Priest's corpse. But how could a freshly dead man's...and then it came clear. The cedar-shake packing in the kiva roof, after moons of dry weather, had caught fire. He could hear people screaming from inside the kiva.

Bad Cast winced, wondering how many might be trapped there, watching helplessly as the fire burned around the plugged exit.

He had helped the old man onto the second level by the time the war chiefs charged into the fight. For long moments, they took the pressure off Crow Woman's little band of warriors where they'd backed against the room block.

Even as Bad Cast watched, the Blessed Sun's trained warriors parried blow after blow, ducked and dodged, and clubbed down their opponents. One red-shirted warrior caught Elder Rattler by the arm, threw her down, and crushed her skull with a single blow.

In a matter of moments, the other elders were likewise struck down.

Bad Cast stared in horror and dragged White Eye back into the shadow cast by the second floor.

"What's happening?" the elder asked.

"The others, they're dead. Killed by the Blessed Sun's warriors."

"And Ironwood's people?"

Bad Cast raised his head to see. "Crow Woman led them into one of the rooms. They can't be attacked, except through the doorway."

"But they can't escape, either."

"No. They're cut off."

White Eye sighed. "Then it's only a matter of time."

A sensation of sudden despair sent an ache through Bad Cast. "So it would appear, Elder."

"The Blessed Sun's warriors need only to hack a hole through the roof of the room where Crow Woman's people are hidden. Through it, they can shoot arrow after arrow."

Bad Cast sat back, heedless of the thick flakes that fell around him. "Then we are all dead."

Wrapped Wrist hadn't meant to become separated. One minute he was behind Crow Woman, and the next an enemy warrior came charging up. Without time to nock his dart, Wrapped Wrist used them as a cluster of short spears, jabbing them into the man's belly. The warrior shrieked, trying to backpedal. By the time Wrapped Wrist jerked his darts loose, Crow Woman was gone, and what seemed like a flood of red-shirted warriors were flocking between him and the other warriors.

As First Moon war chiefs emerged from Burning Smoke's upper room, Wrapped Wrist clambered up the ladder that led to the eastern plaza.

There, too, the battle swirled, Ironwood leading his warriors forward as they fought their way into the plaza. His men seemed to draw from the great war chief's very presence, their actions heroic as they crouched and loosened flight after flight of arrows into the warriors who emerged from the rooms that lined the plaza. The screams and shrieks of wounded men mingled with the falling snow.

"Ironwood!" someone cried. "Leave him to me!"

Wrapped Wrist turned to see a muscular warrior start through the press of the Blessed Sun's warriors. At mention of the name, the red-shirted warriors began to fall back.

"Ravengrass?" Ironwood strode through his ranks of kneeling warriors. As he approached, an arrow drove into Ravengrass's throat. The man clutched at the quivering shaft, turned, and wilted onto the packed clay.

Goaded by shouts of rage, the Blessed Sun's warriors charged. Wrapped Wrist bent, staring down into the kiva. He could see worried Priests picking up ritual clothing, bagging sacred masks, and staring up with fright.

Arrows hissed past his ear as he laid his darts and atlatl aside and grasped the heavy ladder. No ordinary man could have lifted the heavy weight; rung by rung he pulled it from the depths. Below, the Priests were dumbfounded, and in the time it took for them to recover their wits, one of Ironwood's warriors ran up. As the first of the Priests reached to pull the ladder back down, an arrow sliced down through the man's chest.

Wrapped Wrist muscled the teetering ladder into the wind, letting it drop atop the milling enemy warriors.

Ironwood's men shouted, and threw themselves on the disorganized foe.

"Form up!" came the stern order as War Chief Burning Smoke descended the ladder from the third-tier rooms. "We outnumber them! Fight like you've been trained."

Gods, I am no warrior. So what can I do?

Diversion, that was it. Something to take the pressure off Crow Woman and Ironwood.

Wrapped Wrist ducked into one of the plaza-level

rooms and almost tripped over a coal-filled fire bowl. This he dumped into the neat stack of firewood. Room by room, he made his way around the plaza floor; in each he set fire to the woodpiles or dropped the coals in rush matting. He poured grease onto cloth bedding and propped it where the oily flames licked at the dry roofing.

When he emerged again, it was to see Ironwood's men being pushed relentlessly back. Burning Smoke had restored order and spirit. So many warriors.

Wrapped Wrist sucked cold air into his hot lungs. Smoke was billowing from the rooms along the northern wall. Each of the doorways was outlined by a red-orange glow.

What is happening to Crow Woman?

Could he set fire to the other side, too? He crouched, sneaking behind the battling warriors to climb atop the dividing line of rooms.

Flames were rising from the western kiva. Red-shirted warriors lurked to either side of the western room block, bows curved as they periodically released arrows into one of the room doors. He studied the bodies illuminated by the burning kiva. None of the sprawled corpses looked like Crow Woman. So, had she taken refuge in the room?

We are losing.

He suffered a sinking sensation and dropped to his knees. Wild flakes of snow came whipping past, and in the firelight he could see that they were black, tainted with ash and smoke.

"Ripple, you saw it so well." And a knot formed in his throat as he remembered his dead friend's face, and the blood that had pooled under his head and dripped down the half-severed neck.

He raised his hands to the sky, crying, "Ripple? Where are you?"

When he looked back at the high third-floor rooms, it was to see Matron Larkspur as she stood imperiously beside Water Bow and a finely dressed Priest he assumed was Blue Racer.

The battle must have turned enough that they felt safe enough to watch, heedless of the fires that grew one floor down beneath their feet.

The voice seemed to come from the blowing snow. "We come, good friend. Fire...and ice."

Larkspur stood before her room, a buffalo robe over her shoulders. She was heedless of the dirty snow that swirled and twisted from the night sky. Smoke was boiling out of the lower rooms, but she was unsure of its origin. As soon as the fighting was stopped, she'd have her warriors retrieve the big water-storage jars from the south-side rooms to douse any flames.

When she looked at the western kiva, however, her heart sank. Even over the shouts and fury of battle, she could hear the screams of the Priests trapped in that inferno. Smoke and flame rose in a huge curling torch that defied the storm. The doomed inside were no doubt huddled where the ventilator drafted cold air into the blaze.

"Kill them! Kill them all!" she shouted, stepping forward and raising an angry fist.

"Who are these people?" Blue Racer asked, stepping up by her side. He raised an arm protectively as hot air came curling up from the room beneath his feet.

"Ironwood's Outcasts," Waterbow said distastefully. "Matron, we're going to have to consider leaving this place."

She whirled on him. "Why? We're winning." She gestured to where Ironwood's warriors were retreating, their arrows slowed from a shower to a trickle as they backed away from her advancing warriors. Her people needed only to charge, close, and finish them with war clubs.

"We'll put the fires out. Then, you can bet, we're going to take our revenge on the Moon People. I swear, by the time we're done with them, they'll wail for the days when..."

They came from the darkness and storm. The first Larkspur saw was a woman who emerged from the darkness carrying only a stone-headed hoe. Behind her came the rest: farmers with stout digging sticks, hunters with atlatls and hunting darts. Some of the men carried stone-headed axes, others sharp-edged adzes.

Larkspur's warriors stared at them in disbelief, then foolishly waved at them to go away. For so many years, their mere wish had been the barbarians' bane. This time, the Moon People were heedless.

"No!" Larkspur shouted. "Kill them! They, too, are the enemy!"

In the light of the fire, her warriors made perfect targets for the barbarian hunters. The heavy hunting darts, powered by atlatls, sliced through the warrior's shields meant only to stop cane-shafted arrows. Within moments, half of her warriors were screaming as they lay on the plaza, arms, chests, and legs pierced by the long darts. Ironwood's remaining warriors whooped and charged.

Larkspur stared in amazement as her warriors broke and ran, some clambering up the ladders, followed by screaming Moon People. On the roofs they were battered down, and she saw more than one of her warriors leap from the third-floor roof to certain death on the slope so far below.

More and more farmers appeared out of the blizzard night. The Moon People began to identify their dead elders where they lay sprawled on the packed clay. In a wave, the people rushed forward.

"Kill them!" Larkspur screamed. "Kill them!"

She was standing on the edge of her roof, aware that the floor beneath her feet had grown hot. Snowflakes whirled down and exploded in steam.

She stared, dumbfounded, as Moon People flooded across the plazas, picking up her warriors, tossing them alive and screaming into the burning kiva.

"Matron?" Water Bow reached out, placing a hand on her elbow. "It's time for us to leave this place."

"No, I am not about..." She gaped as the woman with the stone hoe appeared on her ladder. The woman leaped onto the roof and hammered Blue Racer across the back. The Sunwatcher ran, screaming, jumping out to land on the lower second-floor roof in the western section. Water Bow scurried in his wake; he tripped and fell as he tried to scuttle down the ladder.

The hoe-wielding woman emerged from Larkspur's room, waving Larkspur's feather holder with its glorious plumage in triumph. In the light, she was a short stocky woman with scars on her forearms.

"Oh, no you don't!"

Larkspur didn't hear him coming. Hard hands grabbed her from behind, and she felt herself lifted. A man was carrying her toward the ladder as she shrieked and kicked, battering at his muscular arms with her fists.

"Shut up," the man growled in a Made People dialect. "I'm tired of Matrons, of Priests, and First People."

"Let me go!" she squealed. "I'll pay you. I can help you."

"We killed your assassin," he growled in her ear. "Takes Falls wasn't worth a jar of turquoise. He told us what you'd paid for the Prophet."

"It's yours. If you'll let me go!"

He'd borne her to the western plaza, where a crowd had formed. She had a glimpse as the Blue Dragonfly Clan kiva roof collapsed inward. Sparks and belching smoke rose as the flames leaped into the swirling snow. A growing roar could be heard as fire jetted from the depths. People screamed in delight as they Danced in the light of the maelstrom.

An image froze, caught between Larkspur's souls. She watched as Blue Racer was tossed high, his body seeming to hang for the briefest of moments before it dropped into the raging flames.

The people cheered.

Then it was Water Bow, his form sent arching into the air. His arms and legs windmilled futilely as he fell into the glowing depths.

A desperate voice called, "No! In the name of the gods, No!"

Larkspur saw Ironwood, pulling at the crowd, trying to drag them back.

"Don't kill them!" Ironwood begged, his one-eyed

face a mask of horror. "We need them alive! They are the way—"

Larkspur never heard the rest. The brawny man who carried her, slung her around. More hard hands clamped onto her legs and arms. She felt the strain as they swung her back and forth. Then she was flying, her body arching high.

Her scream tore as she fell into the scorching heat. Her body hit the angle of the collapsed roof. She tumbled down into pain and flames. Her hair exploded. When she drew a breath, it was filled with searing fire.

Fir Brush stood at the edge of the roof, one hand on Bad Cast's shoulder as she watched the great house burn. White Eye stood on Bad Cast's other side, partially supported by Soft Cloth.

"Another roof just fell in," Soft Cloth told the elder. "The sparks are whirling up into the air. The snow is falling in a red veil that fills the sky. It looks like bloody feathers as it swirls out of the night."

Fir Brush watched mute. How she had arrived here, at this place...it had no form, no shape in her souls. When they had left the kiva that afternoon, the people had had no order, just a quiet desperation. The council had disintegrated without the leadership of the elders. So many individuals had insisted on speaking. Some had argued for war, others for peace.

Some had called for revenge for Ripple's death. Others insisted that he was obviously a false Prophet, or no assassin could have killed him.

In the end, they had trickled away by ones and twos

to climb First Moon Mountain. They had watched the great forest fire as it burned down from the north, felt the change in the wind, and stopped to borrow blankets and clothing from relatives who lived on the mountain.

By the time the first flakes of snow had been whisked across the mountain by the whistling wind, the words, "Cold Bringing Woman's promise" and "Ripple's vision" were passing from lip to lip.

As the temperature dropped, they had crowded toward Guest House, creeping up in the dark, filing past. When one of the Made People stepped out to protest, he was clubbed down. For the most part, the other Made People just watched them pass, like wraiths in the storm.

What amazed Fir Brush was how quiet they had been. Even when they approached the Eagle's Fist, no one had spoken.

"Who comes?" Yucca Sock had called, and Orenda had answered, "The people come, Yucca Sock. Let them pass."

As Fir Brush led the first of them up the ladder, it was to find the western plaza kiva shooting a yellow column of flame into the night.

Later Fir Brush would only remember images, nothing particularly coherent. She would remember the shrieks of rage and horror as the elders were discovered dead. She had seen Crow Woman and Wrapped Wrist as they ran into each other's arms.

She remembered Yellow Petal, shrieking and Dancing as she clutched a red-painted feather holder she'd taken from Larkspur's room. She cradled it to her chest, the eagle, hawk, and macaw feathers waving back and forth. She was leaping as she cavorted with Black

Bush and his teenage sister, Red Thorn. They weren't the only ones. Everyone was looting the place, racing the flames as they burned through roof after roof.

Finally she remembered Ironwood shouting, pleading, as her people found Matron Larkspur, Burning Smoke, and Water Bow. They were dragged kicking and screaming from the smoking rooms.

He was frantic, trying to stop the howling Moon People, as one by one, they threw the First People, screaming into the burning kiva.

In the end, Ironwood had collapsed onto his knees, Pinnacle Great House burning around him. He knelt there, sweaty skin shining in the firelight, head bowed, shoulders slumped in defeat. He might even have died there, consumed with the rest, but Crow Woman and Wrapped Wrist braved the heat and dragged him from the growing inferno.

"What terror have we wrought?" Bad Cast asked.

"The end of our world," White Eye answered. "Come. Someone needs to get me off this mountain before I freeze. The storm is intensifying. We need to seek shelter."

"There is no shelter," Fir Brush said. "Not for my brother, or me, or any of us."

Chapter Twenty-Four

The Unbroken Circle

Oh, yes, at my age, I know exactly what life is.

Life is the flash of a raven's wings in the sunlight. It is the white breath of the buffalo in the wintertime. It thrives in the glowing bellies of the Cloud People as they sail across the sky to melt into the sunrise.

And Death?

Death is no mystery.

It is merely the raven's dark wing.

It reflects from the buffalo's black hooves, stamping out eternity.

It is the crackle of a thunderhead flashing lightning.

Do you really believe there is a difference between a raven's wing and a raven's wing flashing sunlight? A raven is still a raven. Or between a buffalo's white breath and those terrible churning black hooves? It is still a buffalo. Or a glowing cloud and a roaring thunderhead? Both are manifestations of a cloud.

No matter what foolish holy people try to tell you, there is only one animal.

It lives to die.

And it dies to live.

No other truth is as simple.

Or as complex.

Cold settled on the land, deep and unforgiving as violent winds blew the storm on to the south. In its wake, a crystal sky gave way to the promise of sunrise.

War Chief Wind Leaf climbed onto the fourth-story roof and stared out in disbelief at the blue world around him. His breath froze before his face, his eyes on the fields. Snow draped the corn as if carefully laid. Icicles hung sparkling from the long green leaves. Bean plants bowed under the white weight, and the larger squash wore hats of snow.

The harvest! Wind Leaf could feel his heart slow, each beat sodden in his chest as the realization came home. But how far had the storm extended? Was it just here, localized to Flowing Waters Town?

In every direction he looked, the hills leading up to the horizon were a crisp white.

He shivered in his cloak, staring with glum disbelief. He barely heard Matron Desert Willow as she climbed up beside him. This morning she wore a buffalo coat, her arms held snug around her slender body.

"How could this have happened?" Her voice was small in the morning.

"We must tell the Blessed Sun." He couldn't help but take one last look at the end of Dreams. "After that, we need to recall as many warriors as possible. Maintaining order is going to be a problem."

He led the way, taking careful steps on the frozen ladder. He stopped, staring at the guard who sat before the Blessed Sun's door. The man had frost on his hair, streaks of ice where water had melted and then frozen on his clothing or run down into his neck.

Wind Leaf reached out, shoving him. The fellow sprawled dead on his blanket.

"Well, he didn't shirk his duty," Desert Willow murmured. Her voice was oddly detached, as if she, too, were beginning to understand the enormity of the disaster facing them.

"No." Wind Leaf fingered the frost. "This is blood."

Panicked, he ducked into Webworm's quarters, calling, "Blessed Sun, are you...?" He stared at the figure who sat beside the Blessed Sun's bed. She looked regal, a macaw-feather cloak about her shoulders. Long white hair tumbled down her shoulders; he'd have sworn her composed face actually glowed. She raised dark eyes to his, and his heart skipped. He might have been staring into an endless midnight.

"Blessed Sun?" Desert Willow snapped. "Who is this? Why is she here?"

"It's the Mountain Witch," Wind Leaf said, finally catching his breath. He glanced at Webworm's naked body. "And I don't think the Blessed Sun is going to be answering any more questions."

Desert Willow stepped over, her buffalo coat dragging on the floor. She gasped as she saw the slit in her husband's chest, realized that the dark stains were blood.

"Where is his heart?"

"Gone," the Mountain Witch said in formal tongue. "I have drawn it out, sent it away. His souls have been purified and are already on the way to the Blessed Cloud People. By now he is with Cloud Playing and Featherstone. I have finished my duties here."

"Your duties?" Wind Leaf demanded. "What have you done with the Blessed Sun's heart?"

The old woman smiled. "I have purified it." She inclined her head slightly. "A serpent hatched of a cock's egg is the worst kind of evil. Webworm, despite his faults, deserved better than that. Now, with the coming of this morning, my work is finished."

"Your work?" Desert Willow demanded hotly. "Is your work assassination and witchcraft?"

"I am the Witness," the old woman said simply. "Your world is ended." Her dark eyes seemed to swell in her face. "May the gods have mercy on the people."

"Get her out of here," Desert Willow snapped. "Drag her down into the plaza and break her neck. No, burn her alive. Anything, as long as she screams and wails."

Wind Leaf grabbed the old woman's pack, upending it, finding a bloody spindle whorl, little bags of powders, a gleaming black pot full of paste, and several hide-wrapped bundles that sent prickles up and down his arms. He found nothing that resembled a human heart.

"What if she's going to use his heart to witch us?" he growled, emptying pots, searching the rolled hides. Through it all, the Mountain Witch sat, perfectly composed as they ransacked the Blessed Sun's quarters.

Wind Leaf checked outside, looking carefully. The only steps in the frost were his and Desert Willow's.

He ducked back inside, thrusting his face close to hers. "Where's the heart?"

"Where you'll never find it."

"We'll see about that."

Desert Willow raised a restraining hand. "No, we probably won't. There are a thousand things she could have done with it. Perhaps tossed it out the back window to an accomplice, or even sliced it up and eaten it." She pointed. "Look, there's a bloody spindle whorl. You know what witches do with those."

"If she's going to use it to witch us, we have to know, Matron. We have to be able to protect ourselves."

Desert Willow nodded, a new fear in her eyes.

Wind Leaf grabbed the old woman's hand. She didn't resist as he thrust it into the hot coals in the warming bowl. No expression crossed Nightshade's face as her skin burned and her nails began to curl.

It was the odor of cooking flesh that made him relent. "Where is the heart?"

"Gone," she said simply.

He stared, sharing Desert Willow's disbelief. What human wouldn't howl in agony as their hand was subjected to such heat?

Desert Willow frowned, thinking. "You remember the witch boy?"

"The one with the little dog? The one we walled up?"

"Take her down to one of the lower rooms," Desert Willow ordered. "Stake her there so that her souls can't escape, but do it in a manner that doesn't kill her immediately. Then leave her in the dark. Each day, you will go down, ask her what she did with Webworm's heart. When she tells you, she can finally die. Quickly, without more suffering."

Wind Leaf stared at his Matron, envisioning the kind of death this would be. "Stake her?"

Desert Willow was fingering her chin, eyes narrowed as she glared into the witch's eyes. "I'm not in a forgiving mood, War Chief. Stake her to the floor. Drive it through her pelvis, right down through her womanhood." A pause. "She'll talk in the end."

Wind Leaf felt suddenly hot, as if on the verge of sickness, but he nodded. "As you order."

"And do it yourself," she added. "This, I don't want you to delegate."

"Come," Wind Leaf said. "But leave your poisons here. And take off the Priest's robes. You'll die naked."

He watched as the old woman shrugged out of the beautiful cloak, then pulled the white tunic over her head. How she did it with a half-cooked hand was miraculous, but no expression of pain crossed her face.

When they stepped out into the cold, Wind Leaf glanced at the dead guard. Gods, how Powerful was this old hag?

Seeing one his guards on the second floor, he called, "Bring me a heavy stone-headed mallet and a thick wooden stake. And hurry!"

As his guard hastened to his task, Wind Leaf took one last look at the morning, purple and violet now. The final stars were vanishing from the west. "Take a good hard look, witch. It's the last sunrise you'll ever see."

She lifted her eyes to the sky, smiled, and then cast one glance down at the plaza. For a moment her gaze lingered on the wood Trader and Cactus Flower, who had arrived early that day. No wonder—the demand for firewood would be huge.

Wind Leaf shoved her violently into the gloom of the third floor. He had a room in mind, one where no one would hear her scream; and in the end, it would be easy to rock up and seal forever.

Leather Hand climbed wearily up the ladder that led out of the Red Lacewing Clan kiva. His eyes were gritty, his nose burning from the smoke. Time had gotten away from him. Night Sun, by the gods, what motivated that woman?

He stepped out onto the kiva roof, cold hitting him like a wave. He blinked, seeing the dusting of soot-grayed snow that had settled on the curving walls of Talon Town. It frosted the high sandstone cliffs, and occasional flakes, mostly white now, still drifted down from the clearing skies.

Snow? This early in the year?

For a moment the incongruity of it left him stumbling. Only then did the implications begin to sink in.

What does this mean for the harvest?

He shook his head, blinked his eyes, and plodded to the ladder that led up to the room he'd chosen. Once it had belonged to the Blessed Sun. And it would again, when he and Larkspur led the Straight Path Nation back to this canyon.

Snow?

A shiver of unease ran through him, and he puffed a breath into the cold air, watching it frost before him. Gods, it was cold. Not just chilly, but frozen cold. He could see ice where the first flakes of snow had melted and trickled down the cracked plaster walls. Ice was slick underfoot, too.

Ice meant a deep frost.

A premonition of disaster festered between his souls.

No, shake it off.

He was tired, exhausted, after a day and night of battling with Night Sun. That look she had given him would mock his memory for the rest of his life.

Next time, I shall gouge her eyes out. Then she couldn't project that haughty arrogance that drove him half-insane.

She'd almost won, almost driven him too far. But at the last minute, his wits had returned, buffering the anger that had driven him. He had caught himself on the verge of murder and relented.

Dead, you are of no more use, Matron.

He yawned, rubbed the back of his neck, and allowed the terrible cold to seep into his hot body.

Snow? What did that mean for the future? For his future, once he had destroyed Ironwood, claimed Larkspur, and brought his people home?

He bent his head back, feeling light snowflakes as they landed on his face. "Blue God? Am I only to be a ruler of the dead?"

Night Sun's knowing gaze burned in his memory.

"Tomorrow," he promised, "you will beg me to end it."

Yes, tomorrow. And after that, he would discover the extent of the frost. Webworm would be needing him more than ever.

He reached into his pouch, pulling out the carved fetish Webworm had given him. The little serpent coiled inside the broken eggshell. In the storm light, the coral eye seemed to glow with an internal light.

Bad Cast made his way past the Eagle's Fist. Fresh snow covered the bloodstains. He had spent the night at Fir Brush's and had taken Ripple's winter moccasins as well as a blanket for the climb. He nodded to several people who were headed back down the mountain. People were torn, as desperate to see the burned great house as they were to inspect their fields.

Clusters of people hunched in the cold predawn. Their breath hung in frost around their heads. They talked, voices low, as they watched the blue smoke rise into the still air.

Bad Cast found Ironwood standing atop the western plaza by the stairway. The war chief was staring down into the smoking ruin of the kiva.

Heat from the fire had melted the snow here; Bad Cast climbed up beside him.

For long moments he stared down in silence, seeing the black timbers scabbed by white as coals ate into the remaining wood. Dirt and debris had fallen into piles. Heat radiated out in waves that rippled in the cold air. In the gaps between sections of still-burning roof, the corpses could be seen. Where the fire had been hottest, ash and cindered bone remained. A black mass of tangled limbs clustered beside the ventilator shaft. The up-thrust arms, twisted legs, and pulled-back heads could only hint at the agony of their last moments. Open mouths exposed blackened and cracked teeth. Noses were mere holes, the flesh turned to ash, eyes but pits of darker black. When the breeze changed, the odor of charred flesh stung his nostrils; smoke brought tears to his eyes.

"The First People are finished." Ironwood's stare remained fixed on the macabre and grotesquely distorted dead.

"Perhaps we are all finished. My people are trying to save what they can of the harvest. Some are shaving corn from the cobs, seeking to dry it before it rots. Others are cooking green beans and frozen squash, or trying to rig drying and smoking racks."

"It won't be enough," Ironwood said.

"No," Bad Cast agreed.

After a long silence, Ironwood asked, "What will you do?"

Bad Cast glanced to the north, where patchy snow could be seen on the gray slopes of the hills. Burned timber looked like black fuzzy hair. "There's no hunting up there. The game will have fled. Our crops are frozen. Ripple told me to head to the Great River Valley. He must have seen this, too."

Ironwood continued to stare down at the corpses. "I was going to exchange them for Night Sun. Now, I don't know. I suppose I'll take my warriors, see what can be done at Flowing Waters Town. If the frost went that far south, there may be enough confusion that my people can sneak in and free her."

"I pray that the gods go with you, War Chief."

"And with you," Ironwood answered wearily.

"Oh, I think I've had enough of the gods for a while," Bad Cast said. "Their company comes at too high a price."

Chapter Twenty-Five

Wrapped Wrist led the way, picking a trail that wound down through the thinning timber. The route kept to the brushy valleys where lookouts wouldn't be apt to spot them. The Blessed Sun would send any retaliatory war parties up the River of Souls Valley to its confluence with the River of Stones and north into First Moon Valley. Ironwood's small band of warriors hoped to avoid that main force.

If Webworm attacked First Moon Valley, so much the better. Wrapped Wrist's people had already dispatched more than enough scouts to give fair warning. So, too, had hunters gone, bearing their atlatls, to ambush the trails. Those who knew the bow had taken to making war arrows. Everyone expected a terrible retaliation, but this time, the red-shirted warriors would have to fight for every step. Feelings in First Moon Valley were running high. Storage of surpluses from previous years—food that would have tided the people through the current disaster—had been emptied for the Blessed Sun's tribute.

People who faced starvation didn't fear much from a quick death in battle.

Wrapped Wrist glanced behind him, seeing Crow Woman where she trotted warily along. Behind her, the warriors of Ironwood's surviving band carried their round shields, both wicker and leather-bound. Arrows bristled from quivers, and war clubs hung from belts. Yucca Sock and Firehorn brought up the rear, often checking the backtrail to make sure that no one followed.

Ten. That's all we have left.

When, he wondered, had he begun to think of himself as one of them?

The way led down out of the timber, into a broken upland filled with sandstone-capped mesas and juniper-dotted slopes. The drainages here remained damp with runoff from Cold Bringing Woman's storm. Overhead, the midday sun beat down, the temperature pleasant. As was their way, the desert plants were blooming, the sagebrush and rabbitbrush having received enough moisture to flower. A heavy frost might be disastrous to food crops, but it didn't kill the drought-resistant brush.

Topping a rise, Wrapped Wrist caught sight of a man. Immediately he raised his arm, stopping. Behind him, he knew that Ironwood and his warriors were melting into the trees.

The lone figure in the trail was bent under a huge load of sticks and branches. The wood was all gray and sun-bleached, tied into a bundle with a thick leather thong about the middle.

Wrapped Wrist looked around, seeing only the solitary traveler. Assured the man was alone, he trotted over the rise, calling, "Greetings!"

The figure turned, shadowed by the heavy load. "Greetings yourself."

"You have no one to help?"

"Unfortunately. Otherwise I could share this burden. You want to carry half?"

Wrapped Wrist thought the voice familiar, but had to trot closer to squint at the shadowed face. He noticed the patterns on the fire-mottled left arm. "Spots?"

"Wrapped Wrist?" Spots swung his load off his shoulder and let it clatter onto the ground. He grinned, winced as he straightened, and walked into Wrapped Wrist's warm embrace.

"Gods, it's good to see you." Wrapped Wrist patted his friend's back, holding his darts in his left hand. "We thought you were dead."

"Hunting?" Spots asked, indicating the darts. "Bit far to carry meat, isn't it? And wait a minute, aren't those my darts?"

"What are you doing here?"

"I'm a wood Trader." Spots' smile faded. "It's been an interesting moon, let me tell you. We've heard terrible stories about what happened in First Moon Valley. Yesterday morning the first fleeing people passed. They said that Ripple was dead, that all the First People were murdered, that Pinnacle Great House was burned."

"All true." Wrapped Wrist shrugged, wishing he could forget the horrible images in the kiva bottom. "I was there."

"And Bad Cast?"

"He's coming to meet us at Flowing Waters Town. He's traveling with Soft Cloth and the baby. We thought it would be safer that way. Yellow Petal is trying to hang on. You should see the feather holder she has. Black Bush is urging her to go south. There are stories of a valley that didn't freeze. Fir Brush and Slipped Bark might go with her." He looked around. "Where's the Mountain Witch?"

"Captive in Flowing Waters Town. I'm trying to figure out how to free her."

"And Night Sun?" Wrapped Wrist asked.

"The Matron?" Spots shrugged. "The rumor was that she was captured, but I haven't heard of her in Flowing Waters Town."

Ironwood's voice called, "That doesn't mean that Leather Hand didn't take her there." He emerged from the brush at the side of the trail, other warriors rising here and there as if by magic.

Spots smiled weakly. "War Chief. It is good to see you again."

"A Trader?" Ironwood asked. "Does Webworm know you're associated with Nightshade?"

Spots narrowed an eye. "Webworm doesn't know much these days, War Chief."

"Oh?" Ironwood's expression intensified.

"He's dead. No one knows. Desert Willow is keeping it quiet until she can call in enough warriors to ensure Flowing Waters Town's safety."

"Dead?" Ironwood asked. "How?"

Spots went grim. "Nightshade cut his heart out of his body. Nothing could ever have prepared me for the way of it. He lay down, Dancing with Sister Datura, and she cut it, still beating, from his chest. I carried it myself to the equinox kiva fire and watched the serpent crawl out of it as it burned."

Ironwood's expression fell. "She cut out Webworm's...? A serpent was in his heart?"

Spots said soberly. "It had taken possession of his souls. He'd been witched years ago."

"Did he say anything?"

"He wanted to find someone named Cloud Playing."

Ironwood's eyes fixed somewhere in the distance, and he stepped away, shoulders slumping. "Yes, of course he would."

Wrapped Wrist wondered at the man's reaction. He'd swear that watching the First People being burned alive at Pinnacle Great House had taken something out of Ironwood. Or was it just worry about his wife?

"What are the chances of sneaking into Flowing Waters Town?" Crow Woman asked as she walked up. "Are the guards vigilant?"

"Very," Spots answered, studying her intently. "I remember you."

Wrapped Wrist suffered a slight twinge at the interest in Spots' eyes. *Gods, I'm not jealous, am I?*

Spots continued. "A guard was...I killed him the night of Webworm's...since then, Wind Leaf's been a terror on guards."

"But you can get in and out?" Crow Woman asked.

"I'm a Trader. I can get into the plaza, but it's not worth my life to try and climb onto the second floor."

"Night Sun would be somewhere deep in the interior rooms," Yucca Sock said, glancing unsurely to where Ironwood stood. The war chief had a hand pressed to his heart, as if it bothered him. Softness lay behind the war chief's eyes; a faint expression of pain pinched his lips.

"We've got to try," Crow Woman replied. "And we have to do it in a way that doesn't expose us. Wind Leaf and Desert Willow will have everyone watching for us."

Spots cocked his jaw, thought behind his eyes.

From long habit, Wrapped Wrist asked, "You know something?"

Spots gave him a serious look. "I might. For the most part, Traders in Flowing Waters Town are invisible."

"Which means?" Yucca Sock asked.

"Have you ever heard of anyone named Creeper?"

At the name, Ironwood turned, alert again. "Just what would you know about Creeper?"

Leather Hand perched on his knees, his hand on Night Sun's tangled gray hair. Mad rage coupled with a curious respect. He let his fingers smooth her gray locks. They'd gone stiff with age, but he could imagine how sleek they must have been when she was still young and beautiful.

He stared up at the square of sky visible overhead. It beckoned, a deep and crystalline blue.

"I'm so sorry, War Chief," Turquoise Fox said. He stood, a cape over his shoulders, staring down uneasily at the old woman's corpse.

"No, it's all right." Leather Hand stood, head cocked. "I put that slave collar on her as a means of humiliating her. It was to break her spirit." A pause. "It takes a most clever adversary to turn a weapon back upon its wielder."

In the night, she had thrust her fingers under her slave collar, twisted it, and choked herself to death. As consciousness slipped away, the weight of her arm had kept the strangulation tight.

"So dies a Matron," he mused. Even in death her half-lidded eyes had a Power over him. "With her dies the last of her world."

He patted her head one last time, feeling the skull beneath her aged skin. When he rose to his feet, it was with a purpose. "Dead, she is no longer a lure for Ironwood. We need, however, to keep this news from the other captives. I want you to arrange to let the young woman escape. The strong-looking one. She must think she has managed this thing on her own."

Turquoise Fox grinned. "And of course she will run straight to Ironwood!"

"Precisely." He rubbed his hands together. "You know, there's a chance that Ironwood doesn't know where Night Sun was taken. Or perhaps Webworm already has him locked up at Flowing Waters Town. Meanwhile, take what's left of her and find some interior room to stick her in. Preferably an out-of-the-way place. Wall it up, or throw some matting over her. I don't care."

"Yes, War Chief." Turquoise Fox bent to pick up the old woman. A dot of blue caught his eye as a little carved wolf swung loose, dangling on a thong. He considered taking the talisman, then thought better of it. Perhaps she'd earned her guide to the Land of the Dead.

He climbed the ladder into sunlight and looked out at the dawn. The cold air had a bite to it.

Around him, Straight Path Canyon gleamed in the morning. He could see Kettle Town to the east, its squat tiers outlined by snow. To the west, Streamside Town caught the first rays of the morning sun. Across Straight Path Wash, several fingers of smoke rose from the few remaining settlements in the valley. The handful of farmers would have lost what few pitiful crops remained. Leather Hand suspected that within days, they, too, would have left the canyon behind.

He was turning to head for his room when a man climbed the south wall and jogged wearily across the plaza. He wore a woven buffalo-wool cape, a heavy shirt, and thick socks covered his trail sandals, the latter caked with frozen mud.

"Deputy War Chief," the man called, waving. "I have news. Matron Desert Willow and War Chief Wind Leaf order you to come to Flowing Waters Town immediately."

"They have captured Ironwood?" Leather Hand called, propping his hands on his hips.

"No, great Deputy. Ironwood has burned Pinnacle Great House. All the First People, including the Sunwatcher and Matron, are dead. They were tossed into the Blue Dragonfly kiva, burned alive, Deputy. The harvest is lost. People on the verge of panic. The Matron has recalled all able-bodied warriors to Dusk House. You are to report immediately!"

Leather Hand stood in shock. Burned alive? "You are telling me that Matron Larkspur is dead? That all of the First People at Pinnacle Great House are dead?"

"That is correct," the man answered. He'd stopped

on the roof below, chest rising and falling as he panted for breath. "Word is that raiding has broken out all over the land. Farmsteads are burning up and down the River of Souls Valley. Neighbors have turned upon each other. The Matron believes that within days people will begin gathering around Flowing Waters Town hoping for food. She will need all the warriors she can muster to defend the stores."

Leather Hand closed his eyes, swaying as if from a blow. In the eye of his souls, he saw Larkspur, remembered her warm body against his. He had seen the interest in her eyes, fallen in love with her daring smile.

She would have been Matron of the First People. I would have made her so.

Now he was going to have to find another way to become Blessed Sun.

The Blue God's hollow laughter seemed to echo in the thin air, reverberating from the silent canyon walls.

The renowned builder and engineer, Yellowgirl, glanced warily out the door as Creeper came sauntering down the southern wall of Sunrise House. The first level of rooms, freshly plastered, had a clean smell of earth, cedar, and pine. The packed dirt floor was unstained with ash, broken pottery, bits of fiber, or the other detritus that accumulated in a room.

It was a good time for a meeting. Creeper had no fear of them being interrupted. As a result of the frost, all work on Sunrise House was halted, the slaves' efforts dedicated to saving what they could of the harvest.

In the room's rear—partially illuminated by the

midday light that angled in the doorway—sat Copper Ring, Matron of the Coyote Clan, and Wooden Flower, elder of the Bear Clan.

As Yellowgirl stepped inside, Creeper took one look back the way he'd come. No one followed. Four roughly dressed men, trail-worn and streaked with soot and ash, stood talking by the southeastern corner of the building. One tall man seemed oddly familiar, but his back was to Creeper. Out in the fields, people were salvaging the wilting plants.

Creeper entered, a weary weight on his heart. He wasn't prepared for what he would have to say today. He just knew of no other way to save themselves.

"Greetings, Creeper," Yellowgirl said solemnly. "No one saw you come?"

"No," he murmured, nodding to the others. Copper Ring was old, walked with a cane, and had a face like sun-dried leather. Her toothless jaw was undershot, and a mushroom might have admired the shape of her nose. She looked frail, bones like sticks inside her thin arms. Her hair, snowy white, had been wound into a bun and pinned at the back of her head. It may have been a male fashion, but at her age, what did she care?

Wooden Flower, nearly sixty summers old, still had an eagle-like glare in his eyes, though his right arm was withered, the result of some long-ago wound. He wore a tan hunting shirt, yucca socks, and sandals. A gleaming abalone pendant hung on his chest. Distaste—no doubt at the subject they had come to discuss—lay in the set of his mouth.

Together, the four of them spoke for the Made People clans. Just the fact that they were meeting in secret would have had Webworm and Desert Willow shivering at the implications, had they known.

"It is a grim day," Yellowgirl began. "The slaves are in the fields, still trying to pack what they can salvage into the storerooms. No one should bother us."

Copper Ring smacked her brown lips. Being toothless, she had a slight lisp. "It's not good. My lineage elders report that maybe a tenth of the seed jars will be filled. Sometimes the lower ears didn't freeze all the way. The kernels are still green, but better than nothing."

"Thousands of people will be dead or dislocated by spring," Wooden Flower said flatly. "There is no other way of it. Entire villages will be filled with corpses."

"And those who survive will be raiding each other," Yellowgirl added. "People will attack their neighbors for whatever scraps they might be hoarding rather than watch their children slowly die of starvation."

"Remember the Dust People? That was a measure of desperation," Copper Ring added. "And that was before the freeze."

"How did this happen?" Wooden Flower wondered.

"Webworm," Creeper said sadly, and a wound that had opened in his soul began to bleed. "I watched him grow up. He was my closest friend in the world. I loved him. But since he became Blessed Sun, he has become a stranger. Something inside him changed. I do not know this new Webworm. He...he is the fulfillment of the Fire Dog prophecy. I didn't believe it, as you all know. Now, however, after the things I have seen..."

"He changed," Yellowgirl agreed. "Once, he was so likable."

"Bad seed leads to a bad harvest," Copper Ring muttered.

"I have tried to see him for four days now," Creeper added. "Each time War Chief Wind Leaf has prohibited it. Desert Willow only walks between her rooms and her clan kiva. She goes nowhere without Wind Leaf and a couple of warriors as guards."

"They are afraid," Copper Ring added. "Pinnacle House has been burned, the holy Sunwatcher murdered. Runners sent by my people say that the bodies were burned in the kivas. Many of the Made People were killed after the attack, others driven out. The fugitives are on the way here, spreading terrible stories of the Moon People's wrath as they come."

Creeper took a deep breath. "I never thought I would be the one to say this, but it is time that we take action." He knotted a fist, his face a mask of despair. "How did we end up here? What did we do wrong?"

"Nothing." A voice came from the door as a tall man ducked into the room.

Fear's fingers tightened on Creeper's heart. Gods, were they found out? He turned, taking a moment to recognize the big man who blocked the sunlight. The patch over the left eye only fooled him for a moment. "Ironwood? Is that you?"

The old war chief nodded, then bowed to Wooden Flower, who looked shocked, his good hand clasping his abalone pendant. "Greetings, Clan Elder. I hope the Matron is well."

Creeper thought Ironwood didn't look well, a grayness about him, a slump to his shoulders.

Yellowgirl bobbed her head in greeting, but asked,

"What are you doing here? You're declared Outcast. If Webworm hears that—"

"Webworm is dead," Ironwood said firmly. "The Blessed Nightshade, whom you know as the Mountain Witch, cut his heart from his body the night of the storm."

"But we haven't heard this," Wooden Flower insisted.

"Desert Willow doesn't want you to." Ironwood stared from face to face. "She's deathly afraid of what the people will do when they find out."

Yellowgirl asked, "Is that why you're here? Come to lead the Moon People to destroy Flowing Waters Town?"

He shook his head sadly. "I couldn't stop what happened up there. I wanted only to take Blue Racer, Larkspur, and the rest captive. I could have exchanged their lives for Night Sun, used them as pawns while the Made People clans bartered for shared authority. I hadn't counted on the rage of the Moon People."

"Then," Creeper asked, "you didn't attack with the purpose of killing the First People?"

"No." Ironwood gave a faint shake of his head. "The gods, however, had other plans. I have come here only for Night Sun. If you will help me recover her and the rest of the people Leather Hand took, I will leave you to make your own way in peace."

Creeper spread his hands wide. "They are not here."

Ironwood's single eye narrowed. "Not here?"

"Not that we've heard," Copper Ring corrected. "The rumor here is that angry Made People have taken her as punishment for her crimes against them. We

333

have sent out runners to determine if this is indeed the case but have heard nothing."

"Leather Hand captured her. I know that for a fact." Ironwood was frowning. "Why would they want the credit to go to the Made People? What is the purpose of this lie?"

"Things are unsettled," Wooden Flower said. "But then you walk in here claiming the Blessed Sun's been dead for four days, too. And we've heard nothing of that."

Yellowgirl grunted her assent.

"How did you find us?" Creeper asked. "No one knew of this meeting."

"I have friends here." Ironwood smiled. "For the most part they pass invisibly. The least among us are sometimes the greatest."

"However you found out, we must decide what to do about the First People. Perhaps the gods sent you to us as a sign that they must be removed from our lives." Creeper raised his hands, making a decision that deepened the wounds in his souls. "I have come here to recommend that we throw them out of Flowing Waters Town."

"Then do it, old friend." Ironwood nodded. "Their time is past. If you will save Flowing Waters Town from destruction, you must act quickly, and with resolve."

Chapter Twenty-Six

The Moment of Sums

I Dream ...

Dark clouds are passing; veils of rain trail the mountains behind them. In their wake, the air is clean, crisp.

I sit alone on the starlit mountaintop, listening to Wind Mother rustling the wet pines as she climbs the slope. The fragrances of damp trees and grass scent her trailing hem. As she passes, I breathe them into my lungs and hold them for as long as I can before I must let them go; then I turn and reluctantly gaze southward. Far out in the distance, a great darkness swells, pricked only by the winking campfires of the dead.

Am I strong enough for what comes?

I cannot move. What was excruciating pain has become a throbbing ache. Reaching back I can run my fingers over the smooth sides of the stake they have driven through my hips. It pierces my center, running down through flesh, bone, and my womb. My souls writhe around it.

I am an old woman, maybe too old to endure this final trial.

My first teacher, the great Priest Old Marmot, told me that the price of old age was Power. I recall once when he opened his skeletal hands to me and told me he could feel it draining away through his fingers like water through a poorly woven basket. At the time, I was young and so full of Power that it nearly tore my souls apart. I didn't understand. But I believed him.

For more than fifty summers now, I have been hoarding Power, trying to prepare myself for these final heartbeats. It has cost me more than I can tell you. I often left my family to vanish into forest or desert where I could Dance with my Spirit Helpers, or spent days on a lonely hilltop praying until my voice was gone. The people I loved most paid the price. I barely saw my adopted children grow up, and the man I loved with all my heart always had sad eyes.

Only Brother Mud Head's grin widened.

Soon, I will know if it was worth it. The Moment of Sums is almost upon me.

Everything I am, everything I ever hoped to be, is about to be tallied, and when the darkness drains out of my heart, I will know the total of the Light that is left, the Power that I have accumulated. I only pray the sum is not too small to do what must be done.

I rub my face against the dusty floor. We all strive to do so much in life—yet manage so little.

I have spent a lifetime acquiring this one single truth: Spiritual knowing is more a process of unlearning than it is of learning, and I would think it time poorly spent if I did not realize that it is through "unlearning" that I have managed to hold onto the meager dusting of Power that I possess.

Death, Sickness, and Sorrow—my holy trinity of Spirit Helpers—have taught me the only valuable lessons I know.

Because of them, I unlearned what I saw with my eyes.

I unlearned that life is the sole cause.

I unlearned that strength is a virtue.

Were it not for the terrible sacrifices of the weak, the innocent, the infants, death would be meaningless.

I will do well to remember that in the terrifying instant ahead.

Death's meaning—that is the Moment of Sums.

The load of firewood bowed Spots' back as he trudged through the southeast entrance to Dusk House. He looked up, seeing the guard wave him through.

Behind him, Cactus Flower walked with her pack over her shoulder. She shot him a worried look as they made their way to their traditional place across from the great kiva. A party of slaves had carried the bear cage off. Now the space acted as a haunting reminder of the old woman's presence. He dared not guess what Wind Leaf had done to her. He'd seen some terrible knowledge in her eyes when the war chief had led her into the third-floor room. Moments later a warrior had carried a large hammer and pointed wooden stake into that same entrance.

They must have her tied to a pole like a dog.

Well, soon now, he would know, one way or the other. As he laid his wood on the ground, he saw Creeper and Yellowgirl walk through the entrance. Creeper shot a look at the Buffalo Clan guard and gave him a terse nod. The man swallowed hard, glanced nervously around, and nodded in return.

Crow Woman, Yucca Sock, Wrapped Wrist, and others entered single file, what looked like heavy packs slung across their backs. Despite their bowed heads, they were shooting wolfish glances at the walls, taking stock of the situation.

In the southwest, old Copper Ring came hobbling in, her cane tapping the hard ground. Wooden Flower walked behind her, nodding to the Coyote Clan guard at the gate. Behind them came more warriors, all wearing smudged shirts and bearing sacks of this and that over their shoulders.

Spots turned his gaze to the fourth floor. None of the First People could be seen. So far, they had no idea.

War Chief Wind Leaf cupped a corn cake in his callused hand as he scooped bean paste from a corrugated cooking jar beside the warming bowl. He lifted a thinly sliced strip of turkey breast from a warm stone platter and placed it over the beans before he took a bite. As he chewed, he watched Desert Willow. The Matron was occupied with dressing for the day. She had just finished drawing a bone comb through her long glistening hair until it shone. Now she was going through her cedar box, lifting dress after dress, holding it against her naked body, and discarding it to try another.

"I like that one," Wind Leaf told her as she held up a white cotton dress decorated by four-pointed black stars. He liked the way it molded to her body.

"You think?" She smoothed it against her flat belly.

Wind Leaf chuckled. Yes, she was vain. But given the pressure that was brewing around her, she deserved any relief she might find. When he'd taken his final survey the night before, it was to find a hundred new camps dotting the flats above Flowing Waters Town. His warriors reported that refugees by the thousands would be trickling in, looking for food, protection, and salvation.

All things we cannot provide.

He should have been out at first light, checking on his guards, ensuring that the morning bore no threat. But knowing the magnitude of the disaster they faced, he preferred to watch as Desert Willow slipped the dress over her head and wriggled into it like a larva into a cocoon. Who was to blame him for taking a moment to enjoy the sight of this beautiful woman when the whole world would be turning ugly in the coming days?

"What should we do with Webworm?" she asked. "He's starting to stink."

"Our runner should have reached Leather Hand yesterday. He will be on his way as we speak." Wind Leaf finished his corn cake, reached for another, and dipped it in the beans. What a luxury to eat such a delicacy while people picked among the spoiled crops for mere scraps.

"Can you trust him? He was, after all, Webworm's creature."

Wind Leaf rolled the flavor of the smoked turkey over his tongue. "I think he can be persuaded to serve us, provided I approach him correctly."

"And how do you propose to do that?"

"That depends on you."

"Me?" She turned, flipping her shining hair over her shoulder. "I don't even like him."

Wind Leaf arched an eyebrow. "Did you enjoy having me back in your bed?"

A smile curled her full lips. "I have never had to pretend when your staff sends shivers of delight through my sheath."

"Then I propose that Webworm 'die' while fighting to protect some isolated village from raiders. No one need see him leave here; no one but Leather Hand need witness his 'heroic battle' to maintain order and calm. No one need view his corpse until after it is carried back to Dusk House several weeks from now. By then he'll be dead so long no one will be able to tell. His funeral will be a symbol of the sacrifices we must make to maintain the peace."

"Why would Leather Hand agree to this charade?"

Wind Leaf gave her a flat stare, placing it all on this one cast of the gaming pieces. "Because after you name me Blessed Sun, I will name him war chief of the Straight Path Nation. If we name Seven Stars as Sunwatcher, it will give us a unified command." A pause. "And Matron, you are going to need loyal warriors and Priests as you've never needed them before."

She took a deep breath, brow lined with thought. "I will consider this. Not that I have a lot of choice. There are so few First People remaining. In the meantime, how many warriors do you expect to arrive today?"

He shrugged. "Perhaps another ten or twenty."

"When they arrive," she said, "I want you to arrest the Made People clan elders."

"Arrest the...Why?"

"I don't like the looks they've been giving me. I'd swear they're up to something. Their manner worries me. I see the anger behind their eyes. They'll blame me for the early frost, you mark my words." She shot him a challenging look. "I want them taken care of. Quietly. Perhaps with the same mysterious efficiency that was demonstrated when White Cloud Woman was removed?"

"I can take care of the Made People Matrons. We can use this rumor that they have captured Night Sun as part of the excuse. I have a few trusted warriors. They can apprehend them in the night and bring them here where we can quietly dispose of them."

A hard voice behind him said, "I think not."

Desert Willow gasped, eyes large. Wind Leaf twisted, seeing two brown-shirted warriors, bows drawn, as they ducked in. A hardness glittered in their eyes. They were followed by a tall gray-haired warrior, and then Creeper and Yellowgirl ducked into the room.

Wind Leaf scrambled to grab his war club, only to hear the old one-eyed warrior snap, "Don't! Or you'll die."

He froze, staring at the old man. "Ironwood?"

"The very same, Wind Leaf." He shook his head. "You never were very smart."

"Get out!" Desert Willow screamed, finger pointing.

"There will be no more getting out," Creeper said gruffly. "Webworm's body is already being borne to the great kiva for all to see. And you are right: You should have feared the Made People."

Creeper's frigid smile sent a shiver through Wind Leaf. "Creeper? You know me. I wouldn't have carried out her order."

"No," the old man said sadly. "I'm sure you wouldn't. We all know what lies are worth these days."

A tall woman warrior stepped past Yellowgirl and grasped Desert Willow by the arm. "Come on, Matron. We've a special room for you: One where no one will hear you shouting."

"What are you going to do with me?" Wind Leaf watched a short muscular man in a hunting shirt kick his war club out of reach.

"Whatever I'm ordered to," the man said through a thick barbarian accent.

When Wind Leaf tried to struggle, the man's great strength bore his arms back. Ironwood tied them tightly. Then, bound like a captive macaw, Wind Leaf was carried away.

The pine-pitch torch in Spots' hand cast guttered yellow light on the room walls. He knew which doorway Nightshade had been taken through, but once inside, rooms led to other rooms; openings in the floors led down to dead ends. Slanting passages with pole-supported roofs led down in different directions. The place was like a giant rabbit warren.

One by one, he and Ironwood made their way,

passing through storerooms filled with dried turkeys, stacked jars of corn, net bags filled with squash.

"It's like following a tree root down to a buried stone," Spots said. "How do you know which way?"

"Nightshade?" Ironwood cupped his hands and called. The echo reverberated as the war chief seemed to stagger, placing a hand against one of the buff-plastered walls.

"War Chief?" Spots asked. "Are you all right?"

"Just a little dizzy," Ironwood answered, blinking. Sweat popped out on his chest and face. He took a couple of deep breaths. "All right. Let's go down. They like putting prisoners as far down as they can."

Spots lifted his torch, the pine sap hissing as it burned. He had two more in his pack for when this one flickered its last. As he climbed down a tunnel stairway to the next floor, he shot an uneasy glance at Ironwood. The man didn't look well. A gray pallor had crept into his complexion, and his movements were those of a man heavy with fatigue.

The room he entered was empty, four bare walls each cut with a doorway. He cast his light into one, finding nothing but rush matting on the floor. In the next, he found scattered trash, cloth rags, broken baskets, and several smashed pots.

When he inspected the third, he stopped short. Several burials had been placed against the walls. Some of the dead were wrapped in matting, split-feather blankets, and the like. Painted jars, seed pots, and cooking ware had been placed close to the corpses to ease their journeys to the Land of Dead. At sight of the blanket-covered form in the back, his eyes widened. Gods, they hadn't tied her like a dog.

"Nightshade!" Spots ducked through the door, rushing to the old woman's side. A mug of water had been placed just beyond her reach, as had a small bowl filled with dry cornmeal. Her upended pack lay beside its contents. The Wellpot from Cahokia gleamed in the light as if it were a mirror. Bits of stone, animal parts, and Spirit Plants were scattered about, as if trampled upon.

"Brother Mud Head?" she asked groggily. "Have you come to Dance at last?"

"It's Spots, Elder. I came as quickly as I could."

Her eyes were dull as she opened them, a faint smile on her lips. "My young hunter." She barely whispered the words. "Come...too late."

"Nightshade?" Ironwood sank to his knees on the packed clay floor. He was laboring, his breath coming in shallow gasps as if he'd run instead of walked into the room. His hand trembled as he reached out to touch the long stake they'd driven through her pelvis.

"Oh, it's real, War Chief," she told him, smacking her lips. "They didn't want my souls to slip out of my body just yet. I was supposed to confess to witching them with Webworm's heart. If I called back the curse, they would let me die."

"We have to get you out of here," Spots cried, staggering to his feet.

"No," she told him simply. "Leave me like this. All debts are paid." She glanced at Ironwood. "Our world is ended, isn't it?"

Ironwood nodded, shoulders sagging. "It is."

Spots sank back to his knees again, reaching for the cup and placing it to her lips. She drank, spilling water down the side of her face. "Thank you."

"Where is Night Sun?" Ironwood asked. "Is she here, in a room close by?"

Nightshade shook her head. "No, War Chief. The cannibal, Leather Hand, took her to Talon Town. Laid a trap for you."

"Talon Town?"

Spots heard the hope in the war chief's voice. He could see the sudden glitter in the man's eyes.

"Yours was a great love, Ironwood," Nightshade whispered. "Mythic."

"What can I do to help you?" Spots asked as he wrung his hands.

"The Wellpot," she said weakly.

Spots carefully lifted the shining bowl.

"Scoop out a handful," the old woman told him. She watched as he mounded the gray paste on his fingertips. "That's it. Place it on my tongue."

"Elder, you can't survive that much datura."

"It will free my souls from the stake, Spots," she whispered. Her eyes went to Ironwood.

Spots extended his fingers, letting the old woman suck the gob of paste from them. He swallowed hard, watching her roll the concentrated datura seed from side to side in her mouth.

"Elder?" Ironwood asked. "Is there anything you want me to do afterward? Perhaps take you back to Talon Town with me? Or back to the mountain to be with Badgertail?"

"My bones will be fine here, War Chief," she said with a sigh. "Fear not for my breath-heart soul; it is already halfway loose of the stake. Brother Mud Head awaits us."

"Us?" Ironwood made a pained sound as he rubbed his left shoulder. He kept wincing, as if against pain.

She glanced at Spots. "Take the Wellpot and my pack. The Spirits say they like you. Treat them kindly and they will serve you well." She looked at Ironwood. "Do you want Mud Head and me to take you to Night Sun now?"

"You'll take me to her?" Ironwood asked. He sounded confused, his breathing labored. He blinked, shaking his head. Sweat made a sheen on his skin. He looked curiously gray, even in the torchlight.

"She is calling from the Land of the Dead. We can take you to her now, or you can live out the rest of your natural life. The decision is yours."

"She's dead?" Spots asked incredulously. "How can you know?"

Ironwood gasped and closed his eyes, his breath sounding like a great weight was on his shoulders. "If you can hear her...Yes, I understand. Take me to her now, Nightshade."

"Then come, War Chief," Nightshade whispered weakly. "Reach out... Take my hand..."

Spots glanced uneasily at Nightshade. Her eyes had rolled back in her head, her breath exhaling slowly as her souls slipped away.

Her whisper was barely audible. "Let go, War Chief. Embrace the Moment of Sums..."

Ironwood's breath caught, his shoulders hunching as if a hard blow had been dealt to his breastbone. He stiffened, whispering, "Night Sun?" then slumped loosely to the floor. His right eye was half-lidded and dark, and Spots heard him whisper the words, "Oh, my love..."

"War Chief?" Spots grasped his shoulder, shaking the limp body. "War Chief?"

In shadows cast on the walls by the flickering torchlight, he would have sworn he saw Mud Head's ungainly round form Dancing away hand in hand with two human shapes.

Chapter Twenty-Seven

Bad Cast and Soft Cloth had arrived in Flowing Waters Town amid a stream of refugees. Only by demanding that they be allowed to speak to Crow Woman had they finally made it past the barricades that had been thrown up at each gate. Squads of heavily armed warriors kept the crowd at bay and defended the precious food stores.

Once inside, Bad Cast had been taken to Spots and Wrapped Wrist. There, he'd delivered the message that Fir Brush and Slipped Bark were traveling south looking for food. They had left in the company of Spots' sister, Yellow Petal, and her baby, Fresh Stalk. Her husband Black Bush and some of his friends thought they could make it across the mountains to a valley that was rumored to have been frost free. They were traveling light, carrying only a water jar and cooking pot. Yellow Petal had taken her feather holder, swearing it would grace the mantel of her new house.

On the day of Ironwood's funeral, fires were burning in the great kiva. People watched from the galleries, the benches were packed, and outside, guards kept a firm watch on those of the refugees that had been allowed into the plaza.

Ironwood's body had been painted in red ocher and dressed in the finest red war shirt that could be found. A bracelet given him by Night Sun was placed on his wrist, and then he was wrapped in feather cloth and colorfully dyed matting.

Bad Cast was given the honor of helping to bear the ceremonial ladder—emblematic of the climb into the next world—upon which the corpse had been laid. With Crow Woman in the lead, they bore the war chief out of the great kiva, across the plaza, and up to the third floor. Bad Cast heard the whispers of "Ironwood, Ironwood, Ironwood" chanted by the mournful crowd. Then they entered Dusk House, following a route deep into the interior.

They laid Ironwood to rest in a room not far from Nightshade's. The Bear Clan, under Wooden Flower's direction, had shown him a hero's respect. They had dug a shallow trench in the floor into which Bad Cast, Wrapped Wrist, Crow Woman, and Yucca Sock shifted the body. Ironwood's shield, war clubs, arrows, and fending sticks were placed atop him. His kit for making stone tools, his bone stilettos, awls, and other personal goods were laid ready at hand.

Five bowls, one offered by each of the Made People clans and one from the Moon People, were left full of food to help him on his journey to the Land of the Dead. A mug of water and a basket of sacred cornmeal were left close to his head.

"He was the greatest of us," Creeper said.

"Had the rest of us not been looking into the past,"

Wooden Flower added sadly, "we would have seen that he was the future."

Bad Cast bit his lip, remembering Ironwood's expression that day on the high point—how he'd known that a price would have to be paid. What would he have done differently had he known it would be Night Sun, not he, who suffered?

It was Spots who said, "Do not mourn. Last night I Dreamed. He and the Matron are together."

"You know this?" Wrapped Wrist asked incredulously.

Spots just smiled, Spirit Power reflecting from his large brown eyes. With one hand he patted the pack that hung over his shoulder.

Leather Hand watched from the crowd as Ironwood's remains were carried from the great kiva. Wrapped in finery, the body was borne on a ladder perched on the shoulders of strong warriors—members of Ironwood's little band of fugitives. One tall woman walked proudly, head high, as she led the procession up the successive tiers of Dusk House.

Around him, people stood in silence, some with tears streaking down their faces.

"Ironwood!" The name was whispered from lip to lip, people touching their heads or breasts with respectful fingertips.

Leather Hand struggled to keep his expression neutral. He could feel Turquoise Fox's hand tighten on his shoulder, urging restraint.

So, you, too, have eluded me, old enemy?

Just the thought of it left his stomach sour. The reverence and worship in people's eyes sickened and disgusted him. They would pay. He could feel it. The Blue God would be coming for all of them—may she find their stinking souls wanting.

Turning, he made his way slowly through the crowd, watching as people swarmed after the procession, knotting around the stairway as Ironwood was borne upward and into one of the upper-floor doorways.

"What now?" Turquoise Fox asked.

They were both dressed in poorly woven shirts, the hems ratty and frayed. They'd smeared mud on their faces and left their hair loose in the manner of barbarians. Not even their own men would have recognized them. They had only gained entry by bribing the guards at the southeastern gate with pieces of turquoise.

Leather Hand stopped just short of the southern room block. With the crowd's attention on the funereal procession, no one was paying much attention to the bear cage where it stood less than five paces south of the great kiva entrance. Inside Wind Leaf and Desert Willow crouched, looking miserable and forlorn. Two guards, both Made People, stood to either side of the cage, ensuring both the safety and security of the prisoners. Rumors were already circulating that throughout the land, Made People had risen in revolt and anger, murdering First People in their beds, running them down and battering them to death with axes, hoes, and digging sticks.

When the guards looked the other way, Leather Hand motioned Turquoise Fox inside one of the storerooms across from the bear cage. In the dark room, he crouched down and took a deep breath.

"Tonight," Leather Hand whispered, "when it's dark, we will slip out. The guards won't be expecting an attack from this close. Tomorrow morning the Made People will find only War Chief Wind Leaf's headless corpse within."

Turquoise Fox said, "What if Desert Willow won't cooperate?"

"Do you think she would rather share my bed and bear my children in hopes of regaining what is rightfully hers, or remain as a prisoner of the Made People?"

"I think by tomorrow morning, I will be proud to call you Blessed Sun," Turquoise Fox said knowingly.

Yes, I will be Blessed Sun, and may the Blue God show mercy on the Made People, for I shall not.

He was at war with the Made People. Terror was his weapon. He and his men could walk among them, and they would never know. His fingers smoothed the egg-hatched serpent that Webworm had given him.

Something stirred in his heart, as if tightening and coiling.

Chapter Twenty-Eight

Sister Moon's first rays consisted of a pinprick of white light softening the gap between the great stone pillars of First Moon Mountain, then brightening as she peeked through. The shaft of pale white light grew brighter as she cast her glow on the ruin of Pinnacle Great House.

When her round disc filled the space between the pillars, cold luminescence shone off the standing walls, turned the blackened timbers into gray, and cast inky shadows across the skeletonized rooms.

Did she see the corpse of Dreams the same way he did? Spots couldn't help but wonder. He stood at the lip of the collapsed Blue Dragonfly kiva, watching Sister Moon rise between the pillars.

So, you are home.

But where was he?

He stared down into the kiva's midnight depths. Only silence and blackness remained. This place was as empty as his heart, as the hopes of his world.

He and Cactus Flower had detoured here against

the advice of Bad Cast, Wrapped Wrist, and the rest of their heavily armed party. But he'd wanted to see this place one last time. He needed to know, and most of all, to mourn.

This plaza should have been crowded with Priests in costumes, masks, and feathers, offering their prayers to the rising moon. Pahos, drums, and flute music should have been lifting in the still night. Fires should have been blazing, bathing the great house with their own warmth and light. Children should have been laughing, the smell of boiling corn, squash, and beans heavy on the air. Meat should have been roasting in pits, women tending them to ensure the mouthwatering feast was cooked to perfection.

He sniffed, catching only the tart scent of the conifers on the slope below.

In the days after the attack, the First Moon People had removed much of the roof fall, carted the bodies to the edge of the slope, and laid them just below the cliff. There they remained, each with a basket-load of dirt dumped atop it. Other corpses, those of the dead Red Shirts, had been pitched to tangle in the black timber: hideous, flaking caricatures of people, intertwined, with hollows for eyes, noses, and mouths. The snows would come and cover them, and over the years duff and dust would drift down and softly entomb the remains. Charred flesh did not rot, so they would Dance there, frozen in motion.

He turned, staring out at the valley. His people had thought to reclaim this place, rebuild it in their own image. They hadn't lasted a week before the food was gone. Fights broke out, and by the hundreds they had fled, scattering to the north, south, east, and west in search of a place where they could scratch out enough to feed them through the winter.

But where would they go? The deep frost had ruined the entire harvest across a drought-stricken land. Only Yellowgirl's iron control of Flowing Waters Town had kept the place from being sacked.

Across the land was chaos. He had passed Cricket and Seed's farmstead on the River of Souls and found the swollen bodies of a man, a woman, but only three of the children among the burned and looted ruins. He had heard that half the great houses had been attacked, stripped, and set aflame. Terror stalked the land. Traders had been attacked. Bodies lay un-buried along the trails where entire parties of individuals had starved to death in search of food. The rumored valley toward which Yellow Petal and her party had fled for sanctuary was nothing more than a fantasy.

Even wilder stories circulated that Night Sun had been seized by angry Made People who blamed her for the drought. Other rumors said that Ironwood had watched as she was stoically tortured to death. Still other accounts had them alive, traveling in the south with Poor Singer and rallying Fire Dogs to invade the Straight Path Nation to install Cornsilk as Matron. It didn't seem to matter that hundreds had witnessed Ironwood borne to his grave in Dusk House. What was it about people that to believe the impossible seemed more important than to know the truth?

Darker rumors were whispered from lip to lip. Two days after Desert Willow's mysterious disappearance from the bear cage, Creeper had been found dead in his bed, his head missing. In dark places it was whispered that Leather Hand had fathered a child in Matron

Desert Willow, and that Night Sun's own grandson, Ravenfire, had eaten Night Sun's flesh. By some reports, the white-moccasin-clad cannibals were building secret kivas where they ate wombs freshly cut from murdered maidens and Danced to the honor of the Blue God.

Upon one thing, all agreed: While the katsinas and the Flute Player were locked in mortal combat, the Blue God was left free to prowl the land.

Whatever the risks and dangers, tomorrow Spots and Cactus Flower would take the trail east to rejoin Wrapped Wrist and Bad Cast. They would winter in the Great River Valley, and later perhaps their children could return here to reestablish their roots.

He heard the sibilant whispers of the Spirits in Nightshade's pack. They reassured him that coming here had been right. He needed their assurance—he, Spots, who had fled from all that was spiritual.

"Our world is dead," he told Sister Moon. "I only have you to share this night with."

A look At Book Eight:
People of the Nightland

New York Times bestselling authors W. Michael Gear and Kathleen O'Neal Gear weave a gripping tale of prophecy, survival, and war at the edge of an ancient apocalypse.

Thirteen thousand years ago, as the Ice Age wanes and glaciers retreat, a battle for survival begins. The Nightland and Sunpath clans, divided by faith and prophecy, are locked in a brutal war. The Nightland people, thriving along the Champlain Sea, follow their prophet Ti-Bish, who claims Raven Hunter's spirit will lead them through a tunnel in the ice to a promised land—if they destroy the Sunpath people first.

Under war chief Kakala and the fierce Keresa, the Nightland wage relentless terror, yet doubt lingers. Meanwhile, Windwolf, the brilliant Sunpath war chief, struggles to unite his fractured people. Betrayed and outnumbered, he seeks one last alliance with Chief Lookingbill of the Lame Bull people.

Survivor Skimmer, driven by vengeance, escapes slavery and embarks on a mission to assassinate Ti-Bish. But deep in the ice caves, she discovers an ancient power—one that may turn her into Raven Hunter's deadliest weapon.

As war erupts and long-buried forces awaken, the fate of an entire people will be decided in a battle of faith, fire, and blood.

AVAILABLE JUNE 2025

About W. Michael Gear

W. Michael Gear is a *New York Times, USA Today,* and international bestselling author of sixty novels. With close to eighteen million copies of his books in print worldwide, his work has been translated into twenty-nine languages.

Gear has been inducted into the Western Writers Hall of Fame and the Colorado Authors' Hall of Fame —as well as won the Owen Wister Award, the Golden Spur Award, and the International Book Award for both Science Fiction and Action Suspense Fiction. He is also the recipient of the Frank Waters Award for lifetime contributions to Western writing.

Gear's work, inspired by anthropology and archaeology, is multilayered and has been called compelling, insidiously realistic, and masterful. Currently, he lives in northwestern Wyoming with his award-winning wife and co-author, Kathleen O'Neal Gear, and a charming sheltie named, Jake.

About Kathleen O'Neal Gear

Kathleen O'Neal Gear is a *New York Times* bestselling author of fifty-seven books and a national award-winning archaeologist. The U.S. Department of the Interior has awarded her two Special Achievement awards for outstanding management of America's cultural resources.

In 2015 the United States Congress honored her with a Certificate of Special Congressional Recognition, and the California State Legislature passed Joint Member Resolution #117 saying, "The contributions of Kathleen O'Neal Gear to the fields of history, archaeology, and writing have been invaluable..."

In 2021 she received the Owen Wister Award for lifetime contributions to western literature, and in 2023 received the Frank Waters Award for "a body of work representing excellence in writing and storytelling that embodies the spirit of the American West."

Bibliography

Acatos, Sylvio. 1990 Pueblos: Prehistoric Indian Cultures of the Southwest. Translation of 1989 edition of Die Pueblos. Facts on File, New York.

Adams, E. Charles. 1991 The Origin and Development of the Pueblo Katsina Cult. University of Arizona Press, Tucson.

Adler, Michael A. 1996 The Prehistoric Pueblo World A.D. 1150-1350. University of Arizona Press, Tucson.

Allen, Paula Gunn. 1989 Spider Woman's Granddaughters. Ballantine Books, New York. Arnberger, Leslie P. 1982 Flowers of the Southwest Mountains. Southwest Parks and Monuments Association, Tucson.

Aufderheide, Arthur C. 1998 The Cambridge Encyclopedia of Human Paleopathology. Cambridge University Press, Cambridge.

Baars, Donald L. 1995 Navajo Country: A Geological and Natural History of the Four Corners Region. University of New Mexico Press, Albuquerque.

Becket, Patrick H. (editor). 1991 Mogollon V. Report of Fifth Mogollon Conference. COAS Publishing and Research, Las Cruces, New Mexico.

Billman, Brian R., Patricia M. Lambert, and Banks L. Leonard. 2000 Cannibalism, Warfare, and Drought in the Mesa Verde Region During the Twelfth Century AD American Antiquity 65 (1): 145-178.

Boissiere, Robert. 1990 The Return of Pahana: A Hopi Myth. Bear & Company Publishing, Santa Fe, New Mexico.

Bowers, Janice Emily. 1993 Shrubs and Trees of the Southwest Deserts. Southwest Parks and Monuments Association, Tucson.

Brody, J. J. 1990 TheAnasazi. Rizzoli International Publications, New York.

Brothwell, Don, and A. T. Sandison. 1967 Diseases in Antiquity. Charles C. Thomas Publisher, Springfield, Illinois.

Bunzel, Ruth L. 1984 Zuni Katcinas. Reprint of Forty-seventh Annual Report of the Bureau of American Ethnography, 1929-1930. Rio Grande Press, Glorietta, New Mexico.

Bibliography

Cameron, Catherine M. 2002 Sacred Earthen Architecture in the Northern Southwest: The Bluff Great House Berm. American Antiquity 67 (4): 677-696.

Charles, Mona C. 1991 Chimney Rock Barrier Free Trail Mitigation. Contract No. 43-82CS-1-0346. Paper on file at USDA Forest Service, Pagosa District Office, Colorado.

Colton, Harold S. 1960 Black Sand: Prehistory in Northern Arizona. University of New Mexico Press, Albuquerque.

Cordell, Linda S. 1975 Predicting Site Abandonment at Wetherill Mesa. The Kiva 40 (3): 189-202.

--. 1984 Prehistory of the Southwest. Academic Press, New York.

--. 1994 Ancient Pueblo Peoples. Smithsonian Exploring the Ancient World Series. St. Remy Press, Montreal, and Smithsonian Institution Press, Washington.

Cordell, Linda S., and George J. Gumerman (editors). 1989 Dynamics of Southwest Prehistory. Smithsonian Institution Press, Washington.

Crown, Patricia, and W. James Judge (editor). 1991 Chaco & Hohokam: Prehistoric Regional Systems in the American Southwest. School of American Research Press, Santa Fe, New Mexico.

Cummings, Linda Scott. 1986 Anasazi Subsistence Activity Areas Reflected in the Pollen Records. Paper presented to the Society for American Archaeology Meetings, New Orleans.

--. 1994 Anasazi Diet: Variety in the Hoy House and Lion House Coprolite Record and Nutritional Analysis. In Paleo-nutrition: The Diet and Health of Prehistoric Americans, edited by Kristin D. Sobolik. Occasional Paper No. 22. Southern Illinois University at Carbondale, Illinois.

Dodge, Natt N. 1985 Flowers of the Southwest Deserts. Southwest Parks and Monuments Association, Tucson.

Dooling, D. M., and Paul Jordan-Smith (editors). 1989 I Become Part of It: Sacred Dimensions in Native American Life. A Parabola Book. Harper, San Francisco; Harper Collins Publishers, New York.

Douglas, John E. 1995 Autonomy and Regional Systems in the Late Prehistoric Southern Southwest. American Antiquity 60:240-257.

Dunmire, William W., and Gail Tierney. 1995 Wild Plants of the Pueblo Province: Exploring Ancient and Enduring Uses. Museum of New Mexico Press, Santa Fe, New Mexico.

Bibliography

Eddy, Frank W. 1977 Archaeological Investigations at Chimney Rock Mesa: 1970-1972. Memoirs of the Colorado Archaeological Society No. 1, Boulder.

Ellis, Florence Hawley. 1951 Patterns of Aggression and the War Cult in Southwestern Pueblos. Southwestern Journal of Anthropology 7: 177-201.

Elmore, Francis H. 1976 Shrubs and Trees of the Southwest Uplands. Southwest Parks and Monuments Association, Tucson.

Ericson, Jonathan E., and Timothy G. Baugh (editors). 1993 The American Southwest and Mesoamerica: Systems of Prehistoric Exchange. Plenum Press, New York.

Fagan, Brian M.. 1991 Ancient North America. Thames and Hudson, New York.

Farmer, Malcom F. 1957 A Suggested Typology of Defensive Systems of the Southwest. Southwestern Journal of Archaeology 13:249-266.

Frank, Larry, and Francis H. Harlow. 1990 Historic Pottery of the Pueblo Indians: 1600-1880. Schiffler Publishing, West Chester, Pennsylvania.

Frazier, Kendrick. 1986 People of Chaco: A Canyon and Its Culture. WW Norton, New York.

Gabriel, Kathryn. 1991 Roads to Center Place: A Cultural Atlas of Chaco Canyon and the Anasazi. Johnson Books, Boulder, Colorado.

Gumerman, George J. (editor). 1988 The Anasazi in a Changing Environment. School of American Research. Cambridge University Press, New York.

--. 1991 Exploring the Hohokam: Prehistoric Peoples of the American Southwest. Amerind Foundation. University of New Mexico Press, Albuquerque.

--. 1994 Themes in Southwest Prehistory. School of American Research Press, Santa Fe, New Mexico.

Haas, Jonathan. 1990 Warfare and the Evolution of Tribal Polities in the Prehistoric Southwest. In The Anthropology of War, edited by Jonathan Haas. Cambridge University Press, Cambridge.

Haas, Jonathan, and Winifred Creamer. 1993 Stress and Warfare Among the Kayenta Anasazi of the Thirteenth Century AD Field Museum of Natural History, Chicago.

--. 1995 A History of Pueblo Warfare. Paper presented at the 60th Annual Meeting for the Society of American Archaeology, Minneapolis.

Bibliography

Hatch, Sharon K. 1994 Wood Sourcing Study at the Chimney Rock Archaeological Area. Paper presented at the Second Chimney Rock Archaeological Symposium, Anasazi Heritage Center. Paper on file with the USDA Forest Service, Pagosa District Office, Colorado.

Haury, Emil. 1985 Mogollon Culture in the Forestdale Valley, East-Central Arizona. University of Arizona Press, Tucson.

Hayes, Alden C, David M. Burgge, and W. James Judge. 1981 Archaeological Surveys of Chaco Canyon, New Mexico. Reprint of National Park Service Report. University of New Mexico Press, Albuquerque.

Hultkrantz, Ake. 1987 Native Religions: The Power of Visions and Fertility. Harper & Row, New York.

Jacobs, Sue-Ellen. 1995 Continuity and Change in Gender Roles at San Juan Pueblo. In Women and Power in Native North America. Edited by Laura F. Klein and Lillian Ackerman. University of Oklahoma Press, Norman, Oklahoma.

Jeancon, Jean Allard. n.d. Archaeological and Ethnological Research During the Year 1924. Unpublished manuscript on file, Colorado Historical Society, Denver.

--. 1922 Archaeological Research in the Northeastern San Juan Basin of Colorado in the Summer of 1921. The State Historical Society of Colorado and the University of Denver, Denver.

--. 1923 Further Archaeological Research in the Northeastern San Juan Basin of Colorado, During the Summer of 1922. Colorado Magazine 1: 11-28.

--. 1924a Excavation Work in the Pagosa-Piedra Field During the Season of 1922. Colorado Magazine 1 (2):65-70.

--. 1924b Further Archaeological Research in the Northeastern San Juan Basin of Colorado During the Summer of 1922. Pottery of the Pagosa-Piedra Region. Colorado Magazine 1:213-224.

Jeancon, Jean Allard, and Frank H. H. Roberts. 1924 Further Archaeological Research in the Northeastern San Juan Basin of Colorado. Colorado Magazine 1 (2):65-70, (3):108-118.

Jernigan, E. Wesley. 1978 Jewelry of the Prehistoric Southwest. School of American Research, University of New Mexico Press, Albuquerque.

Jett, Stephen C. 1964 Pueblo Indian Migrations: An Evaluation of the Possible Physical and Cultural Determinants. American Antiquity 29:281-300.

Kamp, Kathryn A. 2002 Children in the Prehistoric Puebloan Southwest. University of Utah Press, Salt Lake City.

Komarek, Susan. 1994 Flora of the San Juans:A Field Guide to the Mountain Plants of Southwestern Colorado. Kivaki Press, Durango, Colorado.

Lange, Frederick, Nancy Mahaney, Joe Ben Wheat, Mark L. Chenault, and John Carter . 1988 Yellow Jacket: A Four Corners Anasazi Ceremonial Center. Johnson Books, Boulder, Colorado.

LeBlanc, Stephen A. 1999 Prehistoric Warfare in the American Southwest. University of Utah Press, Salt Lake City.

Lekson, Stephen H. 1988 The Idea of the Kiva in Anasazi Archaeology. The Kiva 53 (3):213-234.

--. 1990 Mimbres Archaeology of the Upper Gila, New Mexico. Anthropological Papers of the University of Arizona, No. 53. University of Arizona Press, Tucson.

--. 2002 War in the Southwest, War in the World. American Antiquity 67 (4):607-624.

Lekson, Stephen, Thomas C. Windes, John R. Stein, and W. James Judge. 1988 The Chaco Canyon Community. Scientific American 259 (1):100-109.

Lewis, Dorothy Otnow. 1998 Guilty by Reason of Insanity: A Psychiatrist Explores the Minds of Killers. The Ballantine Publishing Group, New York.

Lipe, W. D., and Michelle Hegemon (editors). 1989 The Architecture of Social Integration in Prehistoric Pueblos. Occasional Papers of the Crow Canyon Archaeological Center No. 1. Crow Canyon Archaeological Center, Cortez, Colorado.

Lister, Florence C. 1993 In the Shadow of the Rocks: Archaeology of the Chimney Rock District in Southern Colorado. University Press of Colorado, Niwot, Colorado.

Lister, Florence C, and Robert H. Lister. 1968 Earl Morris & Southwestern Archaeology. University of New Mexico Press, Albuquerque.

Lister, Robert H., and Florence C. Lister. 1981 Chaco Canyon. University of New Mexico Press, Albuquerque.

Lomatuway'ma, Michael, Lorena Lomatuway'ma, and Sidney Namingha Jr. 1993 Hopi Ruin Legends. Edited by Ekkehart Malotki. Published for Northern Arizona University by University of Nebraska Press, Lincoln.

Malotki, Ekkehart. 1985 Gullible Coyote: Una'ihwA Bilingual

Bibliography

Collection of Hopi Coyote Stories. University of Arizona Press, Tucson.

Malotki, Ekkehart, and Michael Lomatuway'ma. 1987 Maasaw: Profile of a Hopi God. American Tribal Religions, Vol. XI. University of Nebraska Press, Lincoln.

Malville, J. McKimm, and Gary Matlock. 1990 The Chimney Rock Archaeological Symposium. USDA Forest Service General Technical Report RM-227.

Malville, J. McKimm, and Claudia Putnam. 1993 Prehistoric Astronomy in the Southwest. Johnson Books, Boulder, Colorado.

Mann, Coramae Richey. 1996 When Women Kill. State University of New York Press, New York.

Martin, Debra L. 1995 Lives Unlived: The Political Economy of Violence Against Anasazi Women. Paper presented to the Society for American Archaeology 60th Annual Meeting, Minneapolis.

Martin, Debra L., Alan H. Goodman, George Armelagos, and Ann L. Magennis. 1991 Black Mesa Anasazi Health: Reconstructing Life from Patterns of Death and Disease. Occasional Paper No. 14. Southern Illinois University, Carbondale, Illinois.

Martin, Paul S. 1936 Lowry Ruin in Southwest Colorado. Anthropological Series 23:1. Field Museum of Natural History, Chicago.

Mayes, Vernon O., and Barbara Bayless Lacy. 1989 Nanise: A Navajo Herbal. Navajo Community College Press, Tsaile, Arizona.

McGuire, Randall H., and Michael Schiffer (editors). 1982 Hohokam and Patayan: Prehistory of Southwestern Arizona. Academic Press, New York.

McNitt, Frank. 1966 Richard Wetherill Anasazi. University of New Mexico Press, Albuquerque.

Minnis, Paul E., and Charles L. Redman (editors). 1990 Perspectives on Southwestern Prehistory. Westview Press, Boulder, Colorado.

Mitchell, Douglas R., and Judy L. Brunson-Hadley (editors). 2001 Ancient Burial Practices. University of New Mexico Press, Albuquerque.

Morris, Ann Axtel. 1933 Digging in the Southwest. Doubleday, Doran & Co., New York.

Morris, Earl H. 1917a The Ruins at Aztec. El Palacio 4:3: 43-69.

--. 1917b Discoveries at the Aztec Ruin. American Museum Journal 17(3):169-180.

--. 1918 Further Discoveries at the Aztec Ruin. American Museum Journal 18 (7):602-10.

--. 1919a The Aztec Ruin. Anthropological Papers 26:pt.l. American Museum of Natural History, New York.

--. 1919b Further Discoveries at the Aztec Ruin. El Palacio 6:17-23. Santa Fe.

--. 1921 The House of the Great Kiva at the Aztec Ruin. Anthropological Papers 26:pt.2 American Museum of Natural History, New York.

--. 1924 Burials in the Aztec Ruin. Anthropological Papers 26:pts.3 & 4. American Museum of Natural History, New York.

--. 1928 Notes on Excavations in the Aztec Ruin. Anthropological Papers 26: pt.5. American Museum of Natural History, New York.

Mullet, G. M. 1979 Spider Woman Stories: Legends of the Hopi Indians. University of Arizona Press, Tucson.

Nabahan, Gary Paul. 1989 Enduring Seeds: Native American Agriculture and Wild Plant Conservation. North Point Press, San Francisco.

Noble, David Grant. 1991 Ancient Ruins of the Southwest: An Archaeological Guide. Northland Publishing, Flagstaff, Arizona.

Ortiz, Alfonzo (editor). 1983 Handbook of North American Indians. Smithsonian Institution, Washington.

Palkovich, Ann M. 1980 The Arroyo Hondo Skeletal and Mortuary Remains. Arroyo Hondo Archaeological Series, Vol. 3. School of American Research Press, Santa Fe, New Mexico.

Parker, Douglas. 1994 Chimney Rock Pottery: The Identification of Chaco Ceramics by Petrography and Their Comparisons to Samples from Chaco Canyon. Paper on file with the USDA Forest Service, Pagosa District Office, Colorado.

Parsons, Elsie Clews. 1939 Pueblo Indian Religion. Vols. 1 & 2. Bison Books reprint, Lincoln, Nebraska.

--. 1994 Tewa Tales. Reprint of 1924 edition. University of Arizona Press, Tucson.

Pepper, George H. 1996 Pueblo Bonito. Reprint of 1920 edition. University of New Mexico Press, Albuquerque.

Pike, Donald G., and David Muench. 1974 Anasazi: Ancient People of the Rock. Crown Publishers, New York.

Reid, J. Jefferson, and David E. Doyel (editors). 1992 Emil Haury's Prehistory of the American Southwest. University of Arizona Press, Tucson.

Bibliography

Renaud, Etienne B. 1924 A Pit-House Skull from the Piedra District, Archuleta County, Colorado. Paper on file at the State Historical Society of Colorado, Denver.

Rice, Glen E., and Steven A. LeBlanc (editors). 2001 Deadly Landscapes: Case Studies in Prehistoric Southwestern Warfare. University of Utah Press, Salt Lake City.

Riley, Carroll L. 1995 Rio del Norte: People of the Upper Rio Grande from the Earliest Times to the Pueblo Revolt. University of Utah Press, Salt Lake City.

Roberts, Frank H. H. 1925 Report on Archaeological Reconnaissance in Southwest Colorado in the Summer of 1923. Colorado Magazine 2:2.

—. 1930 Early Pueblo Ruins in the Piedra District, Southwestern Colorado, Bureau of American Ethnology. Bulletin 96.

Rocek, Thomas R. 1995 Sedentarization and Agricultural Dependence: Perspectives from the Pithouse-to-Pueblo Transition in the American Southwest. American Antiquity 60: 218-239.

Schaafsma, Polly. 1980 Indian Rock Art of the Southwest. School of American Research, University of New Mexico Press, Albuquerque.

—. 2000 Warrior, Shield, and Star. Western Edge Press. Santa Fe, New Mexico.

Sebastian, Lynne. 1992 The Chaco Anasazi: Sociopolitical Evolution in the Prehistoric Southwest. Cambridge University Press, Cambridge.

Simmons, Marc. 1980 Witchcraft in the Southwest. Bison Books reprint of 1974 edition. University of Nebraska Press, Lincoln.

Slifer, Dennis, and James Duffield. 1994 Kokopelli: Flute Player Images in Rock Art. Ancient City Press, Santa Fe, New Mexico.

Smith, Watson, and Raymond H. Thompson (editors). 1990 When Is a Kiva?: And Other Questions About Southwestern Archaeology. University of Arizona Press, Tucson.

Sobolik, Kristin D.. 1994 Paleonutrition: The Diet and Health of Prehistoric Americans. Occasional Paper no. 22. Center for Archaeological Investigations, Southern Illinois University, Carbondale.

Sullivan, Alan P. 1992 Pinyon Nuts and Other Wild Resources in Western Anasazi Subsistence Economies. Research in Economic Anthropology Supplement 6:195-239.

Tedlock, Barbara. 1992 The Beautiful and the Dangerous: Encounters with the Zuni Indians. Viking Press, New York.

Trombold, Charles D. (editor). 1991 Ancient Road Networks and Settlement Hierarchies in the New World. Cambridge University Press, Cambridge.

Turner, Christy G., and Jacqueline A. Turner. 1999 Man Corn: Cannibalism and Violence in the Prehistoric American Southwest. University of Utah Press, Salt Lake City.

Tyler, Hamilton A. 1964 Pueblo Gods and Myths. University of Oklahoma Press, Norman, Oklahoma.

Underhill, Ruth. 1991 Life in the Pueblos. Reprint of 1964 Bureau of Indian Affairs Report. Ancient City Press, Santa Fe, New Mexico.

Upham, Steadman, Kent G. Lightfoot, and Roberta A. Jewet (editors). 1989 The Sociopolitical Structure of Prehistoric Southwestern Societies. Westview Press, San Francisco.

Varien, Mark D., and Richard H. Wilshusen. 2002 Seeking the Center Place: Archaeology and Ancient Communities in the Mesa Verde Region. University of Utah Press, Salt Lake City.

Vivian, Gordon, and Tom W. Mathews. 1973 Kin Kletso:A Pueblo III Community in Chaco Canyon, New Mexico, Vo 6. Southwest Parks and Monuments Association, Globe, Arizona

Vivian, Gordon, and Paul Reiter. 1965 The Great Kivas of Chaco Canyon and Their Relationships. School of American Research, Monograph no. 22, Santa Fe, New Mexico.

Vivian, R. Gwinn. 1990 The Chacoan Prehistory of the San Juan Basin, Academic Press, New York.

Waters, Frank. 1963 Book of the Hopi. Viking Press, New York.

Wetterstrom, Wilma. 1986 Food, Diet, and Population at Prehistoric Arroyo Hondo Pueblo, New Mexico. Arroyo Hondo Archaeological Series, Vol. 6; School of American Research Press, Santa Fe, New Mexico.

White, Tim D. 1992 Prehistoric Cannibalism at Mancos 5MTUMR-2346. Princeton University Press, Princeton.

Williamson, Ray A. 1984 Living the Sky: The Cosmos of the American Indian. University of Oklahoma Press, Norman, Oklahoma.

Wills, W. H., and Robert D. Leonard (editors). 1994 The Ancient Southwestern Community. University of New Mexico Press, Albuquerque.

Woodbury, Richard B. 1959 A Reconsideration of Pueblo Warfare in the Southwestern United States. Actas del XXXIII Congreso Internacional de Americanistas II: 124-133. San Jose, Costa Rica.

--. 1961 Climatic Changes and Prehistoric Agriculture in the South-

Bibliography

western United States. New York Academy of Sciences Annals, Vol. 95, Article 1, New York.

Wright, Barton. 1975 Katchinas: The Barry Goldwater Collection at the Heard Museum Heard Museum, Phoenix, Arizona.